YASHIMOTO'S LAST DIVE

BY THE SAME AUTHOR:

Two Hours to Darkness
Smoke Island
The Sea Break
The White Schooner
Towards the Tamarind Trees
The Moonraker Mutiny
Kleber's Convoy
The Zhukov Briefing
Ultimatum
Death of a Supertanker
The Antonov Project
Sea Fever
Running Wild
Bannister's Chart

ANTONY TREW

◆——◆

YASHIMOTO'S LAST DIVE

ST. MARTIN'S PRESS
NEW YORK

Library of Congress Cataloging-in-Publication

Trew, Antony, 1906–
    Yashimoto's last dive.

    I. Title.
PR9369.3.T7Y37   1987   87-16306
ISBN 0-312-01116-4

First published in Great Britain by William Collins Sons & Co., Ltd.

First U.S. Edition

10 9 8 7 6 5 4 3 2 1

The C-in-C Eastern Fleet had further reason
to be perturbed by losses in the Indian Ocean.
Many sinkings by the Japanese were marked
by atrocities. The blood lust of their submarine commanders seems to have grown as
their losses multiplied . . . it was commonplace for ships' crews to be machine-gunned in
boats and rafts.

War in the Southern Oceans 1939–1945
Turner, Gordon-Cumming & Betzler (Oxford University Press, 1961)

One

The clouds obscured the moon and for that he was thankful; it was no friend to a submarine running on the surface. As it was, the darkness was broken by no more than tumbling flashes of phosphorescence along the sides as I-357's bows sliced through the sea. The only sounds of the night were the mechanical clatter of diesels, occasional squeaks from the revolving aerial abaft the periscope standards, and the splash and swish of broken water. Whatever conversation there might have been earlier, there was none now that the Captain had come up. Taciturn, crop-haired, bearded like the rest of the crew, Commander Togo Yashimoto was a strict disciplinarian whose views were well known: the survival of I-357 and all who served in her hung upon a slender thread of vigilance; conversation unrelated to duty diminished vigilance; for these reasons it was, as he emphasized in his standing order book, *a most serious breach of discipline.*

A breeze off the land did something to relieve the torpor of the night, bringing with it the musky, spice-laden odours of tropical Africa. To Yashimoto the smell was a pleasant one, redolent of the Straits of Malacca, waters he knew well, for the submarine was based on Penang, four and a half thousand miles to the north-east. Unless the unforeseen happened, he hoped to be back there by mid-December. That was a little less than a month away. Penang promised several weeks of unbroken nights, freedom from the stress of danger, regular baths, daily shaves, clean clothes, good food and drink with fresh fruit and vegetables, the company of brother officers of his own seniority, and the comfort of Masna's warm thighs, her pleasant chatter and other tender attentions. There would, too, be letters; mostly from his wife

7

in Kure with family news. Indeed, there was much to look forward to. Pleasant as these thoughts were they were soon displaced by others of a graver nature. They concerned a problem which had nagged at him for days. And now as he settled his forearms on the bridge screen to steady the binoculars with which he searched the darkness, the problem once again began to fill his mind. Before dealing with it, however, there was a matter of routine to be attended to.

'Time of sunrise?' he asked, without lowering the binoculars. Fitted with high-resolution night lenses they were standard issue for the Japanese submarine service.

'0526, sir,' replied the officer who stood beside him on the bridge. Ito Kagumi was not only officer-of-the-watch but I-357's First Lieutenant. Ichiro Noguchi, the Acting Sub-Lieutenant on watch with him, had twitched involuntarily at the Captain's question. It was a trap; Yashimoto would have known the time of sunrise before reaching the bridge. The times of setting and rising of the sun and moon were shown on a slate above the chart-table. Lieutenant Sato, the Navigating Officer, chalked them up each morning before going on watch. Yashimoto never failed to look at the chart and slate before coming to the bridge. Nor did he ever fail to make this ritual check with the officer-of-the-watch. And woe betide any who got it wrong. Noguchi had done so on the first few days of the patrol.

'Submarines dive at dawn,' Yashimoto had barked, the frozen stare terrifying the unfortunate Noguchi. 'They dive because daylight is an even greater danger than incompetent officers. To know the time of sunrise is essential to survival.' The Captain's short, thickset body had stiffened, the lower lip jutting aggressively. 'You will therefore, at noon each day, for the next three weeks, give me in writing the times of rising and setting of the sun and moon.'

Yashimoto lowered his binoculars and moved towards the after end of the conning-tower, checking as he went that the lookouts had their night glasses trained on the sectors allocated to them. He felt his way past the periscope

8

standards, reached the anti-aircraft gun-platform abaft the conning-tower, steadied himself against its guardrail and searched astern with binoculars. His mind was not so much concerned with what might be out there in the darkness, as with the problem he had tussled with over the last few days.

The more he thought about it the more certain he became that there was only one solution. Outbursts of hysteria in the control-room could under exceptional circumstances be tolerated, though they were bad for morale and threatened the safety of the submarine. But hysteria while I-357 was under attack, coupled with physical interference with men carrying out their duties at the controls, was an offence of the gravest nature. The young reservist, fresh out of Tokyo University, should never have been drafted into the submarine service; nor would he have been, reflected Yashimoto, but for the influence of an uncle, a rear-admiral, who had distinguished himself in submarines.

Yashimoto was a career officer steeped in the *samurai* tradition, the son and grandson of naval officers, all men of the *samurai* caste. In 1905 his father had fought at the Battle of Tsushima Strait, the greatest sea engagement in the history of naval warfare. In that battle the Japanese Fleet, commanded by Admiral Togo, had sunk six of the eight Russian battleships, captured two, and sunk or captured most of the remaining ships of the Russian Fleet. This for the loss of three Japanese torpedo boats. Against more than 11,000 Russians, killed or captured, the Japanese had lost 117 men. Yashimoto's father had served on Admiral Togo's staff at Tsushima and had in due course given his son the prestigious first name of Togo.

Yashimoto's upbringing and naval training had been dominated by this background. *Bushido*, the way of the warrior, had been evolved by the *samurai*: loyalty, honour, discipline, were the foundations of the warrior code, one which had been fundamental to Japanese naval tradition since the days of the Shimazu warships of the seventeenth century.

Standing by the guardrail with these thoughts in mind, he decided that, for the honour of the Imperial Japanese Navy,

9

for his own honour, and no less for that of the guilty man, he must bring the matter to a conclusion. For him it had been a painful surprise that the offender had shown himself to be no *samurai*; it was the failure of the young man to commit *seppuku*, the implicit admission that he lacked the courage to purge dishonour with that ritual act of disembowelment, which had created Yashimoto's problem. He sighed, shook his head, looked at the luminous dial of his wristwatch. The first pale shades of dawn were showing in the eastern sky. It was time to return to the bridge. On reaching it he spoke to Kagumi.

'We'll be diving in ten minutes. Carry on below. I'll take her down.'

With a brief, 'Yes, sir,' the First Lieutenant lowered himself into the hatch and descended the conning-tower ladder.

Yashimoto put down the binoculars with which he'd been examining the still dark horizon. Turning to Noguchi he said, 'Time of sunrise, Sub-Lieutenant?'

'0526, sir.'

'Good.' Yashimoto nodded approvingly, paused. 'I was on the AA gun-platform a moment ago. There is something knocking against the hull, aft on the port side. Not loud. Possibly a piece of rope or wire caught in a vent. The light is getting stronger. Go along the casing and check. We'll be diving soon so look smart about it.' In a more kindly tone he added, 'Keep a hand on the guardwire as you go. We don't want a man overboard.'

Noguchi had replied with a submissive, 'Yes, sir.' He made his way aft, past the periscope standards, on to the AA gun-platform and down the ladder to the steel casing. With a hand on the guardwire, he moved cautiously towards the stern. He disliked going out on the casing at any time. It always seemed dangerous to him, even when the sea was as smooth as it was now. So he walked slowly, apprehensively, along the steel casing, the bulging ballast tanks beneath him shining wetly in the half light, the sea lapping and gurgling along their tops. He passed the engineroom, the vibrations of the diesels now stronger, reached the after end of the

10

casing and stopped. With one hand on the guardwire stanchion, he leant over the port side. There was nothing to be seen projecting from the vents, nor could he hear the knocking sound the Captain had complained of.

Still kneeling, anxious not to give the Captain the impression that he had skimped the job, he heard the raucous blare of the klaxon.

He jumped up, slipped, but still holding the stanchion pulled himself to his feet and in the faint light of early morning stared in dismay at the distant blur of the conning-tower. It was only seconds since the klaxon had begun to sound but the sharp hiss of air from the vents as the ballast tanks flooded, the cessation of noise and vibration from the diesels as the electric motors took over, and the increasingly bows-down angle of I-357 brought home to him the reality of what was happening.

Terrified, he began a frenzied scramble for the conning-tower, screaming, 'Wait! Wait!' as he went. He reached the ladder to the AA gun-platform, clawed his way up it, the sea foaming and splashing at his feet. Still screaming, he made a rush for the conning-tower hatch between the periscope standards. With awful disbelief he saw that the upper lid was already shut. He was hammering with his fists on its solid top when seas flooding the bridge carried him away.

Soon after Noguchi embarked on his journey along the casing Yashimoto had moved to the foreside of the bridge, put his binoculars to his eyes and begun once again to search the fading darkness. His sudden exclamation of surprise was followed by an urgent, 'Listen.' He gestured towards the port bow. 'Aircraft,' he shouted suddenly, pressing the klaxon button for a crash dive and ordering the lookouts to clear the bridge. With the speed and precision of long practice they dropped into the upper hatch and scrambled down the conning-tower ladders. Having shut the voice-pipes Yashimoto followed, slamming to the upper hatch above his head and ramming home the safety clips before going down the ladder into the control-room. The forward hydroplanes were already pulling the bows down, the rate of dive increasing, the ballast tanks flooding, the sharp hiss of air escaping from them masking other sounds.

'Shut the lower hatch,' he ordered as he landed on the control-room deck. 'Take her down to seventy-five metres.'

'Seventy-five metres,' repeated the First Lieutenant from his station behind the planesmen. Though his eyes were on the clicking needles of the depth gauges he was wondering why I-357's search receiver had failed to detect the aircraft.

Yashimoto picked up the phone to the engineroom. It was answered by the Chief Engineer Officer, Susuma Satugawa.

'Air attack.' Yashimoto's voice was sharp. 'Shut off for depth-charging.' He replaced the phone, knowing that his cryptic order would suffice for both the engineroom and those in the control-room, among them the Yeoman of Signals who at once passed the message to the men in the fore- and after-ends.

The thud of heavy watertight doors closing was magnified by the relative silence which had followed the shutting down of the diesels and the switch to electric motors. It was broken now by the First Lieutenant's report. 'Seventy-five metres, sir.'

'Hold her there. Silent running. Revolutions for two knots. Steer zero-eight-five.' Yashimoto's voice was calm, un-emotional. That was something the crew found reassuring. They were, with few exceptions, young men for whom strong leadership was of special significance.

In I-357 ventilating and air conditioning fans were switched off, the only sounds the faint hum of electric motors at low speed, the subdued voices of men giving and acknowledging orders, and the whirr and click of instruments. The bows-down angle of the dive gave way to a level trim; at two knots the planesmen were just able to hold the trim. The new course, 085°, was ninety degrees to starboard of that which the submarine had been steering before the dive.

The First Lieutenant knew that Yashimoto had ordered silent running in case the aircraft dropped a sonar buoy. The Americans had begun using them in the Pacific. Perhaps the

RAF flying boats based on Kilindini already had them.

Yashimoto leant against the conning-tower ladder, alert but apparently relaxed, a comforting figure to those in the cramped confines of the control-room with its maze of pipes, valves, controls and labyrinth of instruments, a technological Aladdin's cave where dim red lights cast strange shadows on tense, unshaven faces which constantly glanced upwards, listening fearfully for the splash of depth-charges striking the surface before sinking towards I-357 as she moved slowly through the darkness of deep water.

Yashimoto knew what his men were thinking – that at any moment there would be violent explosions which would buffet the submarine with massive blows, rocking the control-room, splintering light bulbs and gauge glasses, water spurting from fractured pipes, short-circuited cables flashing and crackling, the sulphurous smell of burning insulation compounding the ever-present stench of diesel oil; the terrifying noise and chaos of a depth-charge attack like the one they'd experienced a few days before. But as seconds became minutes, and minutes more minutes, nothing happened and gaunt expressions of fear gave way to grins of relief, to eyes which exchanged unspoken messages of congratulation.

At last the Captain broke the silence. 'They could not have sighted us. The crash dive was well executed. I heard the aircraft to port, flying low it seemed. It must have been the morning reconnaissance from Pamanzi or Kilindini.'

Two ratings who had been on bridge lookout when the klaxon sounded exchanged imperceptible shakes of the head. They had not heard the aircraft.

Nor had Yashimoto, for the good reason that there had not been one. The only sound he had heard was a faint scream from the AA gun-platform as he shut the upper hatch.

The unspoken question in many minds was voiced at last by the First Lieutenant. 'Ichiro Noguchi, Captain?'

Yashimoto bowed, gestured solemnly with his hands. 'He was on the after-casing, investigating a peculiar knocking I had heard earlier. When the crash dive came he did not reach the upper hatch.' Yashimoto spoke without emotion, his face impassive. 'He chose the way of honour.'

The First Lieutenant's eyes fixed the Captain's. 'It is better so, Captain.'

To those in the control-room who had so recently witnessed Noguchi's disgrace, his end had come as no surprise.

Before long I-357 was back on her northbound course, making good six knots at a depth of twenty-five metres since there was still insufficient light for periscope observations. Watch-diving routine had been resumed and most of the men off watch had taken to their bunks.

In his cabin – it was a small affair with little more than a bunk, a desk, a diminutive settee, and a washbasin with jugged water – Yashimoto was drafting a brief report on the loss overboard of Acting Sub-Lieutenant Noguchi. Not only would it form an entry in the submarine's logbook but when I-357 reached Penang he intended sending a copy to Rear-Admiral Noguchi, the sub-lieutenant's uncle. He would send it to the Admiral under cover of a personal letter, conveying his most sincere condolences and extolling the officer-like qualities of Ichiro Noguchi, one-time philosophy student at the University of Tokyo.

For these reasons he was attentive to detail in composing the entry. It was important that it should read well. Having completed the task he made his obeisances before the small Shinto shrine mounted on the forward bulkhead of his cabin, commending the soul of Noguchi to the good offices of his ancestors.

It had been an uneventful day: no sightings on the various occasions that I-357 had come to periscope depth, no reports from the hydrophone operators of propeller noises or echoes, nothing but the rhythmic hum of the electric motors, the whirr of ventilating fans and at times the voices of men. In late afternoon, having rested, Yashimoto went to the chart-table where the submarine's position was plotted at hourly intervals. With dividers he measured off the distance covered since the 1700 position. The submarine's course of 355° ran parallel to the Mozambique coast, distant on average some twenty-five miles to port apart from a string of small islands which lay several miles offshore.

For several reasons he had chosen to keep within reasonable distance of the land rather than well out in the broad reaches of the Mozambique Channel. There was plenty of deep water along the coast, much of it 2000 metres and more, merchant ships tended to stay inshore because the British believed it made them safer from submarine attack and, most importantly, the light at Cape Delgado, close on 100 miles ahead, was a focal point for both north and southbound shipping. Running on the surface, I-357 would be off Cape Delgado soon after midnight; Yashimoto had hopes of a target thereabouts, preferably a vessel sailing alone. He was not anxious to tangle again with an escorted convoy. I-357's recent encounter with one had very nearly ended in disaster; as it was he feared that I-362 might have been lost, for her commanding officer, Lieutenant Commander Suzuki, had made no report since that action. I-362 had been placed under Yashimoto's command when they left Penang with orders to attack merchant shipping in the Mozambique Channel.

Earlier in the year Rear-Admiral Ishikazi, with five boats of the 8th Submarine Flotilla, had carried out a highly successful operation in the Mozambique Channel, sinking over 120,000 tons of merchant shipping and crippling the British battleship *Ramillies*. But, as Yashimoto well knew, conditions in the Channel were now very different. Ishikazi had enjoyed the advantage of two armed supply ships, of enemy merchant ships sailing unaccompanied, and the virtual absence of enemy destroyers and other anti-submarine forces, notably aircraft. Yashimoto, with only two submarines under his command, no supply ships and a base plus or minus 5000 miles away, had to operate against well-escorted convoys, patrolling destroyers, and constant surveillance from the air. And since few ships now sailed unaccompanied, easy targets were difficult to find. Yashimoto, a keen and

15

efficient naval officer, found it hard to accept that during the seven weeks since leaving base his two submarines had sunk only four vessels, one of these a coaster off the Chagos islands, on the long outward passage from Penang. Thus the Mozambique operation had yielded only three sinkings so far, no more than 17,000 tons, and I-357 was already homeward bound.

Looking at the slate above the chart-table he saw that sunset was at 1806, moonrise 2034; the clock next to it showed 1801. There was little twilight in the tropics, for the darkness of night soon followed the setting of the sun. The last time I-357 had been at periscope depth Yashimoto had seen storm clouds in the north-western sky. That was where the weather came from. It might be a dark night despite the moon. He decided to surface at about 1930.

TWO

Yashimoto took I-357 to periscope depth at 1930. After a thorough check of the screen of darkness around the submarine, and assurances from the hydrophone operator that there were no propeller noises, he ordered, 'Down periscope – surface.'

The First Lieutenant gave the surfacing orders, the lower hatch was opened by a petty officer, and Yashimoto climbed up the conning-tower ladders, followed by the lookouts.

He eased the safety clips on the upper hatch. When the noise of seas buffeting the bridge ceased, he released the clips, pressure within the submarine then forcing the hatch lid open. Hauling himself clear of the conning-tower he stepped on to the bridge where the last vestiges of sea water were still draining away. Savouring the fresh night air, so welcome after the stale atmosphere below with its odours of diesel, battery gas, human bodies and decaying food, he and the lookouts began probing the darkness with binoculars. Behind the periscope standards the search aerial was turning in its perpetual vigil. Satisfied that all was well, Yashimoto gave the order for the diesels to be started. Charging of the batteries began, air compressors were switched on, and he gave the order for normal patrol routine. It was his custom at night to remain on the bridge with the officer-of-the-watch for the first hour after surfacing; he did this, too, for the hour before the dawn dive.

The sea was calm, its surface still only ruffled by the offshore breeze. Under an overcast sky I-357 slipped through the water at twelve knots, her bows dipping and rising to the undulations of the south-easterly swell. To the officer-of-the-watch, Lieutenant Toshida, the Captain

17

appeared to be in unusually good spirits, certainly more communicative than he had been for some time.

For his part Yashimoto was pleased with the weather, for if the sky remained overcast it boded well for the night; moreover he was glad of the company of Toshida, his Gunnery Officer, a zealous and capable young man for whom he had a high regard. Having remarked that the darkness of the night was accentuated by the banks of cloud which obscured most of the normally starlit southern sky, Yashimoto added, 'Time of moonrise, Lieutenant?'

'2034, sir.'

'Good. Possibly the clouds will hide it.'

'Yes, sir,' replied Toshida quietly. One did not disagree with the Captain, even if one had doubts. Not that Toshida had. He disliked the moon, but his thoughts at that moment happened to be in Matsuyama, on the shores of the Inland Sea. There his wife was expecting their first child. It might already have arrived. Boy or girl? Had it been a safe delivery? Was she well? He would not know until I-357 reached Penang. The uncertainty troubled him. Once more he raised his binoculars in the endless search.

The voice-pipe buzzer sounded. It was the chief tele-graphist, Petty Officer Keda, reporting the receipt of a signal from Penang. The Navigating Officer was, he said, putting it through the cypher machine.

Yashimoto at once announced that he would go down to the control-room.

The signal from the Flag Officer Submarines, Penang, brought such a pronounced wrinkle to the Captain's forehead that men in the control-room wondered what it was about, particularly when he went to the chart-table with Lieutenant Sato, opened the folio drawer, took from it a fresh chart and placed it over the one already on the table.

The Penang signal informed Yashimoto that a damaged British aircraft carrier with two escorting destroyers had passed through the Suez Canal on passage to Durban for refit and repairs. The carrier and its escorts would call at

18

Mombasa to refuel on the journey south, arriving there some time on November 26/27. I-357 and I-362 were to take station off that port not later than midnight on November 25. The chief telegraphist had not yet heard I-362 acknowledge the signal, reported the Navigating Officer.

Yashimoto looked up from the chart-table, the doubt in his narrowed eyes underlined by dark pouches beneath them. 'That is bad news, Lieutenant. Coming on top of I-362's continued failure to report since the convoy attack. Well, this is war. But we shall carry out the attack.'

The Navigating Officer's 'Yes, sir' was unenthusiastic. He had a considerable respect for British destroyers after their recent encounter. Closing his mind to that unpleasant recollection he listened instead to the Captain thinking aloud as he worked on the chart with dividers and a slide rule. 'Distance to Mombasa 485 miles. At twelve knots surfaced and six submerged we make good 216 miles in twenty-four hours. So passage to Mombasa will be fifty-four hours. It is now 2015 on November 20. We have time in hand.' He had worked on I-357's economical speeds. The big 1600-ton submarine was capable of twenty-one knots on the surface and nine knots submerged.

'Current, sir? The . . .' began Sato.

'I am aware of the current,' interrupted Yashimoto with a slight show of annoyance. 'Three knots south-going in the Mozambique Channel. But there is often a counter-current inshore.'

'Yes, sir. Of course.' Sato was now apologetic. 'I only mentioned the current because . . .'

'Because you thought I'd forgotten it.' Yashimoto looked up from the chart, bared his teeth at the young Lieutenant in a humourless smile. 'Inshore is where I intend to go.'

The Captain's aggressive intentions were mirrored by the outward thrust of his lower lip. 'Alter course twenty-five degrees to port. Let me know when we're within five miles of the land. Then give me a course for Cape Delgado.' Yashimoto turned away from the chart-table, looked round the control-room and nodded briefly to the men near him before making his way to the conning-tower ladder. There, he found Lieutenant Torago Nangi, the Torpedo Officer, who had taken over from Toshida when the watches changed at 2000.

In the north-west there were distant flashes of lightning, followed by faint rumbles of thunder. These did not concern Yashimoto unduly as he looked into the darkness. Indeed, thinking about the Penang signal, his earlier sense of well-being became one of near elation. Having disposed of the problem of Ichiro Noguchi in more senses than one, and being free of worry on that account, he was able to give his mind wholeheartedly to what lay ahead. Not only was I-357 homeward bound, but the Penang signal had banished any fear that she might not find a target before reaching her base.

There was certainly a target now – only five days away – and what a target. An aircraft carrier, the dream of every submarine commander. The escort? Two destroyers? Pity about I-362, thought Yashimoto. That could have made things easier. But an arrogant sense of self-sufficiency brushed the difficulty aside. Earlier in the year, off the Marshall Islands, he had sunk an American destroyer and seriously damaged the heavy cruiser it was escorting in company with another destroyer. That attack had been carried out by I-357 operating alone. He was more than ready to meet the new challenge. It was fortunate, he re-minded himself, that I-357 had six torpedoes remaining. Since leaving Penang the expenditure of torpedoes in relation to sinkings had been high, but in a number of instances this had been due to faulty running, technical failures in the weapons themselves. His thoughts went on. There was deep water outside the entrance to Kilindini, the port of Mombasa. That would be in I-357's favour. The enemy's time of arrival off the port was an important factor. If it were during the hours of darkness, so much the better. He preferred a night action. There would be two opportunities for attack, the arrival of the carrier and its escorts and their departure. If conditions did not favour the former he could fall back on the latter. That might in any event be advisable since, on the enemy's arrival, he would have observed the carrier's course when approaching the port. If there was a British minefield she and her escorts would keep to the swept channel.

He was busy with these tactical problems when the voice-pipe buzzer sounded.

'Hydrophone cabinet – bridge. Propeller noises on sector red three zero to four zero, sir. Range five thousand yards. Single screw. Slow revolutions. Closing slowly.' It was the operator on watch reporting from the hydrophone cabinet.

Yashimoto's mind worked fast. Two and a half nautical miles, it told him. Range closing slowly with I-357 doing twelve knots. So they were overtaking a northbound vessel. Single screw. Slow revolutions. A merchant ship.

He called the control-room. The First Lieutenant answered. 'Pass the word for action standby,' Yashimoto's voice had hardened. 'Surface action. Have the gun's crew ready. Tell Lieutenant Toshida I want him up here.'

Yashimoto had not used the action-alarm for fear that its raucous clamour might carry down wind to the target. For the same reason he frowned at the sounds of unusual activity which drifted up through the conning-tower as men below hurried to their stations. Toshida arrived on the bridge, followed by the Coxswain who took over the upper steering position. Yashimoto had already altered course to put the target vessel directly ahead.

In the control-room the Navigating Officer recorded the time in the action log – 2031.

During the next twenty minutes the thunderstorm in the north-west drew nearer, and the range of the ship ahead dropped steadily. By the time it was down to two thousand yards, reports from the hydrophone operator confirmed Yashimoto's belief that the target was a merchant ship. Making good ten knots, it was on course for Cape Delgado, ninety-five miles distant.

The voice-pipe buzzed urgently. 'Still no radar emissions, sir.' Hasumu's report indicated that the vessel ahead, like most merchant ships at that stage of the war, had no radar.

I-357's stealthy approach from astern on a dark night could only be detected visually. What was not good was the storm. The closer it came, the more likely it was that lightning flashes might reveal the presence of the submarine. For that reason a submerged attack would have been better. Yashimoto, however, had no intention of using his remaining torpedoes on a merchant ship; their target would be the aircraft carrier. The ship ahead had to be sunk by gunfire. The sooner the better.

He called the hydrophone cabinet. 'Range now?'

'Twelve hundred yards, sir.' It was the voice of the chief operator who had taken over.

Yashimoto spoke to the First Lieutenant by voice-pipe. 'Gun action stations,' he commanded. Soon afterwards the gun-hatch below the foreside of the bridge opened and the crew of I-357's four-inch moved silently to their stations on the forward platform.

To no one's surprise, for he had excellent night vision, it was Yashimoto who first saw the blurred shape ahead at about the time the hydrophone operator reported the range to be five hundred yards. 'I see it,' the Captain exclaimed to the Gunnery Officer beside him. 'It's dead ahead. Open fire when the range is down to three hundred yards. Aim at the wireless cabin. It's abaft the funnel. We don't want them transmitting an SSSS signal. After that go for their stern gun.' SSSS was the emergency code for *attacked by submarine*.

Toshida passed the range and bearing to the gun's crew. 'Standby for the order to open fire,' he said. 'When I give it, aim abaft the funnel. Knock out that wireless cabin.'

To the Captain he said, 'I've got it, sir. Can't make out any detail. Just a vague shape.' He spoke without lowering his binoculars.

A flash of sheet lightning revealed for an instant the lumbering bulk of a cargo steamer ahead, smoke pouring from its funnel. In that brief glimpse those on the submarine's bridge saw no signs of life round the freighter's stern gun. A rumble of thunder was followed by large, single drops of rain which began to beat a wet tattoo on the bridge.

'Liberty ship,' snapped Yashimoto.

'Range three five zero, sir,' came from the hydrophone cabinet. There was thinly concealed excitement in the operator's voice.

Yashimoto touched the Gunnery Officer's arm. 'Range three five zero. Open fire when you're ready.' He swore softly as the rain began to fall more heavily, misting the lenses of his binoculars. Another sheet of lightning was followed by a roll of thunder. It seemed to those on the bridge that a long time elapsed before Toshida's voice broke the silence with the long expected order to open fire.

The flash and report of the four-inch gun sounded mute and inadequate after the more violent manifestations of the storm. With the shell whining its way across the water Yashimoto waited, tense, keyed up, watching the dim shape ahead as best he could through rain-streaked binoculars. A faint white plume in the darkness marked the shell's fall short of the target. Three more rounds were fired before a burst of flame erupted from the midships superstructure of the Liberty ship.

'Get more hits abaft the funnel,' demanded Yashimoto. 'Then knock out the stern gun.' He spoke into the voice-pipe. 'Revolutions for eight knots.' Turning to the Coxswain he said, 'Steer twenty degrees to starboard.'

Though the gunnery of defensively armed merchant ships was notoriously indifferent, and a trimmed-down submarine a difficult target, especially at night, Yashimoto had no intention of getting too close. With the range under 300 yards and still closing, he brought I-357's bows round to starboard, reducing speed to maintain distance from the enemy ship. It had become a more visible target now, the shell having started a fire amidships. With the submarine falling off to starboard the barrel of its four-inch gun swung to port, holding the steamer steady in the gun-sight; this was happening so swiftly that within less than a minute of the first hit three more rounds had been fired, the first splashing to starboard of the freighter, the next two exploding on the superstructure abaft the funnel. A new sound broke into the night; the shrill hiss of escaping steam. A white plume, illuminated by the light from the fire, reached up from the Liberty ship's funnel.

Lightning flashed once again and for the first time men could be seen round the freighter's gun, its barrel trained on the submarine. 'Shift target to stern-gun.' Yashimoto's shout was urgent. There was a clap of thunder, rain sluiced down, and in that moment an orange flash came from the enemy's gun. A shell screeched towards I-357 and splashed into the sea beyond. 'Port twenty,' shouted Yashimoto. It was vital to present a smaller target.

The submarine's sudden alteration of course, immediately after the unexpected arrival of the freighter's shell, combined to confuse I-357's gun-crew, their next two rounds falling well astern of the target. Toshida's shouted corrections were drowned by another shell splash, this time raising a column of white water just short of I-357's turning bows. It required several more rounds from the submarine before one exploded on the Liberty ship's stern in a vivid sheet of flame. Despite the light from the fire amidships it was too dark to see what damage had been done, though it was soon evident that the stern gun had been silenced. The submarine's last alteration of course having brought her out on the steamer's port quarter, Yashimoto increased speed and altered course to starboard. The clatter of the diesels grew louder, the vibrations more pronounced and, as speed built up sheets of phosphorescent water thrown up by the submarine's bows glittered brightly in the darkness. Yashimoto had increased speed in order to reach quickly a position from which the Liberty ship's waterline would present an easy target. He was watching her through misted binoculars when the lightning came again. The barrel of her stern gun was still pointing to starboard, whereas I-357 was now on the ship's port side. But he had seen something else in the brief moment of illumination, something which made him slap his thigh in sudden exaltation: around the enemy's gun lay the prone bodies of its gun-crew; near them a jagged shell-hole showed in the steel screen at the base of the gun-platform. He shouted down to the gun's crew. 'Well done. You've taught those gum-chewing amateurs a lesson.'

A lamp began to wink from the Liberty ship's bridge.

'Answer them, Yeoman,' commanded Yashimoto.

Takamori, the Yeoman of Signals, trained a signal lamp on the blinking light across the water, clicked out the international signal for *proceed with your message.*

The distant light began its reply.

While this exchange was taking place, Yashimoto ordered revolutions for eight knots and altered to starboard, so reducing the range and putting the submarine on a course parallel with the Liberty ship's.

'Standby to open fire again when I give the word,' he warned Toshida. 'Aim for the waterline. Five or six rounds should sink her.'

The Gunnery Officer passed the order to the gun's crew who had kept the four-inch trained on the enemy ship throughout I-357's manoeuvring.

Moving slowly to the south-east, the thunder and lightning continued unabated though the rain had ceased. Clad in cotton shorts and singlets the men on the bridge and gun-platform were drenched, but the night was humid and sultry and the air temperature still in the high-seventies. To be wet was no discomfort.

'See that, sir?' Toshida's voice was urgent. In the light of the flames amidships the Liberty ship could be seen to be lowering a lifeboat.

Yashimoto called to the Yeoman, still busy with the signal lamp. 'What's he saying, Takamori?' he demanded irritably. 'We haven't time to stay here talking.'

'I cannot read him, sir,' complained the Yeoman. 'He signals badly – and in English.'

'Then forget him. No doubt trying to tell us he's abandoning ship.'

Toshida said, 'Yes. The ship has almost stopped.'

'Typical,' said Yashimoto. 'These western people fight in

a contemptible fashion. Shoot to kill you until they know they have lost. Then they surrender. To save their wretched skins. They do not understand the way of the warrior.'

'You are right, sir.' Toshida was thinking that the dissertation was a long one for the Captain. 'They talk of their God in Heaven, but they do not seem anxious to meet him.'

Yashimoto grunted assent. 'Good. Enough time has been wasted. Now we set course for Mombasa.' With a snort of derision, he added, 'You'll see real action there.' He raised his binoculars again. 'Open fire, Toshida.'

The gunlayer's task was easier now at almost point blank range and with the hull amidships lit up by flickers of firelight. I-357's gun flashed and banged and as if by magic a hole appeared in the freighter's hull a few feet above the water. In less than a minute successive rounds had ripped a series of gashes along the waterline. The heavily laden ship began to list to port.

'Put a couple of rounds into the bridgehouse,' said Yashimoto. He bent to the voice-pipe. 'The enemy is on fire amidships and sinking,' he told the First Lieutenant. 'We will move off now. The flames may attract attention. Revolutions for sixteen knots.'

The First Lieutenant repeated the order. Yashimoto was giving a helm order to the Coxswain when the distant crack of a gun was followed by the rising whine of an incoming shell. A blinding flash of light beneath the conning-tower was accompanied by an explosion which rocked the bridge. Toshida, the Yeoman and a lookout were thrown off their feet. Yashimoto's cry of, 'My God! What was that?' was overtaken by muffled screams from the control-room.

In the faint reflection of light from the Liberty ship's fire one of I-357's bridge lookouts, a young ordinary seaman, could be seen pointing to the stern of the enemy. 'They fired at us, sir,' he complained, in much the same tone as a child might have said, 'They threw a stone at me, miss.'

Three

'Perhaps you two could lower your voices.' The thin man with the long face looked up from the book he was reading, frowned at the offenders.

'Sorry. We were having a discussion.' Galpin, the senior of *Restless*'s two midshipmen, rubbed the side of his nose in a gesture of apology.

'What you were having was a typical wardroom argument, not a discussion.' The thin man tipped his heavily rimmed spectacles straight, glared at the midshipmen and began reading again.

'How would you define a *typical* wardroom argument, sir?' challenged the midshipman with red hair. The emphasis on *sir* was well calculated to irritate Surgeon Lieutenant Philip Kerr RNVR, generally known in HMS *Restless* as 'Docker', a corruption of his name and calling preferred by the wardroom to the more usual 'Doc'.

'Wild assertion followed by flat contradiction ending in personal abuse,' came from a large man with a deep voice. Spreadeagled in an armchair, he had appeared to be asleep. 'It's not original but it will do.' He looked at the wardroom clock. 'Getting on for 2100. Shouldn't you two be turning in instead of making a nuisance of yourselves? You've got watches to keep.'

The Doctor nodded. 'Thank you, Number One. Most helpful.'

'It's a pleasure, Docker. Any time.' The large man pulled himself up in the armchair. 'Midshipmen belong in gunrooms. Destroyers don't have gunrooms. So these young peasants have to come in here with their betters. Appalling really.'

Jeremy Tripp, the freckled, red-haired midshipman frowned. 'Didn't you do destroyer time when you were a mid, sir?'

'Of course. But in those days midshipmen were rather different. Well disciplined, good mannered, quiet – and *clean*. We never argued.' Sandy Hamilton, the First Lieutenant, looking older than his twenty-six years, put up a hand and yawned. 'We were rather a splendid lot really.'

The *clean* struck home. Tropical kit, white shirt, shorts and stockings, was the rig of the day. Those worn by the midshipmen seemed rather more crumpled and grubby than the wardroom's average. Tripp was thinking up an appropriate reply when there was a knock on the wardroom door. A Chief Petty Officer Telegraphist came in, clipboard in hand. He went to the First Lieutenant, passed him the board. 'From SOO, Kilindini, sir.'

The First Lieutenant shook his head as he read the message. 'My God, how absolutely typical. Flaming RAF. Well I suppose we can't win 'em all.' He initialled the message, passed the clipboard back to the Chief Petty Officer. 'Thank you, Duckworth.' He raised an eyebrow. 'Captain not pleased, I imagine.'

Duckworth turned, hand on the wardroom door, nodded. 'He didn't look too happy, sir.' Smiling, he closed the door behind him.

Hamilton ran a hand through a head of tousled hair, stood up, yawned again and stretched. 'I'd better go to the bridge,' he said to no one in particular. 'See how the Old Man's taking it.'

'What is it then that the flying boys have been doing, Number One?' The inquiry in a Welsh sing-song came from the Engineer Officer, Gareth Edwards, a slight, dark-eyed man, who was playing darts with Peter Morrow, an RNVR Sub-Lieutenant. Morrow, whose family farmed at Nakuru, beyond Lake Naivasha, had joined in Kilindini a few days before the ship left for Simonstown.

'That Catalina we've been looking for got back to Kilindini at 1500. She wasn't down at all. Her transmitter had gone on the blink. Some chairborne aviator forgot to inform Navy House.'

'Indeed, and it's a lot of fuel then that we've been wasting.'

'And time, Chiefy. About eight hours while we searched thousands of square miles of ruddy ocean.' The First Lieutenant picked up his cap and made for the bridge.

HMS *Restless* of the 27th Destroyer Flotilla, Eastern Fleet, on passage to her base at Kilindini after a refit and boiler clean in Simonstown, had been diverted earlier in the day to search for an RAF Catalina reported down in the area south of the Comores, the islands in the Mozambique Channel which lay midway between the East African coast and Madagascar. The flying boat's last known position had been one hundred and fifty miles SSW of Moheli Island. Starting from that position *Restless* had carried out a square search, from time to time expanding the area. But it had been a fruitless operation. On receipt of the W/T message announcing the safe return of the Catalina, Lieutenant Commander John Barratt, Captain of *Restless*, had put the destroyer back on course for Kilindini, some 400 miles to the north-west.

It was the second time since leaving Simonstown that the destroyer had been diverted. Several days earlier she had gone to the assistance of a south-bound convoy under attack by submarines between Durban and Lourenço Marques. With the corvettes escorting the convoy, *Restless* had carried out several depth-charge attacks on what seemed promising asdic contacts; but the depth of water was so great that it had been difficult to confirm a 'kill'.

The First Lieutenant found the Captain in the chartroom with the Navigating Officer, Charlie Dodds, a Lieutenant RN whose persistent frown was not surprising in a young man who seldom stopped worrying.

Not sure of the Captain's mood, the First Lieutenant began tentatively. 'Too bad about the Catalina, sir?'

The lean, wiry figure of the Captain turned away from the chart-table. 'Yes, it is.' He stared past the First Lieutenant in an impersonal way. 'I've given SOO our ETA as 2130 tomorrow. If it's wrong, blame the Pilot. He did the sums.'

'Only thing I'm not sure about is the current.' Furrows gathered on the Navigating Officer's forehead. 'For most of today it's been setting south at two-and-a-half knots. The ETA's based on that.'

'I'm going back to the bridge.' Barratt spoke without looking at anyone. 'Need some fresh air before getting my head down. It's a hot night.'

The First Lieutenant nodded. 'Yes it is, sir.' He hesitated. 'Be rather fun getting back to Kilindini, won't it?' The picture in his mind was that of Camilla, the attractive second officer Wren who did cypher duty in Navy House.

Staring at the younger man in a strange, absent-minded way, Barratt shrugged his shoulders and left the chartroom.

The First Lieutenant's voice was apologetic. 'I thought my Kilindini ploy might work.'

'Bit soon isn't it?'

'I suppose so. Wish we could cheer him up. Incredible change though, isn't it?'

'Yes, but understandable. He only got the news six weeks ago. Give him a chance, poor chap. He has to adjust to things.'

'Nothing seems to interest him these days, Pilot. Sometimes I get the impression that his mind is a million miles away. Difficult to get through to him.'

Dodds closed the book on the chart-table – Africa Pilot, Vol III, the Admiralty Sailing Directions – and replaced it on the bookshelf. He turned back to the First Lieutenant. 'How does news get out of Changi, Number One?'

'Haven't a clue. I suppose the POWs operate some sort of grapevine. Can't see the Japanese bothering to notify next-of-kin.'

'No I can't,' agreed the Navigating Officer. 'How long had they been married?'

'About six months I think – that is, when Singapore fell. He never saw her after that.' The First Lieutenant changed the subject. 'Hot and muggy. We could do with another thunderstorm.'

The Navigating Officer was drawing the new course line on the chart. Over his shoulder he said, 'That one this afternoon certainly cooled things down.'

At the point of alteration of course he drew a small circle, noting against it the time, 2049.

There was no moon to relieve the darkness but in the corridors between the clouds the southern sky was bright with stars. From the engineroom skylight came distant sounds, the rhythmic hum of turbines, the purr of ventilating fans and the dissonances of auxiliary machinery. To those on the bridge closer sounds were the splash and rustle of water along the sides, the metronomic *ping* from the asdic's loudspeaker, and the occasional murmur of voices from the men on watch.

Barratt stood at the bridge screen looking into the night, his thoughts in another place, another time, another world: Singapore, the year before, on the terrace at Raffles. A night in some ways not unlike this, he thought; hot, humid, bright with stars, the muted strains of a dance band somewhere in the distance. The slight fair girl sitting beside him, eager and joyous with youth, a bubbling laugh never far away. 'D'you really want to make an honest woman of me, John? Are you sure? With this War and everything?'

'Yes. Absolutely sure. The War's all the more reason. We won't see much of each other, probably. Well – not for some time anyway. Better make the most of it now.'

She laughed. 'You've only known me for three weeks. You're thirty-five. I'm twenty-one. It's completely mad.'

'Good to be mad,' he said. 'Your youth, my rugged old age. What a combination.' That had sounded frivolous, so he'd added, 'I love you, Caroline.' He'd leant towards her, taken her hand and squeezed it. He'd wanted very much to kiss her, but disliked displays of emotion in public. Rather prudish about that, he was.

She'd pushed him away. Laughing, watching him closely,

she'd said, 'I'm told you were a bit wild when you were young. You got into awful scrapes, they say.'

'Who's they?'

She'd looked guilty. 'Oh, somebody who was in the Navy with you in those days.'

'Well, I think I'd describe it as having been a bit high-spirited. Not wild really. Anyway, don't let's discuss my past. Let's do something about our present.'

It was then that she'd looked at him in a calculating way. 'Were you ever married?'

'No. Got near to it once and – well – that came to nothing. I was leading a pretty busy life and – you know – just didn't get round to it. Then the War came.'

All that seemed to have happened a long time ago. Without memories, what was there left? *Won't see much of each other, probably.* He'd not realized how prophetic that was to be. The thought evoked a long-drawn sigh of wretchedness. The signal from the Admiralty said she'd died of fever. What sort of fever? Malaria, enteric, yellow? Not that it made any difference. She was dead. He'd never see her again. Dead in Changi Gaol. What a foul place for anyone to die, let alone a girl like Caroline. Surrounded by those God-awful people with their cold-eyed militaristic dogma that permitted the most ferocious atrocities.

As so often when thinking of her death he had to tussle with confused emotions: feelings of guilt – but for him she might not have been there – of futility because he could do nothing about what had happened – nothing but fulminate and hate. In each hour of every night and day his mind was scourged by thoughts of Caroline. Thoughts of the indignities, the humiliations she must have endured; her loneliness and terror as the fever possessed her; the dreadful, suffering hours as she lay dying, surrounded by Japanese prison guards.

There was nobody with whom he could share his grief, nothing to look forward to, little point in going on with life; yet it was there and had to be lived, and at least the War might provide an opportunity for revenge. That his thoughts were entirely negative, he well knew. But he could not make them otherwise, they couldn't be reasoned away, and that knowledge made things worse.

The discordant rasp of a buzzer sounding on the bridge brought him back to reality. Its urgent summons was followed by the voice of Lawson, the officer-of-the-watch, who was also the destroyer's Gunnery Officer. 'Bridge – W/T office.' A pause, then, 'Repeat that.' Another pause, then, 'Just, *my course is* – good. The bridge messenger will collect it.'

Lawson came over to Barratt at the bridge screen. 'Captain, sir. W/T office reports an SSSS from a US merchant ship, *Fort Nebraska*. She gave her position at 2100 as twenty-two miles east-north-east of Porto do Ibo. The message ended with the words *my course is* – no more after that, sir. Messenger's gone to collect it.'

Barratt came suddenly alive. 'U-boat attack. Transmission interrupted. Poor devils. Steer twenty degrees to port. Revolutions for twenty knots. I'll look at the chart. Tell the Pilot I want him up here double quick.'

Lawson was repeating the orders to the wheelhouse when the messenger arrived on the bridge with *Fort Nebraska*'s signal.

The rhythmic hum of the turbines, the vibrations of the hull, the tumble and hiss of water along the sides increased in pitch as Barratt made his way to the bridge chart-table. He lifted the screen, switched on a light. First he plotted *Fort Nebraska*'s position, then advanced *Restless*'s for the five minutes since 2100. Drawing a line between them, he rolled the parallel rulers on to the compass rose, read off the course to steer – 290° – and measured the distance with dividers – 123 miles. He switched off the light, replaced the screen, moved towards the compass platform. 'Steer 290 degrees,' he called to Lawson.

The Navigating Officer arrived on the bridge. Barratt handed him the *Fort Nebraska* signal. 'Submarine attack, Pilot. I make the course to her position 290 degrees, distance 123 miles. Haven't allowed for current. Plot the scenario in the chartroom and give me a course to steer. Double quick.

After that draft a signal to SOO Kilindini reporting our receipt of the four S. Give her position and ours, and conclude with, 'Proceeding to *Fort Nebraska* position. My course 290°, speed twenty knots. Got that, Pilot? Good. SOO will already have had the four S from the Fleet W/T office – and other ships at sea.'

'Our speed only twenty knots, sir?'

'Yes,' snapped Barratt. 'That's all our fuel remaining will permit. Don't forget we chased around looking for U-boats after that attack on the southbound convoy. Then the Catalina saga. You should know that, my boy. Now get on with it.'

With a breathless, 'Yes, sir,' Dodds made for the chartroom.

Barratt called to Lawson, 'Number One on the bridge. Double quick.'

Double quick was Barratt's variation on the theme of 'at the double'. Midshipman Tripp had dubbed it The Old Man's Signature Tune. The First Lieutenant disapproved. All orders were expected to be carried out at the double. It was not a Custom of the Service to emphasize the obvious. For Barratt, however, they suggested a greater sense of urgency. On this occasion they brought Sandy Hamilton to the bridge in just under sixty seconds. He was dripping, bare-footed and naked but for white shorts and a uniform cap. 'Sorry about my rig, sir,' he apologized. 'I was in the shower.'

The Captain half smiled, became quickly serious. 'We've just picked up a four S from a US merchant ship. Her signal was mutilated. We won't reach the position given for another six hours, but make ready for picking up survivors. Scrambling nets, boathooks, blankets, etcetera. Warn the Doctor. He must put the sickbay on standby.'

'I don't expect we'll make contact with the U-boat, sir?'

'Unlikely, I think. They usually move well clear of a sinking. But if the CO's brave and greedy – and most of these German U-boat commanders are – he may hang around hoping to make a target of whatever comes along to pick up survivors. We'll see.'

'D'you think it's the U-boats we tangled with the other day? The *Gruppe Eisbär* lot operating off Lourenço Marques?'

'I imagine so. Having stirred things between Durban and L.M. they may well have decided to move into the Mozambique Channel.'

Barratt looked at his watch. Five minutes had elapsed since *Fort Nebraska*'s transmission. What other ships and shore stations had picked it up? That reminded him it was time Dodds was back with the draft of the signal to SOO.

As if his thoughts had somehow triggered a response, the phone buzzed. It was the Navigating Officer. 'Course to steer 293 degrees, sir. That allows for a southerly set of two knots. I've drafted the signal to SOO.'

'Right, I'll come down.' Barratt hung up the phone, told Lawson to steer 293°, and went to the chartroom.

Four

With the heat and smoke, the acrid smell and shock of the explosion still about him, Yashimoto knew that he must at once get I-357 clear of the Liberty ship's gun. It was no time to question how an apparently dead gun's crew had come to life, though the puzzle of this nagged at the back of his mind. More important was the reality that the submarine, moving slowly past the sinking ship, could no longer bring her own gun to bear on the enemy's stern gun. The most effective manoeuvre now was to increase speed and take station immediately ahead. Shouting into the voice-pipe, 'Emergency full ahead together,' he ordered the Coxswain to steer fifteen degrees to starboard.

Distant lightning, followed by thunder, came from the storm which had moved away to the south-east, taking with it the rain. The thunder all but coincided with the bright flash and muffled report of the Liberty ship's gun, the screech of the shell rising in pitch as it passed astern of I-357. It was evident that the enemy's increasingly severe list was making it difficult for her gun's crew to train on the submarine with accuracy.

Yashimoto stood at the bridge screen, taut nerves jangling, his mind a turmoil of anxiety as the submarine drew slowly ahead of its adversary. In the flickering light of flames from the fire he saw the name-board on the bridgehouse; *Fort Nebraska*, beneath it the port of origin, *Baltimore*. To his longstanding dislike and contempt for the Americans was now added an immense anger. The shell which struck I-357's conning-tower had been fired after the enemy had given every indication of abandoning ship. They would have to pay dearly for that.

When I-357 was at last in station ahead of the *Fort Nebraska*, Yashimoto ordered *stop engines*. Only three minutes had elapsed since the shell hit the submarine, but to him they seemed the longest three minutes of his life.

From the after end of the bridge he watched the ship astern through binoculars; the plume of escaping steam was still jetting from the funnel, the shrieking hiss now joined by the deep note of the siren, a weird harmony which lent to the scene a Dantesque quality. Turning from it he ordered the officer-of-the-watch to examine the damage done by the enemy shell and report back without delay. Toshida disappeared in the darkness. The voice-pipe call sounded. It was the First Lieutenant, reporting that the explosion at the foot of the conning-tower had caused a number of casualties in the control-room; one man killed and several wounded.

'The explosion was not in the conning-tower,' barked Yashimoto in angry contradiction. 'The shell struck the base of the outer casing. It must have been splinters from that which fell down the tower into the control-room.'

'I see.' There was muted doubt in the First Lieutenant's reply. 'Matsuhito is checking the damage. He will report back shortly.'

'I have already sent Toshida to do that,' snapped Yashimoto, adding, with some petulance, 'I suppose it will do no harm to have two reports.' He went back to the front of the bridge uncertain, confused, worrying about how shell splinters could have caused casualties in the control-room. Was he right in believing that they had been fall-out from the shell-burst at the foot of the conning-tower, in the same way that splinters had fallen on to the bridge itself?

Back from a quick inspection, Toshida brought contrary and more serious news. 'The armour-piercing shell penetrated at the foot of the tower's outer casing, sir. Then went on through the side of the conning-tower itself and burst as it struck the coaming of the lower hatch.'

Yashimoto received the report in stubborn silence, his mind wrestling with its implications. Though insulated from

37

the pressure hull by the lower hatch, the conning-tower was itself a unit of the pressure hull. Once pierced, its watertight integrity had gone. It would mean diving with a flooded conning-tower and relying on the lower hatch to maintain the integrity of the main pressure hull. A holed conning-tower would not only make a crash dive impossible, but would involve some difficulty in trimming when dived.

He was considering these problems when the Yeoman called out, 'She's going, sir.'

Yashimoto trained binoculars on the sinking ship. She was deep in the water now, listing heavily to port and down by the stern, flames from the fire casting flickering light over the desolate scene. But there were more urgent matters to attend to than watch the last moments of the stricken vessel. He ordered Toshida to take over the bridge. 'I will see for myself the damage.' He gestured astern. 'When it has gone, proceed at eight knots, turn slowly to port. I will not be long.'

The contempt in Yashimoto's voice when he'd referred to the ship as *it* instead of *she* warned the Gunnery Officer that the Captain was in a dangerous mood.

Despite an outward show of calm, Yashimoto was dismayed by what he found in the conning-tower. The shell had penetrated both the outer and inner sides of the tower before exploding as it struck the coaming on which the lower hatch lid was seated when shut. The explosion had not only torn away most of the starboard side of the oval shaped coaming but had left a jagged hole in the main pressure hull adjoining it. He trained the beam of his torch on to the hatch lid. Before the explosion it would have been in its open position, standing vertical, clipped back against the inside of the conning-tower. It must have taken much of the force of the explosion for, apart from blast marks and deep scoring by shell fragments, one side of the lid was noticeably closer to the conning-tower than the other. He assumed that the hammer effect of the explosion had warped the lid, twisting it on its massive hinges. With a sense of helplessness, of bewildered dismay, he saw through the shellhole the broken ends of air pressure pipes and electric cables. He saw, too, the fracture marks on the heavy steel hinges of the hatch. Shaking his head, his emotions a mixture of despair and anger, he sent for the Engineer Officer, whereafter he went to the bridge a deeply troubled man. I-357 could not dive. That was the stark reality which now faced him. Nor would she be able to until the damage had been repaired. If it could be repaired? How long would it take? Only Susuma Satugawa, the Engineer Officer, was qualified to answer those questions. As long as the weather remained fine I-357 could run on the surface, but if the weather deteriorated that too would be hazardous with the main pressure hull holed no more than six or seven feet above the waterline. The fundamental problem remained: I-357 could not dive. When daylight came the chances were they would be found by the enemy's air reconnaissance. That would be the end of the submarine and the seventy-five men of her crew. The attack on *Fort Nebraska* had been disastrous. Not, he assured himself, because of any failure on his part. It was due to an incredibly lucky hit by the American ship. The stern guns of merchant ships were 1914-1918 War relics, their crews naval reservists with little training. That they could in almost total darkness score a direct hit on I-357 after their own gun's crew had been knocked out by a shell burst was almost beyond belief. And yet it had happened. He supposed that one or two members of the American's gun-crew had recovered from concussion and managed to lay and train the gun. That, too, must have involved a considerable element of luck.

He was brooding over these hard facts when the First Lieutenant came on to the bridge with more bad news. A leading torpedoman had been killed and three seamen wounded by fragments of metal. The wounded were receiving attention. The dead man's body had been placed in the torpedo compartment. Even more serious was the news that during the gun action, which had lasted less than five minutes, Yochiro Keda, the submarine's Chief Telegraphist, had heard *Fort Nebraska* transmitting a wireless message. It had, he said, been a brief transmission, apparently giving the ship's position but beginning and ending with four Ss. Though Yashimoto appeared to take the news calmly, even phlegmatically, he was shattered by it. The message transmitted by the American ship must bring enemy naval and air units to the scene. Survivors would report having seen a shell burst on the submarine's conning-tower after which, they would say, it had moved away *on the surface*. The brief W/T transmission had made a bad situation a great deal worse.

In the eastern sky the moon came clear of the clouds, revealing to those on the submarine's bridge a lifeboat, several rafts and an odd assortment of floating wreckage strewn across an area where widening patches of fuel oil, dark and sinister in the moonlight, marked the grave of the *Fort Nebraska*.

After that second round, that must have gone way over the U-boat because they didn't see any splash this side of it, and with the list getting worse, Corrigan knew there was no point in standing by the gun with the dead bodies around it.

'We better get to hell out of it, Smitty,' he shouted to the man leaning against the breech of the 5.5 inch gun. 'Get ourselves into a lifeboat.' He'd had to shout to make himself heard above the shrill hiss of escaping steam.

'Reckon I can't make it, Brad. Legs feel kinda weak,' was the hoarse reply.

'Aw, c'mon boy. I'll lend a hand.' In the darkness Corrigan put an arm round the other man's waist. Together they hobbled and staggered across the sloping poopdeck, making for the starboard ladder. They reached it as the lightning came and for a moment Corrigan saw water swirling at the foot of the ladder.

'Jesus!' there was fear and astonishment in the loud oath. 'The well-deck's awash, Smitty. Can't get forward now. She'll be going soon.' It's all right for me, he was thinking, I belong in the water. But Christ! What about Smitty Fredericks?

40

Goddam wound's bleeding. Sharks go for blood like crazy. And I'll be supporting the guy.

But there wasn't time to think that one out. The hull shook, the list increased steeply, the movement now more a series of jerks than smooth like before. The sound of escaping steam had been muted by the deep thrum of the siren, a bizarre duet which deadened thought.

Corrigan remembered the stack of hand-floats on the poop. Shouting, 'Hold on there, Smitty, while I put a float over,' he disappeared into the darkness. With the list too steep to walk without support he had to crawl, hanging on to deck fittings as he went. He reached the stack, flicked open the locking grips and pulled a float clear. He began dragging it back towards the ladder. He hadn't gone far when the hissing sound from the well-deck ventilators rose to a scream, like a gale blowing through rigging. Must be the pressure of water flooding into the holds, forcing out the remaining air, he told himself. Before he could reach Smitty the ship began its final, stern first slide. A slow but irreversible movement, the level of the sea rising until it had covered the after well-deck, then climbing the poop ladder rung by rung. He couldn't see his companion. If only the lightning would come again. He yelled, 'Let yourself down the side, Smitty. Switch on the survivor's light. I'll look after you in the water. You'll be okay.' He kicked off his shoes, switched on the life-jacket's red light, climbed over the guardrail and slid down the side of what remained of the stern above water. When his feet touched the sea he leant forward and plunged in. A strong crawl took him clear of the ship.

He stopped swimming, flipped on to his back and floated. Turning his head he searched the darkness for Smitty's red light, but nothing showed. He shouted, 'Smitty,' several times but soon gave up. There was no chance of being heard above the noise of escaping steam and the siren. He'd have to wait now until the ship had gone before searching for Smitty. So he lay on the smooth sea, rising and falling to the undulations of the swell, wondering about how, when and *if* he and the other survivors would be picked up. Those thoughts were disturbed by the moon breaking through the clouds. It was as if a giant light had been switched on to reveal the scene. The sinking ship seemed closer now that she could be seen, her dying more awesome, whorls of smoke leaping and twisting from the fire, the solitary funnel in its midst like some martyr at the stake. With the stern submerged and the bows high out of the water she slid slowly beneath the sea. Then, where the ship had been, the sea was in turmoil, pieces of wreckage, jets of fuel oil and water, and great bubbles of air bursting to the surface with obscene plops and hisses like gargantuan farts, leaving only the pungent odour of diesel to hang in the air like some invisible mantle.

The turbulence of the sinking was followed by a strange calm, a sudden silence, a tranquillity which Corrigan found comforting. But moonlight and the voices of men soon dispelled the illusion. Because he was looking for Smitty, and couldn't really see properly until lifted by a swell, he focused on the area closest to him. That was where the stern had been, where the dead bodies of the gun's crew lay sagging in the water like black gunny sacks, the air trapped in their clothing ballooning, distorting the shape of their corpses. But there was no sign of Smitty, no one moved, no red light winked, no response to Corrigan's repeated calls.

In and around the widening pools of fuel oil he saw the litter of wreckage: pieces of timber, gratings, hatch-planks, wooden buckets, crates, mooring rope bins, gas cylinders, fire extinguishers and glass bottles. But it was the two lifeboats, some distance from him, which dominated the moonlit scene. One loaded with men, a few of them rowing untidily, was heading for the other which had capsized. Corrigan could see men clinging to its lifelines. Wondering whether to swim towards the lifeboats or make for the hand-float he'd thrown over the side, he heard what sounded like a diesel locomotive in the distance. Soon afterwards, from the top of the next swell, he saw the U-boat, a dark shape on moonlit water. It was a good few hundred yards away, turning in a wide circle.

42

Several swells later he saw that it was moving slowly towards the lifeboats.

He knew from shipmates who'd been in other sinkings what the U-boat was after. Its commander would interrogate the survivors: what ship, where from, where bound, tonnage, cargo, number of crew? Then the Germans would wave, wish them good luck and steam away. Some U-boat commanders had been known to hand cigarettes to survivors, to indicate the direction of the nearest land, to pick a man out of the water and take him on board. Not that Corrigan wanted that. He'd rather take his chance with his own lot.

Thinking about that reminded him of sharks. The sooner he was out of the water the better. There'd been no sign of them yet. They kept away from fuel oil, waited in the waters beyond. Corrigan knew a lot about sharks. A lifeguard on a Massachusetts beach had to. Sharks were attracted by vibrations in the water. For a shark vibrations were worth investigating, especially vibrations from large, irregular and unfishlike shapes. Corrigan knew just about every tactic a swimmer should employ when sharks were about. As a last resort he could defend himself with the sheath-knife on his belt. A blooded shark was always attacked by other sharks. He knew of men who had saved their lives that way. So he didn't feel too bad about sharks, although with wounded corpses in the water and plenty of blood about he reckoned things might go wrong.

Even so, he'd rather stay with his own crowd than be picked up by the U-boat. It had come closer, bows on to him now, maybe a couple of hundred yards from the loaded lifeboat. The rowing had stopped. Someone, the Captain he supposed, was standing in the sternsheets with an arm raised. To Corrigan there was something strangely reassuring about the sleek hull of the U-boat, shining wetly in the moonlight. It represented order and purpose among all that wreckage and devastation. He was aware of the contradictory nature of his thoughts – it was the Germans who'd created the devastation – but there was a bond between seamen which somehow transcended the grim realities of war.

The U-boat came on, moving more slowly. He supposed it was stopping. But it didn't stop. Instead it went steadily on, its bows slicing into the lifeboat, the shouts and screams of the Americans drifting across the water in a frightening dirge. The two halves of the lifeboat, crushed and broken, were thrown aside and began to pass down the length of the submarine. Suddenly, spurts of flame and the rat-tat-tat of automatic fire came from its casing. Disbelief gave way to horror; the U-boat was machine-gunning survivors in the water. Now, less than a hundred yards from him, it was turning to port. With desperate haste he tore loose the tapes of his life-jacket, slipped it off, took a deep breath, duck-dived and began to swim underwater towards the hand-float. Three times he had to come up for air before reaching it: saw the flashing lines of tracer bullets and heard bursts of machine-gun fire. The float with its hanging lifelines was a small, two-foot-square affair, no more than a stout wooden frame over a buoyancy tank. It was designed for swimmers to cling to but not climb upon. Used in that way it could support four men in the water.

Corrigan surfaced on the side away from the submarine, put up a hand and grasped a lifeline. Keeping his chin level with the water he turned the raft just enough to enable him to see the submarine when the swells lifted.

It must have rammed the other lifeboat, the capsized one, while he'd been making the underwater swim to the float. Only its fore-end now remained, the bow pointing forlornly to the sky. Beyond it the submarine was turning to starboard. A powerful beam of light from the conning-tower swept the sea, settling on what remained of the lifeboat. Searchlight, he muttered to himself. Christ help us!

For some time the long black shape, doubly sinister now in the moonlight, continued its grim task; steaming through the wreckage, machine-gunning as it went, then turning to make another run, the beam of light probing the surface of the sea. Once it swept round in his direction. Realizing that the float would be a target he ducked under and began swimming away from it. Never in his life had he swum so far

44

underwater, and certainly never with such urgency. The sound of the submarine's propellers came closer and his terror mounted. But in spite of it he had to come up. With the pressure on his lungs beyond endurance, he surfaced. The submarine was no more than thirty feet away. It must have passed between him and the hand-float, because in the instant of gulping in air he'd heard the rattle of automatic fire and caught a glimpse of men on the casing. The beam of light from the signal lamp had been trained on the side away from him.

In that split second the moonlight had revealed something else, something painted on the side of the black conning-tower: a white rectangle, at its centre, in red, the rising sun of Japan, beneath it, the jagged hole made by the shell he and Smitty had fired. So that was why those bastards were killing everybody. Christ Jesus! The Japs had sunk old *Fort N* and killed most of the gun's crew. Wasn't that enough? They didn't have to massacre the entire crew.

He tried to wipe the oil fuel from his face but realized that it coated his hands and arms and just about everything else. And it burnt his skin and hurt his eyes.

Five

What had promised to be a quiet night in the operations room at Navy House, Kilindini, was interrupted by a spate of incoming signals reporting *Fort Nebraska*'s urgent transmission. The first of these came from the Fleet W/T Office. In no time several more had come in from HM ships at sea, plus two from the RAF, one from the Air Officer Commanding Kilindini, the other from the RAF flying boat base at Pamanzi in the Comoro Islands.

'Here's another, sir.' A tall girl with flaxen hair handed the signal to the Staff Officer Operations, a Commander who sat at a desk on a platform overlooking the plotting table. She was one of two Wrens on duty in the operations room. 'It's from *Restless*,' she added.

'Thank you, Camilla. I've been waiting for this one. *Restless* is all we have within reasonable distance of *Fort N*'s position.' Commander Russel, balding and long of face, took the signal sheet, checked its time of origin, 2109, and read on:

US merchant ship Fort Nebraska *transmitted SSSS at 2102 giving her position as 22 miles ENE of Porto do Ibo. The message ended with quote my course is unquote whereafter transmission ceased. Am proceeding to her assistance at 20 knots. My position 12° 50' S: 42° 56' E.*

Ian Russel, SOO to the Deputy C-in-C, Eastern Fleet, the Rear-Admiral responsible for the control and protection of merchant shipping between Durban and the Equator, passed the signal to a Lieutenant RNVR who appeared to be staring at something over Russel's shoulder. 'Put this on your plot, Jakes, and give me an ETA for *Restless* at the *Fort Nebraska* position.'

46

The Lieutenant's attention at that moment had been diverted from the plotting-table by the statuesque figure of Camilla. It was, to him, quite the most shapely in the business. It looks, he was thinking, particularly good in tropical uniform, and would no doubt look even better without it. Abandoning the pleasant fantasy he took the signal and bent over the plotting-table. A few minutes later he had the answer. 'If the current behaves as it should, I make *Restless*'s ETA 0340 tomorrow, plus or minus five minutes.' He looked up from the plot. 'At twenty knots that's about six and a half hours' steaming time.'

The SOO shook his head. 'The party'll be over long before that. Pity he can't put on more than twenty. Problem must be fuel remaining.' Commander Russel, not the most cheerful of men, tugged at the lobe of his right ear, a gesture known in the operations room to indicate anxiety.

Jakes nodded. 'Has to be that, sir. Long passage from Simonstown, plus extra steaming to and from that convoy shambles off Lourenço Marques, plus chasing around like a blue . . .' he hesitated, coughed. 'Chasing around afterwards looking for the Catalina south of the Comores.'

The SOO moved a hand to the lobe of his left ear. 'Yes. Well, we've nothing available nearer *Fort N* so Barratt'll have to do what he can. The U-boat will long since have gone, but he should be able to pick up survivors.' The SOO went back to his desk, sat for a moment with his head in his hands before looking across to the Wren Petty Officer at the signal desk. 'Pam – make a signal to *Restless*, repeated Captain (D) and RAF (HQ): Your 2109 approved stop. Message ends.'

The Wren finished writing, read back the signal. 'To be encyphered, sir?'

'No. Plain language. Gives away nothing. Get it off right away.'

The SOO flicked a finger at Jakes. It was a gesture which demanded attention. 'This U-boat or U-boats. Must be the same bunch that attacked the convoy on the 16th, 17th. Probably the *Gruppe Eisbär* operating off Lourenço Mar-

47

ques. Evidently shifting their activities further north.' He made a steeple with the fingers of both hands, blew gently through it. 'Some time since they've come to this end of the channel.'

Jakes, who hadn't really been listening all that hard, stopped transmitting private signals to Camilla. 'Yes, sir,' he said. Feeling that something more was necessary, he went on. 'These unaccompanied sailings present easy targets. I wonder we still permit them.'

The SOO nodded gloomily, several times, while he considered Jakes's remark. Did it imply criticism of authority? Was the *we* an indication of collective responsibility? Deciding that it was, he said, 'I've no doubt the Admiral will want to discuss that tomorrow.' He put his hands over his eyes, breathed wearily as if tired by the prospect.

Commander Russel longed for the war to end so that he might return to Naivasha where he had farmed since 1927, the year in which he'd retired from the Royal Navy as a lieutenant. Called up on the outbreak of war, he'd spent a year at sea in an armed merchant cruiser before being appointed to the naval staff in Kilindini. Like all retired officers in the Royal Navy who returned to wartime service he was known as a 'dugout'. Something of a pessimist, he was referred to behind his back as Gloomy Russel.

But for snatched visits to the surface to refill his lungs, Corrigan spent the next ten minutes under water. In this time he had worked his way steadily down-moon in order to get away from anything floating and to hide from the submarine. As long as it was up-moon its lookouts were unlikely to see him.

Because of the swell, and because he did no more than raise his mouth and nose to the surface, he was unable to see the submarine but occasionally the beams of its searchlight swept the water near him and at those times he had gone deeper. When it was near the *woosh-woosh* of its propellers grew in volume. Later, when their frequency quickened, he knew that speed had been increased; when they grew fainter and yet still fainter he assumed the submarine was leaving the scene. Only then did he risk returning to the hand-float.

The top of the wooden frame had been raked by gunfire, the planking partly splintered, some of it hanging over the side. But the buoyancy chamber must have escaped damage for the float remained at its usual height above the surface. Holding on to a lifeline he lifted his head clear of the water and saw the submarine. It was some distance away, still up-moon from him, turning in a wide circle to the west. It must have been going fast because before long it had left the silver path of the moon and was lost in the darkness.

The sound of threshing water broke the surrounding silence. It came from where the huddled bodies lay on the sea. His first thought was that there were, after all, others like him who had somehow evaded the slaughter. But then not far away, where phosphorescent splashes played in the moonlight, he saw dark fins moving among the sagging corpses. Despite the warm water he shivered involuntarily. I better get busy quick, he told himself. Get away from here. Could be a long time before I'm picked up. *If* I'm picked up.

With the sheath-knife he cut through the float's lifelines, took an end and secured it round his waist. Turning on to his stomach he began a slow breast stroke, towing the float, his legs and arms underwater to avoid splashing, his target the rope-bin he'd passed on his journey down-moon.

It was some time before the bin showed up, its staves protruding above the surface of the sea. Thank God for the moon, he thought.

He wasn't tired. The tropical water, warm and buoyant, was kind to the body. But the threshing noises were uncomfortably close and he knew he hadn't much time. The bin was one of several used for stowing mooring ropes. Circular in shape it was a big, cage-like tub. The tops of some of the staves had been shattered and broken. Bullet hits, he supposed.

He had to get the sodden rope out of the bin. He began

by drawing the hand-float against it and tying a lifeline to a stave beneath a cross member. The float would give more buoyancy to the bin and offset his own weight. He climbed in on top of the rope coil and felt the bin tip away from the side where the float was. He fumbled for the bight spliced into the end of the rope, found it and began to pay the rope over the side into the water.

It was a slow business. The seven-inch coir normally had a buoyancy of its own, but it was waterlogged now and heavy. He had no idea how long the task took. At times he stopped to rest aching arms. After what seemed a long struggle he was down to the last few layers of the coil, and finally to the end itself. With a breathless, 'Christ, I thought you'd never come,' he threw it over the side. Free of the weight of the rope the sides of the bin had risen higher above the surface but the planked bottom was still under water. Leaning over the staves he released the lifeline, lifted the float inboard and secured it to the bottom of the crate by its lifeline.

The clouds drifted over the break in the sky, shutting out the stars and the moon, and he found himself in complete darkness sitting on the float in the centre of the rope-bin. Not far away the splashing noises continued but he felt secure inside the wooden cage, the warm water lapping the lower reaches of his body. There was nothing to do now but wait. Thinking again of the slaughter he'd so recently witnessed, a cold anger possessed him.

Satisfied that no one in the water could have survived, Yashimoto gave the order to cease fire. Toshida passed the word to the men on the casing. Taking their weapons with them they moved in an orderly file to the gun-hatch, climbed into it and disappeared below. As they went Yashimoto heard snatches in low voices mixed with muted laughter. Normally he would have dealt severely with such indiscipline, but they were young men and their excitement in the circumstances was understandable. They had been in a fight with the enemy. Several of their messmates had been casualties –

50

one had been killed. In any event there were more important matters on his mind. Matters that had to be dealt with immediately. First of these was to move away. He ordered speed to be increased to sixteen knots and gave the Coxswain a nor-nor-westerly course to steer. This would take I-357 away from the scene of the sinking and closer in to the East African coast.

When he'd steadied the submarine on the new course he turned to the Engineer Officer who had come to the bridge to report. Satugawa said he had examined the shell damage while the survivors were being dealt with. The damage to the main pressure hull and to the conning-tower walls could be repaired but the submarine would have to be in sheltered water. The repairs to the damaged lid and coaming of the lower hatch would be a more complicated operation, involving much time even if continuous shifts were worked. He was not able at that stage to say exactly how long. Possibly three or four days. A lot of improvisation would be necessary in the absence of shore assistance. 'In a neutral port it could soon be done,' he suggested hopefully.

'That is out of the question.' Yashimoto shook his head. 'It would mean internment. The end of the War for this boat and everyone in her.'

'Once the repairs are completed we can dive again, but . . .' Satugawa hesitated, looked past Yashimoto's shoulders as if somewhere out there in the night lay the solution to their problems.

'But *what* Chief?' prompted Yashimoto. The moon had gone and he was checking the darkness ahead, his back to the Engineer Officer.

'It would not then be advisable to go deep again, Captain.'

Yashimoto swung round. 'Why?'

'There would be patched-up holes and fractures, fatigued metal. It would be dangerous to subject them to high pressures.'

'How deep would we be able to dive?'

Satugawa hesitated, frowning at his thoughts. 'At most thirty to forty metres, Captain.'

51

Yashimoto made a long face, hunched his shoulders. 'Well – so long as we *can* dive. That's the vital requirement.'

There was silence after that while he considered what the Engineer Officer had told him. That the repairs would take some time was desperate though not unexpected news. Daylight would come in about nine hours. It would be followed by the enemy's air reconnaisance. *Fort Nebraska*'s brief transmission was an SSSS message. It would have given her position. Such transmissions by merchantmen were well known to the Japanese submarine service. British naval headquarters in Kilindini, more than four hundred miles to the north, would now be planning a search and rescue operation. What they did not know, however, was that I-357 could not dive.

They would assume one of two things: the submarine responsible might have left the area travelling on the surface at high speed, heading out into the deeper waters of the Mozambique Channel to get as far away from the scene as possible before making the dawn dive; their second but less likely assumption would be that the submarine had remained in the area of the sinking in order to attack any vessel, naval or otherwise, which responded to the SSSS message. These thoughts had been in his mind since the moment he'd known the extent of damage caused by the Liberty ship's shell. Now that he'd had time to consider the implications of what had happened a plan of action was suggesting itself. But it would be necessary to work at the chart-table before coming to a decision – and he would have to work fast.

Turning back to the Engineer Officer he said, 'Carry on below, Chief. Make all preparations for the repairs. Assume that we will be in sheltered water.'

Knowing the Captain better than any other member of I-357's crew, and respecting him, Satugawa refrained from asking questions. Of one thing he was certain. Yashimoto would make the right decision. He always did. Saying, 'I'll do that, sir,' he left the bridge.

Yashimoto called the control-room by voice-pipe. The First Lieutenant answered. 'Captain, sir?'

'Inform the Chief Telegraphist that strict wireless silence is to be observed. Listening watch only. Hydrophone and search receiver operators to be especially vigilant. When you have passed these orders, come to the bridge.'

The First Lieutenant came up and the Captain gave him the submarine's course and speed. 'Take over the bridge now,' he said. 'I shan't be long. Make sure that the lookouts are on their toes.' With a last scan of the black wall of night round I-357, he lowered himself into the conning-tower.

Yashimoto stepped off the ladder on to the deck of the control-room and bumped into a seaman kneeling at its foot. There was a bucket of water beside him.

The Captain growled. 'What d'you think you're doing?'

'Mopping up blood, sir.'

The Captain looked down, saw the red lights of the control-room reflected in the dark pool at his feet. He'd forgotten about the casualties. Well, there was no time to worry about them now. He went across to the chart-table, conscious of the eyes which followed him, the gaunt expressions of inquiry on bearded young faces. After the comparative silence of the bridge the control-room was noisy with the clatter of the diesels. The Navigating Officer moved aside to make room at the chart-table. He had been entering details of the gun-action in the War Diary.

Yashimoto said, 'Leave that now, Sato. There are more urgent matters to attend to.' He looked at the chart on the table, *Lourenço Marques to Mogadiscio*.

'Where is the large scale chart for this section of the coast?'

'Underneath that one, sir. Our DR position is on it.'

Yashimoto grunted, pulled clear the chart he wanted, placed it uppermost and switched on the shielded light. From the position Sato had plotted he saw that they were eighteen miles to the east of the Mozambique coast, abeam of Ilha Matemo, one of a chain of small islands which ran parallel to the coast from Porto Amelia in the south to Cabo Delgado in the north, a distance of 135 miles. In the main the islands were close inshore with scattered reefs and shoals abounding in the few navigable passages between them.

Yashimoto worked fast and with complete absorption, for there was little time in which to do all that had to be done. To the Navigating Officer, standing silent at his side, there was something feverish in the Captain's activity; the way in which that formidable man snatched up dividers to measure distances, hurriedly jotted down figures, muttered enigmatically, constantly switching his attention from the chart to the volume of Sailing Directions.

The time was 2132, the sun would rise at 0520; that left Yashimoto with eight hours in which to conceal I-357 from the air search which would begin at daylight. He was not long in making his decisions. He would use, at most, four of the eight hours of darkness left to find a small island, preferably wooded and uninhabited and with enough deep water to manoeuvre close in to its lee on the landward side. This would conceal the submarine from prying eyes to seaward, and give shelter from the prevailing north-easterly monsoon. There would also be the advantage of lying in the shadow of the island when the sun rose. That would make her less conspicuous from the air during the early hours of daylight. Before then the crew would have to carry out the project he had in mind. It was a formidable one.

Close study of the chart and Sailing Directions had persuaded him to concentrate on what looked like the loneliest part of a lonely coast; the twenty-five miles between the islands of Medjumbi and Tambuzi. Little mauve blobs printed against those names indicated the presence of light beacons. They would be invaluable navigational aids. In the twenty-five miles he proposed to explore there were a number of islands from five to twelve miles offshore; the shoals, coral reefs and others navigational hazards on their landward side were sufficiently numerous to daunt searching warships. And he was encouraged by what he'd read in the Sailing Directions: references to mangrove-lined beaches and creeks – Ilha Medjumbi was *wooded, with some tall trees* – Ilha Mionge, *a thickly wooded islet some seventy feet high in places*. Surely he would find what he wanted somewhere among those islands.

The distance to Medjumbi was thirty-three miles – about two hours' steaming at sixteen knots. Once past it, he would tackle the little islets, taking the submarine up through the inshore passages on their landward side.

In an immensely difficult situation he was aware of one potent factor in his favour – the action had taken place off the Mozambique coast. *Fort Nebraska* had been sunk about a hundred miles south of Cabo Delgado; twenty miles north of that cape lay the mouth of the Rovuma River, the boundary between Tanganyika and Mozambique: the former a British colony, the latter Portuguese.

British aircraft and warships could not attack I-357 in Portuguese territory without flouting the International Convention and offending their oldest ally, a still most useful and friendly one notwithstanding her nominal neutrality. It was fortunate, he reflected, that the British were respecters of international conventions.

The risk he ran using Portuguese territory was internment of the submarine and its crew, but that was far less serious than losing them to enemy action. The repairs would take three or four days. If air reconnaissance found I-357 during that time, the British would exert diplomatic pressure on the Portuguese Government to ensure internment. The only way to prevent that was to hide I-357.

Having determined from the chart the course to steer, the Captain picked up the phone to the engineroom. An ERA answered.

'Tell the Engineer Officer to come to the bridge immediately,' said Yashimoto. He hung up the phone, told the Navigating Officer to follow him, and made for the conning-tower ladder.

Six

On reaching the bridge Yashimoto gave the Coxswain the new course to steer and ordered the Navigating Officer to take over the watch from the First Lieutenant. 'Keep a sharp eye on the lookouts,' he said. 'This hot weather can make them careless.' He had scarcely finished speaking when a dark shape came to the front of the bridge. 'Captain, sir. You sent for me.' It was the Engineer Officer.

'Good. I want a word with you and the First Lieutenant.' Followed by the two officers, Yashimoto led the way past the periscope standards to the after gun-platform. Feeling his way in the darkness he touched the twin barrels of the AA gun. They were still hot from recent firing. He waited until Kagumi and Satugawa were close to him before breaking the silence. 'First I must tell you what is to happen before daylight. Then you will get your orders.' He explained where I-357 was heading, what he was looking for, and the steps to be taken to conceal the submarine. He spoke fast, a staccato of clipped sentences, his voice raised against the noise of the diesels. When the Captain had finished Satugawa was the first to speak. 'Repairs are not possible until the boat is stopped and in sheltered water. So it is good to have your news, Captain.'

'Yes,' agreed Yashimoto. 'But I hope you will not now require four days?'

'Hopefully not.' The Engineer Officer's tone was guarded.

'Right,' said Yashimoto briskly. 'Now for your duties. To be attended to immediately.' He spoke first to Kagumi, 'Prepare an inflatable for launching. Check that the outboard engine is in good running order. Take four men as crew: a signalman, two seamen and a mechanician. You'll need a

56

compass, leadlines for sounding, signal torches, boathooks, spare fuel and rope painters. Your duty will be to examine and report on possible hide-outs. You and your crew will carry revolvers and spare ammunition. I'll give you detailed orders when the time comes.' Yashimoto paused, looked up at the sky where the moon had found a break in the clouds, its light illuminating the little group on the gun-platform. He was not pleased to see it. The new compass course would take them five miles clear of the light at Ilha Medjumbi, but they would not be past it until half an hour before midnight – that was still two hours away. After that the moon could be useful.

He shifted his attention to Satugawa. 'Now your duties, Chief. Muster every implement on board that can be used for sawing, chopping or cutting timber, branches or brushwood. For a start begin with the damage control outfits. Take from them the saws and hatchets in each compartment. There are other items which can be adapted. Bayonets and cutlasses, for example. With your lathes, drills, etcetera, it should be possible to turn them into pangas or the equivalent. We want forty of these to be ready by 0130. That gives you four hours. Any problems?'

Darkness hid the Engineer Officer's grim smile. The question was typical of the Captain. Of course there were problems. Many of them, and not the least the time available. But he said, 'I will do my best, sir.'

Yashimoto consulted the luminous dial of his watch. It showed 2147. 'Later than I thought,' he snapped. 'Better get busy.'

The three men left the gun-platform. Yashimoto returned to the bridge, the others to the control-room. The wardroom steward arrived on the bridge with a bowl of rice, dried fish and hot tea.

Yashimoto lowered his binoculars. 'What is our ETA for sighting the Medjumbi light?' he asked the Navigating Officer.

'Twenty-three hundred, sir.'

'Another hour and a quarter.'

57

'Yes, sir.'

The Captain looked to the west, the direction in which the moon would be moving when it passed its zenith towards midnight. The sky there was still heavy with cloud, but the break high in the east through which moon and stars now shone was growing larger. Well, one can't have everything, he decided. We have a calm sea, no more than a light breeze, and a fine hot night. He sighed, took off his cap, ran a hand across a moist forehead. He was tired, but rest was out of the question. Certainly until well into the coming day, if then. Only now, for the first time since the encounter with *Fort Nebraska*, was he able to reflect upon the night's events. So much had happened in so short a space of time. It was difficult to believe that it was just about an hour since I-357 had fired the first shell at the Liberty ship. That seemed to him to have taken place much further back in time.

He had not enjoyed the killing of the survivors. They were seamen, like him and his own men. But Japan and the United States were at war. It was his duty to sink enemy shipping. Similarly it was his duty to do everything possible to prevent the loss of I-357 and her crew once she had been damaged by enemy gunfire. Had the US ship not fired that shell he wouldn't have been compelled to liquidate her survivors. What made matters worse was the deception the Americans had employed. Already on fire and sinking, the Liberty ship had stopped engines, turned out lifeboats, and begun signalling. All those actions suggested a crew about to abandon ship, despite which they had opened fire. In the circumstances he'd had no option but to do as he had. It was either the Americans' lives or those of his men. The *Fort Nebraska* was carrying supplies to the enemy. Her crew were actively engaged in fighting Japan. Those who chose to be warriors must abide by the *bushido* code. They had died in action. No warrior could ask for more.

Much to Yashimoto's relief clouds once more shut out the moon, settling a cloak of darkness over the sea on which the submarine moved steadily in towards the coast.

As so often, it was he who made the first sighting of the winking point of light on the port bow. He did not announce it, waiting instead to see how long it might take Sato and the lookouts to pick it up. In the meantime he checked its characteristics: a white light flashing twice at one minute intervals, range ten miles. Yes, it was definitely Medjumbi Island. His thoughts were interrupted by Sato's voice. 'Red ten, sir. White light flashing twice.' The Navigating Officer's report was followed almost immediately by one from the bow lookout. Yashimoto doubted whether the man had actually seen the light, but let that pass. Instead he growled, 'It's been in sight for close on two minutes. In that time we have travelled nearly half a mile. You men must be more vigilant.'

Sato and the lookouts were silent. The Captain's rebuke was a routine one. The truth of the matter was that no one could compete with his night vision.

But Yashimoto was pleased. The light had been sighted eight minutes ahead of ETA. So the inshore current was with them. Before the night was out it would save him much needed time.

During the approach to the Medjumbi light the Navigating Officer had determined by compass bearing that the current was setting north at two knots: it was the counter-current to which the Sailing Directions referred as 'a possibility at times'. Twelve minutes later he reported the light to be abeam, distance five miles.

Yashimoto reduced speed to fourteen knots. To Sato he said, 'We will make for the inner passage now, between the coast and the islands. Bring her round to port. Remain at five miles from the light.' He moved over to the voice-pipe, called the control-room. The First Lieutenant answered.

'We are entering the inner passage now,' said Yashimoto. 'Is the inflatable ready for launching?'

'Yes, sir, it's on the after-casing. Crew standing by. All ready when you give the word.'

'Good. Come to the bridge, Kagumi. The more eyes here

the better.' Yashimoto thought a lot of the First Lieutenant. Kagumi, small, physically strong, was a first rate officer. Keen, intelligent and dependable, he was a good handler of men.

When the First Lieutenant reached the bridge Yashimoto was at its fore-end, binoculars to his eyes, the Navigating Officer next to him. 'The western sky is still clearing,' observed the Captain. 'What time is moonset, Navigator?'

Sato smiled in the darkness. Wily old bird, he thought. If anybody knows the time of moonset it's him. But he said, '0433, sir.'

'Correct. We may have moonlight soon. The western sky is clearing. It's a mixed blessing. Fine for navigating the inner passage, but bad otherwise. Could make the boat dangerously visible.'

The First Lieutenant said a dutiful, 'Yes, sir.'

Kagumi always agrees with the Captain, thought Sato. But only in words. He's contemptible.

Yashimoto went on. 'At least while it's as dark as this no one on Medjumbi can see us. Not at five miles. Once we're into the inner passage it will be different if the moon comes.'

'It seems from the Sailing Directions,' said the First Lieutenant, 'that the only inhabitants along this part of the coast are likely to be African fishermen. I don't suppose they've ever seen a submarine. Probably wouldn't know one if they did.'

Well done, Ito Kagumi! reflected Sato. There's original thought for you. The Navigating Officer was, like many reservist officers, a university graduate. He disliked the First Lieutenant whom he regarded as a sycophant; a predictable automaton, always doing and saying the right thing. Earlier in the control-room Sato had heard him expressing approval of the Captain's action in ordering the 'liquidation' of survivors. What a word to use when discussing the wholesale killing of human beings. Sato, who'd majored in philosophy, had been appalled by the night's events. To him they seemed a ghastly nightmare. The men in the water, the cold glare of the searchlight illuminating white faces, eyes staring in

60

horror, screaming voices, machine-gun fire ripping into them. Yet Kagumi had approved. Sato's disturbing thoughts were banished by the muffled sound of the Captain's voice from under the canvas screen on the bridge chart-table.

'Sir?' inquired the Navigating Officer.

'We'll be altering to the north again, shortly,' said Yashimoto. 'It looks as if we can find depths of at least five fathoms most of the way up the inner passage. There's a shallow patch west of the Vadiazi Shoal. About three and a half fathoms. We'll trim up for that, reduce draught to a minimum. Once past the shoal we can trim down again. There are two small islets before the Nameguo Shoal. I want you to check on them, Kagumi. We'll put the inflatable into the water soon after we've altered course. You'd better go down now and standby. Got your revolver?'

'Yes, sir.' The First Lieutenant gave the holster a reassuring pat before leaving the bridge.

The Medjumbi light receded and the moon once more shone through cloud breaks which widened as the night grew older. The temperature was in the high-seventies, the atmosphere humid, still and windless above the mirror-smooth sea over which the submarine travelled. To starboard lay the islands, to port the coast, neither more than a few miles distant at any time. Against the background of diesel clatter, silence on the bridge was broken at times by Yashimoto's orders, the responses of the Coxswain, and the voice of the Navigating Officer calling the depths recorded by the echo-sounder. The Medjumbi light grew fainter and in time disappeared. Yashimoto knew from the chart that another fifteen miles of hazardous water had to be navigated before the Tambuzi light was sighted. He hoped they would find a hide-out well before then.

The inflatable had taken station ahead, the note of its two-stroke still audible on the bridge. From time to time the shaded blue lights of signal torches blinked messages between the two craft. More often than not they concerned alterations of course ordered by Yashimoto and repeated to the inflatable by the Yeoman. Sometimes distant fires and the drifting smell of woodsmoke told of African villages. On three occasions native catamarans were sighted; dark, loglike shapes in the moonlight, usually with a single occupant. None was close, which helped Yashimoto's peace of mind.

Within the hour three islets had been checked. In each case the reconnaissance had been brief, Kagumi reporting that they were unsuitable. Then the submarine would get under way again with the inflatable once more in station ahead. Some time after the third island had been found wanting, the light on Tambuzi Island was sighted, an event which caused Yashimoto to sigh with relief. Bringing the submarine up through the inner passage, much of the time in total darkness, had been an exhausting task calling for unremitting concentration. Only when the clouds had cleared sufficiently to allow full moonlight had it become less arduous.

It was after sighting the Tambuzi light that Yashimoto stopped engines for the fourth time and ordered Kagumi to investigate a small islet a couple of miles south-west of the Nameguo Shoal. While the inflatable sped towards it Yashimoto waited, tense and uncertain, and tired with anxiety. The hunt for a hide-out was taking longer than he'd planned, and they hadn't yet covered half the area to be searched. The chances of concealing I-357 before daylight were growing slimmer.

Satugawa came up to report progress. The damage control outfits in the submarine's watertight compartments had yielded ten axes and ten saws: from four of these the engineroom staff had already made two double-handed saws for cutting large timber. There were, in addition, four longhandled wire cutters which could be used on the smaller branches of trees – 'branches that are not more than sixteen centimetres in diameter,' announced Satugawa, always a man for exactitude. A bayonet had been turned into a serviceable panga, seven more would be produced, and he

62

had no doubt the total of forty cutting implements would be ready by two o'clock in the morning.

Yashimoto permitted himself a rare smile. 'That is good work, Chief. I knew you would not fail me.'

Why the *me*, thought Sato. It's *us* surely? Would not the price of failure have to be paid by all of us?

Sitting in the rope-bin in water up to his waist Corrigan found time to think about many things; like the chances of being picked up. Had Jim McManus got off the emergency signal before he and his wireless cabin were blown to smithereens? If a ship did come along, would anyone see him in the rope-bin? Would the calm sea and fine weather last? How long could *he* last without food and water? Where would the current take him? He had no idea of *Fort Nebraska*'s position when she sank. He'd known they were somewhere off the East Coast of Africa, but how far off he'd no idea. In time these doubts gave way to more positive thoughts, for Brad Corrigan was an optimistic young man. There was a lot to be said for the plus things, he decided. After all, he was still alive and well but for scratches on his face and hands, and oil fuel with its horrid stench burning his skin, making his eyes smart and his scalp itch. Not that he could remember how he'd got the scratches. There'd been fuel oil all over the place. In spite of everything he was the sole survivor from a crew of forty-five. That was quite something. He wouldn't have got away with it but for his job before the War. He had to be plenty grateful for that. And finding the rope-bin had been a bit of luck. No way could the sharks get at him now, even if they were threshing about not far away. Greedy bastards. Tearing at dead men's bodies like that. Fighting each other for the best takes.

There were other things, too – like he'd have been in a bad way if it'd been rough. And small things like being able to tell the time because he always wore a waterproof diving-watch. So it could have been plenty worse. Not like for poor old Smitty Fredericks. Nothing had gone okay for him. It wasn't right that it was like that. Smitty was a real good guy. But even if he hadn't been wounded, he wouldn't have got away with it because he was no good in the water and those bastards' machine-guns would have got him if the sharks hadn't.

Pity that 5-inch shell hadn't blown the goddam submarine out of the water. All the same it had made a bloody great hole in the conning-tower. Sure wouldn't be able to dive with a hole like that. Jesus, he thought, that was a lucky hit. He recaptured the excitement of the moment, the flash of flame and the rumble of the explosion, and remembered shouting, 'For Chrissake, Smitty. We've hit the bastard. What d'ya know about that?' and Smitty had screamed back, 'Yeh – I know, Brad. I know. Jeez, man. I saw it, didn't I?' And then they'd struggled to reload the gun and lay and train it. A helluva business that. It was a heavy old gun, and there was the list and all, and Smitty not too good because of the wound, and – anywise, after all that goddam sweat the next round went way over. He supposed he'd over-corrected because of the list. But the real miracle was hitting with that first round.

When the Jap's shell exploded almost on *Fort Nebraska*'s gun the concussion had knocked him out. It couldn't have been too long before he came to. He'd shouted to the others in the darkness then, but got no answer. Not until he'd shouted a second time and heard Smitty's voice sounding kinda funny: 'Who? What's happened?' Smitty had yelled that out like a kid. It hadn't taken long after that to realize that the rest of the gun's crew were dead or unconscious. Corrigan, he'd been gunlayer, remembered shouting to Smitty who was a loading number. 'Say, were we loaded when that Jap shell hit us?'

Smitty had croaked, 'Yeh, sure,' and Corrigan had said, 'Well, c'mon man. Let's go. I'll lay and train. You handle the breech.' It was then that Smitty had said, 'I guess I've been hit, Brad. My left leg don't seem to want to move.'

So Corrigan had laid, trained and fired the gun more or less on his own, with Smitty doing his best to help, which hadn't amounted to much. What they'd been trying to do had been just about impossible in those conditions; total black darkness, the ship listing heavily, bodies to trip over round the breech end of the gun and Smitty just about out. Thinking of all that, Corrigan reckoned it was bloody marvellous they'd fired the shell, let alone got a hit on the conning-tower. That was a million to one chance if ever there was one.

And then, after that, Smitty had somehow crawled to the ammunition rack with him and they'd lifted out another shell and got it into the breech. All of which took time with the list getting steadily worse, and of course the miracle wasn't repeated with the next shot.

He supposed that if he was rescued he'd have to write letters to Smitty's folks in Pittsburg, and to his girl in Baltimore. That wouldn't be easy. Writing letters wasn't his thing.

Moonlight made it possible to watch the inflatable skim across the placid sea, its wake white and conspicuous, the crew dark huddled shapes. Before long it had disappeared behind a headland on the north side of the island.

Yashimoto wondered what Kagumi would find there. Yet another disappointment? No name showed against the tiny black spot on the chart – one of many such in the long chain of islands. But seen from the submarine's bridge, half a mile away, it raised Yashimoto's hopes; the dark silhouette was like that of a crouching monster, the uneven, serrated skyline suggesting bush or trees, its height perhaps a hundred feet above sea level. But height, though useful, was not enough. Was it inhabited? Was there timber? Was the depth of water sufficient to take I-357 close inshore?

Such things could not be known until Kagumi returned.

Seven

Time passed but the inflatable did not return, nor could anything be seen of the land for clouds once again obscured the moon. Bearings of the Tambuzi light, and the depth of water by echo-sounder, confirmed that the current was still setting to the north; Yashimoto countered its effect with the helm and engine orders necessary to keep the submarine in position off the headland around which the inflatable had disappeared.

As the minutes ticked by without any sign of it he became increasingly concerned. Looking into the darkness he kept asking himself what could have gone wrong? The First Lieutenant knew that time was vital; yet more than thirty minutes had elapsed since he left I-357. What could he and his crew be doing?

Yashimoto was wondering what to do next when the sound of the outboard was heard on the bridge. Soon a blue light began to wink in the distance. The Yeoman acknowledged and the light flickered into action again. The signal was brief. 'Message from Lieutenant Kagumi, sir,' reported the Yeoman. 'Reads, good news.'

'Thank you, Yeoman.' The relief in Yashimoto's voice and his *thank you* were a measure of how concerned he'd been. 'Thank you' were words he seldom used.

Kagumi's news was certainly good. 'This island is ideal, sir,' were his excited first words on reaching the bridge. 'In the moonlight I was able to see a good deal. It is about a mile long and a bit less in width. Volcanic in origin I think. The dominant feature is a creek about half a mile long which almost bisects it. The land around the creek rises steeply.

66

There is deep water, ten to fifteen fathoms over most of its length. As much as five fathoms close inshore in some places. On the eastern side there's a cluster of huts. Fishermen and their families live there. About forty Africans. Their catamarans are drawn up on the beach in front of the huts. They are . . .'

Yashimoto interrupted. 'How d'you know all this?'

'We landed by the huts, sir. The people came out. The noise of our engine woke them. I learnt what I've told you with sign language. It was not difficult.'

'Trees, bushes?' Yashimoto's prompting was eager. 'Anything like that?'

'Yes, sir. It's well wooded round the creek. Many trees. Thick undergrowth. Mangroves fringing the water's edge.'

'Any other settlements on the island? Any catamarans apart from those you saw?'

'No, sir. They say there are no people except those in the village.'

Yashimoto shot a questioning glance at the First Lieutenant. 'More sign language?'

'Yes, sir. But the responses were not difficult to interpret.'

The Captain grunted approval. 'Tomorrow we will survey the island. In the meantime – did you see a suitable berth?'

'Two possible berths, sir. One on the east bank, another on the west bank. There's deeper water on the western side.'

'What's the width of the creek?'

'About two hundred and fifty yards at the mouth. Down to about a hundred in the narrows which lead into it. It widens out again after that. Into an oval basin. There's just enough room for the boat to turn there.'

Looking into the night to where the islet lay, a black hump on a dark sea, Yashimoto said, 'You have done well, Kagumi. I shall not forget this. But your work is not finished. You must pilot us in. Take station in the inflatable a ship's length ahead. Use the signal torch as a stern light and I'll follow. Keep to about two or three knots once we head into the creek.'

The First Lieutenant saluted in the darkness, turned on his heels and clattered down the ladder to the casing.

The inflatable's outboard engine spluttered into life, its note rising as Kagumi steered the fast, bouncing, little craft into position ahead of the submarine.

To Yashimoto the task of taking I-357 into a narrow creek he had never seen, without a chart and in almost total darkness, was a nail-biting experience, though in fact he had little to do but ensure that the Coxswain followed the inflatable's blue light. The Navigating Officer kept calling the depths recorded by echo-sounder, the Yeoman stood at the Captain's shoulder reading Kagumi's signals, and a signalman stood by with a searchlight to be used in case of emergency. The bridge lookouts were at their posts but there was little for them to do. The First Lieutenant was proving as efficient as always, warning well in advance of changes in course and speed.

Unable to see in the darkness Yashimoto tried to keep in his mind a picture of the creek as Kagumi had described it. Thus, when the blue light began to swing in a wide circle to starboard and the Coxswain turned the bridge wheel for I-357's bows to follow round, Yashimoto realized that they were heading into the creek. The light ahead began to blink, the Yeoman acknowledged, read the signal aloud: *Dead slow now. Narrows about five hundred yards ahead.*

Yashimoto ordered revolutions for two knots and the note of the diesels dropped to a lower rhythm. With ballast tanks blown to reduce her draught, and engine revolutions sufficient only to maintain steerage way, the submarine moved slowly through the water, the Coxswain turning the wheel as necessary to keep the blue light ahead. On Yashimoto's orders the beam of the searchlight swept the sides of the creek, revealing rocky cliffs, above them wooded slopes which led up steeply from the mangroves fringing the water. The blue light ahead moved to starboard, then held steady on its course for some time before beginning a turn to port; I-357 followed round. Sato reported that the turn had been one of forty-five degrees. Kagumi had just finished the message, *entering the narrows now* when, by good fortune or, as Yashimoto preferred to believe, in response to divine intervention, the moon slipped out of the clouds in the western sky, bathing the scene in silver light, the rocky sides of the narrow channel looming above the submarine, the tangle of mangroves glistening wetly.

Ahead to port Yashimoto saw catamarans drawn up on a small beach, and on the higher ground, beneath clumps of coconut palms, a semi-circle of thatched huts. In front of them dark shapes were grouped about open fires. Some rose and gestured towards the submarine, others remained on their haunches. The musky odour of the little settlement came drifting across the water; the indefinable but unmistakable smell of an African village, a compound of woodsmoke, of long-cooked food, and the sour-sweet smell of human bodies. To Yashimoto these were the reassuring odours of a Buddha-sent haven.

The inflatable's blue light blinked and the Yeoman read the signal aloud: *Stop engines. We leave the narrows now to turn sharp to starboard around the bluff.*

The diesels stopped and I-357 began to lose way. As they followed the blue light round to starboard Yashimoto saw that the creek had widened out into an oval basin. He was wondering where the berths were of which Kagumi had spoken, when the inflatable signalled: *Suggest you turn bows to seaward. Good berth south of the bluff. We go there now. Will take mooring lines when you've turned.*

Yashimoto decided there was sufficient room in which to turn the bows to seaward using one propeller to go ahead and the other astern: *Standing turn* as they called it at the submarine base at Yokasuko. It required the use of the electric motors as the diesels could not be put astern. Now clearly visible in the moonlight the inflatable had stopped close in on the western side, just south of the bluff; there the bank ran straight for several hundred feet before curving round the head of the creek.

This is the berth, winked the blue light. *Depth of water ten*

69

metres. Shoals rapidly three to four metres from the bank.

The submarine finished its turn, bows to seaward, the inflatable came alongside, took the end of a mooring line which had been lowered into the water from the fore-casing and towed it inshore. Two seamen jumped on to the bank, hauled the line ashore and made it fast to the trunk of a tree.

At the submarine's end the mooring line was taken to the capstan on the fore-casing, the offshore bow anchor was dropped and the capstan began to turn, warping the bows in towards the bank as the anchor cable was paid out.

The process was repeated with a stern line and stern anchor until the submarine was alongside, the port saddletanks close to the mangroves which lined the bank. The difficult, improvised manoeuvre had been completed within ten minutes of leaving the narrows. Soundings with hand lead-lines gave the average depth of water in which I-357 had moored as eight metres. In the shallowest part, towards the bows, there was just under three metres beneath the keel. The Navigating Officer reported that the tide was rising. High water was, he said, still three hours away.

'What's the rise and fall?' demanded Yashimoto.

'About four metres, sir.'

Yashimoto said, 'Good,' and ordered partial flooding of ballast tanks in order to reduce the submarine's above water profile.

The inflatable came alongside and the First Lieutenant reported to the bridge. Somewhat perfunctorily, for he had more important matters in mind, Yashimoto congratulated him on the night's work. Having done that, he came to the point. 'There will be no rest for the crew until well into daylight tomorrow. The inflatable is to proceed immediately to the mouth of the creek. Crew it with a petty officer and two ratings.' The orders were delivered in Yashimoto's customary staccato of clipped sentences, the voice high-pitched. 'They will take with them a machine-gun, rifles and ammunition. They will ensure that no catamaran leaves the creek. Warning shots are to be fired across the bows if any attempt to do so. If these are disregarded the catamaran's occupants are to be killed. Is that understood, Kagumi?'

'Yes, sir.'

'The occupant of any catamaran or other small craft entering the creek from seaward,' continued Yashimoto, 'is not to be interfered with. But once in he will not be permitted to leave. Is that clear?' Kagumi having said it was, the Captain went on. 'Another inflatable is to be brought up from below and prepared for launching.'

Kagumi brushed a mosquito from his forehead and stifled a yawn. A tired man, he managed a dutiful, 'Yes, sir.'

'See to these matters at once. Then assemble the officers and petty officers in the control-room. I shall give them their orders.' Yashimoto looked at his watch. 'It is now 0135. We are an hour behind schedule.'

Mechanically, his mind busy with the problem of carrying out the Captain's orders at the speed clearly expected of him, the First Lieutenant mumbled another 'Yes, sir,' and left the bridge.

The Captain stood at the base of the conning-tower ladder, one foot on its lower step. Tired though he was, and deeply worried, he managed to look relaxed and confident as he unfolded his plans for the night, occasionally consulting the single sheet of notes he held in one hand. 'It is necessary', he began, 'to conceal I-357 from aerial observation while repairs are taking place. These may occupy four days.' He paused, his dark eyes searching the faces in front of him. 'The time is now close to two o'clock. The sun will rise at five-thirty. So we have less than four hours in which to complete the first stage of our task. It will require hard work, hard work without rest, for the next few hours.' He paused again, this time the lower lip protruding and the eyes narrowed. 'But let me assure you that it will be completed.' He glanced at his notes before continuing: 'The saws, axes, pangas and other tools for your task are being made ready for issue on the after-casing. Working parties are to draw their tools before proceeding ashore. I will now give details of those parties, their duties and the allocation of tools.'

71

Yashimoto went across to the chart-table, placed one sheet of notes on it and picked up another. For some moments he regarded the officers and petty officers in the control-room in silence, his expression inscrutable. Some were standing, others sitting, a few crouching on their heels; all looked tired and anxious, their eyes submissive, their clothing scanty because of the heat.

'Time is short,' the Captain said. 'I will be brief and you will act swiftly. When a party has been detailed the officers and petty officers concerned will at once leave the control-room, select and muster their men, draw their implements and proceed ashore. The First Lieutenant will be in general charge. Any difficulties or disputes in selecting personnel and equipment, or in regard to other matters, must be referred to him.'

Yashimoto proceeded to detail the various parties, their duties, the names of the officers and petty officers responsible for each, and the implements to be drawn.

The cutting party of twenty men was the largest, and the first to go ashore by way of the gangway planks brought up from the torpedo compartment to bridge the gap between the submarine and the bank. Their first task, Yashimoto had stressed, was to cut leafy branches and brushwood. The felling of trees would come later. Lieutenant Toshida was in charge, with the Coxswain as his deputy. The appointment of these two men, both regarded by the Captain as outstanding, indicated the importance he attached to the work of the cutting party.

Before they left the control-room he emphasized that nothing was to be cut within several hundred yards of the submarine; where cutting did take place it was to be spread over a wide area. 'The slopes of the creek are thick with trees and bushes, and the shoreline with mangroves,' he told Toshida. 'For our needs less than one per cent of what is available will be sufficient. See to it that what we take leaves no scars to be seen from the air.'

Next to go were the sentries: a party of seven men under the senior watchkeeper, Lieutenant Matsuhito. His responsibility, explained the Captain, would include the men on duty in the inflatable at the entrance to the creek. The sentries were to take up positions on shore to prevent any approach to the submarine. They would, in addition, man the second inflatable for mobile duty as required.

He then named the eight men who were to carry the branches and brushwood from the cutting sites to the submarine: 'They're strong men,' he said, his dark eyes on Lieutenant Sato who was to take charge of the group.

A camouflage party of ten men under the Engineer Officer was to see to the placing of the foliage once the carriers had delivered it on board.

Various other duties were allocated: an officer, a petty officer and a dozen men were to rest until dawn when they would be required for reconnaissance and relief sentry duties. They were, he said, to form a spare crew pool. Three mechanicians under the Chief Engineroom Artificer were to remain on board for maintenance duties; three seamen under the Torpedo Gunner's Mate would stay on board for general duties. The Chief Telegraphist, the search receiver and hydrophone operators, were to maintain listening watches, wireless silence being observed.

Finally Yashimoto stressed the dangers of malaria and the importance of taking the quinine tablets which had been issued to the crew on a weekly basis throughout the patrol.

In a perverse way he had enjoyed the briefing, notwithstanding the serious situation, for it was one which fully engaged his passion for detail and his considerable energy and determination.

In spite of Sato's reservations about the Captain and the enterprise in which they were now involved, he had to concede that Yashimoto was handling the matter in masterly fashion. Every contingency appeared to have been taken care of, every man in the crew given a task. The Captain was indeed a formidable man, decided the Navigating Officer: as capable as he was ruthless.

*

The last of the shore parties having left, Yashimoto gave his attention to the casualties. The first problem to be dealt with was the disposal of the body of the dead torpedoman. For this purpose he sent for Petty Officer Hosokawa, the Boatswain's Mate. 'I want you to see to the burial of Leading Torpedoman Takiko. This must be done before daylight. Take two seamen with you in the inflatable. See that the body is securely weighted before you put it over the side. He is to be buried between the headlands. Be sure this is done with proper ceremony.'

Without any clear idea of what 'proper ceremony' might be under such unusual circumstances, PO Hosokawa bowed himself out of the Captain's cabin.

Yashimoto's next move was to visit the wounded in their bunks in the fore-ends. One man was critically injured, a fragment of steel having penetrated his chest and apparently lodged in a lung. He had been in great pain until the Coxswain administered a morphine injection. Now deeply sedated, he breathed noisily through the rime of blood about his lips and nostrils. Of the remaining casualties one had a head wound, the other a shattered forearm. The wounds had been treated by the Coxswain. Yashimoto spoke to the men, expressed sympathy, and in a show of encouragement told them he hoped to have them back in Penang before too long. Presumably wondering what period of time that might be, they muttered their thanks and Yashimoto returned to the wardroom to attend to more pressing matters.

Eight

During the remaining hours before dawn the crew of I-357 worked with furious energy on the wooded slopes of the creek. Toshida's twenty men, stripped to the waist, toiled in the moonlight, cutting, chopping, clipping and bundling, developing unfamiliar skills as the hours passed, sweat pouring from their bodies, blisters forming on their hands, arms and shoulders aching. They were spurred on by Toshida, a shadowy figure moving among the trees, encouraging and cajoling; and by the Coxswain, a barrel-chested, loud-voiced man who used more forceful methods, cursing and joking, demonstrating the proper uses of axes and pangas, the sharpening of blades with files and hillside stones, and the binding of cuttings with the lianas which hung like ropes from the older trees.

No sooner were the bundles stacked in the shadows beneath the trees than bearers would appear, hoist the heavy loads on to their shoulders, and set off once again down the hill up which they'd come. These were Yashimoto's 'strong men'.

Activity on the hillside was matched on the submarine's casing where the camouflage party worked at a blistering pace, covering and draping the casing and saddletanks, the conning-tower, the guns and gun-platforms with foliage.

I-357's two stewards were continuously on the move, carrying mess-tins of rice and fishmeal to the working parties on shore and refilling watercans. Each time they returned to the submarine they would report progress on the cutting sites to the Captain. On several occasions he sent the First Lieutenant ashore to check the work being done, particularly to ensure that cutting was widely dispersed over the area, and that no lights of any sort were shown.

Slowly but surely with the passing of the hours the submarine took on the appearance of a long green mound. What little water there was between the saddletanks and the mangroves lining the banks had been covered with branches supported by inflatable rafts and lifejackets, pellet buoys and other floatables which, like the gangplanks, would rise and fall with the tides.

By dawn the last touches of camouflage had been added; not far from the submarine's berth four sizeable young trees had been felled, carried on board and 'planted' – one on the forward gun-hatch, one on either side of the periscope standards, and another just abaft the AA gunplatform. Towards sunrise I-357 had so effectively disappeared under her leafy camouflage as to become a part of the creek itself.

Other than the sentries who had been instructed to conceal themselves at daylight and remain at their posts until relieved, the shore parties had returned on board by the time the eastern sky grew lighter. The officers and petty officers were again ordered to the control-room to be addressed by the Captain. When the Coxswain reported that all were present, Yashimoto came from the wardroom and took up his usual stance at the conning-tower ladder; looking around, he smiled approval at the sweat-stained, bearded faces, at the tired bloodshot eyes which regarded him. 'You and your men have done well,' he said, emphasizing the commendation with a respective nodding of the head. 'The honour of the Emperor and the Imperial Japanese Navy has been safe in your hands. May Buddha reward you.'

As if regretting the emotional nature of this benediction he added, 'Working parties will rest until 0930. The half hour thereafter will be for breakfast. Orders for the day will be issued at 1000. Nobody will go on to the casing without the duty officer's permission.' He paused, his tired mind fumbling with what he had to say while he looked at his notes. 'All

76

hatches will be left open to ventilate the boat. The branches covering us will improve conditions on board.' He hesitated, surveying his audience in silence before saying, 'You may carry on.' As the officers and petty officers moved off to attend to their various commitments, he beckoned to Kagumi who stood by the door of the W/T office. The First Lieutenant came across.

'I'm afraid there's no rest for you, Kagumi.' The Captain smiled sympathetically. 'Take two men from the spare pool and go over to the huts in an inflatable. Bring back a couple of catamarans and secure them astern. I have plans for them. With your sign language,' Yashimoto grinned, 'tell the Africans that no catamaran is to leave the creek until we have gone. Make sure they understand the penalties. Stress that it is only for a few days. After that we shall have gone. They may fish in the creek, but not beyond the narrows. Before dark each evening their catamarans must be drawn up on the beach in front of the huts. Our sentries will be on guard there.' He stopped, rubbed his eyes with a knuckled fist, yawned. 'You and your men must go ahead. Return not later than 0700.' When Kagumi had gone the Captain sent for the Navigating Officer.

Sato arrived, gaunt, weary-eyed, his khaki shorts crumpled and dirt-stained, his bare arms and torso scratched by the branches he had handled during the long hours of darkness. 'You sent for me, sir?'

Yashimoto nodded, his eyes elsewhere, as if engaged more with his thoughts than with the dishevelled young man in front of him. 'Ah, Sato,' he said as if surprised at the Navigating Officer's presence. 'I have an important duty for you. To be completed by 0700. Take an inflatable and crew with two men from the relief pool. I want you to travel right round the seaward side of this island. Chart it as you go. Record the salient features, the presence of ravines and water courses, the estimated height of the hills and so forth. Mark the wooded, bush-clad areas, and the location of beaches. Look out especially for signs of human habitation. See to it that you and your men are well armed, and be sure

77

to return by 0700. When you do, I expect to be shown a useful map of the island.' Yashimoto smiled with his teeth, a familiar but humourless gesture. 'It has no name on the chart, but let us call it Creek Island.'

Sato was pleased, flattered. It was an interesting assignment and tired though he was an exciting one for he shared the dream of every navigator – to chart uncharted territory.

'I will see to that at once, sir.' He saluted and was about to go when Yashimoto said, 'Keep close to the shore on the journey round the island. That way you are less likely to be seen.' Sato saluted again before making for the forward hatch.

With a final look round, the Captain made for his cabin. He sat at the small desk, head in hands, his mind full of questions. Had he thought of everything that should be done? What was going on out there in the Mozambique Channel? Had enemy units arrived at the position given by *Fort Nebraska*? The approximate times of the morning and afternoon reconnaissance flights over the Mozambique Channel were well known to the Japanese. Would the RAF now cover the coastline and islands? The morning flight was likely to be on its way. Kilindini was about 400 miles to the north, Pamanzi, the RAF base in the Comores, some 300 miles to the south-east. It was unlikely that enemy aircraft could be over the creek much before eight o'clock that morning, but sooner or later they would cover that part of the coast. They would find some pretext to explain to the Portuguese why they had overflown Portuguese colonial territory. Searching for survivors?

How long, he wondered, would it take to make good I-357's damage? Everything else was subordinate to that. During the passage up the coast Satugawa and the Chief Engineroom Artificer had carried out a detailed examination and agreed on what had to be done. The work was to begin when the rest period ended at ten o'clock that morning.

He got up heavily, the weight of exhaustion upon him,

and knelt before the Shinto shrine. He had not been there long before his prayers were interrupted by the distant sound of three shots fired in rapid succession.

Nine

Shortly before three o'clock that morning *Restless* reached the position given in *Fort Nebraska*'s signal: twenty-two miles east-north-east of Porto do Ibo. In spite of bright moonlight and a glassy sea there was no sign of wreckage or oil slicks, nor did a five mile square search yield any results. Barratt was in the chartroom discussing the problem with the Navigating Officer. 'How accurate is our position, Pilot?'

'Depends on the current, sir. I allowed for a two knot southerly set.' Dodds's forehead creased into a huge frown. 'If in fact there's a counter-current, the position is not reliable.' He looked at the chart before going on. 'Wreckage and oil slicks could be north of us in that case. Trouble is, I've had to work on DR and a moon-sight with a dodgy horizon.'

'Any W/T beacons within range?'

'The two we might have used have shut down. So that U-boats can't use them.'

'What about soundings?' Barratt looked up from under bushy eyebrows, the lined, hollow-cheeked face showing signs of strain.

'Too deep and uniform round here, sir. All much the same – around the thousand fathom mark. If the sky remains clear I should get good star-sights at dawn. But that's another two and a half hours away.'

Barratt turned, folded his arms, leant against the chart-table. 'Pretty bloody useless really, isn't it?' he said gloomily. 'But not hopeless. The light at Porto do Ibo has a ten mile range. We should be within twenty-five miles of it now. That means about fifteen miles from the range limit. Give me a course for Porto do Ibo. Once we've sighted the light we'll know where we are and which way the current is setting. Then we'll be in business again.'

'Good idea, sir.'

'I do have them occasionally, Pilot. Now give me that course.'

A more or less cheerful grin replaced Charlie Dodds's frown as he bent over the chart-table. The Captain might be tired but his mood seemed better than it had been for some time.

In due course the light at Porto do Ibo was sighted broad on the port bow. Had the destroyer's DR position at 0300 been correct the light should have been sighted dead ahead. As it was *Restless* was eight miles west-nor-west of the DR position. Successive bearings of the light indicated a northerly current of just under two knots. Applying this to *Fort Nebraska*'s position at 2100, Dodds estimated that the wreckage would already have drifted thirteen miles to the north; that would be nineteen miles north-east of *Restless*'s present position. He reported this by phone to the Captain who had returned to the bridge.

'What we don't know, Pilot,' there was a note of scepticism in Barratt's voice, 'is how long the gun action lasted and how far *Fort N* may have travelled after her four S.'

'Quite so, sir.' Dodds was on the defensive. 'But I had to make assumptions, and the position she gave seemed as good as any.'

'Calm down, Pilot. I'm not getting at you. Simply thinking aloud.' Barratt coughed. 'Sorry. Give me a course and distance for your estimate of the wreckage position, work on a two knot northerly set. Double quick. I suspect the survivors would like to see us.' He put down the phone, joined Geoffrey Lawson at the bridge screen. Lawson, *Restless*'s Gunnery Officer, was officer-of-the-watch.

The watches changed at 0400 that morning. Soon afterwards the Navigating Officer reported that traces of the *Fort Nebra-*

81

ska sinking should be sighted soon if the assumptions made were correct.

Conscious of the possibility of a U-boat in the vicinity, Barratt phoned the A/S and radar cabinets. 'We're in the sinking zone now,' he warned. 'May well be a U-boat sniffing around. Keep everything on the top line.'

But there was no sign of wreckage or oil slicks despite the good visibility which persisted with the moon now low in the western sky.

'It seems the assumptions made were not correct,' said Barratt tartly. 'We'll do another square search. Start the plot.'

The Navigating Officer said, 'Yes, sir.' He decided against adding that the plot had been running since a position had been established off the Porto do Ibo light. The Captain had enough to worry about without being reminded of things he'd forgotten.

The square search was not long in yielding results. Halfway through the second leg the First Lieutenant made the sighting. 'Green – three – zero. Distant object, sir.' He had taken over the watch from Lawson at four o'clock that morning.

Barratt and the starboard bridge lookout focused night glasses on the bearing.

'For object read objects,' said the Captain. 'I see several bits and pieces and various things which look like sacks. I wonder what cargo she was carrying.' He put down his glasses. 'Starboard fifteen, Number One. Revolutions for ten knots. Steady her when the wreckage is ahead. Must be the best part of a mile away.'

The First Lieutenant passed the orders to the wheelhouse by voice-pipe, the distant hum of the turbines dropped to a lower key, and the destroyer's bows swung to starboard.

'Yes. I suppose so, sir. I've told the Bosun's Mate to get his party to standby the scrambling nets.'

'Don't think we're going to need them. Don't see any lifeboats,' said Barratt. 'They probably set out for the coast six or seven hours ago. It's within thirty miles. There's no wind. In these conditions they could row at a couple of knots I suppose.'

The First Lieutenant checked with night glasses. 'Yes. They'd make for the land. No point in hanging around.' He added, 'Those aren't sacks, sir. I think they're bodies. I can see survivors' lights. A few. Just visible.'

Barratt wiped the sweat and heat mist from the eye-pieces before raising the binoculars. 'Yes. There are red lights. Funny shapes if they are bodies. Can't really make out what they are.' He added, 'But those are definitely survivors' lights. I can see the edge of the oil slick now. We'll be into it soon.' He lowered his glasses. 'Revolutions for three knots, Number One.'

The First Lieutenant passed the order to the wheelhouse. 'These chaps were probably hit in the gun action,' suggested Barratt. 'We'll have to check if some are alive. There don't seem to be many.' Aware of the risk of presenting a sitting target to a submarine his senses were keyed to *pings* from the bridge's loudspeaker. Subconsciously he was waiting for the *ping* to change to the deeper, more sonorous *pong* of an underwater contact.

As if reading the Captain's thoughts the First Lieutenant said, 'I expect the U-boat's on its way, sir. Looking for another target.'

'I dare say, Number One.'

Standing together at the bridge screen they spoke quietly, rarely lowering the night glasses.

Restless had almost reached the beginning of the oil slick when Barratt exclaimed, 'Good God! There's somebody sitting in the water waving at us.' He spoke into the wheel-house voice-pipe. 'Stop engines. Coxswain on the wheel.'

Over his shoulder he called, 'Scrambling net over the port side, Number One. Double quick.' The First Lieutenant went to a voice-pipe. Barratt kept his glasses trained on the waving arms. Very odd, he said to himself. How on earth does he do that Christ on the water act?

'Coxswain on the wheel, sir.' The report from the wheel-house was repeated by the First Lieutenant. With engines stopped the only sounds on the bridge now were the whirring undertones of fans and auxiliary machinery, the *pings* from the bridge-speaker, and the lap and murmur of the water along the sides. Into this comparative silence there came suddenly a new sound, one that drowned all others: the high pitched scream of escaping steam from *Restless*'s squat funnel. The engineroom was getting rid of excess boiler pressure.

Pale opalescent light began to appear on the eastern horizon as *Restless* drifted slowly towards the man in the water.

It looked like the beach at Sandport, but somehow it wasn't. But one thing was for sure – the guy in the motor cruiser was shooting at him. He'd best be careful, or he'll hit me. Guess I must get out of this. Swim over to that girl on the diving float. He tried to swim but couldn't, his legs were tied together, wouldn't move. The girl in the red costume was waving like crazy. What did she want? She was standing up on the float. Didn't look in any trouble. But they did that sometimes. He was wondering about her when the water splashed in his face.

He came to with a start. Where the hell? What's going on? The rope-bin had listed over to one side so that the water was lapping his face, his head and shoulders against the submerged staves. He felt around him, touched the staves on the high side, threw his weight that way and corrected the list. Now he was sitting upright again. So it had been a dream. Pity. The girl looked cute.

The illuminated dial of his watch showed thirty minutes after four. The moon was low in the sky, but still giving light up-moon. Not that there was anything to see there. Four-thirty. He'd been in the water for more than seven hours. How much longer? Could be days, he supposed. Maybe for ever. Better to have been machine-gunned perhaps? For Chrissake, why had he ended up in a ship like old *Fort Nebraska*? Without an escort you never had a chance going it alone against a submarine. He'd joined the naval reserve to get into a fighting ship, not a Liberty ship. 'You take what we give you, buddy,' the Chief Gunner's Mate at the training base had retorted when he complained. He wondered if he'd ever see Sandport again? What was Mary Lou doing right now? With some other guy perhaps? And Dad and Mom? What would the time be now in Massachusetts? Five hours west of Greenwich, UK, wasn't it? But what's the longitude around here? Must be well east of Greenwich. So what. I don't know. There's worse problems, anyway. Goddam thirst. Surrounded by water and thirsty. That's plain stupid. Why can't the rain come like it did before? This stinking fuel oil. Burns my skin. Smarts my eyes. Must have a pee. No problem. No point in opening the flies. Just pee – like that. Yeh, that way feels kinda good. I needed that.

The sound of splashing water? Goddam sharks still at it. Can't see them, they're way down-moon. It's dark there. Guess they won't trouble me so long as there's enough dead guys to eat.

Jesus! What's that noise? Coming from the dark side? That high-pitched hissing. Hurts the eardrums. Not too far away. Jesus! It's a ship. It's a goddam ship.

He began to wave his arms and shout. 'Hey, ship ahoy, ship ahoy! Hey you guys, I'm here.'

When he realized there was no way he could be heard above the noise of escaping steam he stopped shouting. But he didn't stop waving.

Barratt looked aft from the wing of the bridge, saw the man climb the scrambling net on to the iron deck. Splattered with fuel oil and without a lifejacket he ignored the hands which reached down to help him inboard though he must have been in the water since nine o'clock of the previous night. Powerful looking chap, pretty tough customer, decided Barratt. He went to the wheelhouse voice-pipe. 'Revolutions for five knots, port ten,' he ordered. Turning to the Yeoman he said, 'Standby the starboard ten-inch. We'd better take a close look at what's left in the water.' He went to the starboard

85

wing of the bridge, called out, 'Expose now.' A powerful beam leapt from the signal lamp, the long finger of light probing the sea to starboard. It settled on one corpse, moved at Barratt's request to another, and another, and another. There was little left to see: tatters of mutilated flesh, torn lifejackets and broken white bones. In all about a score of corpses were examined. Feeling physically sick, Barratt said, 'That'll do, Yeoman.'

The rapid clatter of feet on the rungs of the bridge ladder told of someone coming up in a hurry. It was the First Lieutenant. 'We've got him on board, sir. His name's Corrigan. He says he's the sole survivor. One of the stern-gun's crew. He's a US naval reservist. Haven't had time to interrogate him properly.' He took a deep, noisy breath. 'He says it was a Jap submarine, not a German U-boat. Claims that his gun scored a direct hit at the foot of the Jap's conning-tower. The submarine then rammed the two lifeboats and machine-gunned the survivors. It apparently made several runs after that, using a searchlight and machine-gunning the wreckage and anything else showing in the water. It did this for about ten minutes.'

'My God, how typical.' Barratt's voice rose in sudden anger. 'How did this chap get away with it?'

'Haven't got round to that yet, sir. He's in the sick-bay, they're cleaning him. Getting rid of the fuel oil. The doctor wants to examine him.'

'He looked pretty fit to me as he came over the side. Did he say what the submarine did after the machine-gunning?'

'Yes, sir. He saw it heading away down-moon, running on the surface. It was soon lost to sight. He thinks it can't dive.'

Barratt was silent, thinking. 'Down-moon at say 2130 last night,' he said. 'Down-moon at that time would have been west. Towards the coast. Funny.'

'That might have been the submarine's initial course, sir. It could have altered later. For all that Corrigan says, it may have dived.'

Barratt shrugged, lost himself in another silence. At last

he said, 'I'm going to the chartroom, Number One. I'll make a signal to Captain (D). In the meantime steer 010°. Revolutions for sixteen knots.' With a final, 'Over to you,' he left the bridge.

Ten

In the operations room at Kilindini the third officer Wren on duty in the morning watch wrote on the signal pad with one hand while holding the phone in the other. When the voice at the far end announced, 'Message ends' she replied with, 'I'll read it back.' She did so, got an 'Okay love' from the Petty Officer in the Fleet W/T Office, tore the sheet from the pad and took it through to Cookson, the RNVR Lieutenant in charge of the watch.

'From *Restless*,' she said. 'They've picked up the *Fort N* survivor.'

He threw his head back, an eyebrow raised in mock alarm. '*The* survivor. Sounds odd.' He took the signal, read it aloud, looked at the Wren in surprise. 'So it wasn't a German U-boat,' he said. 'Haven't been any reports of Jap submarines in the Mozambique Channel for at least six months. That last attack – the southbound convoy – was attributed to *Gruppe Eisbär*.'

She frowned, wrinkled her nose. 'Aren't the Japanese dreadful. Killing survivors like that. It's unspeakably brutal.'

'Yes, they're a bloody lot,' he agreed. 'But marvellous that *Fort N* scored a direct hit. I expect that's why the poor sods were massacred.'

'You shouldn't call them sods.' Her tone was censorious. 'They're dead.' Since her relationship with Donald Cookson was a good deal closer than their respective ranks she had few inhibitions about his seniority.

'You know what I mean, Jane,' he protested. 'Where's Hutch? He should see this.'

'Gone to the loo. In the meantime *Restless* says she

proposes to remain in the area. Requests orders. Shouldn't you do something?'

Cookson patted the front of his mouth to hide a yawn. 'Have a heart. I've only had the signal for about forty-five seconds.' He reached for the phone. 'SOO will have to deal with this. It's addressed to Captain (D).'

He glanced at the clock over the wall-chart. It showed 0449.

The Staff Officer Operations lived with a number of other officers in the big white house down the path from Navy House. When Cookson read him the signal he said, 'Acknowledge it, repeated Deputy C-in-C and RAFHQ. Instruct *Restless* to remain in the area until further orders. That's all. I'll inform Captain (D).'

Deep in thought, Commander Russel hung up the phone and sat on the edge of the bed, his back to the mosquito netting, contemplating his feet. 'Strange that Barratt should be involved. The mills of God no doubt.' He nodded agreement as if someone else had made the remark, before reaching for the silk dressing gown which hung on the back of the door.

With a uniform jacket over his pyjamas the SOO stood at the top end of the operations table, billiard cue in hand. Pointing with it to the miniature model of a merchant ship on the many times enlarged chart, he said, 'That's the position *Fort N* gave in her four S signal.' The cue moved northwards to a tiny grey warship. 'That was *Restless*'s position at 0435. Where she found the wreckage, twenty-six miles east of Ponto Pangani, picked up the survivor and saw evidence of the machine-gunning.' He moved the cue back in a southerly direction. 'The survivor last saw the submarine here. Surfaced and heading down-moon at about 2130. At that time down-moon would indicate a westerly heading. In other words, in towards the coast.'

Captain George Reynolds, short title Captain (D), a large, rotund man with mischievous blue eyes and a bucolic face, was the administrative authority for the destroyers, frigates and corvettes of the Eastern Fleet's escort forces based on Kilindini. He looked up from the chart. 'This chap Corrigan. I wonder how reliable a witness he is? You can't see much when you're in the water at night. At least I couldn't and I'm more buoyant than most.' He chuckled fruitily. 'Of course mine was nasty cold Atlantic – *and* rough. Corrigan, one of the Yank's gun-crew, claims a direct hit on the conning-tower. I wonder? It was a night action. Wasn't it perhaps the flash and report of the submarine's gun immediately forward of the conning-tower?'

The SOO nodded. 'Survivors' reports can be dodgy. Rather like witnesses of a road accident. Depends a lot on what they think they saw.'

'Trouble is,' said Captain (D), 'non-submariners tend to regard the whole bridge structure as the conning-tower. They don't realize that the tower inside all that free-flooding space is on about the same scale as one cigarette in a packet of twenty. If *Fort N* did secure a hit the odds are against it being on the conning-tower itself.'

'On the other hand there was no point in massacring the survivors, unless . . .' The gloomy aspect of the SOO's face was heightened by shadows from the wall lighting.

'Unless what, SOO?'

'Unless the Japanese captain decided he must take steps to prevent it being known that the boat was damaged. But for Corrigan *we* wouldn't have known, would we?'

'Possibly. But I think it's more likely that the Jap was simply working off his rage at being hit. It isn't the first time their submarines have murdered survivors from merchant ships.' Captain (D) sighed. 'They tend towards the barbaric, you know.'

The SOO frowned at the little ships on the operations table as if they were somehow responsible. 'However improbable, I do feel we shouldn't dismiss the possibility that Corrigan may be right. As I see it we're confronted with simple alternatives. One, that the submarine cannot dive – two, that it can. If the latter case I imagine it will remain on

90

the surface until dawn, using darkness to move well away from the sinking. If it can't dive it's in trouble unless it can somehow evade air cover.' He turned to the Flight Lieutenant who represented the RAF in the operations room. 'What do you say, Hutchison?'

'It certainly will be in trouble if it can't dive, sir. The Catalinas take off shortly on routine dawn patrols.' He looked at the wall clock. 'In about fifteen minutes. One from here, the other from Pamanzi. We'll concentrate them on the area to be searched – and put two more Cats in the air if necessary. Incidentally we've just heard that a Cat from Pamanzi was sent off shortly after the sinking to look for survivors in the position given in *Fort N*'s signal. It got there a few hours later. Searched in heavy rain but found nothing.'

'I see.' The SOO looked doubtful. He pointed the billiard cue at the RNVR Lieutenant. 'Plot the furthest-on right away, Cookson. One radius at twelve knots from 2130, the other at twenty knots. That'll give us the Japs' furthest-on at both economical and maximum speeds.'

'More likely to be the former.' Captain (D) mopped his forehead with a large handkerchief. 'Our Nippon friend is a long way from base. Maximum speed burns up the fuel.'

Cookson measured off the radii from *Fort Nebraska*'s position, plotted the furthest-on circles. The Flight Lieutenant jotted details on the notepad on which he'd already written the position co-ordinates. He looked at the SOO. 'Will two Cats do?'

'Yes, I think so. At least until we've briefed the Admiral. Important to cover the furthest-on areas first. Fortunately we have *Restless* down there.'

The Flight Lieutenant picked up the phone marked RAF. 'Duty Officer, 290 Squadron,' he said.

Captain (D) leant over the operations table. 'If the submarine can't dive it'll opt for concealment during daylight. Not too difficult on this bit of coast.' He pointed with a large finger. 'We'll put *Restless* on an inshore search right away. She can sniff round the coastline and islands. If the Admiral agrees we'll ask 290 Squadron for a third Catalina to support her directly. Of course using the air means over-flying Portuguese territory.'

'We've standing permission to overfly, sir, if we're looking for survivors.'

'Thank you, Hutchison,' said Captain (D). 'I'd forgotten that.'

The SOO snapped a finger at the RNVR Lieutenant. 'Draft the signal to *Restless*, Cookson.'

While Cookson was busy with the signal Captain (D) and the SOO went out on to the verandah. Below them a thin curtain of mist rose from the water between Lukoni and Port Reitz, revealing as it lifted the hazy outline of warships at anchor.

Captain (D) looked at the dawn sky. 'It's going to be a hot day, Ian.'

The SOO nodded absent-mindedly. 'I'm sorry in a way that *Restless* is down there. Not going to help Barratt.'

'What are you driving at?'

'You know – his wife's death in Changi.' The SOO's expression of gloom deepened. 'He's just seen the remnants of a massacre. A Japanese one. That on top of the other business.' He shrugged. 'Could be too much.'

Captain (D)'s head moved up and down in slow affirmation. 'I see what you mean. On the other hand it may help him work off steam. The possibility of coming to grips with the little yellow men. I'd hate to be one of them if he does.' He looked at his watch, yawned noisily. 'Another two hours to breakfast. Dear me. Don't think I can hold out that long. You coming, Ian?'

'I'll come down later, George.' The SOO looked puzzled. 'Thought you were on a diet. Getting rid of some of that blubber?'

Captain (D)'s rubbery face arranged itself in a cheerful smile. 'Came off it yesterday. But I don't intend to overdo things. Couple of eggs, sausages and bacon, toast and marmalade, coffee, a little fruit perhaps – nothing excessive.'

The SOO shook his head. 'You're incorrigible.'

George Reynolds and Ian Russel had been term-mates at Dartmouth.

For Barratt the twenty minute interval between the despatch of his signal to Kilindini and the receipt of Captain (D)'s reply was a busy one. His first action was to put *Restless* on a north-westerly course and increase speed to twenty knots. 'We'll close the land,' he explained to Charlie Dodds. 'And make northerly progress. Let me have ETAs at Cape Delgado for the submarine. One at twelve knots the other at sixteen. And an ETA for *Restless* at twenty knots.'

The Navigating Officer made for the chartroom.

Barratt had an open mind about the extent to which the submarine might have been damaged. While he had reservations about survivors' reports, particularly where night action was concerned, he was influenced by Corrigan's evidence that it had last been seen heading down-moon. That meant towards the coast, and that was why Barratt was taking *Restless* in that direction.

Other considerations influenced him: if the submarine could still dive, as he thought likely, it would get away from the scene of the sinking with its evidence of a massacre, and hunt for its next target. Unescorted ships kept close to the coast; Cape Delgado was a focal point for shipping; once off it a change of course was necessary; what better place for targets than its approaches?

Looking at the chart to decide on his course of action he had noted that the boundary between Tanganyika and Mozambique was the Rovuma River, its mouth some twenty miles north of Cape Delgado. If the submarine could not dive, the coast south of the Rovuma River was not only neutral territory but so studded with small islands, bays and inlets as to be an almost ideal hiding place.

That thought triggered another: the German cruiser *Königsberg*, when evading pursuit by British cruisers in the 1914-18 War, had holed up in the Rufigi River south of Dar-es-Salaam, only to be found and destroyed there later by HMS *Hampshire*. Perhaps, thought Barratt, the Rovuma

93

River could be to the Japanese submarine what the Rufigi had been to the German cruiser.

His thoughts were interrupted by the arrival in the chart-room of the Coxswain. Behind him at the door stood a young man with tousled hair, bloodshot eyes and scratches on his face and arms. The deeply tanned, muscular body seemed too large for the white shorts and vest he wore. 'Leading Seaman Corrigan, USNR, sir,' announced the Coxswain. 'The doctor says he's in pretty good shape but needs a rest.'

Barratt said, 'Come in, Corrigan. Glad to hear you're all right. I won't keep you long, but your answers to one or two questions may be very important.' The Captain nodded towards the Chief Petty Officer. 'You may carry on, Coxswain.'

The ten minute chat with Corrigan put a question mark over Barratt's belief that the submarine could still dive. When he explained to the American why it was unlikely that the conning-tower itself had been damaged, Corrigan disagreed with a good deal more vigour than was customary between officers and ratings in the Royal Navy.

'Got a picture of a submarine here?' he challenged. 'I'll show you right where that shell went in.' As an afterthought he added, 'sir.'

Barratt took from the shelf a copy of *Jane's Fighting Ships*, found the section dealing with the Imperial Japanese Navy, turned the pages until he came to those dealing with submarines. 'Here's an "I" class built just before the War.' He pointed to it.

Corrigan looked at the photograph closely, took a pencil from the chart-table. 'The shell went in right here.' He indicated the point of entry with the pencil. 'Dead in line with the space between the two periscopes. And that's where the conning-tower is.'

Barratt was taken aback. 'You've served in submarines, then?'

'No, sir. But we were shown over a couple when we did

our gunnery course. And we had blown-up diagrams of enemy submarines. For points of aim, you know.'

Barratt frowned. 'You're not telling me you aimed to hit the conning-tower?'

Corrigan's scratched face broke into a grin. 'No, sir. It was a dark night with flashes of lightning and there was just the two of us. Me and Smitty Fredericks and he was wounded. I just aimed in the general direction of the midships super-structure. I guess it was a dead lucky hit.' He shook his head in disbelief of what had happened. 'But later, when I was about thirty feet from the submarine, in bright moonlight, I saw right good where that shell went in. Take it from me, Captain, that Jap can't dive.'

Barratt was thoughtful, looking at the photograph in *Jane's* and then at the chart. At last he said, 'If you're right, Corrigan, we have a sporting chance of finding him.'

'I'd like to be around when you do, sir.'

The Captain nodded sympathetically. 'I can understand that.'

He went on to question the American about the machine-gunning, and the direction in which the submarine had headed as it left the scene.

Having confirmed what he'd told the First Lieutenant, Corrigan added, 'You know why those . . .' He hesitated on the edge of obscenity. 'Why they killed my buddies, sir – I'll tell you. It was because they knew they'd been hit real bad. That submarine couldn't dive. If that news got out their number was up. That's why they killed like they were goddam butchers.'

'Thank you, Corrigan. What you've told me is most help-ful.' He looked at the young man with quizzical eyes. 'What was your job before the war?'

'Lifeguard, sir. On the beach at Sandport, Massachusetts.'

The Captain smiled. 'That explains a lot.' When the American had gone, Barratt put *Jane's Fighting Ships* back in the rack. 'Did you hear that, Pilot?' he asked Dodds who was working at the chart-table.

'I heard most of it, sir.'

95

'He seems pretty sure the Jap can't dive.'

Dodds looked up from the pad on which he'd been making notes. 'Yes, he does,' he said in an offhand way, adding, 'I've got those ETAs ready, sir.'

Soon after Corrigan left the chartroom Barratt sent for the First Lieutenant. 'I need you for a council of war,' he said when Sandy Hamilton arrived. 'Captain (D)'s signal orders us to remain in the area and search the immediate coastline.' Barratt straightened up from the chart-table and stretched his arms. 'I intend to interpret that fairly liberally. Two Catalinas on routine AM patrol are taking off about now. They'll be showing up in a few hours' time. The Pamanzi chap first because he hasn't got so far to come. Right. Now for the ETAs, Pilot.'

The Navigating Officer checked his notes. 'For the submarine, ETA Cape Delgado at twelve knots will be 0630, at sixteen knots 0330. No allowance for current, and . . .' he tapped nervously on the chart-table with the fingers of one hand, '. . . I've assumed that he left the sinking position at 2130, and that at twelve knots he'll have had to dive at dawn . . .'

'Which is now,' put in the First Lieutenant. 'The sun was beginning to poke its rim above the horizon when I left the bridge a few minutes ago.'

'He's likely to have dived,' said the Captain. 'Unless he can't – in which case he won't be there. He'll have gone inshore to hole up. What's our ETA Cape Delgado?'

'0835 at twenty knots, sir.'

'I see.' Barratt pinched the bridge of his nose with thumb and forefinger, cleared his throat and bent over the chart-table. 'So the Jap is well ahead of us at either speed, and we . . .' He nodded at some indivulged thought. After a brief silence he said, 'If this submarine *can* dive I think we can more or less forget him until his next sinking. I'm going to assume that he can't, that Corrigan's right. As far as I'm concerned it's more a gut feeling than anything else. Probably because I want to believe that he can't dive. If he's stuck on the surface he'll try to hide. That'll give us a sporting chance. Where he can go, we can. Our draughts are much the same.' He coughed, took out a handkerchief, wiped his mouth. 'We'll start at the Rovuma River mouth. It's about twenty miles north of Cape Delgado. When we've checked it thoroughly we'll work south. He won't be north of the river. Too risky. Tanganyika is British territory. If he has to hide he'll stick to the Mozambique coast. Somewhere between where *Fort N* sank and the Rovuma River. Perhaps in the Rovuma.' Barratt turned from the chart-table. 'What d'you chaps think?'

'Portuguese neutrality, sir? If we operate close inshore?' The First Lieutenant sounded doubtful.

'They are very much our friends, Number One. And it's a pretty deserted coastline. Not much more than a thin sprinkling of African fishing villages along the bit we're interested in. We're looking for survivors from the *Fort N* if we're asked. You, Pilot. What's your view?'

'If Corrigan's story is correct . . .' He sounded doubtful, shrugged. 'I suppose it gives something to go on. But the hide-out, if there is one, won't be in the Rovuma River, sir. I'd thought of that too. So I read it up in the Sailing Directions. There's a sand-bar across the mouth. Even at high tide there isn't enough water for anything but a ship's boat to cross it.'

There was a sudden silence. The Captain sighed, his face reflecting disappointment. 'So that rules out the Rovuma.' He looked down at the chart. 'Well, there's a lot of other places south of it that are promising. *And* there's a couple of things in our favour.' He turned to face them. The grey of his eyes was accentuated by the shadows beneath them. A very tired man, thought the First Lieutenant. Doesn't get enough sleep.

'Yes, two things,' went on Barratt. 'If the sky remains reasonably clear we'll have moonlight tonight. Secondly, there'll be catamarans on the move in and around the islands. Some of the Africans in them may have seen the submarine.' The expressions of doubt exchanged between Hamilton and

97

Dodds irritated him. 'Or have you forgotten how we found the *Coimbra*?'

The *Coimbra*, a Portuguese coaster, had run aground on a coral reef south of Dar-es-Salaam some months earlier and given a position which was badly in error. *Restless* had found the little ship by questioning African fishermen. Barratt had mentioned moonlight and the *Coimbra* because he sensed that Hamilton and Dodds were lukewarm about an inshore search and sceptical of Corrigan's report that the submarine could not dive. At another time, in other circumstances, he might have shared their reservations, but the massacre of *Fort Nebraska*'s crew and his preoccupation with what had happened in Changi Gaol combined to influence his judgement; to fill him with a blind determination to find the submarine, a resolve more emotional than rational.

Something in the First Lieutenant's voice, in his expression, a restrained cynicism, suggested that he was aware of this. 'We'll be using the motorboat will we, sir?' he said. 'To contact the catamaran people?'

'We will indeed, Number One. I've told the PO Tel to observe wireless silence – listening watch only. Once we've reached the mouth of the Rovuma River and begun our search to the south we'll shut down on radar as well. No point in advertising our presence for the benefit of the Japs' search receiver.'

The Navigating Officer shuddered as if assailed by an icy wind. 'Navigating at night, close inshore, sir – through those narrow passages between the islands – coral reefs and sandbanks?' He hesitated, the frown lifting his eyebrows.

Barratt stared at him. 'Well,' he said bluntly. 'So what?'

'Radar would be a big help, sir.'

'We managed very well without it until quite recently.' The Captain's brusque manner made it clear that the matter was not arguable. 'I've no doubt we'll do so again.'

Eleven

At first light Kagumi and his men set out on the journey to the African village. The inflatable was halfway across the creek when the sound of rifle shots came from the direction of the narrows. Kagumi realized they must have been fired by the sentries on the other side of the bluff. He opened the throttle wide and headed for the narrows, the inflatable bumping and spraying its way across wind-rippled water. Once round the bluff he saw the drifting catamaran, the body of an African slumped over the stern, blood oozing from his head, an arm thrown out over the outrigger. Two men with rifles stood at the water's edge.

The bigger man answered. 'He was paddling the catamaran out of the creek, sir. Three times we shouted to him to stop, but he wouldn't. When we fired a warning shot he paddled faster. So we had to . . .' He shrugged, as if unwilling to complete the sentence.

Kagumi accepted that it was nobody's fault. The sentries had obeyed orders. It was unfortunate that the villagers did not yet know that it was forbidden to put to sea. The warning shot must have caused the African to lose his nerve. Had he made a slightly later start the incident could not have taken place. Unfortunate, decided Kagumi, but war was war.

With the catamaran and its dead occupant towing astern, he steered towards the huts under the palm trees. Their inhabitants would realize now the importance of obeying the orders he was about to give them. On balance, he concluded, the incident was probably a good thing. He was sure that would be the view of Yashimoto, whom he could see standing

99

under the leafy branches which concealed I-357's periscope standards.

Yashimoto lowered his binoculars. It was evident what had happened. Not for the first time he congratulated himself on having a First Lieutenant as capable and quick thinking as Kagumi. An excellent officer, he could always be relied upon to do the right thing at the right time. It was unfortunate that an African had been killed, but the example set would do no harm. Though the goodwill of the villagers was desirable, they could not be permitted to go out to sea. Once on the fishing grounds they would meet other fishermen and the news that a submarine was hiding in the creek would soon spread. The safety of I-357 and her crew had at all times to be paramount.

A good deal happened on board in the next few hours. Kagumi returned with two catamarans in tow, an African in one of them. The catamarans were secured astern of the submarine, and the African was taken on board.

'The villagers understand your orders, sir,' Kagumi reported. 'Though some of the women moaned and wailed when I handed over the body.' A deprecatory laugh came from the First Lieutenant. 'Trying to explain in sign language what had happened wasn't easy. But in the end the message got through.'

'The African you brought back?' inquired Yashimoto.

'He can speak a dialect which is possibly English or South African. He has worked on the gold mines in South Africa, near a place he called Goli. Apparently many Africans from Mozambique do so.'

Yashimoto permitted himself a rare smile. 'How did sign language tell you that?'

'He pretended to dig, picked up a stone, held it against the gold-coloured anklets the women wore. He pointed to himself several times, said, "Goli, South Africa," and again went through the motions of digging.' Kagumi paused. 'After that . . .'

Yashimoto held up a peremptory hand. 'That will do, First Lieutenant. Why did you bring him across?'

'Hasumu was studying English at university in Yokahama before he was called up,' explained Kagumi. 'It is possible that he will understand the African. I thought that might be useful.' The First Lieutenant had difficulty in concealing a yawn. The gesture was not lost on Yashimoto. 'You have done well, Kagumi,' he said. 'Now take a rest. It must be a long time since you slept.'

The inflatable with Sato and his crew got back to the submarine at half-past seven that morning. Yashimoto's concern at their late return was mollified by the quality of the chart the Navigating Officer had made. He was also much relieved by Sato's report that there were no signs of human habitation other than the huts in the creek. Looking at the chart it struck Yashimoto that Creek Island was shaped like a wolf's head: the creek its mouth, the bluff the big fang which shut out the view from seaward. Perhaps he should have called it Wolf Island. 'Later,' he told Sato. 'You must complete the chart with soundings in the creek and its approaches.'

The hills which enclosed the creek and the bluff which jutted into the narrows not only hid the submarine from seaward but provided shelter from the prevailing wind. The steep, wooded slopes rising up from the water's edge would, he realized, cast shadows over the creek through most of the day. An enemy warship attempting to enter must, on rounding the bluff, come within point blank range of the submarine's forward torpedo tubes; finally, the creek was so narrow, its sides so high, that bombing runs by aircraft would be difficult. For purposes of defence, decided Yashimoto, Creek Island could scarcely have been better. The disadvantages were that the hills, and the leafy camouflage on the conning-tower, limited the function of the search receiver, while the hydrophones could only be effective over a restricted sector where the narrows led into the creek's basin. Distant warning of a ship approaching would be difficult at night.

The advantages the island's geography conferred on the submarine were shared in quite different ways by the African fishing community. Small wonder, thought Yashimoto, that they had sited their huts where they were.

A short time after sunrise that morning the seven sentries guarding the land approaches to I-357, and the petty officer and men from the inflatable on duty in the creek, returned on board having been relieved by personnel from the spare crew pool with Sub-Lieutenant Nikaido in command in place of Lieutenant Matsuhito.

At about eight o'clock the operator on the sound receiver reported the approach of an aircraft on a southerly bearing. Three short blasts were immediately sounded on the bridge siren and all activity in I-357 ceased. In accordance with orders the sentries at once took cover. Camouflaged with foliage, the inflatable at the creek entrance nosed into the bank to hide under overhanging branches.

The atmosphere in the control-room became tense, no one moving, many eyes looking at the deckhead as the distant drone increased in volume until it passed overhead in a crescendo of sound, only to become steadily fainter as the aircraft drew away.

'Flying low.' The Captain spoke in a subdued voice. 'No more than a few hundred feet, probably. If he does not circle and return soon, all is well.'

The First Lieutenant nodded assent. During the next few minutes tension in the control-room slowly diminished. Yashimoto looked towards the cabinet where the sound operator sat, staring blankly, his hands pressing the headphones to his ears. 'Do you still hear it, Hasumu?' he demanded.

The operator shook his head. 'It has gone, sir.'

The Captain turned to Kagumi. 'Sound the carry-on, First Lieutenant.'

The long shrill blast of the siren travelled down the conning-tower to the control-room.

*

Within thirty minutes the performance was repeated. This time the aircraft came in from the north and passed over the creek on a southerly heading. Again it gave no indication of having sighted anything untoward. Whether it was the first aircraft returning or another, Yashimoto did not know. Because of the time, and the direction from which it had come, he assumed its base was Kilindini – there was no means of telling. The sentry on duty beneath the foliage on the after gun-platform had reported that both aircraft were Catalinas.

Wearing greasy, sweat-stained khaki shirt and shorts, the pouches under his tired eyes darker and more prominent than usual, Yashimoto addressed the officers and petty officers gathered in the control-room. Their dishevelled, soiled appearance, their weary faces, matched those of their commanding officer. Standing well clear of the conning-tower from which came sounds of hammering and drilling, he began by explaining that strong tropical sunlight would by the end of the day have withered much of the submarine's leafy camouflage. 'We'll have to put fresh layers on top,' he said, running his tongue across his lower lip. 'This will mean another night of hard work. But we shall begin it well rested. Until midday all men not otherwise employed will clean and tidy the boat. After so many weeks at sea it is dirty and foul-smelling. This is not your fault. It is unavoidable on a long patrol. But now we have the opportunity to wash-and-brush-up . . .' The Captain stopped, showed his teeth in a dry smile. 'The litter, the grease, the peelings, the food droppings and waste material – all must be collected and made ready for disposal tonight. Each compartment is to be scrubbed and washed down with sea-water, then sprayed with disinfectant. Mess-tins, plates, cutlery and mugs must be scoured and stowed away neatly. The filth, the untidiness, the foul smell in the boat must be gone by noon. After that . . .' His voice was drowned by the high pitched whine of an electric drill in the conning-tower where the lower half of a man's body showed on the ladder. Yashimoto frowned at the First Lieutenant. 'Tell him to stop that confounded noise until I've finished.'

103

Kagumi shouted up the conning-tower and the drilling stopped. Yashimoto said, 'The engineroom department makes excellent progress with the repairs. That is good, but they must not silence your Captain.' With a self-conscious grin he cleared his throat and straightened his cap. 'All men not detailed for special duties will rest until 1830. Sunset', he added, 'will be at 1823. Working parties for tonight will be the same as they were in the early hours of this morning.' Looking round at the tired, grubby faces, his manner softened. 'I realize that in this heat we would all like to swim but that's not possible. Apart from the danger of sharks, nobody may go on deck during daylight hours unless sent by the duty officer. The risk of detection from the air is too great. Further reconnaissance by aircraft may not take place until late in the afternoon, but we cannot take chances. They may come at any time.' He glanced at the sheet of notes on the chart-table, went on: 'Now an item of good news.' Yashimoto's mouth smiled but not his eyes. 'The First Lieutenant tells me that the Africans draw their water from a spring behind the huts. Tonight an inflatable goes across with empty drums. Tomorrow we wash ourselves and our clothing in fresh water. That will be a luxury.'

Not quite accurate, thought Sato: *We* will wash *our* clothing, the wardroom steward will wash *yours*. But I do give you credit for having restricted yourself to the daily ration of four mugs of fresh water a day while we were on Pacific patrols.

Yashimoto folded the sheet of notes, placed it in his shirt pocket. 'That is all,' he said. 'You may carry on.'

Restless had rounded Cape Delgado and set out on the last leg to Rovuma Bay when radar reported an aircraft approaching from the north. Not long afterwards it could be seen ahead, the distant speck growing steadily larger. When close the Catalina began to fly in a wide circle, the noise of its engines masking all other sounds, the boatlike fuselage gleaming in the sunlight.

Over his shoulder the Captain called, 'Make our pennant numbers, Yeoman.'

The Yeoman aimed an Aldis lamp and its shutter began to click. An answering light blinked from the aircraft. The Yeoman passed the pennant numbers, the Catalina acknowledged, adding, 'Any joy?' The Yeoman repeated the message aloud.

Barratt said, 'Make – Not yet but getting warmer. Strict W/T silence imperative. Please inform Captain (D).'

The shutter of *Restless*'s lamp chattered busily. The Catalina acknowledged with, 'Will do. Can we assist?'

Barratt shook his head emphatically as the Yeoman repeated the message. 'Make – Thanks but please keep clear. Your presence draws attention to us.'

With a final, 'Will do,' the Catalina climbed away on a southerly course.

In a quiet aside Geoffrey Lawson, the officer-of-the-watch who shared the bridge with Sean O'Brien, said, 'Pretty unfriendly, weren't we? The only thing that's getting warmer is the weather.'

'Well, I wouldn't be knowing about that, Geoff, but I think the Old Man's right in not wanting to advertise our whereabouts. In the Western Approaches we learnt . . .'

'Here we go again,' interrupted Lawson. 'And what was it *we* learnt in the Western Approaches?'

O'Brien looked across to where the Captain sat in his chair on the compass platform. 'To keep a low profile if you hoped to find a submarine before it found you. Remember Max Horton's golden rule? *Cut the cackle?*'

'I wasn't in the Western Approaches – and anyway he's *Admiral Sir* Max Horton to you, my lad.' Lawson raised a disapproving eyebrow. 'Never forget – there are few more lowly forms of marine life than a Sub-Lieutenant RNVR.'

'Ah, and that sounds like the good old RN,' said O'Brien, one eye still on the Captain. 'But it's fine to know that some of us do it for the pleasure and not the money.'

*

The river had pushed a semi-circle of brown silt far out into Rovuma Bay, and it was there that *Restless* reversed course and began her search to the south.

The heat of an already oppressive day was tempered by a light breeze from the south-east which rustled the surface of the glittering sea. A few miles to starboard the coast showed thinly through the heat haze, the swell breaking on its off-shore reefs throwing up sheets of white foam which seemed to hang lazily in the air.

With few exceptions the men on deck, their bodies deeply tanned, wore only white shorts. To those on duty on the bridge, however, no such licence was permitted. 'I'm not having a lot of half-nude gorillas on my bridge,' Barratt had informed the First Lieutenant on joining the ship in Colombo, thereby ending the dispensation granted by the previous captain.

Cape Delgado was rounded an hour after leaving Rovuma Bay, and the destroyer's progress to the south became painstakingly slow. The many alterations of course and speed in the inshore passages between the islands and the mainland, and the stops to lower and recover the motorboat and skimmer, were responsible; the former was used to investigate promising islets and inlets, and the latter to question catamaran fishermen. For this task Peter Morrow, armed with a photograph of a submarine, was proving invaluable. The recently joined Sub-Lieutenant, born and brought up in Kenya, was fluent in Kiswahili, the *lingua franca* of the coast Africans. This, combined with an easy-going manner, ensured his rapport with the fishermen.

In the chartroom Dodds divided frowning attention between the plotting table where a stylus traced the destroyer's course through the channels between the islands and the mainland – every reef and sandbank, every shoal and shallow for him a threat of imminent disaster – and the echo-sounder which recorded the depths of water through which *Restless* passed. And finally, the tide-tables which served only to compound his worries.

106

At noon, looking a vastly troubled man, he reported to the Captain that average speed made good since Cape Delgado was only 6.3 knots.

The Captain was in a wing of the bridge examining an Arab dhow through binoculars. 'Not bad, Pilot,' he said, 'when you consider how we've been buggering about.'

With its lateen sail filled by the south-easter, the dhow was making up the coast in the narrow channel between the mainland and the islands off Cape Nondo where mangrove swamps gave way to bushclad slopes which in turn led to a hilltop where a baobab tree stood in solitary grandeur.

The Captain lowered his binoculars, pointed to it. 'See that,' he said. 'I expect the skipper of that dhow uses it as a leading mark. Just as his Arab ancestors have done for the last thousand years.'

Not bad for the Old Man, thought Charlie Dodds, almost poetic. 'I expect so, sir,' was his dutiful reply.

Twelve

By early afternoon the pattern of the search had become established. The motorboat and skimmer were now no longer hoisted inboard on completion of a mission, experience having shown that time was saved if they were left in the water to follow *Restless* until needed to investigate; the destroyer's speed reduced to that of the motorboat, the slowest of the trio.

Radar had been shut down after passing Cape Delgado on the journey south; to compensate for this the number of lookouts had been doubled. When near the small port of Mocimboa da Praia, a northbound coaster was sighted by the masthead lookout. Barratt altered course to seaward to avoid being seen inshore; not that he was unduly worried on that account. The 'searching for survivors' story could always be used.

Barratt was in the chartroom when Duckworth arrived in person to deliver a signal from Captain (D).

'With W/T silence, I couldn't acknowledge it,' he explained as he handed it over.

'Of course not, Duckworth. They'll understand.' Barratt read the signal and with an exclamation of annoyance put it in the chartroom clip. Addressed to *Restless*, repeated Deputy C-in-C, it read: *Return here if no contact by sunset today*.

Barratt raged inwardly. How on earth could he be expected to complete a thorough search of the coast in the twelve hours which had elapsed since Kilindini's signal ordering it that morning. There were still fifty-five miles of coastline and islands to be checked before they reached Matemo Island, twenty miles off which *Fort Nebraska* had gone down. There were another forty miles of coast south of that where a damaged submarine could have hidden. A worthwhile search was only possible in daylight. With almost a hundred miles still to be done, at an average speed of about six knots, there wasn't a hope of finishing before sunset the following day.

The whole thing was preposterous. He saw the hand of the SOO behind the recall signal. Russel didn't like him, they were on different wavelengths. And he didn't much like Gloomy Russel for that matter. A dreary individual, decided Barratt. He suspected that the incident which had sparked mutual dislike had taken place soon after *Restless* arrived in Kilindini from Colombo with other units of the Eastern Fleet. He, Russel and others, had gone off to the flagship in the same motorboat. In accordance with custom the coxswain had gone alongside the starboard gangway to disembark the Captains of *Restless* and *Resister* who were piped on board and saluted by the officer-of-the-watch and his minions. Russel, though senior in rank to Barratt, had remained in the motorboat with several other officers until the coxswain took it round to the port gangway where they disembarked, their arrival on the quarter-deck not qualifying for the cere-monial 'pipe' since they did not command ships. Later, on the return journey to the shore, Russel had remarked, somewhat sardonically, that using different gangways for officers arriving at and departing from the flagship in the same boat struck him as a monumental waste of time, particu-larly with a war on.

Barratt had replied, 'It is a very old custom, pre-Nelson in fact. Perhaps it has something to do with the scroll on the wall in the Captain-of-the-Fleet's office?'

'Oh really, what?'

'I'm not sure of the exact wording, but approximately, it reads: *It is the custom of their Lordships to give preference to those who serve at sea.*'

Turning a gloomy eye on him, Russel had remained silent. Later, Barratt regretted the remark. As Staff Officer Opera-tions Russel was on the shore staff. Older than Barratt, and a good deal longer on the retired list he was, notwithstanding

109

his rank, less suitable for command. It was not surprising, therefore, that he had been given a shore job. Barratt knew this, and knew too that Russel was happy to be in Kilindini, not too far from his farm at Naivasha, whence his wife made her not infrequent visits to Mombasa. The incident had been trivial enough, but Barratt felt it was reponsible for Russel's chilly manner.

As for *Restless*'s recall, he thought it likely that Captain (D) and the SOO had agreed that Catalinas could carry out a more effective search than a destroyer; and they were probably right, he conceded privately. But that wasn't going to change his plans. He'd already made up his mind. *Restless* would not return to Kilindini until the search had been completed. Nor would he break wireless silence to plead, argue or explain.

Something which Captain (D) and SOO didn't know, and would never know, was what the search meant to him. From the moment Corrigan had reported that the submarine was Japanese, Barratt's determination to hunt and find it had become an obsession. He had been presented with an opportunity to do something about what had happened to Caroline. For this reason he no longer saw the submarine in the context of prosecuting the War against the enemy. It was much more than that – nothing less than a personal matter between himself and the Japanese. There had for a long time been in his mind an indelible image; the harsh face of the commandant of Changi Gaol. The image persisted but the face now was that of the commander of the Japanese submarine. And because the imagery was a product of hatred, the face was not a pleasant one.

By late afternoon there was to Barratt's tired eyes a wearying sameness about the coastline and its islands; blue seas lapping dazzling white beaches fringed with coconut palms; the higher ground bushclad, with clumps of indigenous trees overlooked at times by feathery casuarina trees. On the seaward side of the islands the surf curled and foamed where the swells broke on the reefs. There were glimpses of

110

palm-thatched native huts, the only other signs of human activity the catamarans fishing off the reefs.

The water was so transparent in the shallows that rocks and coral reefs could be seen from the bridge, dark shapes against the sandy bottom where shafts of sunlight danced to the music of the sea.

In the skimmer, Peter Morrow had got the average time of interrogation down to a few minutes per catamaran. 'It's a fine art,' he'd explained to anyone prepared to listen during a snatched sandwich in the wardroom at midday. 'You flash the photograph, say, "Seen one of these?" The African stares at it, shakes his head, grins and offers you a fish. You refuse politely, saying, "May your catamaran bear many fish and your wives many children". With these courtesies done, you open the throttle and speed away. The whole thing takes just under three minutes. I need a beer, Docker. What about you?'

But as the hours passed and the motorboat and skimmer bustled about their respective duties, their reports uniformly negative, Barratt's spirits sagged and the enthusiasm of the morning gave way to disenchantment. Of course they'd never find the wretched submarine. Why had he ever thought they would? Even if it couldn't dive, the places to hide were so many, it was like looking for a needle in a haystack.

The Engineer Officer, Gareth Edwards, who'd served in submarines, had not helped Barratt's mood when he came to the bridge in the afternoon. In the course of a discussion he had pointed out that a hole in the conning-tower did not necessarily mean a submarine couldn't dive. 'With the lower hatch shut,' he explained, 'you *can* dive. The holed conning-tower itself becomes a free-flooding area. But you can trim the boat to look after that.'

'Surely there must be some problems, Chiefy. With a ruddy great hole in the conning-tower.'

Edwards said, 'Yes, indeed. The surfacing drill is affected, and crash dives are not practical. But neither of these prevent the boat from diving. They are what you might call operational inconveniences.' Barratt had not chosen to answer, but his resolve had remained unshaken. He would stick to his instinct. For him the deciding factor was the massacre of *Fort Nebraska*'s survivors. If the Japanese submarine could dive, what was the point of that senseless killing? So the search went on; and would go on, if necessary, until nightfall on the following day.

Towards sunset a Catalina was sighted some distance away. Flying low over the islands, heading north, it turned towards *Restless* as it came closer. A few minutes later it had passed about a quarter of a mile away to port. Barratt watched the flying boat through binoculars, annoyed that it had come so close; but it neither circled nor attempted to signal and he was grateful for that.

Soon afterwards there was a heavy rainstorm which drenched the bridge and everybody on it; but since it lowered the temperature and countered the oppressive heat it was more than welcome.

Hutch Hutchison put down the phone. 'The duty officer at Base says Catalina Freddy-Orange's ETA is 2205. It will have covered the coast between here and Port Amelia on both the outward and return legs.' He looked at the clock above the wall chart. 'Let's see. Time 1800. It should sight *Restless* soon if she's still in the Cape Delgado area.'

The SOO said, '*If* is the operative word. It would be interesting to know exactly what Barratt meant by "not yet but getting warmer".'

Captain (D) blew his nose noisily. 'Presumably means that he was on to some sort of clue. But what sort? That's the sixty-four dollar question. Any ideas, Haddingham?'

Jim Haddingham, a Lieutenant Commander on Captain (D)'s staff, was Flotilla Navigating Officer. 'Not much in the way of hiding places between Rovuma Bay and Cape Delgado,' he said. 'But the chart shows plenty of possibles south of the Cape.'

The SOO stroked his chin with thumb and forefinger. 'His

112

request to the Catalina to keep clear because it was drawing attention to *Restless* . . .' He looked at Captain (D). 'What d'you make of that?'

'Pretty obvious isn't it? He didn't want attention drawn to *Restless*'s presence.'

The SOO looked unconvinced. 'Presumably anybody who could see the Catalina circling was likely to have seen *Restless* anyway.'

Captain (D) shook his head. 'Not necessarily, Russel. A submarine concealed behind an island or in a creek might see the aircraft circling without being able to see what it was circling over. If the aircraft's signal lamp was flashing he'd know it was talking to a surface vessel.' He turned to Haddingham. 'You and Barratt were at Dartmouth together. What sort of chap is he? I know him as a reliable but . . .' He pursed his lips. 'Let's say a run-of-the-mill destroyer captain. But then he's only been with us since we got here and ceased to operate as a flotilla.'

'He's an odd sort of a chap,' said the Flotilla Navigating Officer. 'Not the type one noticed much in those days. Quiet, a bit bookish, didn't shine at games though he was a good cross-country runner. Used to enter for them all and win 'em all.'

'I can believe that,' Captain (D) nodded understandingly. 'He's one of those gaunt, wiry types. They usually are good runners.'

Haddingham waited for Captain (D) to finish, before saying, 'It was later that he began to be noticed, I suppose.'

'In what way?' Captain (D)'s head was cocked on one side.

'He was inclined to be accident-prone. Ran into bits of trouble. Odd sorts of scrapes. For example, as a sub-lieutenant in destroyers he got involved in a mock duel with a midshipman in Valetta. Fought it out on the iron deck with Very pistols. Both young men rather tight. One of the Very flares landed in the sternsheets of a motorboat coming alongside the starboard gangway. The Captain's dinner guests were in it. So was the Captain.'

113

Captain (D) chuckled. 'He was not amused, I dare say. Anything else?'

'Other incidents of that sort, you know. Usually after he'd had a few drinks. He wrecked a pin-table in a Chatham pub on one occasion. Told the publican that a notice on the machine invited payment of sixpence in return for three playing balls. He pointed out that it had jammed and failed to deliver the balls although it had got his sixpence. The gross breach of contract had, he said, compelled him to take steps to recover the sixpence.' Haddingham laughed. 'The pubkeeper reported him and the story got into the local press.'

Captain (D) looked mildly surprised. 'He doesn't strike me as that sort of man. Rather quiet, I thought. He left the service as a Lieutenant, didn't he?'

Haddingham said, 'Yes. He did. With about six years between his stripes. He had a frightful car smash when his ship was in Portsmouth. Coming back from a hunt ball somewhere in the country. A cabinet minister's daughter was his passenger. Her face was badly cut up. The police said he'd been drinking. There was a hell of a row. He left the Service not long afterwards. Went into the family wine business. That was a few years before the War began.'

'Shouldn't have thought the family wine business was the best place.' Captain (D) was lost in thought. 'I suppose most of us did some rather stupid things when we were young. Bad luck though, that car accident. Both for the girl and his naval career.'

'There were other scrapes. He was, as I've said, accident-prone,' continued Haddingham. 'But to his credit, he was popular with the lower deck. Very good with them. Always ready to help men in trouble. Never threw his rank about.'

The SOO fanned himself with a signal pad. 'You seem to know a lot about him.'

'I got to know him well in the training cruiser. And later on the Subs' Course at Greenwich. He was an amusing chap, and a good friend. Never let you down. I liked him. He was

114

a funny mix. Half quiet and reserved, half rather wild. Our paths crossed several times after that.'

The SOO said, 'I've always wondered how he got command of a fleet destroyer.'

Captain (D) said, 'I know the answer to that. Made a name for himself at Dunkirk. Got his DSC there. The V & W he commanded shot down a couple of aircraft and took off a lot of people.'

'I see.' The SOO looked gloomily through the open french windows down to Kilindini harbour where the long stretch of water reflected the light of the setting sun and the camouflaged hulls of warships at anchor.

Thirteen

An interested spectator of the day's events was Brad Corrigan. Wearing white shorts from the ship's clothing store, he spent most of the day on deck watching the comings and goings of the motorboat and skimmer, gleaning something of what was happening from scraps of conversation around him.

The American's bloodshot eyes, the scratches on his face and upper body, were reminders of the long night in the water; apart from these he seemed in good shape. Convinced by what he had seen that night, he did not believe the submarine could have dived. For him the search made sense, he admired the thorough way in which it was being conducted, and had a burning desire to be involved. He would have liked to be in the skimmer, the outboard engine screaming its head off, its propeller throwing up plumes of white foam as it leapt and bounced over the sea.

His interest had been heightened by the low-flying Catalinas, the sound of their engines deafening as they flew overhead. All in all he reckoned the Limeys were doing a good job. If they didn't find the Jap it wouldn't be for want of trying.

Some time soon, he reckoned, he'd request to see the Captain again. Ask him couldn't he, Corrigan, maybe go along in the skimmer and lend a hand? The Captain seemed okay. A hard face, but when he smiled it changed a lot, made him look a nice guy.

There's no one in the ship can want to find that submarine the way I do, soliloquized Corrigan. Sure I've got a grudge. Yeh, a real bad grudge. I saw the sons of bitches killing

116

my buddies, didn't I? Gunning them down like they were animals.

That adds up to one helluva good reason for wanting to get stuck into the bastards. I'll put it to the Captain that way. Maybe he'll understand. Give me the okay to go along. I need to get into that act real bad.

When the sun had gone and the twilight glow in the western sky had given way to night, the motorboat returned to *Restless*. The Gunnery Officer who'd taken it away put in the negative report that had become all too customary.

Barratt had shrugged, concealed his disappointment. 'We'll tackle the southern section tomorrow,' he said. 'It looks promising on the chart. More islands and broken coastline than we've had today. Now that we've got into the routine it should . . .'

The shrill voice of the starboard lookout broke into the sentence. 'Skimmer approaching, sir. Ahead to starboard.'

It couldn't be seen in the gathering gloom, but the high-pitched whine of its engine grew steadily louder. Moving through the water at slow speed *Restless* showed no lights until the Chief Bosun's Mate directed the beam of his torch on to the sea. The skimmer came out of the darkness, manoeuvred alongside and was hoisted on board. Morrow ran up to the bridge, found the Captain on the compass platform. 'Sorry, sir. No joy,' he said.

'There's a lot to be done yet.' Barratt spoke quietly, didn't lower his binoculars. 'We're only half way.'

Morrow thought the Captain sounded despondent, almost as if he didn't really mean what he was saying.

Barratt decided that *Restless* should stand out to sea that night. With revolutions for fifteen knots and radar and asdic operating, the destroyer settled down on a fifteen mile patrol line, three miles to seaward of the islands of Tambuzi and Metundo, the light on the former in sight most of the time. Some time after eight o'clock, satisfied that the ship was on station, he handed over the bridge to Geoffrey Lawson.

117

After a modest meal in his sea-cabin he made his first attempt at sleep in the twenty-four hours since *Restless* had picked up *Fort Nebraska*'s signal. To Barratt it seemed a good deal longer. Exhausted and depressed he lay on the settee, turning constantly, the pillow moist with sweat, the humid heat too much for the fan which whirred above his head. Sleep just wouldn't come. Too many thoughts in his head. Through it kept passing pictures of all that had happened during those twenty-four hours. Inevitably, they were accompanied by questions and uncertainties. Was he carrying out the search in the most efficient manner? Was there anything more he could and should be doing? Closer co-operation with the Catalinas? Why? In what way? They were searching as thoroughly as they could. So was *Restless*. The only sort of co-operation possible was the exchange of more signals. With what object? There was nothing to say. To have aircraft circling and flashing messages morning and evening was a sure way of making a nonsense of the search.

Captain (D)'s signal? Surely to God the operations room couldn't imagine there'd been enough time to complete the search. They've got bloody great charts, he told himself, the Catalinas will have reported where we were AM and PM. So they know the approximate rate of our search. Why call it off less than half way through? Can't they see from the chart that the Jap is just as likely to have looked for a hide-out to the south of *Fort N*'s sinking position as to the north?

Tired though he was he could formulate only one response to these conjectures and rhetorical questions: *Restless*'s search would continue. Only if the southern section yielded nothing by the end of the following day would he set course for Mombasa. To call a halt now was as unthinkable as it was indefensible. A dialogue with Caroline took shape in his mind.

'But why did you give up half way?' she was saying.

'Because of the signal. Captain (D) ordered me to return.'

With a small frown, a lifting of the eyebrows, she said, 'But surely you didn't have to answer. W/T silence and all that. You could have gone on, couldn't you?'

'And disobeyed orders?'

'Why not? Nelson did. He said he couldn't see the signal. You could say you hadn't received it.'

'So I let you down?'

'That's for your conscience to decide. I don't know. I'm dead.'

And so the interminable mental wrangle had gone on, and her *Why not? Nelson did*, kept repeating itself until, at long last, he fell asleep.

But for a gentle roll, an occasional creak in the superstructure and the distant murmur of machinery, there was little indication in the wardroom that *Restless* was at sea. The few officers there were reading, talking or idling in other ways. One of them, the Engineer Officer, sat on a settee, hands clasped behind his head, legs stretched out in front of him. He made a second attempt to get the Doctor's attention. 'And what would be the important book that so engrosses the Doctor?' he asked, the sing-song Welsh accent exaggerated for the occasion.

The Doctor looked up, frowned. 'It's a scholarly work by a German gentleman,' he said. 'You would not have read him.'

'Ah. And which one might that be?' The Welshman covered a yawn with a large hand. 'Thomas Mann maybe, or Mr Einstein?'

'No. From its title you might conclude that I have here a treatise on constipation. But it is not so, though some might describe the work as related to that complaint.'

'*Mein Kampf*,' came from a fair man with a square face who was playing chess with a midshipman. The square face belonged to Andrew Weeks, a Lieutenant RNVR who had graduated from Oxford not long before the War began.

The Doctor turned to look at him. 'Very good, Andy. Nothing like a classical education. And now, for a hundred dollars, my next question. Who was the author?'

Midshipman Galpin's hand went up. 'Adolf Hitler, *sir*.'

'You weren't asked, precocious youth.' The Doctor frowned, went back to his book.

The Torpedo Officer, John Taylor, a small thin man with black crinkly hair and dark eyes, threw a last dart at the board before slumping into an armchair next to the sprawling figure of Sandy Hamilton, who opened an eye to see who the newcomer was.

Taylor said, 'Sorry if I've disturbed you, Number One.'

'Not at all. It's a pleasure. One always enjoys being disturbed, particularly when dreaming.' The First Lieutenant shifted his legs and rearranged himself in the chair.

'Camilla was it?' suggested Taylor.

'Officers and gentlemen don't discuss ladies in the wardroom.'

'Sorry, Number One. I must apologize for the lapse.' The Torpedo Officer's sigh was exaggerated. 'She's very beautiful.'

'Pipe down, little man. That's enough.'

Taylor smiled. 'Now that you're awake. May I ask you a question?'

'Yes. If it's not about politics, religion or women.'

Taylor leant towards the First Lieutenant, lowered his voice. 'A bit odd that the Old Man has ignored Captain (D)'s signal, isn't it?'

'What d'you mean?' There was a cautionary note in the First Lieutenant's reply.

'You know what I mean. Sunset was two hours ago. We haven't the slightest clue where the ruddy submarine is. And yet here we are farting up and down a patrol line when we should be legging it for Mombasa.'

The First Lieutenant, his eyes on the chess players, didn't reply. Slowly, and with some effort, he levered himself out of the armchair, yawned and stretched.

Taylor said, 'You haven't answered my question, Number One.'

The First Lieutenant stared at him. 'I'm not in the business of criticizing the Captain's decisions,' he said. 'Nor should you be.'

He looked round the wardroom, tapped his mouth to hide another yawn. 'I think I'll turn in,' he announced to no one in particular as he went to the door. He, too, wondered what the Captain was up to.

It was not long before the voice-pipe on the bulkhead above Barratt's pillow whistled him awake. It was the officer-of-the-watch. 'Captain – bridge. Radar contact – small target, dead ahead, bearing steady, range eight miles, closing slowly.'

'Good. I'll be up in a second.' Barratt rolled off the settee, blinked at the single red light allowed in his sea-cabin, looked at the time, course and speed indicators on the bulkhead and set off for the bridge. *Small target* was probably a coaster, but it could equally be a surfaced submarine. *Dead ahead, bearing steady* and *closing slowly* meant it was on the same course as the destroyer which was overtaking.

It was some time before the range had closed sufficiently for the A/S cabinet to classify the target as 'small ship, single screw, reciprocating engine'. So it wasn't a submarine.

Nor were several other reports that brought Barratt to the bridge that night.

Fourteen

By sunset I-357's crew were ready for another night of hard work. Rested and refreshed, most of them having slept through the afternoon, there was much chattering and laughter as they made ready their equipment before going ashore. There was now an addition to their ranks. Kasuki, the man who'd received a headwound from a shell splinter, had been passed fit by the Coxswain. With a bandage round his head the young able seaman was questioned by the Navigating Officer to whom he had expressed his keenness to join the shore party. 'I feel good,' he told Sato who, with the First Lieutenant's permission, then detailed him to work with the carrying party.

In accordance with Yashimoto's orders the forenoon had been devoted to cleaning up the submarine below decks; the results were remarkable. The litter had gone from compartments which had been washed down and made ship-shape enough for an admiral's inspection; the foul smells of rotting food and hot unwashed bodies had given way to those of disinfectant, tinged with the ever-present odour of diesel oil. The foliage spread over I-357 made conditions on board more tolerable than they would otherwise have been. Open hatches and sea breezes from the creek blowing through the different compartments did much to check the high temperatures of the Tropics. The excellence of the crew's morale was in part due to this, but in the main it came from the knowledge that a dangerous situation had been averted: the Captain had found a safe hiding place, the repairs to the conning-tower were going ahead, and enemy aircraft had failed to spot the submarine. In a few days they would be putting to sea again, bound for Penang with all the pleasures

122

and comforts that promised. For this they had to thank their Captain, a man for whom they had the greatest respect. He was, they knew, a highly efficient naval officer; calm under all conditions, however difficult and dangerous; they saw him as someone who always acted decisively, always made the right decisions.

They knew they were lucky to have a man like Commander Togo Yashimoto as their Captain. It increased the chances of survival in a service in which few survived.

Throughout the day the sounds of hammering and the whine of high speed drills came from the conning-tower where the repair party under Hayeto Shimada, the Chief Engine Room Artificer, worked with unremitting effort. Lack of space restricted the number of men who could be in the conning-tower at any one time. To offset the heat in that confined space they were relieved at intervals by men who had been resting. The work having begun soon after I-357 arrived in the creek, the initial task of dismantling was well advanced.

The aircraft alarm signal was sounded twice during the afternoon. In mid-afternoon the first Catalina came in from the south; the second came from the north an hour or so later. But on this occasion it had been noted by a sentry that the Catalinas had different identification letters. The presence of two aircraft over the islands was to Yashimoto evidence of unusual air activity. Was this because the British suspected that I-357 was hiding somewhere on the coast? Or was it for some other reason such as searching for survivors? He inclined towards the latter.

The southbound Catalina which arrived in late afternoon flew low over the creek, skimming the trees on the summits of the surrounding hills. It had climbed away, its engines screaming, turned steeply and then flown back along the length of the creek, after which it continued its journey to the south. Worried as he was by its apparent interest in Creek Island, Yashimoto congratulated himself on the steps he had taken to conceal the submarine. He acknowledged to himself, however, that the configuration of the creek also helped: less than seven hundred yards long, most of it little more than a hundred wide, much of it shadowed by the steep slopes of the surrounding hills, it was no easy target for observation from an aircraft which could be over it for no more than fractions of a minute.

After the working parties had gone ashore, Yashimoto and the Engineer Officer met in the wardroom to discuss the progress of repairs. They sat together at the wardroom table, drawings of the conning-tower and its casing before them. To smoke was a luxury not permitted below decks under normal conditions, but with fresh air now passing freely through the boat they were enjoying cheroots which had been bought by the Captain in Penang.

Satugawa was explaining the problems involved in carrying out the work. 'Nothing has been easy,' he said. 'The armour piercing shell – it was probably a 5.5 inch – having passed through the outer casing, penetrated the wall of the conning-tower at its junction with the main pressure hull before bursting. That has left a large jagged hole at the point where the two surfaces meet at an acute angle. It also destroyed most of the starboard side of the lower hatch coaming. This makes the repairs very difficult. We have to restore the integrity of the main pressure hull and rebuild the lower hatch. Damaged air pressure pipes and electric circuits have also to be repaired. We've cut away most of the broken steel. Next we have to make a start on patching the pressure hull and conning-tower and rebuilding the lower hatch. To do this we have to cannibalize other parts of the boat without weakening the structure. It is a long, slow business. Finally there is the damaged hatch lid itself. Removing it has taken longer than expected.' The Engineer Officer's tone became apologetic. 'It is a heavy steel fitting, designed to withstand great pressure. The explosion put exceptional stresses on the lugs to the hinges. This distorted them and also the hinge pins. To remove them we have had to drill and chisel before getting the lid out for straightening and repair of the hinges.

Soon we will make a start on cutting and bending three-eighth steel plating to fit over the shell holes, then bolt them into place. Reconstruction of the tower hatch and hatch lid, and shaping the steel plating will require very high temperatures. We do not have a furnace on board but we can set up something ashore. Build it with stones, fuel it with dry timber and diesel oil, and use compressed air cylinders to blow it since we haven't got bellows. That was the Chief ERA's idea. All this will take time. Many hours will be required to achieve the temperatures necessary. The steel must be worked while it's white hot. This will involve constant reheating and measurement controls. Since we do not have the equipment of a foundry, there will have to be a lot of improvisation. A process of trial and error. Learning as we go, so to speak.'

The line of Yashimoto's mouth hardened. 'I cannot accept failure,' he said decisively. 'I must have your assurance that the work can be done.'

Satugawa avoided the Captain's penetrating stare. 'It can be done,' he said. 'But it is difficult to estimate how long it will take.'

Yashimoto pursed his lips, exhaled, his eyes on the smoke ring climbing to the deckhead. 'Today is the twenty-first of November.' He spoke slowly, very deliberately, as if each word was being weighed. 'We have been ordered to take up station outside Mombasa not later than midnight on the twenty-fifth. The carrier and its escorts are due on the twenty-sixth or twenty-seventh. The journey to Mombasa will take two days. To be on station in time we must leave here by midnight on the twenty-third. Can you get the work done by then, Chief?' Yashimoto's pouched eyes bore into the Engineer Officer, who held up his hands as if fending off an attack.

'If we fail,' Satugawa lifted his shoulders in a gesture of doubt, 'it can only be because we have attempted the impossible.' Aware of the ambiguity, he quickly added, 'I do not believe we are attempting the impossible.'

Yashimoto took the cheroot from his mouth, examined its

burning end before tipping the ash into a saucer. 'The fitting of outboard engines to the catamarans. Any problems there?'

Satugawa at once relaxed, the change of subject appeared to please him. 'There is no problem, Captain. The work will be completed before daylight, of that you need have no doubt.'

Yashimoto nodded approval, his eyes on a picture of the Emperor hanging on the wardroom bulkhead. 'Good,' he said. 'The catamarans will be less likely to attract attention from the air than inflatables.'

As daylight took over from night *Restless* left her patrol line to steam towards the coast between Tambuzi Island and the Nameguo Shoal. Barratt was anxious to get on with the search of a cluster of small islands between the shoal and Cape Ulu, about ten miles south of Mocimboa da Praia. That the chart gave no names to many of them suggested they were likely to be uninhabited but for small communities of African fishermen.

The day promised to be like its immediate predecessors, hot with a cirrus-laced sky, the blue sea smooth, its only movement the undulations of a swell which came in from the Mozambique Channel to break on the reefs guarding the coast and islands.

The motorboat and skimmer were lowered and the routine of the previous day was soon in full swing. Barratt sat in his seat on the compass platform, a tennis hat on his head, face and arms brown against his tropical uniform, his binoculars constantly in use. On the bridge with him were Taylor and O'Brien the watch-keepers, with the Yeoman, a signalman and the lookouts, while the Navigating Officer made periodic dashes between the chartroom and bridge, alarm written large on his face. With *Restless* steaming at slow speed, Barratt kept to the deep water channels, occasionally venturing too far from them for the comfort of Charlie Dodds who would make agitated reports about shoaling water, the state of the tides and currents.

*

By eight o'clock in the morning when the watches changed, the motorboat had visited most of the islands off Cape Ulu without success; in that time the skimmer had questioned the occupants of catamarans fishing off the shoals and reefs in the channels. The skimmer, like the motorboat, drew nothing but blanks, but the search went on.

In early afternoon the skimmer was sighted coming in from the direction of Tambuzi Island with something in tow. When nearer the tow could be seen to be a catamaran. 'What on earth's that all about?' exclaimed Barratt who was watching through binoculars. The skimmer and its tow drew closer until a solitary African could be seen sitting in the catamaran's sternsheets steering with a paddle. The sizeable bow-wave made by the makeshift craft and its outrigger suggested that it was travelling a lot faster than usual. The crew of the inflatable, clad only in shorts, their tanned bodies almost as brown as the African's, grinned happily as the skimmer and its tow turned in a wide circle before edging in towards the destroyer. A painter was made fast and with the skimmer and catamaran safely alongside, Peter Morrow came up a rope ladder on to the deck where the hoisting party was standing by. 'Keep this lot towing alongside, Chief, while I report to the bridge,' he called over his shoulder to the Bosun's Mate as he made for the fo'c'sle ladder. Moments later he arrived breathless on the bridge.

'What's that catamaran doing alongside?' Barratt shot at him.

Side-stepping the Captain's question, Morrow said, 'Permission to hoist the skimmer and catamaran, sir.'

'The catamaran, why?'

'I've made a deal with Katu, its owner, sir. The African sitting in it.'

'What sort of deal?'

'Clothing, tobacco, food. That sort of thing, sir. All barter, no cash. He's agreed to spend the afternoon with us if we'll hoist his catamaran on board and return him with it to these fishing grounds this evening.'

'May I ask why he should spend the afternoon with us?'

Looking rather pleased with himself, Morrow said, 'I think he may know something about the submarine, sir. It's a long story. He can't be rushed. I'm afraid this is the only way to handle it. Can I bring him on board and get on with the hoisting?'

With sudden decision Barratt said, 'Yes. In double quick time. When that's done, bring him to the chartroom.'

With its owner in attendance, fussing lest it be damaged, the catamaran was hoisted and stowed forward of the after-screen, the mast and outrigger unshipped and placed along-side it.

In Kiswahili, Peter Morrow spoke to the African. 'Come with me now, Katu. We go to the Bwana M'Kubwa. First we talk with him, then I give you the clothes, the food in the tins, and the tobacco.'

Katu looked about him uncertainly before following the Sub-Lieutenant along the iron deck, the African's lean muscular body, naked but for a loincloth, shining like oiled mahogany.

They went up to the chartroom where the Navigating Officer was watching the echo-sounder, a pencil between his teeth and a frown on his forehead.

Morrow said, 'You wait here one minute, Katu. I go fetch Bwana M'Kubwa.'

The shore parties had returned on board well before sunrise on 22 November, the beginning of the submarine's second day in the creek. With five more hours of darkness available than on the first night, the frenzied work rate of that occasion was no longer necessary. The cutting of foliage and brush-wood had been more selective, more deliberate, and by two o'clock in the morning all that was needed had been cut and carried down to the submarine. Bright moonlight through most of the night helped to get the work done in good time.

Some two hours after cutting had ceased the men working

on the casing under the Engineer Officer had finished laying and placing new material to camouflage the submarine. Among other things they had replaced the trees on the conning-tower and over the gun-platform with fresh ones.

The sun which had been overhead for so many hours during the preceding day had dried most of the foliage, the leaves curling and fading under its heat. Yashimoto had insisted that the old foliage should not be removed. 'Put the freshly cut stuff on top of it,' he said. 'Build irregular mounds and leave gaps where the colour of the withered leaves will break up the uniformity. That way you create a camouflage which looks even more natural.'

Daylight proved the Captain's point. The long, foliage-covered mound, lumpy and irregular with trees 'growing' upon it, now merged with the wooded banks of the creek more convincingly than before.

On his return from a visit to the Africans' huts, the First Lieutenant had reported that the camouflage was particularly good when seen from the opposite bank.

Kagumi had gone over to the settlement at eight o'clock that morning to see the Headman, and to return the African he had brought back the day before in the hope that he and Hasumu might understand each other. That hope had not materialized. 'He speaks a language he calls Fanaglo,' Hasumu had reported to the First Lieutenant. 'At least the word sounds like that. From his attempts to explain by mimicry, I think it may be the language of the mine labourers and their white overseers. It is definitely not English. Though mine is poor I know enough to be sure of that.'

The main purpose of Kagumi's visit had, however, been to talk to the Headman about an incident which had occurred during the previous night: Lieutenant Matsuhito, the officer responsible for sentries had, in the course of his rounds at midnight, checked on the men detailed to patrol the boundaries of the little settlement and guard the catamarans drawn up on the beach near the huts. He had found one of the men asleep in a drunken stupor. Having formally arrested the man, Matsuhito replaced him with one of the catamaran's crew. The offender was brought back to I-357 and placed in his bunk, his wrists handcuffed to its rail.

Within the limitations of sign language, in which he was becoming increasingly proficient, Kagumi had discussed the incident with the Headman. What he had gleaned from the grey-haired old African would be given in evidence later in the morning when the Captain dealt with members of the crew brought before him as defaulters. That weekly disciplinary ritual was two days late, having been deferred by the pressure of events.

With the use of a photograph from an illustrated Japanese periodical, Hasumu had learnt from the African who had spent the night on board that there were no sharks in the creek; presumably the currents, the sandbars outside the entrance, and the rich harvest of fish off the shoals and reefs were responsible for that. It was evident that he was right, because a number of African children had been seen swimming from the beach in front of the huts that morning.

After a discussion with Yashimoto about the prisoner who would be appearing at Captain's Defaulters later that morning, Kagumi raised the question of swimming; might it not be possible, he asked, to permit a limited number of men to swim at certain times under controlled conditions?

Without hesitation Yashimoto had turned down the suggestion. 'Under no circumstances,' he said, his tone and expression indicating displeasure. 'By day it is out of the question. We could not risk having men in the water anywhere near the boat. At night the same applies. The beach where the Africans bathe is in front of the huts. Even if we wished to, how many men could we ferry over there? How soon could we get them back in an emergency? Catalinas patrol at night. We know that from our experience in the Mozambique Channel. An aircraft might drop a flare over the creek.' Yashimoto shook his head vigorously. 'I cannot permit swimming. A supply of fresh water was brought on board last night. Each man can now have a bucketful a day. That is luxury enough, Kagumi. We are at war.'

The bearded face of the First Lieutenant, his short erect figure rigidly at attention, reflected discomfort. 'Quite so, sir,' he said in a low voice. 'I should not have made such a suggestion.'

Yashimoto's manner softened. 'You must not hesitate to make suggestions which you believe to be in the interests of the crew. That is your duty. In this case you overlooked the reality of our situation. The men must wait for Penang. There they can swim as much as they like.' A burst of hammering from the conning-tower made Yashimoto pause. 'I will be happy when that is done with.' Frowning, he inclined his head in the direction of the noise. 'Satugawa's men make good progress. He tells me the forge is almost ready. All that's needed now is a bellows. He hasn't got one, but he intends to use an air pressure cylinder with a nozzle on the end of a flexible steel hose. It should work well. An ingenious man, our Engineer Officer.'

'He is indeed, sir,' agreed Kagumi, anxious to make amends.

Fifteen

The Swahili ended his long and colourful explanation – it had been accompanied by many gestures – with a shrug of his shoulders, after which he stared at the dial of the echo-sounder, apparently fascinated by the digits which clicked and changed as if moved by an unseen hand.

Peter Morrow spoke to the Captain who was leaning against the chart-table. 'He's added quite a bit to what he told me this morning, sir, but it's rather complicated. While he was fishing a reef off Cape Ulu yesterday evening a man he knows from another village was fishing close to him. His name was Cassim. Cassim told Katu that he had heard from Mahmoud – he's another catamaran fisherman –' Morrow smiled apologetically '– that Mahmoud's brother, I'll call him X because Katu didn't know his name, while fishing a reef south of the Nameguo Shoal two nights ago had seen a huge fish go by. Its fin was, according to X, as high as a chief's hut. He was in darkness and it was in the moonlight, so it could not see him. He – that's X, sir – said it was growling as it swam . . .'

'Heading which way?' interrupted Barratt who was staring at the Swahili as if he were the manifestation of a miracle.

After a brief exchange with the African in Kiswahili, Morrow shook his head. 'He says Cassim didn't tell him that.'

Chin in hand, eyes on the chart, Barratt nodded with slow deliberation as if confirming an unspoken thought. A long silence followed before he said, 'It looks as though the man we need to see is X. Ask Katu if he can take us to him right away.'

There was another lively discussion with Katu after which

Morrow said, 'He tells me he doesn't know where to find X. They are not friends. But he knows where Mahmoud lives and can take us there. He says Mahmoud will not be fishing until this evening.'

Barratt was silent, his face a picture of doubt. 'Ask him if Mahmoud's village is on the coast, or on an island. And how far from here? Show him where we are on the chart. See if he can identify the place.'

The Navigating Officer, an interested onlooker, pointed to a cross he'd pencilled on the chart a few minutes earlier. 'That's our approximate position,' he said, standing aside to make room for Katu and Morrow. The latter launched into an explanation in Kiswahili, pointing to the cross Dodds had made.

The African peered at it, looked up at Morrow, peered again, shook his head, said something which caused the Sub-Lieutenant to explode with laughter. 'Sorry, sir,' he said. 'When I tried to explain where we were on the chart, Katu said, "No, Bwana, the ship is not there. It is on the sea." When I told him about a chart, what it was etcetera, he said, "This picture is no good, Bwana. The paper cannot be the sea. A man will not catch fish on paper." But he says Mahmoud's village is on a little island – about an hour's sail from here in a fair wind. That must be about four to five miles, sir.'

Barratt said, 'Good. Bring him up to the bridge and we'll see how he shapes as a pilot. If he wants to head for shallow water, you'll have to take him with you in the skimmer for the rest of the journey. If you find Mahmoud, bring him back if you can. Strike the same sort of bargain you did with Katu.'

Restless headed down a narrow channel between two reefs several miles off a coast which shimmered and danced in a tropical mirage, the palm trees lining the beaches magnified and distorted by refraction. Katu had explained that once through the channel there was deeper water which would lead to Mahmoud's islet, a mile or so along the coast. The destroyer was moving slowly ahead when an urgent warning came from Dodds: the water was shoaling rapidly. Barratt put both engines astern and *Restless* backed away into deeper water.

After a brief consultation the skimmer was lowered, its crew boarded and with Katu beside him Morrow opened the throttle wide and the little inflatable bumped and sprayed its way over a sea ruffled by the south-easter. The African gripped the skimmer's handrail as if his life depended upon it, though his benign expression suggested to Morrow that he was enjoying the experience of travelling over water many times faster than he could ever have done before.

Within the hour the skimmer returned and was hoisted on board. Once more in the chartroom with Katu, the Sub-Lieutenant was explaining what had happened. 'Good news, sir,' he beamed. 'We found this guy – I mean this man Mahmoud. Katu told him he wanted to see X about the "huge fish" he'd seen a couple of nights back. Mahmoud told him it was not necessary to see Moroka – that's X's name – because he, Mahmoud, had later and more important news. Moroka was, he said, a very ignorant man. The so called "huge fish" was a big boat like a whale, not known in the islands but it was clearly a boat and not a fish. It had been seen by two men – one of them Mahmoud's cousin – who had been fishing a reef close to the shore on Maji Island. That was after midnight two nights ago. The same night that is, that Moroka said he saw the "huge fish". The boat they saw was off the island for some time. Then a rain squall came and later they saw the boat disappear round the northern side of the island and that was the last sight they had of it. They don't know where it went after that.'

There was a gleam in the Captain's eyes that Morrow had not seen before. 'Did you find out where Maji Island is?' he asked the Sub-Lieutenant.

'A few miles south of us, according to Mahmoud.'

Barratt examined the chart with a magnifying glass. He shook his head. 'The name Maji doesn't appear anywhere here. But there are a good many unnamed islets.' With some

134

irritation he added, 'Why didn't you bring Mahmoud off to the ship?'

'Not necessary, sir. Katu says he knows Maji Island well. It has a sheltered, deep-water creek and a fresh water spring. "Maji" is the Swahili word for water. The island has a small settlement of fishermen, he says; several families apparently. He has friends among them. He says he will take us to the island after we . . .' Morrow smiled.

'After we what . . .?' interrupted Barratt.

'Give him the presents we promised.'

'Oh those.' Barratt looked relieved. 'For God's sake see that he gets them in double quick time.'

Within the cramped confines of I-357's control-room the weekly ritual of Captain's Defaulters was taking place. It had begun at ten o'clock that morning; within ten minutes three men had been dealt with, the most serious offence involved concerned the loss of a panga. The rating responsible had dropped it over the side while working on the casing at night: he had offered to dive for it but Satugawa, who gave evidence on his behalf, had forbidden this in view of the ban on swimming.

The Captain warned the man to be more careful in future and ruled that the value of the panga would be deducted from his pay. Charges against the other two defaulters were of a minor nature; one concerned failure to clean utensils properly when cook-of-the-mess, the other a breach of censorship in a letter written for posting on return to Penang. Warnings and five days' stoppage of leave in Penang were imposed by the Captain in both these cases.

These defaulters having been dealt with, the men in the control-room braced themselves for the real business of the day: the appearance of the man whose offence had been the subject of widespread discussion since the early hours of morning. Whereas defaulters normally stood in a discreet line behind the Coxswain, who stood to the left of the Captain, the principal offender on this occasion was nowhere to be seen.

Bearded chin out-thrust, Commander Yashimoto turned to the Coxswain. 'Is that all?' he inquired, knowing perfectly well that it was not.

The Coxswain, CPO Okudo, cleared his throat. 'No, sir. Able Seaman Saigo Awa has still to appear.' He spoke in the formal, measured tones he reserved for these occasions.

The Captain turned to the First Lieutenant. 'Have the prisoner brought before me,' he ordered in a stern voice. The Coxswain passed the word to the Yeoman, who in turn passed it to a leading torpedoman whence it reached the torpedo compartment.

Soon afterwards the handcuffed prisoner was marched in between two armed guards. He was a tired young man with hollow cheeks and bloodshot eyes. He looked round the control-room with a frightened expression as the escorts jostled him into position in front of the Captain.

'The charge, Coxswain?' inquired the Captain who had himself framed it an hour earlier.

The Coxswain nodded deferentially, referred to his clipboard. 'Able Seaman Saigo Awa is charged with criminal neglect of duty in that during the night 21/22 November 1942 while on wartime sentry duty on Creek Island, he did – One, absent himself from his place of duty. Two, partake of intoxicating liquor while on duty. Three, thereafter desert his place of duty in order to sleep.' The Coxswain looked up from the clipboard. 'The prisoner was subsequently arrested by Lieutenant Matsuhito who found him asleep and in an intoxicated condition.'

A silent but perceptible ripple of shock swept through the control-room: the thirty or so men crowded into it, drawn from each branch in the submarine, had been ordered to attend on the instructions of the Captain.

It was evident to those watching that what was taking place was more in the nature of a court martial than the routine appearance of a defaulter before the Captain.

Yashimoto's dark eyes held the prisoner's in an unwavering stare. 'How does the prisoner answer the charges?' he asked.

The wretched young seaman looked away, hung his head, mumbled something.

'Speak up.' Yashimoto spoke sharply. 'I cannot hear you.'

'Guilty, sir.' It was little more than a whisper.

'Have you got anything to say in mitigation, Able Seaman Awa?' The Captain's tone had become conciliatory.

In a low voice, his eyes averted, Awa said, 'It was a hot night, sir. My throat was dry. I wanted water. There were Africans sitting by a fire in front of the huts. I went to them and asked for water. But they couldn't understand Japanese. So . . .' he shrugged helplessly. 'I made a cup with my hands and put it to my mouth. After that they filled a container from a gourd and passed it to me. I thought it was water. It was the same colour as water and they were drinking it. I swallowed some. It tasted nice, quite sweet, and I was very thirsty so I drank some more. When that was gone, they filled the container again. They were very friendly, sir. I could see they wanted me to enjoy it. And I felt good and drank some more. Then I felt a bit funny and I went down towards the beach carrying my rifle. That is the beach where the catamarans were. My head was splitting. I suddenly felt dizzy so I sat down with my back against a coconut palm. Next thing I knew Lieutenant Matsuhito was shaking me awake . . . I know I have done wrong, sir.'

Yashimoto looked towards Matsuhito. 'You found this man and arrested him, Lieutenant?'

'That is correct, sir.'

'Do you wish to say anything?'

'No, sir. Except that he did not really come awake. He was in a drunken stupor. We put him in our catamaran, brought him back to the boat and placed him in his bunk. He did not appear to be aware of what was happening.'

'Thank you, Lieutenant.' Yashimoto turned to the small but formidable figure of the First Lieutenant who stood immediately to his right. 'You investigated this matter, Lieutenant Kagumi. Have you anything of importance to add to what I have just heard?'

'Only to say, sir, that the prisoner's explanation accords

with what I heard from the village Headman in my discussion with him this morning. Since we had no common language with which to communicate, it was difficult for me to determine whether the men round the fire understood that the prisoner was asking for water when he approached them. The Headman indicated that Able Seaman Awa asked to be given some of the liquid they were drinking.'

'What were they drinking?'

'Fermented coconut milk, sir. The Headman gave me some to taste. It is the colour of water and of a pleasant though strong flavour. Evidently highly intoxicating. The Headman's gesture made that quite clear. The native name sounds like *kaola*. The Headman's miming told me that they never drink it before going fishing.' The First Lieutenant smiled. 'I suppose it could be difficult for a drunken man to manage a catamaran.'

Yashimoto uttered a curt, 'No doubt.' Looking once again at the hapless offender he said, 'Lieutenant Sato – this man is in your division. Would you care to say anything on his behalf?'

Sato came from where he'd been standing beside the hydrophone cabinet. 'Yes, sir. Awa is a good man. Hard working, able and conscientious. He has never given any trouble. I would strongly recommend clemency in his case, though the offence is serious.'

There was a flicker of animosity in the Captain's eyes as he said, 'I rather expected that from you, Lieutenant.' There was a brief silence during which he took a note from the pocket of his uniform shirt. Glancing at it, he looked round the control-room with a slow, deliberate stare. 'The offences with which Able Seaman Saigo Awa are charged would, in terms of the Naval Discipline Act, be extremely serious in peace time.' He paused, his eyes travelling over his audience. 'In time of War, with this submarine disabled in an operational area and hunted by the enemy's air and surface forces, the offences are of the utmost gravity. The purpose and duty of sentries is to safeguard this boat, and all who serve in her, while members of the crew work night and day to repair action damage and conceal the boat from the enemy. Within the next few days the repairs should be completed. We will then leave the island to take up station off Mombasa where we shall attack a British aircraft carrier and her escorts. After that attack we will return to our base in Penang.' Yashimoto stopped, surveyed once again the tense faces watching him. 'But that will only be possible if our vigilance is never relaxed. Particularly, I would add, the vigilance of our sentries.'

The Captain spoke in an aside to the First Lieutenant who nodded assent. Yashimoto tightened his lips, half closed his eyes. 'The sentence I have to pass on you, Able Seaman Awa, must be such as to ensure that you can never again fail in your duty, and that others will be aware of the consequences should they be tempted to do so.'

The Captain's body stiffened as he drew himself to attention. The officers and petty officers ranged behind him followed suit. In the sudden absence of human speech the background sounds of ventilating fans, of generators and air compressors at work in the engineroom seemed to grow in volume. It was not long, however, before the Captain's voice again commanded attention. Speaking slowly, each word carefully weighed, he said, 'Able Seaman Saigo Awa, I find you guilty on all counts with which you have been charged, and to which you have pleaded guilty. Since the Japanese Empire is at War your gross neglect of duty in an operational area leaves me with no option but to condemn you to death. The sentence will be carried out after sunset this evening. May Buddha rest your soul.'

Saigo Awa, sobbing uncontrollably, was led away. The Captain went to his cabin, and the officers to the wardroom. The remainder of those in the control-room drifted off in shocked silence, for Awa was an inoffensive and pleasant young man, a hairdresser's assistant before the War, whose skill with hair and beards had been much in demand by the crew.

Sixteen

The more he thought about it the more Barratt realized that Katu's story presented him with a difficult decision, particularly against the background of Captain (D)'s recall signal. Much though he wanted to believe that Moroka's 'huge fish' and Mahmoud's 'big boat like a whale' were the Japanese submarine, he felt the stories, second and third hand as they were, smacked too much of fishermen's tales. The Catalinas had been searching the islands and coastline morning and afternoon during the last two days. Surely they'd have seen the submarine if it had been in the creek at Maji Island?

If, however, the fishermen's reports were correct, if they had seen the submarine – and with every fibre of his being he hoped they had – then a number of possibilities had to be weighed. The reports concerned something seen on or about midnight on November 20, the night of *Fort Nebraska*'s sinking. It was now afternoon of the 22nd. If the submarine's crew had repaired the shell damage it would already have left Maji Island. But if they had not, and it was still there, what were *Restless*'s possible courses of action? That was Barratt's problem. He dismissed the notion of closing the island in daylight to investigate. The submarine Captain would have placed lookouts to warn of ships approaching. According to Katu the island had a deep water creek. To steam into it without knowing its configuration and the depths of water would be to risk stranding *Restless*. To go in without knowing exactly where the submarine lay meant running the risk of a close range torpedo attack. Should he take *Restless* to a position off the entrance to the creek, clear of a possible line of torpedo fire, while he asked Kilindini for aircraft to check if the submarine was in the creek? That course of action he dismissed for two reasons: if in their searches so far the Catalinas hadn't sighted it, it was either because it was not there or wasn't visible from the air. But the more compelling reason was a psychological one: at the back of his mind he feared that the Catalinas might find and destroy the submarine. That was not what he wanted. His emotions had become too involved; it had become a matter of honour, a moral obligation, that he personally should exact retribution from the Japanese.

Though he would probably have been evasive on the point, he was not yet prepared to inform Kilindini of what he had learnt from Katu; to hand to others the opportunity which might shortly be his of finding and attacking the submarine. Influenced more by emotion than reason he decided to take *Restless* out to sea for the remainder of daylight, keeping clear of the area where Katu said the island lay. When darkness fell he would bring the destroyer close inshore and set about investigating Maji. He'd plan the detail during what was left of the day.

Restless had steamed some distance out to sea when a Catalina was sighted coming up the coast from the south, well to seaward of the islands. Much to Barratt's relief it made no attempt to close the destroyer or exchange signals. It had no sooner gone than Peter Morrow arrived on the bridge with a new problem. 'It's about Katu, sir,' he explained. 'I told him of the change of plans. That we wouldn't be asking him to take us to Maji Island until some time tonight. He wasn't pleased. Said we'd promised to put him and his catamaran back on the fishing grounds this evening. If he's away tonight his wife may think he's drowned or, worse still, that he's spending the night with a girl friend on another island.'

'I see. Same all over the world, aren't they? Did you give him those clothes and the other stuff?'

'Yes. He's very happy about that.'

'I thought he might be. Look, Morrow. Tell him we'll double the quantity of everything, if he stays with us tonight.

In the morning we'll return him to where you found him. See him right away.'

The Sub-Lieutenant disappeared. Back on the bridge a few minutes later he reported that Katu had accepted the arrangement. 'He says his wife won't think bad things once she's seen the loot.'

'That RAF Pamanzi signal, Hutchison. In what position did their Catalina sight *Restless* at 1720 today?' Captain (D)'s well-fleshed face glowed with perspiration as he dabbed at his forehead with a large handkerchief.

Hutchison pointed with a cue to the position on the plotting table. 'Here, sir. Ten miles east of Medjumbi Island.'

Captain (D) got up from his chair, leant over the table. 'I don't understand what Barratt is up to. Yesterday morning he made his "getting warmer" signal to the Catalina. Stressed the importance of W/T silence. That sounded as if he was really on to something. *Restless* was then between Cape Delgado and Rovuma Bay, heading north. Late that evening a Catalina sighted her about forty miles south of Cape Delgado. So what takes Barratt down there? Yesterday evening we instructed him to return if he'd not made contact by sunset. He didn't acknowledge our signal. We've no idea where he was or what he was doing during the night. But we do know he was off Cape Ulu this morning.' Captain (D) shook his head, pointed with a podgy finger at *Restless*'s 1720 position. 'And here he is late this afternoon ten miles out to sea and thirty miles from Cape Ulu.' He grunted disapproval. 'Doesn't make sense. He's chasing round like a madman. What's your view, SOO?'

Commander Russel took off his spectacles, massaged his eyelids, put the spectacles on again. 'Quite extraordinary really. The "getting warmer" suggested he was on to something. Presumably he knew where the Jap was. A clue of some sort. But *what* sort, if it has him charging up and down the coast for thirty-six hours, and now takes him well out to sea? Where, incidentally, I should have thought he could safely have broken W/T silence.'

142

Captain (D)'s blue eyes, set deep in the bucolic face, reflected perplexity. 'I don't think we can let him go on with this Nelson act. Ignoring signals, etcetera. The Admiral's becoming restive. So am I.'

Russel nodded gloomily. 'Yes. I think we've got to rein him in. *Restless*'s fuel must be running low, and she's still a day and a half's steaming from here. Apart from anything else, we must have her back by the 25th to augment the escort force for the carrier. That's absolutely essential now that we know Japanese submarines are busy at this end.'

Captain (D) lifted himself out of the chair. Head up, hands clasped behind his back, he walked to the french windows. 'Well, that decides it. We'll pull him in.' He looked over his shoulder to the signal desk. 'Pam, take a signal.' The Wren said, 'Aye, aye, sir,' arranged a signal pad in front of her, picked up a pencil, patted her hair, smiled expectantly.

Unclasping his hands Captain (D) scratched the back of his neck, looked thoughtful and began. 'To *Restless* repeat Deputy C-in-C and RAFHQ, from Captain (D). Message begins – Return to base forthwith. Acknowledge – message ends.'

'That should see him here by daylight on the 24th.' The SOO looked at the wall-clock. It showed 1853. 'I expect he'll have some sort of story to tell.'

'It'd better be a good one.' Captain (D)'s eyebrows bunched in a threatening manner, one quite out of keeping with his genial nature. 'Well, I must organize my sundowner,' he said. On his way to the door he glared disapproval at the ancient punkah which squeaked intermittently as it flapped. 'Sounds like a gull trying to take off after it's eaten too much,' he said. 'Do get somebody to oil the ruddy thing.'

At the far end of the room Second Officer Camilla Lacey WRNS raised limpid blue eyes from the operations log she'd been entering. 'We've reported it to the Fleet Engineer's office, sir,' she said.

'Good heavens! Can't somebody get up there with a can of Three-in-One? I wouldn't have thought it was an engineering job.'

Hutchison looked up at the punkah, waved a dismissive hand. 'I'll see to it, sir,' he said airily.

When Captain (D) had gone he went across to Camilla's desk. 'I'm no good at heights.' He spoke in an undertone. 'But I'll be happy to hold the ladder if you'll go up.'

'I'm sure you will, Flight Lieutenant Hutchison RAF – but I won't.'

'Oh, well. Can't win 'em all.' He managed an exaggerated sigh before going back to the operations table.

By evening forbidding clouds had massed above the creek, shutting out the sun and hastening the coming of night. On Yashimoto's orders repair work had ceased at sunset, to be resumed only when he gave the word. In the absence of the now familiar banging and clattering the only sounds were those of the submarine's auxiliary machinery, for there was an otherwise strange silence in I-357 where men sat about in twos and threes, waiting in sombre mood for what was to come.

Before the time of sunset Lieutenant Sato had gone to the search receiver cabinet where the prisoner had been placed after sentence was passed. The Lieutenant waved aside the armed sentry at its entrance and entered the cabinet. Able Seaman Awa was sitting on the operator's stool, head in hands, his back to the entrance, his elbows on the wooden ledge beneath the instruments.

'Able Seaman Awa,' Sato called. The young man turned, his eyes red, the flesh round them swollen. In spite of the heat he was shivering. Sato put a hand on his shoulder. 'Have courage. You go to a far better place.' He spoke softly. 'Your ancestors will be there waiting for you. With them you will find eternal peace.'

There was scarcely room for one person in the cabinet, and with the Lieutenant standing in its entrance, any view those in the control-room might otherwise have had of Awa was blocked.

'I have come', continued Sato, 'to ask if you have any messages for your family. I shall be writing to them.' He

144

lowered his voice to almost a whisper. 'You may be sure I will speak well of you, Awa. You have been a good man.'

In a broken voice Awa said, 'Please tell my mother and father and my sisters that I love them – I think of them always –' His voice petered out and he began to sob.

'I will do that.' The Lieutenant reached out, took Awa's right hand in a firm grasp. It seemed to Sato moist, limp and lifeless as he pressed the sedative tablets into it. Continuing to whisper, he said, 'I see you have water here, Awa. Swallow these now. They will help you.'

Awa withdrew his hand, turned once more to the instrument panel. He took the mug of water from the ledge with one hand while the other went to his mouth.

Once again the Lieutenant placed his hand on the prisoner's shoulder. 'I will be with you until the end, Awa. May Buddha bless you.'

It was not long before the shrill whistle of a boatswain's call was followed by the Coxswain's voice: 'Men detailed for ceremonial and special duties muster on shore.'

Shafts of moonlight shone through shifting cloud patterns as the cortège led by the sturdy figure of Togo Yashimoto, followed by the First Lieutenant, the Engineer Officer and Gunnery Officer, made its way through the trees. In spite of the heat all wore their formal uniforms as they marched, the officers with sheathed swords at the carry.

They were followed in turn by a ceremonial party of twelve ratings drawn from different departments, their rifles at the slope. Ahead of them marched the Coxswain, Yoza Okudo, carrying an unsheathed naval cutlass over his shoulder.

Led by Lieutenant Sato, the prisoner and armed escort followed the ceremonial party. Behind them came four petty officers headed by the Chief Engine Room Artificer. The rear was brought up by four ratings carrying signal torches, and two men marching in tandem with a folded stretcher over their shoulders. Yashimoto's attention to detail had been meticulous.

From the assembly point abreast the submarine, the Captain led his men through the trees bordering the creek to a small clearing opposite the bluff. Calling the procession to a halt, he ordered the torchbearers to stand at the four corners of a square which had been marked with stakes earlier in the afternoon. The ceremonial party then took station facing each other on two sides of the square. Yashimoto, his officers and the Coxswain marched between them to the far end to form the third side, while the petty officers under Hayeto Shimada completed the square, its corners now marked by the blue lights of the signal torches.

The prisoner and his escorts marched into the square and halted at its centre. Lieutenant Sato took up his position to the right of the condemned man.

At Yashimoto's command, 'The prisoner will kneel,' Awa, wearing shorts and a vest, his hands handcuffed behind his back, was assisted into a kneeling position by the escorts who bent his shoulders forward until he faced the ground. As he knelt he had given a last despairing look towards Sato, but the Lieutenant had already closed his eyes.

Yashimoto nodded to Kagumi. 'Carry on, First Lieutenant,' he ordered.

The First Lieutenant spoke over his shoulder to the Coxswain who stood a few paces behind him. 'Proceed with your duty, Coxswain,' he said in a firm voice.

With the cutlass slanted over his shoulder the Coxswain marched to the centre of the square. There he stopped, facing the left hand side of the kneeling figure. With legs apart and both hands on its hilt he lifted the cutlass high above his head.

The moon rode clear of the clouds to reveal Yashimoto standing rigidly at attention, bearded chin out-thrust, dark eyes staring ahead. He raised his right arm with the stiff movement of an automaton, held it aloft, then dropped it sharply. Reflecting the light of the moon, the cutlass described a gleaming arc, the dull thud of cleavage scarcely audible as the prisoner's head fell from his body and rolled to one side. The corpse collapsed in a twitching heap and the moon, as if satisfied that justice had been done, withdrew once more behind the clouds.

By eight o'clock that night those members of the crew who attended the execution had resumed their normal duties; for some it was with the foliage and camouflage parties; for others it was sentry duty; and for the rest, duties on board.

The prisoner's corpse, its head beside it, had been carried down to the bluff on a stretcher, loaded into a motorized catamaran and taken out to sea where it was dumped beyond the headland east of the creek. No ceremony, no last rites, accompanied the disposal of Able Seaman Awa's remains; there was, however, some concern that the head, not weighted with a large stone as was the body, had remained afloat until retrieved; to be weighted then with a shackle, whereafter it sank quietly into the sea.

Not that Awa had been forgotten, nor was likely to be; the affair was too dramatic, too recent for that. As it was, his execution was the subject of whispered discussion among the crew, ashore and afloat, for most of that night. Those who had not witnessed it, and they were in the majority, asked in awesome undertones for details: how had Awa behaved at the end? Had the Coxswain severed the head with a clean blow? Was there much blood? What was the Captain's demeanour? These and many other questions were put and answered during a long night.

Togo Yashimoto, but for Saigo Awa the principal character in the drama, had in the solitude of his cabin spent some time kneeling before the Shinto shrine. Dressed in a ceremonial white kimono, he had addressed his prayers variously to the Emperor, the Gods of Nature, Buddha and Awa's ancestors, consigning the young man's soul to their safe keeping that he might find eternal peace. For himself he asked only for guidance in the difficult task of safeguarding I-357 and her crew so that they might continue to wage war on behalf of the Emperor, for the greater glory of the Imperial Japanese

Navy and the Empire it served. Of one thing he was certain – with or without divine assistance, there was no longer any danger of sentries sleeping at their posts.

Seventeen

Barratt lay on the bunk in his sea-cabin staring at the single red light in the deckhead. It was there because the human eye adjusted more quickly to darkness after red light than after white – and that was important to destroyer captains in wartime whose nights involved many sudden visits to the bridge. He had always found the cabin depressing – the dog-box he called it – but his mood this night was more one of frustration and anger than depression. It had been triggered by Captain (D)'s signal ordering *Restless* to return *forthwith*, and made worse by the peremptory *acknowledge*. He had no intention of returning to Kilindini forthwith, nor of acknowledging the signal. This, he knew, was insubordination but on receiving the signal his decision had been immediate and instinctive.

Handing it back to the CPO Telegraphist he had said, 'Wireless silence is to be maintained, Duckworth.'

Duckworth's expression was one of disbelief. 'We are ordered to acknowledge, sir.'

'I expressly forbid that, Duckworth. We will continue to observe W/T silence. The responsibility is mine, not yours.' There was unusual severity in the Captain's tone. He liked Duckworth, but having made his decision he was not going to have it challenged by the telegraphist, or anyone else for that matter.

Duckworth had looked at him in silence for a moment before shaking his head and leaving the sea-cabin.

Barratt was quite clear in his own mind as to what he was doing, the risks he was taking. His decision could involve him in a court-martial; dismissal from the Service perhaps, or at least dismissal from his ship. He was prepared to take those risks. After all he was a *dug-out* who'd go back to the family wine business when the War was over, not a career officer. The knowledge had, not unnaturally, influenced him. The more he thought about Katu and Mahmoud's stories, the more he began to feel there was now a real chance of finding the submarine. He was in no mood to forego the opportunity to investigate the creek at Maji Island that night. *To return forthwith* would involve just that– to *acknowledge* could disclose *Restless*'s position to the Japanese. A reply to Captain (D)'s signal would have to wait until daylight.

Having once again thought through the problem he looked at the luminous dial of the cabin clock. It showed 1927. Time to get on with plans for the night.

The Captain's day-cabin, large, spacious and within easy reach of the bridge, was unusually crowded. Barratt had swung his desk chair round so that he could face the others; Charlie Dodds was at the dining-table with the chart, Peter Morrow and Katu sat together at his side, while the First Lieutenant was on the settee with Geoffrey Lawson.

'This is the outline scenario for tonight,' explained Barratt, a certain tenseness in his manner. 'We'll reach the coast ten miles south of Cape Ulu at 2300. That right, Pilot?' He looked across to Dodds.

'Yes, sir. I've plotted the position. Six miles WSW of a nameless speck on the chart which, from what Katu says, seems likely to be Maji Island. We'll close the coast from the south, passing in north of the Vadiazi Shoal. There's a channel there with sufficient water at low tide to get us within a mile of the coast.'

'Thank you, Pilot. Next point. We're experiencing typical Doldrums weather. Calm sea, mild breeze, barometer steady on FAIR. A threat of rain perhaps.' Barratt looked at his notes. 'Pilot tells me – and he'd better be right –' the Captain favoured Dodds with a theatrical glare '– that the moon rises at about eight tonight and sets shortly before seven in the morning. That can be helpful in some ways, but a bloody nuisance in others. Fortunately there's a lot of cloud about so hopefully we'll have some help from that. Without navigation lights, with the coastline as background, and radar and *ping* shut down, *Restless* shouldn't be easy to spot. It'll be a useful test of the camouflage Simonstown's painted all over us. Never liked it myself. Bit too Picasso, I'd say.' He stopped, took a silver cigarette case from his pocket, looked at it and put it away again. 'Now I intend to take the ship no closer to the island than three miles but it'll depend on the moon. At about that distance we'll lower the motorboat and skimmer plus Katu's catamaran.' He glanced at Dodds. 'Got his okay on that, Morrow?'

The Sub-Lieutenant said, 'Yes, sir. After a bit of an argy bargy. Your promise fixed it. A new one if we lose his.'

'Quite a businessman your Katu, isn't he?' Barratt smiled at the African who smiled back though he couldn't understand a word of the conversation.

'Very reasonable chap really,' defended Morrow.

'Right. Now let's get back to *Operation Maji*.' Barratt looked once more at his notes. 'The shore party will consist of Katu, Peter Morrow, Brad Corrigan and Angus McLean the signalman.'

'Corrigan, sir?' The First Lieutenant appeared to be mildly shocked. 'The *Fort N* survivor?'

'None other,' said the Captain firmly. 'He says he wants to be involved. So involved he's going to be. Brought up on boats, useful man in the water, and he has an account to settle with the Japanese.'

'But he's not RN, sir. Isn't that a problem?'

'He's US Navy, Number One. Seconded by me to the Royal Navy as from now. Any objections?' Barratt's bright-eyed stare was accompanied by a three finger drumming on the wooden arms of the desk chair.

The First Lieutenant changed the subject. 'So there'll be four in the shore party?'

'No. Five.'

'Who'll be the fifth member, sir?'

'I will.'

The First Lieutenant started, jerked his head back. 'The

151

ship, sir. You don't mean you'll leave the ship?' he looked at the Captain incredulously.

'I do mean that, Number One. You will be in command in my absence. That should please you. Every Number One reckons he can do it better than his Captain. Now, where were we? Ah, yes – the motorboat. Leading Seaman Hind and two ratings will crew it. Having embarked the shore party – and with the catamaran and skimmer in tow – it will leave *Restless* at 0100 and head for Maji Island. The Pilot has drawn a rough plan of the island based on what Katu has told him. The important thing is the creek. It's apparently a fairly long, narrow affair. Katu reports deep water but for shoals off the mouth on the northern side. The entrance faces north-west if his information is correct. On the assumption that it is, we'll land on the southern side at about 0130. The shoreline there is screened from the creek by the hills which enclose it. Once ashore we'll take it from there, depending on what we find. Have I reported Katu correctly on this, Morrow?'

'Yes, sir. That's about it. His description is based on catamaran experience of course. Destroyers and catamarans are not quite the same thing . . .'

'Good point, Morrow,' said Barratt drily.

The Sub-Lieutenant grinned. 'So he's a bit vague on whether *Restless* could get in and out.'

The Captain nodded. 'The shore party will transfer to the catamaran when we're within a mile of the island. But that will depend on the state of the moon at the time. If it's behind cloud we'll go in closer before making the transfer. If not, we'll have to do it further out.'

The briefing went on for some time. It was followed by a general discussion and a question-and-answer session during which a number of modifications were made to Barratt's operational plan. Closing the proceedings he said, 'See to it that everything's on the top line, Number One. Side-arms, fighting knives, signal torches, Very pistols, flares, first-aid kit, water bottles, the Pilot's plan, extra paddles – the lot to be in the motorboat by midnight. Shore party and motorboat's crew to muster port side in the waist at 0030 for final briefing. Dark clothing, faces and other exposed flesh blackened – remember your jungle warfare drill. To repeat. We'll be off Cape Ulu at 2330. In position three miles off Maji Island at 0100. That's when the party begins in earnest.'

At sea *Restless*'s wardroom, usually empty by ten-thirty at night, was on this occasion anything but that. In groups of twos and threes its occupants were discussing Operation Maji with varying degrees of interest, enthusiasm and disapproval. A fairly general complaint was put by Sean O'Brien. 'Why is a recently joined, wet-behind-the-ears, adolescent RNVR like Morrow the only officer the Old Man's chosen for his shore party? Bloody unfair I reckon.'

'Not much mystery about the *why* of it, is there?' said Jeremy Tripp. 'Morrow speaks Kiswahili.'

'Why Angus McLean?' chipped in Midshipman Galpin. 'What can he do that I can't?'

'Make and read signals for starters,' suggested the Gunnery Officer.

'You know a good deal about deer stalking do you, Galpin?' The Torpedo Officer's twisted smile concealed a verbal trip-wire.

'I don't follow, sir?'

'Angus McLean was a top poacher in the Highlands before Hitler became a bloody nuisance.'

Galpin blinked. 'I don't see the point?'

'I dare say that's why the Old Man didn't choose you. Galpin's not too bright, I can hear him saying.' The Torpedo Officer drew on his cigarette, smiled again. 'But let me explain, dear boy. Any man who can repeatedly get close enough to stags at night to kill them, is a man who can see and move like a cat in the dark. Got it?'

'How did the Old Man know McLean was a poacher?' There was a note of injured disbelief in Galpin's voice.

'The entire mess-deck knew it. Just like we know all about you, young Galpin. And that, I may say, isn't too *kosher*.'

153

In a corner of the wardroom the First Lieutenant and the Doctor were talking in subdued tones.

'It worries me, Docker.' The First Lieutenant leant closer. 'It's the second signal from Captain (D) that the Old Man has ignored. You just can't do that sort of thing, you know. He's been *ordered* to return forthwith. *Ordered* to acknowledge. And he doesn't do a damn thing. By now the Admiral is probably in the picture. There'll be hell to pay.'

The Doctor drank the last of his beer. 'He doesn't appear to be worried. In fact I've seldom seen him in better form.'

'It may seem to be better form, Docker, but to me it's rather disturbing. He's all worked up, excited, something I've never seen in him before. Quite honestly I think he's halfway round the bend.' Inadvertently, the First Lieutenant had raised his voice. He looked round the wardroom to see if anyone was listening. It seemed no one was. They were all too busy with their own conversations.

'Sure you're not just a little put out, Number One?' A friendly smile accompanied the Doctor's inquiry.

'Put out. Good God, no. Why?'

'Because you're not in the shore party?'

Sandy Hamilton shook his head with unusual vigour. 'On the contrary I'm very glad I'm not. Do you realize, Docker, that the Old Man is leaving the ship – abandoning his command – to land an armed party on a Portuguese island. All this on top of his refusal to answer signals. Maji Island may be remote but it happens to be neutral territory – *inhabited* territory according to this man Katu. As tactfully as I could, I warned the Old Man of the dangers of infringing Portuguese neutrality. He more or less told me to mind my own business. The whole thing is crazy. I honestly think he may be a bit – well, you know.'

The Doctor shrugged. 'I don't see any symptoms. His judgement may have become blunted. The *Fort Nebraska* corpses were a pretty horrifying sight. That on top of his wife's death in Japanese hands. Could be enough to push him over the top, I suppose. One hopes not. But the human brain is a delicate mechanism.' The Doctor paused, looked away, tapped the rim of the empty tankard with his finger-nails. 'What d'you think he'll do if the submarine *is* in the creek?'

The First Lieutenant regarded his feet with a dismal stare as if they were somehow responsible for a situation which he found profoundly disturbing. 'God alone knows,' he said. Looking up he was suddenly more cheerful. 'Fortunately, I don't think the question will arise. I can't believe it's there. Difficult to imagine how a bloody great submarine – all three hundred plus feet of it – could be lying in a creek in one of those tiny islets without a Catalina spotting it. They've been doing a very thorough snoop during the last forty-eight hours. Low flying, circling, you know.'

'They certainly have,' agreed the Doctor. 'But what about Katu and Mahmoud's reports?'

'I accept that they may have seen something. Possibly even the submarine. But that was two nights ago. We don't know what the damage was. The repair of a shell-hole in the conning-tower casing should be within the capabilities of a submarine's engineroom staff. They might have fixed it that night – they had about nine hours of darkness in which to do the job. That would explain why the Catalinas haven't found it. It's probably many hundreds of miles away by now.'

The Doctor leant back in the armchair lost in thought, his hands clasped behind his head. 'What are we going to do – the ship, I mean – between now and midnight?'

'What we're doing now. Mess about at sixteen knots, five miles off the nearest land.'

The Doctor laughed wryly. 'Too bad if the Jap's doing the same thing. We might tangle.'

'I shouldn't worry about that, Docker. We're pinging away. I think we'd spot him first.'

'Haven't we shut down our *ping*?'

'Not yet. We will when we close the land at midnight.' The First Lieutenant looked at his watch. 'Well, it's getting on. I'd better go up on deck and see what progress the Coxswain's making with gear for the assault boys. See you later.'

The Doctor nodded. 'Don't think I'll turn in till they've gone. I'd rather like to see our desperadoes disappear into the night.'

Eighteen

Clipboard under arm, the Chief Telegraphist went into I-357's wardroom, acknowledged the presence of the First Lieutenant with a formal bow, and handed a signal to Lieutenant Matsuhito whose duties included those of cypher officer. The Lieutenant unlocked the safe under the settee and took from it the cypher machine. Watched by Keda he tapped away at the keys, stopping after each group to note with pencil and pad the words which came up on the display:

From Flag Officer Submarines, Penang, to I-357 and I-362. ETA carrier now 27/28 Nov. Acknowledge.

Gesturing towards the door of the Captain's cabin, Matsuhito handed the message to Keda. The Chief Telegraphist went to the door, heard the Captain's 'Come' and entered. Yashimoto, in a cotton singlet and shorts, was sitting at the small desk alongside the bunk examining his teeth in a hand mirror.

'Signal for you, sir,' said Keda.

Yashimoto put down the mirror, took the signal and read it, his eyebrows gathering in a frown as he did so. 'Tell the First Lieutenant I want him,' he said.

The First Lieutenant closed the book he was reading, rubbed his eyes and sighed before following the Chief Telegraphist back to the Captain's cabin. There was scarcely room for three men in its limited space but with Keda standing, his back to the door, Kagumi was able to sit on the settee beside the Captain. With a peremptory, 'Read this,' Yashimoto thrust the signal at him. Watching the First Lieutenant closely he said, 'We cannot break wireless silence.' A smile displaced the frown. 'But the news is good.

We have one more day in hand. We may need it.' The sharp, clipped sentences were delivered in a tone which never varied. 'The British carrier is now due at Mombasa on the 27/28th. We shall have to take up station outside the port by midnight on the 26th. In three days. So . . .' he paused, pinching his nose as if taking snuff, '. . . we must have left here by midnight on the 24th. Repairs and tests must be completed within the next forty-eight hours.' He looked again at the signal which lay on the desk, drummed on it with his fingers as if seeking inspiration. Evidently none came, for he waved a hand in a gesture of rejection. 'No. We cannot acknowledge the signals. We cannot break wireless silence until we are out at sea – *and* able to dive.' He glanced at the Chief Telegraphist. 'Right. You may carry on, Keda.' To Kagumi he said, 'Tell the Engineer Officer I wish to see him at once.'

Kagumi opened the door and the distant sound of drilling, hammering, scraping, and the clanging of metal, grew louder, the smell of diesel oil more pungent. Having told Satugawa to report to the Captain, he went ashore by way of the forehatch, walking awkwardly across the litter of branches and foliage which covered the casing and gangplank. Followed by two armed seamen he made his way in the darkness along the bank to where the catamarans lay astern of the submarine. They boarded the nearest catamaran, cast off, paddled it clear, and started up the outboard. With Kagumi at the tiller they set off on the inspection round. Until the Awa incident, Kagumi had performed this duty between one and two in the morning. On Yashimoto's orders, issued soon after Awa's execution, it was to be carried out twice during the hours of darkness; once before midnight and once again before sunrise, the times to be varied so that no pattern was established.

Near to midnight the Engineer Officer finished his discussions with the Captain. Yashimoto had opened the proceedings with the signal from Penang. Satugawa read it and passed it back. The Captain gave him a searching look. 'Can you have

158

us ready for sea by midnight on the 24th?' Yashimoto's lips tightened as he waited for the answer.

Satugawa avoided the Captain's stare by focusing on the Shinto shrine set in the bulkhead above the desk. 'We have completed repairs to the outer screen around the conning-tower,' he said, evading the direct question. 'That was not difficult. We are dealing with an almost flat surface in a free-flooding area. We are now making progress with repairs to the hull and to the conning-tower. They are critical because both form part of the pressure hull.'

'I am aware of that, Chief. But you are not answering my question.' Yashimoto tapped petulantly on the desk. 'You have an extra day. Can you complete by midnight on the 24th?'

'Captain, there are problems. We can, I believe, solve them. Within the time available, I hope. But this, the time factor, I cannot guarantee. If I could explain . . .' Satugawa looked sideways at the Captain as if anxious to avoid direct confrontation.

'Yes, yes. Do so.' Yashimoto's impatience was, it happened, due to the Penang signal rather than to any shortcomings on the part of the Engineer Officer for whom he had the highest regard.

Satugawa paused, seemed to be choosing his words. 'Well – as to the damage to the pressure hull and conning-tower. We have to bend sections of three-eighth high tensile steel plates to the exact angle of the surface to which they will be bolted. This work is being done in the foundry ashore. We have templates, but the problem is to bend the steel, while white hot, to the shape of the templates. We do not have the proper equipment, the presses and so forth. The work has to be done manually, with hammers and an improvised anvil. Blacksmith' work, which involves much trial and error. But I hope to have the plates ready for fitting some time tomorrow night.'

Yashimoto's face puckered, contracted, the fleshy folds beneath his eyes bulging. 'And the hatch coaming and the lid? You haven't mentioned them?'

159

Satugawa looked unhappy. 'They are my major worry.' His eyes once more sought the Shinto shrine. 'We have serious problems there. In the case of the coaming, building it up for fitting is proving difficult. A lot of adjustment is necessary. In the case of the lid we have problems. There is distortion and the flange is buckled. The thick steel is proving difficult to straighten. Then, unfortunately, the fractured hinge broke off at its base while it was being treated . . .'

'How treated?' interrupted Yashimoto, his lower lip protruding beneath the threatening eyes.

'The hinge had been brought to white heat in the furnace. A mechanician was trying to hammer it straight on its seat when it broke off. We had not realized how deep into the metal the hairline fracture had gone.'

Yashimoto glared at the Engineer Officer. 'Surely that *should* have been realized,' he snapped.

'Without X-ray equipment it is not possible to determine the depth of a hairline fracture.' Satugawa was standing his ground. He had come up the hard way, started life in the Navy as a stoker and by dint of sheer drive and a good brain had climbed the difficult ladder of the engineering branch. A Chief ERA at the beginning of the War, the highest non-commissioned rank, he had been promoted to Warrant Engineer Officer and later to Engineer Lieutenant. At thirty-nine – six years older than the Captain – he was the oldest member of I-357's crew.

While he respected the Captain's ability, his skill in matters concerning seamanship, submarine handling and naval warfare, he had long been critical of his bland refusal to acknowledge, or perhaps understand, the problems of the engineroom.

Detecting the change in Satugawa's attitude, Yashimoto adopted a more conciliatory tone. 'So – about the hatch, Chief? You said the flange on the lid was buckled and there was distortion. Tell me about this?'

'It is the problem of restoring the lid to its designed shape. At least sufficiently to get it shut with a reasonably effective seal. The pumps can deal with normal leaks, but not with

160

bad ones at depth. I don't think it will be too difficult to get a passable seal. We have already made some progress with trueing up the lid. The real problem is the hinge. We have to build up a new one by cannibalizing certain engine parts, then fix it to the lid. With the restricted equipment we have, that is going to take time.'

'How much time?'

Satugawa looked the Captain squarely in the face. 'I don't know. All I can guarantee is that we will do everything possible to finish on time. All being well we should be able to carry out flooding tests by sunset on the 24th.'

Yashimoto smiled, his eyes softened, and he leant forward to give the Engineer Officer's shoulder a playful slap. 'That's what I wanted to hear from you, Chief. You keep the best news for last, you old rascal.'

Satugawa relaxed, realized that the confrontation was at an end. He leant back against the bulkhead. 'I did say, *all being well*, Captain.'

Yashimoto got up, took a bunch of keys from his pocket and opened a cupboard under the bunk. From it he took a bottle of *saki* and two small cups, handpainted with flowers. 'You know I never drink at sea, Chief. But we are in harbour now and we have something to celebrate.' He put the cups on the desk top and filled them. Passing one to the Engineer Officer, he raised his own. 'To I-357 and all who sail in her,' he said, bowing gravely.

Satugawa returned the bow before putting the cup to his lips. Having drunk from it, he held it away to examine the pattern. 'These are beautifully decorated, Captain,' he said. 'Where did you get them?'

'My wife's work. She is a talented woman. Not only at painting. Her flower arrangements have won many prizes, and her garden is much admired. When I am worried, when the harsh realities of war trouble me, I like to think of her arranging flowers and working in her garden.' He looked away, sighed. 'It is the gentle, beautiful things of life which bring peace to a man's soul.'

'Quite so.' The Engineer Officer sipped the *saki*, in his

161

mind a picture of Able Seaman Awa's severed head bouncing away from the stump of a neck which squirted blood – little jets of it, silvered by moonlight.

Nineteen

The atmosphere in the operations room in Kilindini was uncomfortable, less because the punkah was no match for the humid heat of equatorial night than for the failure of *Restless* to acknowledge the recall signal. Perspiring freely, elbows on the desk, Captain (D) mopped his face with a moist handkerchief. 'I simply cannot understand Barratt's failure to acknowledge,' he wheezed.

'Perhaps his transmitter's gone on the blink,' suggested Hutchison.

Captain (D) directed a frosty look at the Flight Lieutenant. 'Destroyers have several transmitters, generators and back-up systems. The only time they can't transmit is when they've sunk.'

The SOO tugged at an earlobe, looked gloomily down the length of his unusually long nose. 'Remarkably like insubordination, I'd say. Been drinking perhaps. Haddingham said Barratt's scrapes were usually associated with that sort of thing.'

'May I say something, sir?' The question came from the RNVR Lieutenant at the operations table.

Captain (D), checking the file copy of the unanswered signal for possible ambiguity looked up in surprise. 'Yes, Jakes. Of course. What?'

'Well, sir, it's a little awkward but I . . .' he hesitated. 'I wondered if Lieutenant Commander Barratt might not be the victim of a compulsive obsession.'

Captain (D) frowned. 'What on earth are you talking about, Jakes?'

'It's a psychiatric disorder, sir. Can be brought on by shock though it's normally deep-seated and chronic.'

163

'Good God, Jakes.' Captain (D) looked at the Lieutenant in dismay. 'Don't tell me you're one of those.'

'No, sir. But in the club a few days ago I read an article on the subject in a periodical. Now I wonder if his wife's death, plus the massacre of *Fort Nebraska*'s crew . . . if the shock of those could have triggered a compulsive obsession.'

'To disregard signals, I presume.' The SOO gave another imitation of a pelican looking down its beak.

Jakes shook his head. 'To find and destroy the Japanese submarine.'

'You may be right, Jakes. But this is an operations room of the Royal Navy not, thank God, a psychiatric ward.' Captain (D)'s cheeks bulged as if building up a powerful head of steam. '*Restless* has failed to acknowledge her recall, dammit,' he exploded. 'She's required here in advance of the carrier's arrival. The Chief Staff Officer tells me he will have to report this to the Admiral if we've not heard from Barratt by midnight. That is exactly one hour away. For his sake I hope we do hear from him by then.'

It was after Captain (D) and the SOO had left the operations room that Camilla flounced across to Jake's desk. 'I heard all that,' she said with a disapproving twitch of her nose. 'Makes me angry. Why can't they give the poor man a chance? He must have a good reason for not replying to their signals. Why not give him the benefit of the doubt?'

'What doubt?' Jake's voice was flat.

'Oh, you men! Why not assume that he knows what he's doing? He probably knows where the submarine is. Believes that in a day or so it'll put to sea. It may be in some small harbour or inlet on the Mozambique coast. In neutral territory, so he's hanging around waiting for the wretched thing to come out. But he knows it won't if the Japs know he's there. Hence wireless silence.'

'If he knows where it is, why doesn't he tell us?'

'I've just told you why.' Camilla's voice did its best to reflect despair.

'You've heard my theory, Camilla.'

164

'Your *Reader's Digest* quote?'

'It wasn't the *Reader's Digest* as it happens.'

'Well, whatever it was, I wasn't impressed. Nor were Captain (D) and SOO. *Restless*'s Number One is Sandy Hamilton. He wouldn't go along with anything stupid like . . .' She frowned, searching for the words. '. . . rank insubordination or whatever it was Old Gloomy called it. Sandy is a well-balanced, level-headed, ambitious, young naval officer.'

Jakes nodded, a half smile about his lips. 'And, rumour has it, a certain lovely lady's boy friend.'

'He's nothing of the sort,' she flashed. 'Simply a nice man who happens to be a good friend.'

Jakes beamed good-naturedly. 'Who was seen with a certain young lady week-ending down the coast at the Tuna Inn?'

'You horror. I don't know why I bother to speak to you.' Tossing her head with just the right touch of outraged dignity, she went back to her desk.

A light breeze from the shore ruffled the surface of the sea to help cool what would otherwise have been a humid, breathless night, with stars glittering brilliantly in a break in the southern sky. Against the dark background of the land *Restless* moved slowly through the water; without lights of any sort she was invisible but for the pools of phosphorescence which tumbled and glowed along her sides as the engines were put astern.

From a wing of the bridge the Captain looked down to where men had gathered on deck abreast of the motorboat which hung from turned-out davits. 'Standby to lower,' he called, before going back to the compass platform. To the dark bulk of a man standing there, he said, 'We're three miles off Maji Island now, Number One. Pick us up here at 0500, unless we send up a flare before then.' With a dry laugh he added, 'Which I sincerely hope we won't.' He searched the darkness round the ship with binoculars. 'Right. She's all yours. Take care.'

'Aye, aye, sir. I will.' The First Lieutenant followed Barratt to the top of the bridge ladder. 'Good luck, sir. We'll keep our fingers crossed.'

'Thank you, Number One.' The Captain tugged at the webbing belt which held a holstered revolver. 'This Wild West gear is bloody uncomfortable,' he complained as he started down the ladder. 'Almost as bad as having to look like a ruddy boot-black.'

The strangely assorted tow of small craft moved in towards Maji Island, which was not yet visible in the darkness. Coxed by Leading Seaman Hind the motorboat led the way with the catamaran and skimmer on a short tow astern. Corrigan was in the skimmer steering with a paddle, the outboard engine still tipped clear of the water. The landing party's approach was silent but for the low rumble of the motorboat's engine and the gentle swish and slap of the sea against the hull. No one spoke but for whispered exchanges between Morrow and Katu.

Piloted by the African, the trio of small craft headed in towards the southern side of the island. Katu had explained that the coastline was rocky but for three small beaches; the one for which they were heading – already named Recce Beach by the Captain – another in the north, and a third on the western side of the island.

They had gone some distance when Katu pointed ahead. He made a whispered report to Morrow. 'It's the island, Bwana.'

The Sub-Lieutenant spoke to Barratt, told him what Katu had said, adding, 'I can see it now. He says we must steer more to port.'

Barratt checked with binoculars, picked up the dark blob on the port bow and ordered the change of course. Soon afterwards Katu spoke again. Morrow did an almost simultaneous translation. 'He says we're not far off now, sir.'

'Right. Stop engines, Hind. We'll haul the tow alongside and make the transfers.'

*

166

Katu was first into the catamaran; Morrow went next, then Barratt followed by Angus McLean. Darkness concealed a weird-looking crew, their faces and other exposed flesh blackened, their dark clothing a strange assortment of blue shorts, cut down bell-bottoms, rugger jerseys and other non-uniform items. All were bareheaded and the two blonds, Corrigan and Morrow, had blackened their hair. Tucked away somewhere or hung about them were revolvers, fighting knives, torches, binoculars, Very pistols and flares.

The outrigger kept the catamaran on an even keel in spite of the uncertain movements of a crew who'd never manned one before, though they'd had a dummy run earlier that night, climbing in and out of the primitive craft stowed on *Restless*'s upper deck. Long and narrow, scooped from a single log, the hull required its four occupants to sit in line: Katu in the stern, ahead of him the others in the order in which they'd boarded. All had paddles. Before leaving the motorboat Barratt had a last word with Corrigan, who was alone in the skimmer. 'Remember the drill. Don't use the outboard. Paddle in behind us. Remain close. It's dark and won't change unless the moon gets through the clouds. When we've beached the catamaran you stay afloat nearby. Within sight of the catamaran if possible. We'll aim to be back on the beach by 0430. Sunrise is at 0525. You okay on the pre-arranged signals or do you want to go through them again?'

'I guess I'm okay, Captain,' said the American.

'Remember, a red Very light means trouble. And that means a high-speed getaway. I hope we won't need that. Paddling's a lot quieter. And better for the body.' Barratt cleared his throat. 'Even if it is a bit of a bind.'

'Okay, Captain. It's a deal.' The note of confidence in the American's voice reminded Barratt that for both of them this was more than an exciting, perhaps daunting adventure. They had personal scores to settle. Behind all they were doing lay a primitive but fundamental urge. The desire for revenge.

*

167

Cloud banks shut out the last of the stars as the catamaran moved over the sea in a silence broken by the splash of paddles and the occasional murmur of voices. Long before the others, Angus McLean sighted Recce Beach, a pale smudge at the base of the black hump ahead. Soon after its sighting, a plaintive cry came to them across the water. Barratt was saying, 'For God's sake. What's that . . .' when Katu cupped his hands and answered with an equally weird cry.

'For Christ's sake stop him, Morrow,' snapped Barratt. 'This isn't the Swiss Alps.'

Having spoken to the African, Morrow said, 'It's a catamaran fisherman, sir. Katu says the man heard our paddles and is asking who it is and where from. In reply Katu gave his name and village. They do this exchange of greetings on the fishing grounds.'

With binoculars trained on where the sound had come from, Barratt said, 'I don't see anything there.' His words were almost overtaken by McLean's. 'About thirty degrees to starboard, sir. A hundred yards or so, I reckon there's something on the water.'

Having said, 'You're a bloody marvel, McLean,' Barratt ordered, 'Stop paddling. Give Corrigan two blue flashes. We'll transfer to the skimmer. Morrow – tell Katu that once we've left the catamaran he must take it across to his chum and stop the yodelling. The other man may be a Maji fisherman. What he tells Katu might save us a lot of trouble. The important thing is we can't afford to hang about too long. Tell Katu we'll wait here until he returns. But he's got to get back in double quick time. Got that?'

'Aye, aye, sir. I'll fix that.'

'And,' went on Barratt, 'tell Katu not to say a word about us, or what we're after. He's out fishing on his own. Normal drill. Right?' As he spoke the skimmer came up from astern. Barratt told Corrigan what had happened, and the shore party transferred to it while Katu, now alone in the catamaran, paddled off in the distance.

*

168

Barratt checked the minutes as they ticked by: five, six, seven, eight, nine. At the tenth minute, tense and impatient, he growled. 'I wish he'd bloody well hurry up. It's already 0132. We're ten minutes behind schedule.'

'Africans observe a polite routine when they meet in the bush,' explained Morrow. 'I imagine it's the same at sea. They ask where you're from, what tribe, who's your chief, how many wives have you, how many children, how many are daughters? How are your cattle, your crops, have you had rain, etcetera? It's really quite a rigmarole. I expect that . . .'

'It's nae so different in the wild parts of the Heelands,' interrupted McLean. 'When strangers meet they . . .'

'This is no time for lectures on African and Scottish culture,' interrupted Barratt. 'We've a job to do.'

A few minutes later paddling could be heard. It was soon followed by the catamaran's arrival alongside. Katu spoke to Morrow at some length, whereafter the Sub-Lieutenant said, 'All's well, sir. He says the other guy, Obudo, is not from Maji. He's from the coast. A fishing village about six miles from here. Katu asked him if he'd seen any strange ships, something like a big whale. But Obudo hadn't. Nor had he seen any Maji fishermen recently. He told Katu there were usually a number of Maji catamarans on these fishing grounds, but none over the last few days which puzzles him. He thinks it may be an outbreak of malaria in the village. Or something like that.'

'I see.' Barratt was silent, deep in thought. After a while he said, 'I wonder what the devil *something like that* could be?' Then he was all action again. 'Let's get back into the catamaran. Time's precious.'

About five minutes after they'd landed the moon came out and for the first time Corrigan saw the catamaran where they'd drawn it up against a rock ledge at the far end of the beach; the only indication of its presence was a mast looking like a bare tree pole, which was precisely what it had been before Katu cut it down for his craft.

Worrying about the moon, Corrigan paddled the skimmer close inshore where it wouldn't be too visible. When he found a good place at the opposite end of the beach, he put the anchor over the side and the skimmer swung to in the lee of the rocks. He patted the bulging gunwale affectionately, thankful that the skimmer was all black rubber. That thought prompted another and he ran a hand lightly over his forehead. The sticky feel of the blacking was reassuring. The luminous dial of his watch showed 0217. If all went well the others would be back by 0430. Two and a quarter hours to wait. He yawned, wriggled into a more comfortable position on the bottom boards, his back against the skimmer's side, his eyes on the beach. At regular intervals he put a hand over the side to feel the water. It was a 'keep-alert' drill he'd learnt on the beach at Sandport. He reckoned the water was just right. In the middle-seventies, probably. Great to be in the water right now, he decided, knowing it wasn't possible. On the messdecks they said there was good swimming in Kilindini harbour; shark nets, floats, diving stages, the lot. He'd have to wait for that. They'd be there in a few days.

He wondered what would happen to him in Kilindini? Passage back to the States in a homeward-bound ship, survivor's leave? Three weeks in Sandport? His watch told him it was November 23. With luck he might make it in time for Christmas at home. Great. The folks would like that. So would he. Three weeks' leave. Jeez! Go places with Mary Lou. Take her down to New York. Maybe get married if her parents could be persuaded. Not likely, they weren't keen. Said she was too young at eighteen. That was what they said, but it wasn't what they meant. They'd told other folks in Sandport that she could do better for herself than marry a lifeguard. How better? Something up market – like a bond salesman?

He could hear the mosquitoes buzzing around but they weren't worrying him like usual. The blacking, he supposed. He yawned, dipped a hand in the water once more, sprayed his face with it. He wasn't tired, he'd had a good rest in the afternoon. The Captain had made all the shore party do that.

170

The trouble now was lack of movement. He shifted his position on the bottom-boards, moved a couple of feet forward. Thinking about the Captain sent him off on another track. Barratt was a nice guy. Quiet but tough and determined, he reckoned. Good man to be with in a bad situation. They'd told him on the messdecks about his wife dying in Changi Gaol. That explained a lot. Why they both felt the same way about the Japs. Branded on his mind, the nightmarish recollection passed before his eyes like a film on a big screen: the dark bulk of the submarine cutting through the water, the cold glare of the searchlight sweeping the sea, settling on the huddled shapes, the tracer bullets racing towards them, kicking up spurts of foam to find the range before smacking into the white faces in the water. Jesus, he thought. Only three nights back. Unbelievable that it had happened only three nights back.

He looked at his watch again – 0232 – wondered how the shore party was getting on. Had they found anything? The big whale? No way of telling. Just have to wait. There wasn't much action for him sitting there in the skimmer. He'd rather have been with the guys on shore. But at least he was involved now, and the Captain had chosen him for the job when there were plenty of others in the ship who reckoned they were better qualified. So luck was on his side, and it was early days yet. If the submarine was there things were going to happen, and whatever they were he was likely to be in on them.

The moon drifted behind the clouds. He was glad of that. It was good for the men ashore – and good for him. A seabird called, a sudden shrill cry, the first sound he'd heard for a long time other than the constant lap and murmur of the sea.

Twenty

That night Yashimoto ordered the Navigating Officer to complete his chart of the island with lines of soundings in the creek and through the narrows. When Sato had gone, he wrote up his report on the trial and punishment of AB Awa.

The shore parties returned on board an hour after midnight bringing with them a casualty: a seaman had gashed his thigh with a panga. Yashimoto suspected a self-inflicted wound; a ploy to escape the gruelling work of cutting timber in a tropical jungle on a sultry night. But the wound was so severe, and the men who had witnessed the incident so certain that it was caused by a branch which had deflected the panga blade, that he accepted reluctantly that it was an accident. He administered an injection of morphine before sterilizing the wound with a red hot knife blade, whereafter he dressed and bound it.

Tired by a long and taxing day – it had included Awa's execution – Yashimoto climbed on to his bunk and lay there with the reassuring thought that for the first time since the sinking of *Fort Nebraska* he could go to sleep knowing that for I-357 and her crew the outlook was good. Satugawa's statement that flooding tests should be possible by sunset on the 24th was the prime reason for Yashimoto's peace of mind. Another was the behaviour of the Catalinas; on neither the morning nor afternoon flights had they shown any particular interest in Creek Island. A final comforting thought was the certainty that sentries would now be at their most vigilant. Within forty-eight hours I-357 should be at sea again, bound for Mombasa to arrive in time for the attack on the British carrier. Once clear of Creek Island he would acknowledge

172

FOS's signal, report I-357's position and confirm that she would be on station in time.

After the attack he would set course for base. The thought of Penang conjured up attractive images, prominent among them the lovely face and shapely body of Masna. With that stimulating fantasy he fell into a sound sleep. It was not to end until he was called at seven-thirty in the morning in accordance with the instruction in his Night Order Book.

Katu led the slow, upward trudge across the slope of the hill with the others close on his heels. Thick bushes, rocks, loose stones and the steep incline made the going slow and the climbers sweat profusely. To these discomforts were added the attentions of countless insects which buzzed and protested as progress was made through the undergrowth. The shore party were about half way to the summit when the moon came through the clouds and the pace was quickened. Katu, never having approached the village except by way of the creek had, until then, been moving tentatively, feeling his way in the darkness, stopping at times to find a way round when thickets halted progress.

He and Morrow, brought up in the African bush, were adept at silent movement; McLean, too, excelled in this, though he'd learnt the art in a different environment. Barratt was the amateur of the party, and each time he trod on a dry twig or displaced a loose stone he cursed under his breath. The slow, upward journey across the slope had taken almost half an hour when they reached a clearing from which could be seen the moonlit tops of trees on the far side of the hill. Katu stopped, waited for Morrow to catch up. 'We will come to the village by following the ravine,' he explained. 'That way we will not be seen because the trees are thick behind the huts.' He pointed ahead to a clump of tall casuarinas. 'The top of the ravine is behind those trees. Not far now.'

Saying, 'We must stop here, Katu. I will tell Bwana M'kubwa of this.' Morrow repeated to Barratt what the African had said.

Barratt wiped the sweat from beneath his eyes with moist

173

fingers. 'Right. We'll separate now. You go ahead with Katu to the huts. Don't show yourself there unless he gives you the okay. When he's learnt what he can, rejoin us at the casuarinas not later than 0400. We're due back on the beach by 0430. That gives you an hour and a half. Should be enough.'

Morrow said it was, adding, 'If you're not here when we get back, sir, do we wait for you?' The Captain's sweat-streaked, blackened face struck the Sub-Lieutenant as particularly villainous in the moonlight.

'Not long after 0400. Say five minutes. Same drill for us. If you're not here by then we'll carry on down to the beach.'

Morrow spoke to Katu. The two men moved away through the undergrowth and were soon lost to sight.

Though they had reached the top of the hill, Barratt and McLean found that the thickly wooded summit shut out any view of the creek. According to Katu it lay directly below them. Eager for a sight of it the two men moved through the trees in a direction away from the ravine. Before long they reached a clearing where an outcrop of rock thrust upwards to almost the height of the trees. They climbed it and for the first time saw the creek; a long stretch of water, silver in the moonlight, its mouth on the north-western side of the island leading to narrows into which poked a rocky bluff. Beyond the bluff the narrows ended and the creek opened out into an oval basin. From their vantage point they saw that Maji was shaped like a horseshoe, its open end the entrance to the creek. The slopes of the hills enfolding it were densely wooded and on the eastern side a beach led to a clearing where native huts were fringed by palm trees. The dark hulls of catamarans were drawn up on the northern end of the beach.

To Barratt the anti-climax was like a kick in the stomach; nowhere in the moonlit scene was there a submarine. The entire creek, its most distant point little more than a thousand yards from them, lay open to inspection and clearly it had no exciting secrets to hide. If the submarine had been there it had gone. *If* it had been there? 'Nothing here,' he said to McLean in a subdued voice. 'So much for the big whale. All that bloody effort for nothing.'

Sensing the Captain's thoughts the signalman said, 'Ah, weel, sir. It was worth the try. It's a bonny creek but there's nary a place for a submarine to hide. Too easy for Catalinas to have seen it.'

Barratt was pondering this truth when the sound of an outboard engine reached them. Moments later its source was apparent. A catamaran with mast and outrigger, but no sail, was travelling at a fair pace down the narrows, its outboard engine throwing up a plume of foam, white in the moonlight.

Surprised and puzzled, they watched it. During the last forty-eight hours they'd seen many catamarans in and around the islands, but never one with an outboard engine. It was heading for the bank on the western side of the creek, some distance north of the bluff. The note of the engine dropped and it ran its bows against the fringe of mangroves lining the shore. Two dark shapes came from the shadows and stood on the bank facing the catamaran. A minute or so later it had backed away, turned and headed down the narrows. It had not gone far when the performance was repeated, this time at the foot of the bluff where a single dark shape left the treeline and moved towards the water. When close to the catamaran the dark shape knelt, evidently talking to its occupants though nothing could be heard at that distance. Once again the catamaran backed out. This time it made for the shore on the opposite side of the creek. Fascinated, they watched the frail little craft's progress. The first stop on the eastern side was in front of the huts where its bows were run up on to the beach. Two shadowy figures went down to it. It was apparent that they were talking to the men in the catamaran. Barratt and McLean, both watching through binoculars, muttered a simultaneous 'See that?'

For Barratt, what they had seen was like a shot of adrenalin. The distant figures which had gone down to the beach had rifles slung over their shoulders.

In a low voice McLean said, 'There's something funny going on there, sir.'

'There certainly is.' Barratt's matter-of-fact tone concealed excitement. 'But just *what*, it's difficult to make out. Let's hope Morrow and Katu have the answer.'

'They'll surely have heard the outboard,' said McLean.

The two men kept watch as the catamaran continued its journey. Having pulled out from the beach, it motored a short distance down it until, at the southern end, it again stopped; a man came to the water's edge. He, too, was carrying a rifle.

Once more what looked like a brief discussion took place. The catamaran's outboard engine burst noisily into life and it made its way across the creek to the opposite side. There it was lost to Barratt's eyes in the shadows cast by the trees lining the bank.

'See anything?' he asked the signalman.

Without lowering his binoculars McLean replied, 'Aye, sir. It's gone alongside the bank. There's two other catamarans there. Moored next to each other.'

Barratt strained at the binocular eyepieces. He wasn't sure but thought he might have seen the dim outline of catamarans. 'I can't really make out anything,' he admitted. 'Keep watching. Let me know what's happening.'

Soon afterwards McLean said, 'One man has already stepped on shore. Now – another's beginning to follow. The third man's standing in the sternsheets.'

Barratt, tense, waiting for more, could hear nothing but McLean's deep breathing.

'Aye, sir. He's on shore now,' came from the signalman at last. 'They're moving into the trees. Three of them, walking in single file.' Shortly afterwards he added, 'I see the faint glow of a fire. It's reflected in the tops of trees somewhere up the slope from where they landed.'

'A camp fire, d'you think?'

'Could be that, sir.'

Barratt put a hand to his forehead. 'Just let me think about this for a moment, McLean.' He muttered something to

176

himself, then said, 'I can't make it out . . . unless . . .' The sentence was left unfinished.

'And what is that, sir?' prodded McLean.

'Unless they were sentries. The other people – the men in the catamaran – could be checking to see that all is well. But the question remains, who are they? Surely African fishermen don't post armed sentries? Katu may have the answer when he gets back. The point is, if the lot we've been watching aren't fishermen who the hell are they? Portuguese officials? Police? Fishery control? Recruiting agents for the mines and plantations? Something like that?' Barratt answered the rhetorical questions. 'Highly improbable, I think. So we're left with the sixty-four dollar question. Who the devil are those people?'

McLean was thoughtful. 'Maybe survivors, sir,' he said.

'Survivors? What sort of survivors, McLean?'

'Japanese, sir. Perhaps that submarine – the big whale – didn't make it into here. Maybe the crew did. In inflatables. Could be they've a camp in the trees.'

'I wonder if you're right, McLean.' Barratt paused. 'You may well be. They'd have seen the Catalinas. If they are Japanese they'll be afraid they may be pulled in by the Portuguese.' He relapsed into silence. Quite suddenly, in a voice that had risen, he said, 'Know what? Katu's yodelling chum, the one fishing offshore tonight. Remember, he couldn't understand why he'd not seen any Maji fishermen recently.' Barratt dropped his voice again. 'That would fit with Japanese sentries wouldn't it?'

'Aye. I dare say.' McLean was cautious. 'For preventing men from the village going out to fish, you mean?'

'Yes. Just that.' Barratt looked at his watch. 'We've an hour left. I suggest we stay here until it's time to get back to the casuarinas. Maybe we'll see something else going on in the creek.'

'Aye, and that's a good idea, sir. We'll nae be finding a better place for watching.'

They were silent for some time, each busy with his own

177

thoughts until Barratt said, 'I hope to God that Morrow and Katu haven't run into those sentries.'

'Katu will be going in alone will he not? From the direction of the spring. That's at the back. At the foot of the ravine. The sentries seem to be stationed on the beach side of the huts. He should be okay. A black man and all. Just one of the African fishermen.'

'Fair enough for Katu, but Morrow is white. He can't pass himself off as one of them.'

'He'll be fine, sir. He's looking black enough and he speaks the lingo.'

McLean's confidence was infectious. Barratt changed the subject. 'Those catamarans on the west bank – apart from the one we saw moving around – I suppose they're for the use of the outfit in the woods, whoever they are?'

'Aye. That could be it,' agreed McLean.

Making themselves as comfortable as they could on their rocky perch, they settled down to watch. But the night had other plans; clouds crept up on the moon and the watchers were once more in total darkness.

They'd gone someway down the ravine when Katu stopped, grabbed Morrow by the arm. 'Listen,' he said urgently. Morrow heard the sound of the two-stroke engine, a distant high-pitched snarl. It came from the general direction of the creek, grew slowly louder, then stopped.

'That's an outboard engine,' he said. He was explaining what that was when Katu interrupted. 'I know, Bwana. I have already seen such things in Mocimboa da Praia.' Katu's tone implied concern that he should be thought so ignorant. 'They push a boat through the water,' he added by way of putting the matter beyond doubt.

From where they were in the wooden ravine it was not possible to see into the creek, so they continued their slow but silent descent towards the spring. Katu stopped at frequent intervals to listen. By the time they reached the foot of the ravine the sound of the outboard had started and stopped several times; on each occasion it appeared to be increasing in volume.

While still in the trees which bordered a small clearing Katu stopped suddenly and pointed ahead. 'The spring,' he whispered. In the moonlight Morrow saw a rough stone canopy in the centre of the clearing. Listening intently, he could hear the murmuring bubble of the spring which the canopy shielded from the sun. Katu came close, spoke into the Sub-Lieutenant's ear. 'Not far now, Bwana.'

Keeping to the trees, they moved round the clearing with Katu still in the lead. They had not gone far when he stopped, held a finger to his mouth, moved behind the trunk of a tree and gestured to Morrow to do the same. They had almost reached the edge of a big clearing in which could be seen the tall trunks and bunched heads of coconut palms. Beyond them a semi-circle of huts stood above a white stretch of beach which reached down to the edge of the creek, its water margin silvered by moonlight. For Morrow an otherwise captivating scene was jarred suddenly by the distant silhouette of two men walking towards each other from opposite sides of the beach. It was not possible to catch anything more than glimpses of them through the gaps between the huts and the palm trees, but those glimpses were enough to imprint on his mind an indelible image: the men carried rifles over their shoulders. When they met they conferred briefly before turning to march back in the directions whence they had come. Who they were he had no idea. What they were was pretty obvious.

Twenty-one

When the sentries were out of sight Katu left Morrow with a final, 'You wait here, Bwana. I come back soon.'

The African was moving stealthily forward when the clouds closed over the moon and its pale light went as if at the touch of some heavenly switch.

Thank the Lord for that, breathed Morrow, peering into the black wall of night and seeing nothing. The sentries had been walking close to the water's edge, about fifty yards in front of the huts, the entrances to which must have been on the beach side for nothing but blank walls had faced him before the moon went.

Katu would be all right, he decided. Even if the moon came again and he was seen, it would not matter. It was normal practice for Africans to leave their huts during the night to relieve themselves; tribal culture did not embrace modern conveniences.

The Sub-Lieutenant leant against the tree trunk, alert, watching the darkness, his senses finely tuned. Before he'd seen the armed men on the beach he'd regarded *Operation Maji* as an exciting adventure. The sort of thing he'd read about as a boy. But it was more than that now, more complex, more worrying. He was, though he would not have admitted it, fearful of what might happen: that he might be the target for those rifles? Bizarre pictures of the shattered corpses of the *Fort Nebraska* survivors passed through his mind, and he recalled Brad Corrigan's description of the horrors of that night. From where he stood all that could be heard was the water lapping the beach. Was the Japanese submarine somewhere in the creek? The men with the rifles made sense if it was. They'd be Jap sentries. Some of the men who'd massacred the survivors. No mercy could be expected from such people. Waiting behind the trunk of the palm tree he worried increasingly about what might happen, about things that could go wrong. In spite of the hot night he shivered, felt for the revolver at his hip. Its touch was only partly reassuring.

Was this Japanese submarine they were hunting the one which had attacked the southbound convoy? The one *Restless* had attacked, thought then to be a German U-boat? He recalled the excitement of the occasion, his first real taste of action. Difficult to believe that it had happened less than a week ago.

There hadn't been much to see. Too dark for that. But a merchant ship near them had been torpedoed, they'd heard the explosion, and *Restless* had made an asdic contact soon afterwards. Sean O'Brien, the ASCO, had classified it as *submarine*, and Barratt, deciding on a counter-attack, had taken *Restless* in at high speed, dropping a pattern of depth-charges set shallow. The usual but always spectacular fountains of foaming water had leapt high in the air as explosion after explosion rumbled and thudded, the surface of the sea trembling, convulsed by the forces beneath it, the destroyer shaking to the pounding of her own charges. What followed had been unusual and immensely satisfying. The bows and then the top of the conning-tower of a submarine had shown briefly in the long white beam of *Restless*'s searchlight. Morrow had been on the bridge, seen it happen, heard Barratt's shouted, 'Port twenty,' the destroyer heeling over, swinging hard to starboard, and the First Lieutenant's urgent phone warning to Geoffrey Lawson in the gunnery control-tower, 'Port quarter – two hundred yards – submarine surfacing.'

But all signs of the submarine had gone within seconds of its breaking surface. The convoy had gone on, leaving *Restless* to try to regain asdic contact. Whether the submarine had broken surface because of a loss of trim, or whether the depth-charges had sunk it, they were never to know. All attempts to regain contact in waters of great depth failed. An hour later they'd abandoned the search.

A sudden noise from somewhere behind him caused Morrow to stiffen against the trunk of the palm tree. Revolver in hand he edged himself slowly round it, his eyes searching the darkness. The noise came again, louder this time and unmistakably from the direction of the spring. He relaxed. It was the croaking of a bull-frog. Grinning at his jumpiness, he forgot his fears, reflecting instead on his good fortune in having been chosen for the shore party. That more reassuring thought was soon banished by a low whistle from the darkness ahead – a short and a long. It was repeated and he knew it must be Katu, so he whistled a long and a short in response; the agreed challenge and reply for *Operation Maji*. He could neither see nor hear the African approaching, but less than a minute later Katu was at his side. He was not alone.

'This man', he whispered, indicating the dark shape near him, 'will come with us, Bwana. I will tell you later of him. He is Aba Said.'

Thanks to the newcomer who led, the journey up the ravine and over the hilltop to the casuarina trees was safely accomplished in total darkness and good time. A tall, lithe young man, Aba Said seemed to glide rather than walk over the rough terrain.

'He know every track, every bush, every stone on Maji. He live in this place all his life,' Katu explained to Morrow. That it was so, was soon evident. The route the young African chose to reach the casuarinas was a good deal easier than the one they'd taken for the journey down to the huts.

They waited at the casuarinas for some time before a theatrical hiss from Katu was followed by his, 'They come, Bwana.' Minutes later Morrow, every nerve strained, heard the faint scuff of feet – the Captain's, he decided with a private smile – followed by the whistled code to which he at once replied.

It was a weird meeting, the only means of recognition familiar voices which identified shapes in the dark. Morrow began to explain who Aba Said was when the Captain interrupted. 'Tell me about him later. No time now. Seen any sentries? Men with rifles?'

'Yes, sir, on the beach in front of the huts. Two of them.'

'Did they see you?' The Captain threw the question at him like a missile.

'Definitely not, sir. I stayed in the trees.'

'And Katu?'

'He went to the hut of his friend, Aba Said's father. He says he could not have been seen.'

Barratt said, 'Thank God for that.' In what seemed an afterthought he added, 'Did he find out who the armed men were? What it's all about?'

So the Captain didn't know. Morrow experienced an almost uncontrollable desire to laugh, to relieve the tension. This was his moment and he was going to enjoy it. 'Yes, sir,' he said quietly. 'They are Japanese. From the submarine in the creek.'

'My God, I don't believe it.' The pitch of Barratt's voice rose. 'McLean and I have searched every inch of that damned creek with binoculars. What's more in bright moonlight. Where is it? Submerged?'

Morrow told him.

The darkness of a cloud-covered sky persisted, but with Aba Said leading them down a winding track through the undergrowth the journey to the beach presented few difficulties other than that of walking silently.

They couldn't see the skimmer when they reached the catamaran, but Corrigan's reply to the coded whistle travelled softly across the water, and soon they heard the faint splash of paddles approaching the beach. The skimmer grounded and Corrigan's 'Hi' sounded in the darkness. Barratt quickly briefed the American, told him the submarine was there, adding, 'We've crew for you. An African, Aba Said. He's a Maji fisherman. Brought up with paddles. Follow us out when we leave the beach. When we give you the signal, close us.'

The catamaran was launched, the shore party climbed in

183

and paddled away from the beach in silence. It was not until they'd covered the first mile of the journey that the Captain said, 'Now, Morrow. Let's have your story.'

The Sub-Lieutenant began by explaining Aba Said's presence. 'Katu recruited him to take his place when he returns to the fishing grounds this morning. He says that Said knows every inch of the island, all the tracks to the beaches, where the sentries are, the Japs' daily routine, etcetera. I think he'll be very useful.'

'He certainly will.' Barratt's voice was hoarse with supressed excitement. 'Now give us the gen about the submarine.'

To the accompaniment of splashing paddles and creaks and groans from the mast and outrigger, Morrow repeated what Katu had told him: the submarine's arrival at the creek three nights before; the camouflaging before dawn; the crew's daily routine; the shooting of the Maji fisherman; the Japanese ban on fishing, and the consequent shortage of food; the execution of the sentry who'd drunk *calao* with the villagers; the sounds of mechanical work on the submarine night and day; the spiral of smoke rising from the trees each day, and the distant glow of a fire at night.

A question and answer session developed, Barratt showing particular interest in precisely where the submarine was berthed, how she was lying in relation to the narrows, the direction in which her bows faced? Was any part of the boat visible in daylight? Where were the sentries posted? Were they checked on day and night and, if so, at what times?

In the course of an almost simultaneous translation Morrow tossed the questions and answers to and fro, clearly enjoying his role until Barratt cut him short. 'That's a very useful report. Now tell Katu that I think he's done a marvellous job. I'm deeply grateful. Tell Aba Said that *he* will be well rewarded for *his* services. Go to some trouble to reassure him by saying that his people will not have the Japs around their necks much longer. Tell him I intend to see to that.'

Morrow said, 'I was about to mention something important, sir. Something Katu told me he'd heard from Aba Said's

184

father. When the Japanese officer came to show them the head of the sentry he said that if the Africans behaved themselves they'd soon be fishing at sea again because the submarine would be leaving before long.'

Barratt's euphoria, induced an hour earlier by Morrow's calm announcement that the submarine was in the creek, drained away as if sluice-gates had opened. In an agony of uncertainty he wondered if he'd at last found the submarine only to lose it? Was this the day of the Japanese officer's *before long*? With a deep sense of urgency and foreboding he knew that he must get back to *Restless* as soon as possible. Morrow was saying something. Barratt wasn't sure what it was because he wasn't listening, he was too upset. 'Sorry,' he said. 'I didn't get that. What did you say?'

'That Katu was no fool, sir.'

'Meaning what?'

'He told Aba Said's father that we would want to know when the submarine was leaving. The old man said he'd light a fire near the casuarinas to warn us when they saw it was getting ready to go.'

Barratt laughed with relief. 'My God, what a man. He certainly isn't a fool. One thing though. How will they decide when it's getting ready to leave?'

'The Japs will have to shift all that camouflage, sir. Said's father told Katu it would mean a lot of work.'

'When you settle up, see to it that Katu, and Said's dad, get an extra five pounds of tobacco. They've done a great job.'

Morrow grinned in the darkness. 'I thought you'd be pleased, sir.'

'That's an understatement. Now let's get cracking. Double quick.' On his orders paddling ceased, the skimmer was cast off and the outboard lowered into the water. The two small craft gathered speed as they headed for the rendezvous, bumping and spraying, their outboard engines screeching in high-pitched harmony.

Restless was sighted at about the time the first pale light of dawn appeared in the eastern sky. Not long afterwards

185

the skimmer and catamaran were alongside. Their occupants clambered on board, tired and bedraggled but exultant, their blackened faces streaked with sweat. The catamaran and skimmer were hoisted, Barratt went to the bridge, engine-room telegraphs rang, the note of the turbines rose, and the destroyer began once again to cut through the warm waters of the Mozambique Channel.

Twenty-two

Refreshed by undisturbed sleep Yashimoto washed in the handbasin in his cabin – thanks to the village spring the daily allowance of fresh water had been doubled – pulled on shorts, a vest and canvas shoes, and went to the wardroom where he ate his customary but frugal breakfast, a handful of rice and a cup of black tea. His first stop after the meal was at the chart-table in the control-room where he checked the times of moonrise and set printed on the slate in Sato's neat hand.

He is certainly a good navigating officer, conceded Yashimoto, conscientious and reliable, yet I don't really like him. It is not what he says but the way he looks at me, that critical light in his eyes, the mouth slightly twisted. Oh no, it's not what he says, it's what he thinks that worries me. These wartime officers, some of them university graduates like Sato, lack the naval outlook. They've not been brought up in the *samurai* tradition, their minds are filled with philosophical abstractions, many of them Western in origin. He shrugged away the unpleasant train of thought; there were more important things to worry about than Sato's shortcomings. The progress of repairs, the programme for the flooding tests, the disposal of the sick and wounded before departure. The moon would rise at about nine o'clock on the 24th, setting some twelve hours later. If the sky were not clouded it would help him take the submarine out of the creek. But for a line of sandbanks to the north-east of the entrance the water was deep fairly close inshore. Once clear of the headlands he would be able to dive if necessary, though he intended running on the surface until dawn in order to make good time to Mombasa.

It was still less than three days since he'd sunk the *Fort Nebraska*, yet so many things had happened that he thought of that incident as being much longer ago, more like weeks than days. His thoughts turned to the latest problem; Kagumi had come to his cabin that morning with bad news: a mechanician had collapsed with a high temperature and hallucinations; another case of malaria, bringing the total to three. There was no sick-bay in the submarine, nor any other facilities for nursing the sick. For those reasons he had decided it would not be practical to keep them on board for the long journey back to Penang. Other arrangements had to be made. He had not yet told Kagumi, but that would be attended to later in the day.

Attracted by the sound of men at work in the conning-tower, the source of his major problem, he went to the ladder and looked up. A man stripped to the waist was kneeling astride the hatch crouched over an electric drill, its high whine deafening as it bit into the steel. The Captain called out, 'Good morning, Taisho.'

The engineroom artificer stopped the drill, looked down. 'Sir?'

Yashimoto said, 'Work going well, I trust?'

The frown left the artificer's sweat-streaked face. 'Yes, sir. The coaming should be ready to take the lid by sunset.'

'And the lid? I see it's not in place.'

'At the foundry, sir. There's more to be done to make it the way it should be. The Chief ERA says it must be back on board for fitting and testing soon after sunset.'

A humming sound came from outside the conning-tower, followed by an abrasive screech. 'What's that, Taisho?' Yashimoto had to shout to be heard.

'They're working on the damage at the foot of the conning-tower wall. The angled plates are ready for bolting on. They're trimming up. Getting rid of rough spots on the surface around the broken metal.'

'H'm,' Yashimoto grunted. 'Still a lot of work to do then?'

'Much has already been done, sir. We should be ready for pressure tests by tomorrow evening.' The ERA's confident tone heartened Yashimoto. With men like these, he thought, everything's possible. He was about to go to the fore-ends to see how the sick and wounded were getting on when the Navigating Officer appeared.

'I have completed the chart, sir.' He handed it to the Captain. 'Petty Officer Nomura and a seaman came with me in the catamaran last night. There was a good deal of moonlight during the first part of the night. Otherwise accurate fixes would have been difficult.'

Yashimoto placed the chart on the table, switched on the light. He spent some time studying Sato's plan of Creek Island, now neatly studded with soundings.

The Captain looked up at him, smiled approval. 'Very good. This will be a great help. I see the sandbanks extend further west than we'd thought. That means a ninety degree turn soon after clearing the mouth of the creek.'

'Yes, sir. There's not much room to spare, though plenty of water if you keep to the channel I've plotted.'

'What was the tide doing when you took these soundings?'

'It was rising, sir. Two hours of high water. But I've allowed for that. The depths plotted are for mean low water.'

Yashimoto's head moved up and down, slowly, very deliberately. 'So, at midnight tomorrow, what margin will I have in the basin?'

Sato looked at the chart over the Captain's shoulder, thought for a moment. 'About a metre more than the plotted depths. Say an average depth of thirty metres around its centre.'

'That should be sufficient for the tests. We can always boost the pressure by pumping compressed air into the tower.' Yashimoto patted the Navigating Officer's shoulder. 'Creek Island has been good to us, Ishii Sato. Strange – but fortunate – that the basin should have water so much deeper than the narrows.'

'Not really, sir.' Sato was mildly shocked by the Captain's unusual familiarity. Yashimoto had never before used his first name, nor touched him physically. 'The island is volcanic in origin,' he went on. 'The basin is the old crater. Its rim

189

the steep hills around it. One would expect depth in the centre.'

Yashimoto frowned but said nothing. To him Sato's remark, accompanied by the crooked lip smile, smacked of condescension – *one would expect*. Indeed! But the Navigating Officer had produced a most useful chart and it was not the moment to rebuke him. The Captain decided to let the matter pass.

Before Yashimoto could carry out his intention of visiting the fore-ends, the Engineer Officer and Hayeto Shimada, the Chief ERA, came into the control-room. Stripped to the waist, both men looked near to exhaustion, their faces grimy and perspiring, dark shadows under their eyes. Yashimoto knew that they had worked through the night for the last three nights, snatching what rest they could during the day – and that was not much.

'All going well, Chief?' he asked Satugawa.

The Engineer Officer nodded. 'Progress is satisfactory, sir. We go back to the foundry shortly. It is necessary to get something to eat.' He put his hand to his mouth to hide a yawn. 'Sorry,' he smiled apologetically. 'It's the heat. Makes a man tired.'

'*Work* and heat,' corrected the Captain. 'And lack of sleep.'

Satugawa shrugged. 'The work has to be done, Captain. There is no other way.'

'I know.' Yashimoto sighed. 'We all suffer from lack of sleep. But that will soon change.'

Sato at the chart-table heard the Captain's remark and smiled sardonically. Confounded hypocrite, he thought. He's just had six hours of undisturbed sleep, and we all know it.

Yashimoto was speaking again. 'The pressure tests tomorrow night, Chief. We continue on schedule?'

The Engineer Officer wiped the sweat from his forehead, turned tired eyes on the Captain. 'Yes, sir.' The tone was resigned.

*

190

His on-board inspection completed, Yashimoto went up to the casing by way of the gun-hatch rather than disturb the men at work in the conning-tower. Once on the casing he stepped carefully, choosing his way through the litter of trees and branches, the dry tinder cracking under his feet as he made his way across the gangplank to the bank. It was his custom each morning to visit the foundry-site to see how work was progressing and to encourage the men. It was a chore he enjoyed because it enabled him to escape from the confinement of the submarine with its abiding odours of battery gas, diesel oil and human sweat, and it provided an opportunity for exercise. He always combined it with a brisk walk about the hillside to check that the cutting party of the night before had not left 'scars' which might be visible from the air. Physical exercise had become imperative for Yashimoto ever since Masna, in a moment of intimacy, had chided him about his weight problem. This she had done with a taunting slap on his bare but ample stomach; much as he enjoyed sharing her bed, he had resented the Malaysian girl's diminution of his dignity. Dignity was something to which Yashimoto attached great importance. Determined to surprise her, he had been dieting throughout the patrol, supplementing this with daily exercises in his small cabin.

Half an hour later, coming down the hillside through the trees, he met Satugawa on his way back to the foundry.

'That was quick work, Chief,' said the Captain cheerfully. 'You should have had a rest. Even a short one helps, you know.'

Satugawa shook his head. 'Not possible, Captain. I have had a wash and breakfast. They refresh a man. I told Shimada to rest for two hours. After that he will relieve me at the foundry. Then I will take a rest.'

Yashimoto was in the midst of praising the work of the engineroom staff when Satugawa held fingers to his mouth in a gesture for silence. The distant drone of aircraft engines grew steadily louder, the sound coming from the south. The two men listened intently. Though nothing could be seen from where they stood under the trees, they stared anxiously at the fragments of sky which showed through the leafy canopy.

Yashimoto looked at his watch. With a frown he said, 'Morning reconnaissance.'

Satugawa nodded agreement. Their heads turned slowly to follow the sound of the aircraft they could not see as it passed to the westward. When it had faded into the distance, Yashimoto said, 'Never closer than a mile, I'd say. And not as low as usual.'

'It reminds me, Captain. Something I must discuss with you. The tests tomorrow night.'

Yashimoto's head came up in alarm. 'Nothing wrong is there?'

'No. It's not that. It's a question of method. Before we move the boat to the centre of the basin we will have to strip off the camouflage. That will be quite a task. Once in position in the basin we will flood tanks and submerge. Say, to twenty-five metres. Then check to see how the repairs stand up to pressure. But that pressure will be entirely external.'

Yashimoto's face arranged itself in a puzzled frown. 'And so? What of it?'

The Engineer Officer avoided the challenging stare. 'If that test is satisfactory we have to make another. With the boat surfaced, we will shut the upper and lower hatches, flood the conning-tower and raise the pressure in it by pumping in compressed air. The angled steel plates – those to be bolted into position over the cavity where the main pressure hull meets the vertical wall of the conning-tower – those plates are outside. The correct place, since external pressure will force them against the cavity in the pressure hull which they cover when the boat is submerged. It is necessary, however, to subject them also to *internal* pressure. Something equivalent to the stresses imposed by the explosion of depth-charges – the whiplash effect.'

Yashimoto continued to frown, pinching his nose between thumb and forefinger. 'Yes, Chief. We have discussed this before, though not in such detail. What is the point you want to make?'

Satugawa looked into the trees, away from the Captain's disconcerting stare. 'The second test will be the most exacting. If it fails – I don't think it will –', he added hurriedly, 'but if it fails we shall need another day in the creek. During that time the boat must continue to be concealed from observation from the air. For this reason I think we should reverse the testing order. Make the second test first.'

'I don't follow.'

'We can make the second test while still alongside and without removing the camouflage. That's the point, sir.'

Yashimoto gazed at the trees, fingered his beard. 'It's a good point, Chief. Yes – we'll do that.'

Satugawa's face showed relief. 'I think it's the logical thing to do, Captain.'

After a brief chat about progress of the repair work they parted, the Engineer Officer going off in the direction of the foundry while Yashimoto made for the submarine. He was in good spirits. It was nine o'clock, the real heat of the day had not yet come, and under the trees the early morning air was still cool. To talk with the Engineer Officer was always reassuring; the man was so intelligent, so competent, that it could not be otherwise. Yashimoto had little doubt that the coming tests would be successful. Buoyed by these thoughts he began to hum a simple, repetitive folktune, one which his wife Akiko often sang when she was doing the things she enjoyed, like working in the miniature garden, or painting, or arranging flowers. It would be marvellous to get home, to be with her again. Absolutely marvellous. But Kure and the Inland Sea were far away, and the war in the Pacific at a difficult stage. It seemed that I-357 would be based on Penang for a long time to come. He sighed, was momentarily sad, until pictures of life in Penang, Masna in so many of them, restored his cheerful mood.

Soon we sail, soon we sail, he hummed, putting the words to Akiko's folktune: *At dawn we dive, at dawn we dive* he added, as he walked beneath the trees with a new bounce to his step.

*

193

Barratt arrived on the bridge looking like a coal-heaver, every visible part of him blackened and streaked with perspiration. Saying, 'I've got her, Number One,' he turned *Restless* away from the island and set course for the south-west, towards the coast and clear of the channel used by coasters and dhows making for Mocimboa da Praia. 'I'll brief you in a moment,' he said. 'But there are a few things that won't wait. Tell Dodds I want him up here. Double quick.'

The First Lieutenant went to the phone, spoke to the Navigating Officer who soon came clattering up a bridge ladder. He made for the dusky figure in the Captain's chair. 'Sir?' He did his best to look as if the Captain's appearance was normal.

'Out there on the starboard bow,' Barratt pointed. 'There are three tall casuarina trees on top of that hill. See them, Pilot?'

Dodds stared in the given direction. 'Yes, sir.'

'We'll remain on this course until they are difficult to see. Then we'll turn on to a patrol line, two or three miles of it, which keeps them in sight. Got that?'

Dodds said he had.

'I want you to standby to fix our position, and plot the patrol line when I give the word.'

'May I use radar, sir?'

'No you may not. Radar is shut down and will stay that way. Use the old bow and arrow.'

A prodigious frown accompanied Dodds's mild, 'Aye, aye, sir,' as he went to the compass platform.

Barratt kept the casuarina trees under close observation, first with the naked eye and then, as the distance increased, with binoculars. Though the trees were tall and on high ground, their image was blurred by distance and early morning mist. When five miles from them Barratt decided to go no further. 'Get a fix *now*, Pilot,' he ordered, 'and plot the patrol line.' He turned to the First Lieutenant. 'I want a masthead lookout, Number One – plus doubling up the bridge lookouts, and two officers on the bridge until further notice. Object of the exercise? – to keep the casuarina trees under observation. What to look for? – smoke near the trees by day, fire at night. Reason why? – there is a Japanese submarine in the creek and Katu has a pal on the island who will light a fire near the casuarinas if the Jap begins to move. When you've got those lookouts posted I want you to take over again so that I can clean myself and get something to eat.'

The First Lieutenant's astonishment was manifested by an unbelieving frown and a delighted grin. 'D'you mean to say it really is there, sir?'

'It is, Number One, and I trust it doesn't leave before we're ready to deal with it.'

Much happened during the next few hours while *Restless* steamed up and down her patrol line on a glass-smooth sea, the heat growing more intense as the sun climbed into a cloudless sky. On Barratt's orders the shore party had been told to rest until further orders. He himself, changed and breakfasted, had gone back to the bridge at eight o'clock. In the chartroom he briefed the First Lieutenant on the shore party's expedition, sketching in the details of what they had seen, and what Katu had heard from Aba Said's father.

'What's the plan, sir? Are we reporting this to Kilindini?'

Barratt shook his head. 'No. Not yet. That Jap won't be tempted out if he knows we're here. W/T silence is imperative. As to a plan . . .' He shrugged. 'There isn't one yet. I think I've got the beginnings of an idea. Prefer not to talk about it until it's taken some sort of shape.'

'Neutrality's the problem isn't it?' The First Lieutenant eyed him keenly. 'Pity the islands are Portuguese. If they were ours the RAF could bash the Jap.'

Barratt was looking at the casuarinas through binoculars. 'Could they?' he asked in a disinterested way. He put down the binoculars. 'Those trees are showing up better. Mist must be lifting.' His manner became suddenly businesslike. 'Now, Number One. Next item on the agenda. Get Morrow to see that the loot due to Katu is placed in his catamaran by 0800. Have the catamaran and motorboat ready for lowering at

195

that time. The motorboat is to tow Katu back to his fishing grounds.'

'Do you want Morrow to take it away, sir?'

'No. He's to rest with the others when he's dealt with Katu. Put a petty officer in the boat.'

With the catamaran in tow and a waving, smiling Katu and his possessions in it, the motorboat shoved off and made for the fishing grounds north of Tambuzi Island. The petty officer in charge had orders to return to *Restless* as soon as possible.

It was clear to those on the bridge that the Captain was in an uncommunicative mood. For most of the time he sat hunched in the chair on the compass platform, the white tennis hat tipped forward to protect his eyes from the sun. Occasionally he used binoculars to check on the casuarina trees, but for the most part he sat silent, deep in thought, gazing into space.

'I wish the Old Man would go and get his head down. He looks clapped out,' the First Lieutenant said to Lawson, the officer-of-the-watch.

'Not surprising. He's been on the go for most of the last twenty-four hours.' Through binoculars Lawson was examining a coaster coming in from seaward, P O R T U G A L in large white letters painted along its side. It was on a course likely to take it several miles clear of *Restless*. 'I imagine that little chap is heading for Mocimboa da Praia.' He put down the binoculars.

'He must wonder what we're doing here,' said the First Lieutenant. 'He's by no means the first coaster or dhow to have seen us in this neck of the woods in the last few days.'

'Does it matter? Remember the Old Man's story? If asked, we're looking for *Fort Nebraska* survivors. Men last heard of on a raft which may have drifted ashore on an uninhabited island.' Lawson went on, his voice lowered. 'Fantastic, isn't it? That submarine being there, I mean. I never really thought it would be. Did you, Number One?'

'No. To be honest I didn't. Have to give the Old Man full marks for following his hunch.' The First Lieutenant looked across to where the Captain sat. 'Can't imagine what he's going to do next. He still refuses to break W/T silence. There'll be one hell of a row when we get back.'

Lawson raised his binoculars again. 'I suppose we'll hang about until the Jap decides to leg it, whenever that may be. Then we'll pounce.'

'I wouldn't put my money on that, Geoff. If the Jap does move it'll be under cover of darkness. The Old Man says the distance from the huts to the submarine is about four hundred yards. They're apparently on opposite sides of the creek. Could be difficult to see what's going on in the dark at that distance. But even if the Africans do see, it'll take time to get somebody up to the casuarinas to light a fire before the boat shoves off. And more time before we've steamed round to the other side of the island.'

'Have you told the Old Man what you feel?'

'No. Hadn't thought it through until about five minutes ago. But I will tell him. Once we . . .'

The First Lieutenant's sentence was interrupted by a loud, 'Hear that,' from Barratt who was pointing to starboard.

Almost immediately afterwards the starboard lookout reported, 'Aircraft – green one three zero – flying low – distant.'

'Catalina.' Barratt spat the word as he glared at the flying boat through binoculars. 'I wish he'd bugger off.'

The Catalina came closer, its fuselage glinting in the sunlight, the roundel and squadron letters clearly visible, engines muffling all other sounds. It passed over *Restless*, wobbled its wings in salute, and climbed steeply before flying on to the north.

Twenty-three

The unwelcome visit of the Catalina provided the opportunity for Hamilton to tell the Captain of his misgivings. 'We're patrolling a line to the south of the island, sir. We can see the casuarinas but we can't see the entrance to the creek because it's in the north shielded from us by high land. If there's any hitch, if the Africans are late in spotting what's happening and getting the fire going at the casuarinas, the Jap may get clear and dive before we've had time to cover the distance to the entrance. Isn't that a bit of a snag?'

Barratt blinked weary eyes at the younger man. 'It certainly, is, Number One. It's been worrying me. But there's no easy answer. To really bottle up the sod we should take station outside the entrance to the creek. But if we do that we'll be seen and he won't come out. Said's dad says there's a skimmer on guard duty at the mouth of the creek and we know there are sentry posts along the narrows. So what do we do? By keeping a low profile here we've a chance of catching Mister Bloody Nippon with his pants down. Show ourselves at the entrance and he won't lower them. I haven't gone to all these lengths, W/T silence, shut down radar, ignoring signals, in order to blow it all by strutting about where we can be seen.'

It was an unusually long dissertation for the Captain, but the First Lieutenant sensed that he'd been glad of the opportunity to discuss the problem.

'It is a difficult situation, sir. I wonder . . .' He hesitated. 'I wonder if it wouldn't be a good idea to pass the buck to Kilindini. Tell them where the Jap is and ask for orders. At least *Restless* will get the credit for having found the boat.'

With a dismissive flourish of his hand Barratt said, 'I don't give a damn about the credit, Number One. My objective is to destroy that submarine and her crew. For the last time, let me make it quite plain. We are not, repeat not, going to break W/T silence.'

The First Lieutenant looked away. 'I see, sir,' he said quietly, adding, 'And the signal of recall?'

'That's my business, Number One.' Barratt's manner had become frosty. 'You needn't worry. Your yardarm's clear.'

The rebuke was not lost on the First Lieutenant. 'Sorry, sir. I didn't mean to butt in. It's only that – well . . .'

'Well what?'

'I'm worried about what the consequences might be for you, sir.'

Barratt got up from the Captain's Chair, stretched and yawned. 'Leave the worrying to me, Number One,' he said with a thin-lipped smile. 'I'm going to have a rest now. I'll think about the problem of where we should be, north or south of the island. That and sleep are my major preoccupations at the moment.'

The First Lieutenant shook his head as he watched the Captain go down the bridge ladder. Poor chap, he thought. Glad I'm not in his shoes. He joined Lawson at the bridge screen. The Gunnery Officer regarded him quizzically. 'Did you tell him what you thought?'

'Yes. He's as worried about it as I am. But it's not easy.' The First Lieutenant repeated what the Captain had told him.

'So what happens next?'

'We stick to the patrol line for the time being. He's gone down to have a rest and think about it.'

'Not surprised. Long time no zizz for him.'

The First Lieutenant focused binoculars on the distant trees. The mist had gone and the stark silhouette of the casuarinas was visible with the naked eye. 'I'm worried about the Old Man,' he said.

'Yes. He looks absolutely knackered.'

'It's not that. The trouble is . . .' The First Lieutenant

lowered his voice. 'This thing's become a personal vendetta.'

'Changi Gaol?'

'Of course.'

'Incredible, Peter. No, I can't think why. Is that all? Good.'

Hutchison put down the phone, looked at the inquiring faces round the table in the operations room. 'That was the Squadron duty officer. They've received a signal from Dar-es-Salaam. He says G-for-George has just landed there with engine trouble. Being checked now. Its Captain says he flew over *Restless* at 0815 this morning, eight miles south-east of Cape Ulu. She was steaming at about 15/17 knots on a north-easterly course. Neither he nor the ship made any attempt to communicate with each other. Otherwise everything appeared to be normal. Except . . .' Enjoying the moment, Hutchison paused. 'Except that a few miles north of *Restless* he sighted her motorboat towing a catamaran with a lone black man in it. They were heading for Tambuzi Island.'

'Where's that, Jakes?' The question came from a four-ring Captain RN with sandy hair, sunken cheeks and friendly grey eyes.

'Here, sir.' The RNVR Lieutenant pointed with the cue tip to a black dot on the wall chart.

'Motorboat towing the catamaran *away* from *Restless* – extraordinary,' said Captain (D).

'Some sort of rescue operation, I imagine,' said the four-ring Captain. 'Catamaran in trouble. *Restless* sends help. Lone African requests a tow home. The RN in its AA role.'

'For me, *Restless* gives the impression of having withdrawn from the War,' said the SOO.

A perspiring Captain (D) glared at the punkah. 'The squeak's stopped but the performance is pathetic.' He puffed out crimson cheeks. 'Can't make out what Barratt's up to. He's been down *there* for the best part of twenty-four hours. In the area generally – along the coast and among the islands – since early on the twenty-first. That's – let's see.' He glanced at the calendar. 'About fifty-four hours plus.' Unfolding a

200

clean linen handkerchief he began a systematic mopping of his face and neck.

The SOO squinted down the length of his nose. 'Since when,' he said, 'we've heard from her once. The signal informing us that she'd picked up the *Fort Nebraska* survivor. She neither acknowledged nor replied to ours of the twenty-first, nor that of the twenty-second recalling her.'

Hutchison held up a hand as if asking to be heard. 'In fairness to Lieutenant Commander Barratt, sir – he did exchange Aldis lamp signals with Catalina S-for-Sugar in Rovuma Bay on the twenty-first. Passed that "Getting warmer, W/T silence imperative" message.' The Flight Lieutenant looked across to Camilla at the far end of the room, to be rewarded with the faintest smile of approbation.

The four-ring Captain – James Pelly, the Admiral's Chief Staff Officer – short title CSO – looked relieved. 'Oh well. I'm glad he did that.' Pelly was for the first time involved in what had become known at Naval HQ as *The Barratt Business*.

Captain (D) exchanged a barely perceptible smile with the SOO. They both knew that Jim Pelly had distinguished himself in destroyers earlier in the war. There was little doubt where his sympathies lay.

'And that', said the SOO, 'was the last we heard from him. I need hardly remind you, sir . . .' He regarded the Chief Staff Officer with the lugubrious expression of a spaniel, '. . . that we require *Restless* here before midnight on the twenty-sixth. The carrier arrives AM on the twenty-seventh.'

'Twenty-eighth,' corrected the CSO. 'The signal amending her ETA came in this morning.'

The SOO's eyebrows arched. 'Why haven't we had it, Jakes?'

'We have, sir.' Jakes looked mildly surprised. 'With the first batch this morning.'

'I wasn't shown it.'

'You initialled the clipboard copy, sir.'

'Did I?' The SOO's tone suggested he hadn't. 'Well,

anyway, *Restless* has to be here to augment the forces available to carry out an A/S sweep in advance of the carrier's arrival – and to help with close escort for the last fifty miles in.'

Captain (D)'s expression was bleak. 'Trouble is, CSO, the Flotilla has dispersed: two are at sea off Diego Suarez, there's one in Mahé, one refitting at the Cape, and one with that last southbound convoy. That leaves me with only two fleet destroyers for escort duties, *Rampage* and *Restless*, plus a couple of corvettes and three A/S whalers. We're pretty thin on the ground just now. With the Japanese resuming submarine operations in the Mozambique Channel this represents a bit of a headache.'

'Yes,' the CSO agreed. 'I'm sure it does. But now, about *Restless*. I know it's difficult to understand Barratt's failure to reply to signals, particularly the recall signal. Of course his behaviour seems incomprehensible but . . .' He paused, twiddled the signet ring on his finger. 'The man must have a reason. I think, gentlemen, that he knows where the submarine is. He's waiting for it to put to sea. When it does he'll attack it. That's why he's going to a great deal of trouble to ensure it doesn't know *he's* there. I can't think of any other explanation that makes sense.'

'So what do we do, CSO?' Captain (D) spread his hands in a gesture of despair.

The CSO gazed hopefully at the wall chart, examined his fingernails, smiled amiably. 'I think we give him one more chance. Tell me,' he turned to Hutchison. 'If this weather holds, any reason why a Catalina shouldn't land on the sea close to *Restless*?'

The Flight Lieutenant said, 'None at all, sir. No problem. But I don't understand.'

'Good.' The CSO smiled again. 'I suggest that you, SOO, or Captain (D) if he'd prefer it, join the Catalina for tomorrow morning's reconnaissance. It means an early start,' he warned. 'But if *Restless* is still down there the Catalina lands close to her, and you ask the destroyer to send across a boat. When it arrives you request transfer to *Restless*. You have orders from the Admiral which you have to deliver in person. Once on board you ask Barratt what the deuce he's playing at.' This time the CSO smiled with his teeth but not with his eyes. 'If you're dissatisfied with his reply you have my authority to relieve him of his command and hand it over to the First Lieutenant. You inform him that *Restless* is to return here forthwith and you remain in the ship to see that she does. You send Barratt back in the Catalina. I think that's probably the best way of tackling a difficult situation.'

The SOO shifted in his chair, looked uncomfortable. 'I do think it would be more appropriate if Captain (D) went, sir.'

Captain (D)'s blue eyes twinkled with pleasure. 'I shall be absolutely delighted to do so,' he said. 'Always wanted to sample a Catalina.'

A phone on the SOO's desk rang. He picked it up. 'SOO speaking. Oh yes. Who from? DNI Whitehall. Good, let's have it?' The SOO directed a blank look at the faces round the table as he listened to the voice at the other end. 'Very good. Thank you.' He put down the phone. 'That was Godley – Fleet Intelligence Officer. The reply from the Director of Naval Intelligence has come at last. His Portuguese oppo reports that there is no Japanese submarine in any Mozambique port. Nor has there been since the War began.'

Hutchison looked at the wall clock – 1115. Don Tuke would be taking off at noon. There was just time enough.

The hyper-active state of Barratt's mind made sleep impossible and though close to exhaustion he abandoned the attempt not long after reaching the sea-cabin. Awake, he contemplated the deckhead above his pillow with tired eyes, seeing nothing but the red light and the pictures in his mind: the tree-covered submarine lying against the bank below the bluff, its bows, according to Aba Said's father, facing the end of the narrows. The image of the Japanese Captain's face, formerly that of the commandant of Changi Gaol, replaced the submarine; the slanted eyes arrogant, the hoarse voice mouthing absurd pidgin English: *Boat is gleen like tlee*

– enemy think is cleek – bow tubes command nallows – high land plotects boat flom enemy bombs, also guns. So, English captain, what can you do? Nothing - you must wait.

Barratt cursed aloud. The imagery was so real, his anguish so fierce, that his body shook with emotion. There won't be any forcing of the narrows, any attack from the air, my nasty little yellow man, but by God you're going to pay for what you've done.

He dismissed the imaginary conversation, shook away the images: that sort of thing was silly, unnecessary, led nowhere. What was needed now was constructive thought. He got off the bunk, helped himself to a glass of water, sat on the settee thinking, his head buried in his hands. Within the next few minutes he'd made up his mind. What had been the beginnings of an idea ever since *Operation Maji*, began to take shape.

That, he said to himself, is how I shall do it.

'You sent for me, sir?' The First Lieutenant, stood in the doorway of the sea-cabin.

'Yes.' Barratt's half smile enlivened an otherwise listless face, the eyes red with exhaustion. 'I'm working on an idea, Number One. A plan of attack. If I can sort it into practical shape I'll tell you about it. The time's short, and there's a lot to be done. To develop the idea I'll have to chat to Taylor, to the TGM, the Coxswain, the Shipwright, Aba Said, Morrow and maybe others. I'll see them in my day-cabin. There's more room there. So don't be disturbed by the various comings and goings. First two on my list are Taylor and the TGM. Get them to report to me there in ten minutes, will you?'

The First Lieutenant began to say something, but stopped in mid-sentence. After a moment of strained silence, the two men avoiding each other's eyes, he said, 'Aye, aye, sir,' and went along the passageway. Barratt waited before following him down the ladder which led to the wardroom and officers' accommodation.

*

'That's roughly what I have in mind.' Barratt swung his chair round from the desk, handed a sheet of notepaper to the RNVR Lieutenant sitting on the settee near him.

Restless's Torpedo Officer, John Taylor, examined the rough pencil sketch before passing it to the Torpedo Gunner's Mate who sat near him. 'Doesn't look too complicated, McGlashan. What d'you think?'

With a non-committal, 'We'll see, sir,' the Petty Officer took the sketch. After a minute or so of frowning concentration he looked up. 'A bit unusual, I'd say. But it should work.'

Barratt seemed pleased. 'You'll see from the notes I've made that the overall weight mustn't exceed two hundred pounds. Any difficulty there?'

The TGM shook his head. 'It means bleeding out about half the charge. But Amatol is stable enough. No problem there, sir.'

The Torpedo Officer agreed. 'The buoyancy drum – size, rate of sinking, etcetera – is the only difficult part,' he said. 'And the primer will have to be modified. Both will involve a good deal of trial and error. We'll need the motorboat for that.'

Barratt glanced at the clock on his desk. 'You can have the motorboat and anything else you need, Taylor. But time is the essence of the contract. It's now 0945. Report back to me if you have any serious problems. You should finish testing and have the thing ready by 1600. Think you can manage that?'

The Torpedo Officer turned to the TGM. 'That gives us about six hours. We should have it ready well within that time. What d'you think, TGM?'

'Aye, sir. We'll have it ready.'

The note of confidence was sweet music to Barratt.

Next to be called to the day-cabin were the Shipwright, Petty Officer Trewhela, known to the ship's company as 'Chippy' – and the Coxswain. Once again the Captain opened proceedings with a pencil sketch; the requirement this time was less exacting. 'A sort of stretcher, made of wood,' he explained.

'It's got to be strong enough for the job. Allow for rough handling, but keep the weight down.'

The Shipwright, a West Countryman with beetling eyebrows, tufts of hair growing from his cheekbones, and fierce dark eyes which belied his good nature said, 'Leave it to me, sir. There's no problem.'

'I'd like you to see to the fastenings, Coxswain, and the release and flooding gear.' Barratt took the sketch from the Shipwright, passed it to CPO Gibbs. The Coxswain studied it briefly. 'Rope strops, Senhouse slips, toggles and lanyards. Should be straightforward.'

'The handling will probably be in complete darkness. Keep the toggles and Senhouse slips plumb on top of the float where they can be found by feel.'

'We'll watch that, sir.'

'Let me know if serious problems arise. I want you to have everything on the top line by 1600. All the bits and pieces – yours and the torpedo department's – to be on deck for assembling by 1600, at which time report to me.'

'Forward of the quarterdeck screen, sir?' suggested the Coxswain.

'Yes. That'll do fine. Pass the word to the TGM.'

'Aye, aye, sir.'

Last to come to the Captain's cabin were Peter Morrow and Aba Said, the latter still goggle-eyed after a rambling inspection of the white man's strange ship. Barratt's formidable series of questions about Maji Island, the Japanese submarine, the routine of its crew, particularly that of the sentries, were put to the African by Morrow who relayed the answers to the Captain.

Do the Portuguese authorities come to the island? The last time was three years back when a police official came to make inquiries about a wanted man. Where is the nearest Native Commissioner? At Mocimboa da Praia. Do the Maji people go there to see him? Not much. Usually to report births and deaths, though sometimes this is long after the event. Do they pay taxes? No. We are too poor.

206

The interrogation finished, Barratt said, 'Tell him I am very grateful for this information. Also that we will return him to Maji before daylight tomorrow. Tell him, also, that I may need his help against the Japanese tonight. If he gives it he'll get the same reward as Katu did.'

Morrow told Aba Said what the Captain had said; the young African alternately frowned and grinned, the former whenever the Japanese were mentioned, the latter in a big way when Morrow got on to the subject of rewards. 'He likes the idea of the loot, sir,' explained the Sub-Lieutenant, 'but he's anti-Jap anyway. The fisherman they killed that first morning was his brother.'

The discussions at an end, they left the cabin about the time the shrill note of a boatswain's call sounded over the ship's broadcast to be followed by a disembodied voice announcing the time – 'Ten hundred'.

Exhausted but relieved, decisions made and plans in hand, Barratt stretched out on the settee. With his mind at rest he fell asleep.

Twenty-four

An hour later than expected the motorboat returned to *Restless* in mid-morning and was hoisted inboard. Its Coxswain, Petty Officer Benham, reported to the First Lieutenant that Katu and his catamaran had got safely home.

'Home?' said the First Lieutenant. 'I thought our contract was to deliver him to the fishing grounds off Tambuzi Island?'

'He lives on a little island a few miles beyond Tambuzi, sir. Mr Morrow told me that Katu was afraid he'd be in trouble with his wife for being absent without leave. When we got to the fishing grounds he kept pointing to this island we could see three or four miles ahead. I could tell from his antics that he was worried, wanted to get there quick. So I towed him to it. His old woman and some kids came running down to the beach. She was shouting at him before he got ashore. Like she wasn't too pleased. Then when they helped haul the catamaran ashore, she saw what he had in it and she started laughing and patting him on the back.'

The First Lieutenant said, 'Typical woman. You'll have to take the motorboat away again shortly, Benham. Lieutenant Taylor and the TGM want it for some tests or other. Don't ask me what they are because I haven't a clue. Captain's idea.'

To an audience of men off watch, not short of cheerful and ribald asides, the motorboat drew away from *Restless* and made for sheltered water in the lee of a low-lying islet south of the patrol line. Before leaving, it had been loaded under the supervision of the Torpedo Officer, the Coxswain and the TGM. Among the items lowered into it were a number of empty oil drums of various sizes, lengths of rope, shackles,

208

and Senhouse slips; last of all was a heavy, rounded object concealed by a service blanket. There was much speculation and helpful advice from onlookers, including improvisations from *Roll out the Barrel* and *Life on the Ocean Wave*.

The Torpedo Officer pretended not to hear, while the Coxswain gave the audience a stony stare, easily interpreted as *you lot just wait until I get back aboard*. The TGM's two finger gesture required no interpretation.

On *Restless*'s bridge the officer-of-the-watch gave wheel and engine orders, turbines whirred and the destroyer gathered way, a tumbling swirl of foam at her stern.

Late that morning Hutchison drove Camilla to the Mombasa Club in his ancient Jeep. After a swim they sat talking in the shade of large, shiny-leafed, tropical trees, enjoying a pre-lunch drink.

'You remember what Haddingham said about Barratt being wild, doing mad things? All that stuff?'

'I do.' Camilla's calm blue eyes contemplating him over the rim of her glass mesmerized Hutchison. He looked at her with blank adoration.

'Well,' she prompted. 'Go on.'

He sighed, pulled himself together. 'Haddingham liked him. Regarded him as a good friend. He wouldn't have said what he did about him unless he'd meant it.'

'Where is this leading to, Hutch?'

'Well, he's presumably still capable of doing mad things. Particularly since he's lost his wife. The *Fort N* business on top of it.'

'I don't think it necessarily follows, but go on,' she said coolly.

'We've both met Barratt briefly. I liked him. Don't know about you, but to me he seemed a decent sort of chap.'

'Oh, come on, Hutch. Get to the point.'

The Flight Lieutenant took a deep breath, looked away. 'I thought he should be warned about CSO's plan for tomorrow. Told that the Great and the Good are not amused by his Nelson act. If Captain (D) goes down there in the

209

morning . . .' He shrugged, tasted the Pimms. 'The consequences for Barratt could be extremely serious.'

'So?'

Camilla's level gaze again deflected his thoughts for a
moment; sighing, he once more collected them. 'I felt something ought to be done. I had a word with Peter Ward. Don
Tuke is flying this afternoon's Catalina to the south. Took
off at noon. I thought . . .'

A burst of raucous laughter came from the nearby pool.
Camilla put on sunglasses, looked across. 'Charles Peaslake,'
she said. 'Would be him, wouldn't it.' She turned back,
sampled her Pimms once more. 'What did you think?'

'I'd like to get your reaction.'

'Why mine?'

'Because you spoke out in his defence the other day. And
because you have a more than passing interest in *Restless*.'

'Have I?' She was a picture of wide-eyed innocence.

'Yes. Sandy Hamilton is Barratt's Number One. If Barratt
really is haywire, puts up a monster black, some of the mud
may stick to Hamilton. Why didn't he intervene, etcetera?'

'Mixed metaphors, Hutch. But I get the drift. I *have*
worried about that – the mud, I mean. But I'm sure Barratt
is intelligent enough to know the consequences of what he's
doing.'

Hutchison looked doubtful. 'I wonder. People's emotions
often upset their judgement. He's every reason to be
emotionally mixed-up right now.'

She tapped the rim of her glass with well-manicured finger-
nails.

'I wouldn't do that, Camilla.' He pushed her hand aside.
'Every time the glass rings a sailor drowns at sea.'

'Rubbish,' she said, but stopped tapping. 'Look, Hutch.
If something really helpful to Barratt is being done, I'm all
for it. Let's leave it at that.'

The motorboat headed for the break in the reef. Beyond it
a strip of blue sea lay placid as a lake, the white margin of
beach shimmering in the noonday sun. In the channel through

the reef the sea was shallow, gnarled mounds of coral looming beneath the keel before falling away into the deeper waters of the lagoon.

The motorboat nosed slowly in, the bowman sounding with a leadline, calling the depths. At two and a half fathoms anchor was dropped. It took time after that to assemble the odd-looking contraption which quickly became known as The Rig. When it was ready it was lowered over the side, an operation accompanied by noisy exertion and muttered oaths from the TGM and the two torpedomen assisting him. The Torpedo Officer stood by with a stop-watch offering encouragement and advice. Midshipman Tripp, at his side, was responsible for entries in the notebook.

Several changes had to be made with the flotation gear, various sizes and combinations of empty drums being tested before it was decided to concentrate on two of medium size.

'Between them they give positive buoyancy plus a useful margin,' said the Torpedo Officer. 'Flooding one will provide the negative buoyancy needed. It's a question then of timing the rate of sinking and adjusting the flooding accordingly.'

'Not so easy,' said the TGM. Like the others he wore only shorts, his brown body glistening with perspiration, his hair wet and matted.

So the tests went on. Time and again the TGM would pull a lanyard and call, 'Flooding *now*.' The Torpedo Officer would start the stop-watch; after an interval of time the TGM would announce, 'Bottomed *now*,' the Torpedo Officer would give the sinking time and the midshipman would record it. Then would begin once more the laborious business of raising the sunken rig, securing it alongside, lifting the flooded drum on board and emptying it. That done, the whole process was repeated. And repeated it had to be, many times, before Taylor shouted. 'Marvellous. That's just what we need – exactly two minutes. Well done, TGM. Now for the swim.'

The TGM looked up, an eyebrow raised. 'Safe here, is it, sir?'

'Absolutely. Sharks won't go through shallow channels to get inside a reef. Not even to eat sailors.'

'Are *you* going to swim, sir?' inquired the midshipman with a note of disbelief.

'Of course I am. So are you. Petty Officer Benham will take over the stop-watch and notebook.' The Torpedo Officer looked round. 'Right. We have four swimmers; you Tripp, the volunteers – Corrigan and Wilson – and myself. Let's get starko for a start.'

Following the Torpedo Officer's example, the swimmers took off their shorts and stood nude but cheerful waiting for the next instalment.

'Fine-looking lot,' observed the Torpedo Officer with a sardonic smile. 'Now we come to the drill. We get into the water first. Hang on to the starboard side, waiting and watching. When the PO shouts *GO* we swim flat out, parallel to the beach. When he shouts *STOP* we stop . . .'

'Logical,' observed the midshipman.

The Torpedo Officer glared at him, '. . . and tread water. You, Tripp, will then measure the distance covered by each swimmer. For our purposes we'll take the average of the three.'

'How will I know the distances?' inquired the midshipman.

'Because, my lad, before the swim begins you will have swum to the beach and taken station opposite the motorboat. When you hear *STOP* you will drop a marker, stride smartly forward – a stride to a yard – until you are opposite the first swimmer when you will drop another marker. He'll be the slowest. Ditto the second, ditto the third. He'll be the fastest.'

'What do I use for markers, sir?'

'These.' The Torpedo Officer stooped, picked up a small linen bag. 'Tie this round your waist until you're on the beach. It contains four small pieces of wood.'

'Jolly good.' Tripp took the bag, peered into it. 'Clever. I wonder who thought of it?'

The Torpedo Officer ignored the impertinence.

*

212

At three o'clock in the afternoon Barratt woke from deep sleep, pleasantly shocked to find that it was so late. After a shower and change he went to the bridge where the Navigating Officer was on watch with Midshipman Galpin. Whereas the sky had been clear of cloud when last seen by Barratt it was now seven-tenths overcast, dark masses of cumulo-nimbus moving in from the north-east, the screen of rain beneath it rent by distant lightning.

'What's the barometer doing?' he asked the Navigating Officer.

'Falling, sir. Nothing dramatic but I think we'll be getting that rain before long.'

With a non-committal, 'H'm,' Barratt went to a wing of the bridge, looked along the side. 'I see the motorboat's been hoisted. When did they get back?'

'About an hour ago, sir.'

'Is all well?'

'I believe so. Lieutenant Taylor and the TGM are busy with the rig now.' Dodds pointed aft. 'You can see them forward of the quarterdeck screen. The Chief ERA and some of his people are giving a hand. Cutting and welding.'

'Good. Any idea how the Shipwright's getting on?'

'He's modified that wooden frame. The TGM has tested it for buoyancy. Says it's okay, sir. Looks a bit like a sledge now.'

'I'm glad to get the news,' said Barratt drily. 'Nobody else seems to have thought of telling me.'

'Your orders were that you were not to be disturbed, sir. Unless wanted on the bridge.'

'Ah, yes. My fault. Number One about?'

'In his cabin resting. He's got the last dog-watch. He's a bit short of sleep. Up all night while you were away with the shore party – and most of today.'

'Of course. I'd forgotten that. Inconsiderate of me. Glad you mentioned it, Dodds.' Barratt trained binoculars on Maji's skyline where the casuarinas stood stark and solitary against bundles of grey cloud. Taking the strap from his neck he folded it round the binoculars, put them back in the bin marked 'CO'. 'I'm going to see how Torps and company are getting on. Be back soon.'

When the Captain had gone Dodds went to the bridge chart-table where a midshipman was plotting the destroyer's position. 'Not bad,' he said looking over the young man's shoulder. 'Could be neater. Your numerals are too large. Small is beautiful, Galpin.'

'I do my best, sir.'

'I suppose so,' said Dodds absent-mindedly. 'The Captain's looking a lot better since his rest.'

Galpin nodded, a faraway look in his eyes. 'I wonder if the messman's going to give us mangoes tonight. Last lot were absolutely marvellous.'

The Navigating Officer grunted disapproval. 'Food and women. All you mids ever think of these days.'

'I didn't say anything about women, sir.'

'No. But you think about them, Galpin.'

Barratt was in his day-cabin making notes for the night's briefing when the bridge phone rang. It was the officer-of-the-watch, Lawson, to report that the storm had broken. There was heavy rain, though the thunder and lightning were still some distance away. 'The casuarinas are no longer visible, sir. Nor the island.'

'Is it blowing?'

'Yes. About force six. More in the squalls.'

'Awnings furled, ventilators trimmed?'

'Yes, sir.'

'Good. I'm coming up.' Barratt resented the interruption; the briefing notes were complicated, required concentration. He'd hoped the storm would pass astern but obviously it hadn't. For God's sake, why now? he thought on his way to the bridge. I'd have welcomed it tonight, but not yet. Heavy rain not only shuts down visibility but puts out fires. So much, then, for the Headman's signal if it were made now. Barratt panicked. The submarine might be about to leave, was already leaving? *Restless* was on the blind side of the island, at least five miles from the entrance; more when she was at

214

the seaward end of the patrol line. Anything from fifteen to twenty minutes steaming at twenty knots. Fuel remaining was getting dangerously low so full speed was out, even for a short time. If the Jap *was* ready to go, the storm might be all that he was waiting for.

He made for the bridge, the rain slapping into his face, its sizzling roar shutting out other sounds. By the time he reached the compass platform, drenched but determined, he'd made up his mind. 'Port fifteen, revolutions for twenty knots,' he ordered, raising his voice as he spoke down the voice-pipe. To Lawson he said, 'A/S and radar to resume normal sweeps. Navigating Officer on the bridge, double quick.'

Lawson passed the orders to the A/S and radar cabinets, and to the wardroom.

Almost immediately the bridge-speaker began to relay the high pitched *pings* of asdic transmissions; the bridge radar repeater, the PPI, came to life, reflecting in green light the sweep of the scanner and the echoes it portrayed, an electronic picture of the coast and islands glowing and fading with each sweep.

A breathless, frowning Dodds arrived on the bridge. 'Sir?'

'I'm shifting the patrol line to the west,' Barratt told him. 'We'll settle for a position from which we can cover the creek entrance by radar without being seen from the creek. According to Aba Said, the sandbanks immediately to the north-east of the entrance are awash at low water. The deeper water, the channel to Mocimboa da Praia, is several miles north of Maji. Aba Said has fished that area for years. From what he says the submarine, if it comes out, will have to head north-west and won't be in water deep enough to dive to periscope depth for about a mile.'

'Surely the Japs will see us, sir. Once we're in position west of the entrance?'

'There's high land on either side. The headlands. We'll have three miles and a headland between us and them.'

'If they do see us I imagine they won't come out?' Dodds

215

put his belief as a question, adding, 'Knowing they're protected by Portugal's neutrality while in there.'

Barratt shrugged, said, 'This rain shows no sign of stopping.' Like everyone else on the bridge he was soaked. The rain was cool and refreshing and oilskins insufferably hot in the tropics, so no one wore them. To Dodds, the Captain was a strange sight: cap-less, his clinging white shirt and shorts browned by the tan they covered, his hair plastered against his skull, his face quaintly serious as he concentrated on the PPI, gobules of rain dripping from the end of his nose.

Unhappy at the forced change of plan at such short notice, Barratt's emotions were confused. He was as upset by his failure to foresee what a tropical rainstorm might have done, as he was anxious about the consequences of shifting *Restless*'s position. It was an advantage that radar would cover the mouth of the creek, and from what Aba Said had reported it was unlikely that the transmissions would be picked up by the submarine – the trees 'planted' over the search receiver, plus the high land round the creek, should mask them. *Restless*'s asdic transmissions would be outside the range of the enemy's hydrophones. So the Japanese shouldn't know she was there. If, however, they had a lookout on the headland, she'd be sighted once the storm passed; in that case the submarine would remain in the creek. Suspecting that their hide-out had been discovered, the Japanese would be doubly alert. *Restless* would have lost the advantage of surprise.

These were the things which worried him. However, by the time *Restless* was in position several miles to the west of the headland, optimism had overcome misgiving and he began to feel that the rainstorm was not, perhaps, the disaster he'd imagined. As it was he now had two workable options: if the submarine came out he'd sink it by gunfire before it could dive. That would save a lot of toil and sweat. If it wasn't ready or willing to leave, he would carry out his original plan during the coming night. Though it was the more difficult option it was the one he favoured and to which, for largely emotional reasons, he felt committed.

216

The important thing now was to get on with the briefing notes. Once the rain stopped and visibility was back to normal he'd go to his cabin and finish them.

Twenty-five

Making good ninety knots, the Catalina on the southbound leg of the afternoon patrol had passed well to seaward of the islands of Temba, Zanzibar and Mafia during the three hours since take-off at Kilindini. If speed was maintained it would be turning in towards the coast near Cape Delgado at about 1550. Its pilot, Flight Lieutenant Donald Tuke, knew that not long afterwards it would cover the area between Tambuzi and Medjumbi where *Restless* had been seen that morning.

A quiet, straightforward, and well-liked man, Tuke was not altogether happy about what he'd been asked to do, more particularly since Hutchison had insisted that secrecy was paramount. 'That's why a lamp signal's no good,' the Flight Lieutenant had said. 'It could be read by others on board, and that's the last thing Barratt would want. He'd be most upset if it was talked about. It contains information confidential to him personally.'

Hutchison had handed over the sealed envelope shortly before take-off and, since Hutch represented the RAF in the operations room at Navy House and enjoyed the confidence of the RN, Tuke had had neither the time nor the inclination to question the wisdom of what he'd been asked to do. It was only when thinking it over during the long boring hours flying down the coast that questions occurred to him which he realized he should have put to Hutchison. What, for example, was the message about? Why hadn't he told him that? Who was it from? The RN? *Confidential to him personally*. What did that mean? Something concerning Barratt's personal affairs? Possibly to do with the death of his wife? It was known in the Squadron that Barratt had requested patrolling Catalinas to keep clear of his ship while he searched

218

for the Japanese submarine – one, incidentally, which every-body else believed had long since left the area. And yet, despite Barratt's known aversion to RAF visitations, here was G-for-George about to make one at Hutchison's request. Tuke wished he'd asked Hutchison that. *Secrecy was paramount*: that sounded more like something operational than personal. So what was it all about?

He gave up. He would do what he'd been asked to do, what he'd undertaken to do. But he'd have felt a lot better if he'd known the answers to those questions.

At 1550, shortly before passing over Tambuzi, G-for-George flew into a heavy rainstorm, obliging Tuke to fly on instruments. With visibility down to zero he decided to abandon the attempt to find *Restless* on that leg. He would, instead, fly on to Porto do Ibo, the southern limit of his patrol, before reversing course and looking for the destroyer on the northbound leg. That would involve another hour's flying during which time the rainstorm should have moved on to the south-west. Having made this decision he asked the navigator for an ETA at a position midway between Med-jumbi and Tambuzi islands. The navigator worked on the chart, jotted the answer on the pad and passed it back – ETA 1710.

An officer in *Restless* who welcomed the Captain's decision to establish a new patrol line was Sandy Hamilton. The First Lieutenant was told of it by the wardroom steward who called him at five with tea and the latest news. Having had four hours' sleep and a shower, Hamilton did a quick change. While doing so he thought about the Captain's decision. It was one which took a major worry from his mind, for it implied that Barratt had abandoned whatever wild-cat scheme he'd harboured. Not that Hamilton really knew what it was – the Captain kept his cards close to his chest – but the tests carried out earlier in the day by the torpedo party had provided some sort of clue and it was one which appalled the First Lieutenant. If Barratt had in mind what it suggested, it confirmed Hamilton's belief that the Captain had lost all sense of proportion in his determination to destroy the submarine.

But the decision to cover the entrance by radar looked as if he'd now decided to wait for the Jap to come out before attempting an attack. Hamilton hoped that Barratt would now decide to break wireless silence and put Kilindini in the picture. That *Restless* had found the submarine would repair some of the damage done in ignoring Captain (D)'s signals, something for which there was no longer any excuse.

Sandy Hamilton finished his cup of tea, munched the last of the shortbread, and made for the bridge.

It was the heaviest rainstorm he'd experienced for a long time and when it had passed, going almost as suddenly as it had come and taking with it the hail and the wind, Petty Officer Hosokawa emerged from the bushes under which he'd been sheltering, shook himself like a dog and studied the sky. 'Come on, boys, the storm is over,' he called over his shoulder.

Two soaked, bedraggled, young men with rifles and bandoliers came from the bushes. Shaking the rain from their bodies, brushing it from their faces with their hands, they laughed at each other's discomfort.

'You're as wet as fishes,' said the Petty Officer.

'It was fine,' said one of the seamen. 'Makes the body cool.'

Hosokawa adjusted the webbing which held his revolver, and looked at his watch. 'Past five o'clock,' he said. 'Time to patrol. Lieutenant Toshida will be coming to check soon. Let's get on with it, boys.'

They followed the Petty Officer down to where the catamaran was drawn up on a sand strip, its stern under overhanging trees, the bow end afloat. They manhandled it into the water, lay their rifles fore-and-aft, and climbed in. The patched brown sail was unfurled to flap idly in the breeze while the Petty Officer pulled the starting lanyard. After several abortive attempts the two-stroke spluttered uncertainly before screaming into life. Hosokawa took the tiller, opened the throttle, and the catamaran gathered way. Once clear of the inlet he headed for the mouth of the creek.

For Hosokawa these creek patrols were the highlights of the day. Always he steered to the eastern side, towards the headland that jutted furthest to seaward. On reaching it he would turn the catamaran and make for the headland on the western side. The journey across the mouth of the creek completed, he would head down the narrows to pass in front of the huts. Then he'd turn and make for the bluff. The patrol ended, the catamaran would return to the inlet where it would once again be drawn up on the sand.

The sentries had been placed at the mouth of the creek to stop Maji fishermen putting to sea, and to give warning of vessels approaching. Apart from the fisherman killed on the first morning, nothing untoward had happened and the sentries had found their duties uneventful. But the execution of Able Seaman Awa and the regular inspections carried out by Lieutenant Toshida – plus Lieutenant Kagumi's surprise checks – ensured that there was no slackness. Nor, in fact, was there any lack of volunteers for a duty which provided escape from the confined and fetid atmosphere of the submarine, and the hard work of cutting, carrying and laying camouflage.

As always, Hosokawa turned the catamaran short of the mangroves at the foot of the eastern headland and set course for the western headland. The breeze, now from the northwest, had freshened and the petty officer, a sailorman to his fingertips, switched off the engines and trimmed the sail to the wind. The clouds had moved away, the sun was low in the western sky, and in the aftermath of the storm the worst heat of the day had gone. The catamaran's gentle motion, the cry of seabirds, and the quiet swish of water against the hull induced in Hosokawa a pleasant feeling of well being.

The end of a strange interlude was in sight; the repairs to I-357 were almost completed, the tests would take place late the next day, and the submarine would leave the creek soon afterwards, for Mombasa and Penang. He was thinking of Penang and the pleasantries of life there when he heard the faint thrum of aircraft engines. Instinctively he reached for the starting lanyard, heaved at it several times before the outboard came to life. Opening the throttle, he steered for the inlet while a seaman got busy furling the sail. He was doing this when he shouted, 'A ship.' Pointing to the west, he added, 'The plane is circling round a ship.'

Hosokawa looked, saw the sunlight reflected on the distant aircraft as it banked in a tight turn. Beneath it he saw the ship silhouetted against the western sky. Soon afterwards the headland had shut out the view as the catamaran bustled down the creek towards the inlet.

But the brief glance had been enough. The dark shape on the skyline was a destroyer, the circling aircraft a Catalina. He turned the catamaran sharply to port, opened the throttle wide and headed for the bluff. Within a few minutes he had rounded it, boarded I-357, and hurried down below to knock on the door of Commander Yashimoto's cabin.

Soon after the rainstorm had passed in a last flurry of hail, *Restless* turned on to the new patrol line.

Barratt was about to go down to his cabin to get on with the briefing notes when a call on the radar voice-pipe sounded. Dodds answered, repeated the operator's report: 'Radar echo, red zero-nine-five, seven thousand yards, opening, classified small surface object.'

Barratt hurried to the port side of the bridge, trained his binoculars on to the bearing. Their powerful magnification brought closer the dark bulk of the far headland, short of it the stick of mast with its furled sail, beneath it the hull and outrigger of a catamaran, a tell-tale fluff of white at its stern.

'Must have an engine, sir,' Dodds called from the compass platform. He, too, was using binoculars.

'An outboard,' said the Captain. 'Made in Tokyo, no doubt.'

'You think they're Japs, sir?' The question was almost a yelp of surprise.

'Yes.'

'D'you think they can see us?'

'Unlikely from sea level at seven thousand yards, but possible. We hadn't seen the catamaran until radar picked it up.'

Barratt felt a strange exultation, a desire to make known his emotions, to shout, 'Thank God'. Instead he offered a silent prayer of thanks. He had been haunted by the thought of an anti-climax – the possibility that the submarine might have left during the rainstorm while *Restless* was shifting station to the west of the headland. That would have made a nonsense of the long search of the last few days and the final triumph of the find. It was the sort of uneven-handed trick that Fate might have played.

But that hadn't happened, the Japanese submarine was still there and he was convinced that the catamaran crew, their eyes at sea level, had not sighted *Restless* against the cloudy, rain-streaked sky of late afternoon. Had they done so they wouldn't have continued their journey across the mouth of the creek to the further headland.

So what was he going to do? Wait, maybe for days, for the submarine to come out; break W/T silence, inform Kilindini, request orders? Or press on during the coming night with what he had in mind?

Torn between these options he went to the PPI, watched the sweeping scanner trace its picture in phosphorescent light, saw the moving green speck turning short of the distant headland, imagined Japanese faces, sinister and evil. He gripped the bridge coaming more tightly.

The faint sound of an aircraft's engines broke into his thoughts. It was followed immediately by reports from the bridge lookouts, from the officer-of-the-watch, and from the radar office. 'Aircraft, green three-three-zero, six thousand yards, closing fast, flying low.'

Wondering why it had not been picked up earlier, Barratt realized that it must have come up from the south-east, close to the water, screened from the destroyer's radar by Maji Island. It was soon sighted, a Catalina flying at no more than a hundred feet above the sea. Making for *Restless* it pulled up in a steep climb as it drew close, passed overhead with a noisy roar then, banking steeply, it began to circle the ship. An Aldis lamp winked from the fuselage.

The First Lieutenant came clattering up the ladder on to the bridge. Barratt, scarcely aware of his arrival, glared in frustration as *Restless*'s signalman gave the 'go-ahead'. The Catalina's lamp winked again and began, slowly by naval standards, to transmit its message, the signalman calling aloud the words as he read them: *Stand – by – for – urgent – message – drop*.

The signalman acknowledged, lowered his Aldis lamp. 'Any reply, sir?'

'None.' Barratt's voice was flat, hostile. 'Let him get on with his bloody drop. The quicker the better.' He turned to Dodds. 'Stop engines. Slow astern together.'

The Navigating Officer passed the order to the wheelhouse. The note of the turbines dropped. Seconds later the ship shuddered as the astern turbines took over.

Barratt turned to the First Lieutenant. 'Get a couple of hands to standby in the waist to pick up the drop. Double quick.' The order was barked, a measure of the Captain's anger.

The Catalina completed another wide circle round *Restless* before drawing ahead. With engines throttled back it flew straight and level into wind, a few hundred feet above the sea. Shortly before crossing ahead of the destroyer it released a canister, its long be-ribboned tail fluttering down behind the container until it splashed into the sea on *Restless*'s port bow.

The Catalina passed over once more, waggled its wings in salute, climbed steeply and flew off to the north. Barratt gave it a last long look of disgust. 'I wonder whose bright idea that was? It's completely buggered our low-profile act.'

A bridge phone rang. Dodds answered, listened, his eyes on the sea. 'Will do,' he said. He hung up the handset, went across to the compass platform where the Captain sat looking wet and depressed. 'Canister's recovered, sir,' he said. 'Number One's bringing it to the bridge.'

Barratt frowned, shrugged. 'Have it sent down to my cabin. I'm going to change into something dry. Put the ship back on the patrol line, revolutions for sixteen knots. Over to you.'

'Aye, aye, sir.'

Barratt got up from the chair, had a last look round the horizon and went below.

Dodds felt sorry for the Captain, understood how he felt about the Catalina. What message could be so urgent that it had to be dropped by canister rather than transmitted by W/T? All HM ships at sea maintained a listening watch whether or not they observed wireless silence. Kilindini knew that. Why resort to a method which so blatantly drew attention to *Restless*'s presence? Particularly since it was known to be the last thing Barratt wanted. The Japs, only a few miles away, would certainly have heard the Catalina and seen it circling.

It was a bridge messenger and not the First Lieutenant who brought the canister to the day-cabin. Barratt thought he knew why. He'd ignored Sandy Hamilton when he'd come to the bridge during the drop. It hadn't been deliberate; it was simply that he'd been too upset by the Catalina's intrusion to think of anything else at that moment. He'd make amends later. Have a friendly chat with Number One. Send for him shortly.

But now for the canister. He unscrewed the lid, removed the waterproof bag, took from it the sealed envelope, opened it and took out a sheet of notepaper. Unfolding and smoothing it, he laid it on the desk blotter. Frowning as he read, he exclaimed, 'Bloody cheek,' pushed the message away, looked despairingly at the silver-framed photograph on the desk top: Caroline and himself outside Raffles. He picked up the notepaper, looked at it again. The printed heading made clear whence it had come; the members' reading and writing room of the Mombasa Club. It bore that day's date, 23 November, 1942, but there was no name or signature to

225

indicate its origin. Once again he read the typed message: *Afraid your Nelson act not going down well at Navy HQ. Captain (D) coming down in tomorrow morning's Catalina to board you – leaving here 0400 unless you have by then responded to the recall signal. Situation serious. This message is unofficial, personal and strictly confidential, its existence unknown to Navy HQ. Best of luck.*

Barratt had no idea who was responsible. It wouldn't be Captain (D), or the SOO, or for that matter anybody reasonably senior in the Royal Navy. Too unorthodox for that. Might be an RNVR or a Wren, not that he knew anyone in Kilindini well enough for them to bother much about him. Or was it RAF? After all, the pilot of the Catalina must have known who gave it to him to drop. He realized that the anonymous sender was trying to be helpful. It was a friendly act. And it had already achieved something: it had made up Barratt's mind finally. Once Captain (D) arrived matters would be taken out of his hands. There was no point now in considering the alternatives. It would have to be *Operation Maji – Mark Two* and it would have to be that night.

The clock over the desk showed 1728. Another seven or eight hours. He'd have to put Number One in the picture, finish the briefing notes, and get the act together.

Tomorrow morning's Catalina – leaving here 0400. He managed a humourless laugh. With any luck it would all be over by 0400.

Twenty-six

'You sent for me, sir?'

'Yes, Number One. Sit down.'

The First Lieutenant lowered his considerable bulk on to the settee. Barratt turned the desk-chair to face him. 'Time for us to have a chat,' he said. 'There wasn't an opportunity on the bridge with that Catalina messing about.' The Captain's smile was warm, friendly. 'I've had to make a decision. Like to discuss it with you.'

'Orders in the message drop?' suggested the First Lieutenant, his eyes on the canister at the far end of the settee.

'Information, not orders, Number One. The message has affected my decision. But I want to give you an appreciation of the situation as I see it – and the possible courses of action I've had to consider.' Barratt paused. 'Now – for a start – we know exactly where the submarine is and, thanks to last night's recce and the gen from Aba Said and his dad, we have a good idea of what goes on in the creek. You can take it as read that the Catalina's recent performance has told the Japs that we're sitting here waiting for them. So they won't come out. Simple as that.'

The First Lieutenant nodded agreement. 'Neutral territory. Warship puts in for urgent repairs. Safe haven until she's ready for sea. The Japs are on a good wicket.'

Barratt glanced at the First Lieutenant with a doubting frown before going to a scuttle to look across the sea to where the dark hump of Maji Island reared itself above a dusky skyline. In the spacious, well-furnished day-cabin the only indication that the ship was at sea was the distant hum of turbines and the occasional creak of the superstructure as *Restless* responded lazily to the ground swell.

227

Barratt went back to his desk. Resuming where he'd left off he said, 'Now for the possible courses of action.' His eyes were on a pastel of the Singapore waterfront on the opposite bulkhead. It had been a present from Caroline.

During the minutes that followed he outlined the options, dealing last with that of breaking wireless silence to inform Kilindini of the situation and request orders. Almost before Barratt had finished, the First Lieutenant broke in. 'I take it that's what you'll do, sir. Has to be the soundest course of action. *Restless* has done her stuff. Found the submarine, bottled it up in the creek. Your signal will pass the buck to Captain (D) and Co.' Sandy Hamilton appeared happier and more relaxed than for some time.

In a quick but decisive way Barratt said, 'There's not going to be any passing the buck, Number One. I will break W/T silence, but only to inform Kilindini that we attack the submarine before dawn tomorrow.'

The First Lieutenant showed surprise. 'I thought you regarded W/T silence as imperative, sir? To preserve the element of surprise. The Japs will pick up the transmission, won't they?'

Barratt took a cigarette from the silver box on his desk, was about to offer one until he remembered that Hamilton didn't smoke. He put the cigarette in his mouth. 'I rather hope they do.' He lit the cigarette. 'It doesn't matter now. The Catalina destroyed any element of surprise we might have had.'

'So they won't come out knowing we're here?' It was half a question.

'I don't suppose they will. But that's not going to interfere with my plan of attack.'

The First Lieutenant's concern showed in his face. 'You're not going to take *Restless* into the creek are you, sir? Infringe Portuguese neutrality? Present the Japs with a sitting target?'

'No, Number One. I shan't do any of those things.'

'May I ask, then, how you do propose to attack?'

'You may. That's why I sent for you.' Barratt cleared his

throat before going on to outline briefly but with much conviction how the attack would be carried out. 'So that,' he said finally, 'will be *Operation Maji Mark Two*.'

The First Lieutenant's changing expressions as Barratt unfolded his plan had conveyed surprise, anxiety and disbelief. Now he said, 'May I be frank, sir?'

'Please do.'

'I think it's a . . .' He hesitated, as if embarrassed by the thought of what he'd been about to say. '. . . it's a very unsound plan, if I may say so. It involves the Admiralty and our Government in an open breach of Portuguese neutrality. Quite apart from that, I think it's a highly dangerous operation, tactically unsound, bound to involve us in casualties and . . .' He took a deep breath before finishing, '. . . and almost certain to fail.'

The Captain stubbed out the cigarette, got up from the chair and began pacing the cabin. 'Well – you've certainly been frank, Number One.' He stopped, regarded Hamilton with challenging eyes. 'There are a couple of things you ought to know. First, your precious neutrality. Maji is, I suppose, nominally Portuguese territory. In all other respects it's a tiny island, seven thousand miles from Portugal, about a mile long, six miles off the coast, inhabited by a handful of African fishermen. The Japanese are in there without authority. They've closed the creek, forbidden the Africans to go to their fishing grounds, and they've already killed the only poor devil who tried. They are terrorizing that little community, Number One, interfering with their freedom and their livelihood. Four days ago those Japanese massacred the survivors of a US Liberty ship. Yesterday the Japanese Captain summarily executed one of his crew. Beheaded him. The man is a psychopath. And that's being polite.'

Barratt leant against the bulkhead, folded his arms, his eyes still on the First Lieutenant. '*Restless* will deal with that. I'm going to destroy that submarine and, hopefully, its Captain and some of his wretched crew. We shall be doing the Portuguese Government a favour, intervening on their behalf, freeing their helpless people. D'you for a moment imagine they would take a serious view of neutrality in such circumstances?'

Barratt directed a dark frown at the First Lieutenant. 'Of course they wouldn't.' He began pacing again, stopped at a scuttle, looked out to sea. 'That's my answer to your neutrality question. Now your other problem, Number One. It's evident that you disapprove of the operation. You're perfectly entitled to do so. And to express your views to me *privately*. But I happen to be Captain of *Restless*. I make the decisions. They are my responsibility. No one else's. If you wish I'll give you a letter confirming that. Acknowledging that you have warned me against the dangers, diplomatic and otherwise, of this operation. That will clear your yard-arm. And since nobody on board will know about it, you'll be doubly protected.'

The First Lieutenant's expression was strained as he got up from the settee. 'That won't be necessary, sir,' he said stiffly. 'I'm sorry you thought it might be. You are my commanding officer. I shall carry out your orders. Give you every possible support, notwithstanding my personal feelings. But I felt it was my duty to point out the dangers and possible consequences of what you have in mind. It was no more than that. It was certainly not self-interest. If you must know, it was because I was worried about how this could affect *you* – your naval career.'

In a voice suddenly subdued, Barratt said, 'I haven't got one, Number One. I'm a dugout. A wine merchant in RN uniform. But I do appreciate what you've just said.' His manner softened, he held out a hand. 'And I'm sorry if anything I've said hurt you.'

With some awkwardness the First Lieutenant took the Captain's hand.

'Under tension one says things one doesn't mean.' Barratt shrugged. 'Now sit down and I'll tell you what I want done before tonight's briefing. We'll hold it at 1900 in the ward-room, so have it cleared by then. I'll give you a list of the people I want. When you approach those I've marked "Shore Party" emphasize that every member is to be a volunteer.

230

Stress that any man who feels he can't volunteer will not suffer in any way. Nor will I think any less of him. And his messmates won't know because we shan't tell them. Got the hang of that?'

'Yes, sir.'

'Right. Carry on now. Pass the word for Corrigan to report to me right away.'

With a faint raising of eyebrows the First Lieutenant said, 'Aye, aye, sir.' He went to the door, turned and looked at Barratt in a strange way before lowering his head to pass through the doorway.

Yashimoto's narrow, pouched eyes fixed the Petty Officer with a doubting stare. 'You are certain it was a warship and not a coaster, Hosokawa?'

'Yes, sir. The silhouette was sharp. Two guns forward, two aft. Bridge superstructure well forward, thick funnel immediately abaft it. Searchlight platform amidships. No mistaking. It was a destroyer.'

'The Catalina was circling it, you say?'

'Yes, sir.'

Yashimoto tapped with a pencil on the small desk beside the bunk, his mind preoccupied, his eyes on the Petty Officer who stood inside the doorway, cap under arm. Eventually he asked, 'D'you think they could have sighted the catamaran?'

'Possibly, sir. We were under sail when we spotted them. *If* they saw us, I suppose they'd think it was a native vessel coming in to the creek from the fishing grounds.'

'I hope you're right, Hosokawa. But we know that the Catalinas have been flying over this area twice a day since we arrived. The coastline and its islands are in Mozambique, neutral territory. In spite of this the RAF overfly it regularly. Why?' With a shrug and a grunt, he added. 'But that's my problem, not yours.' He pressed with thumb and forefinger on his eyelids. 'Should the destroyer attempt to enter, wait until she is in the narrows before firing the Very lights. There will be moonlight from ten o'clock tonight if the sky continues to clear. But in any case you'll hear the ship, the sound of

231

her machinery, once she's in the narrows. She'll have to pass close to your post at the inlet.' He paused, looked at the portrait of the Emperor as if seeking inspiration. 'So – abandon the catamaran patrols, keep your post fully manned until further orders, and be especially vigilant tonight.'

Hosokawa said, 'We will do that, sir.'

Yashimoto relaxed momentarily, showed ivory-white teeth in a taut smile. 'You have done well, Hosokawa,' he said. Then, once more the disciplinarian, he added, 'Return to your post immediately. Tell your men that the destroyer is to receive a hot welcome if it attempts to come in.' The dark eyes had narrowed, the lower lip thrust forward. 'Request the First Lieutenant to see me at once.'

With a deferential, 'Aye, aye, sir,' Hosokawa bowed himself out of the cabin.

Kagumi listened attentively as the Captain broke the news that a British destroyer had been sighted to the west of the headlands guarding the entrance to the creek. A Catalina had been circling it.

'That must have been the aircraft heard by the conning-tower sentries ten minutes ago, sir. I did at once report to you.'

'Yes, yes.' Yashimoto's tone was impatient. 'I know you did. I assumed it was the usual late afternoon reconnaissance. Now we know it was more than that.' He fingered his neatly bearded chin, trimmed each day with the same ritual ex-actitude that he used in clipping his close-cropped head. 'We will at once prepare for an attack from seaward. Pay close attention to what I say.'

Kagumi said a dutiful, 'Yes, sir.' He would have liked to have added, 'I always do.'

'The Torpedo Officer is to muster his men in the fore-ends, one watch to be closed up until further orders, the other to remain on standby. Inform him that a British destroyer *may* attempt to force the narrows tonight.'

'Yes, sir.'

Yashimoto's fingers beat their customary tattoo on the

desk top. 'Next – enough camouflage is to be removed to give the forward gun a clear arc of fire covering the basin. An arc of fire for the AA gun on the after platform is also to be cleared. It should not be necessary . . .' A knock on the door stopped him in mid-sentence. Frowning, he called 'Come'.

Lieutenant Sato came in. 'Sorry, sir. Top secret from Flag Officer Submarines, Penang. I've just decyphered it.'

Irritated by the interruption, Yashimoto snapped, 'Read it.'

'ETA enemy carrier at Mombasa now AM 28 repeat 28 November. Acknowledge.'

'We can't acknowledge. There's a British destroyer outside the creek. But we can thank our Gods for this.' Yashimoto's sour manner switched to one of almost boyish exuberance. 'It means an extra twenty-four hours. That's a lot under present conditions. Thank you, Sato. You may carry on.'

When the Navigating Officer had gone Yashimoto, still looking pleased, said, 'Where was I?'

'The arcs of fire, sir?' prompted Kagumi.

'Yes. Now the matter of sentries. We've only one machine-gun post in the narrows. It's halfway between the inlet and the bluff. That's not enough. Issue machine-guns right away to the bluff sentries, also to those on the beach by the huts and to Hosokawa's post at the inlet.'

'Our establishment of machine-guns is only four, sir. This will mean issuing all of them.'

'I am well aware of that. Do as I say.'

Kagumi, realizing that he had offended, uttered a submissive, 'Yes, sir.'

'If the destroyer tries to come in, if they are foolish enough to risk giving our torpedoes a target at point blank range . . .' Yashimoto dismissed the idea with a contemptuous flourish of his hand. '. . . *if* they're foolish enough to do that – then their upper deck, and the bridge especially, are to be raked with machine-gun fire as they steam down the narrows.' The Captain was thoughtful. 'Of course they may risk sending in a fast motorboat to reconnoitre – or even a whaler under

233

sail.' He peered at Kagumi with narrowed eyes. 'The whaler would be silent, difficult to see in the dark. Warn the sentries accordingly. We must take no chances. Any craft of any sort that enters is to be machine-gunned, and the sentries must not hesitate to use rocket flares to illuminate if there's no moonlight. Stress the vital importance of giving us early warning with Very lights.'

The First Lieutenant managed a 'Yes, sir. I'll see to that,' before Yashimoto continued: 'There are to be no inspections of sentry posts tonight, Kagumi. No catamaran patrols until further orders. Guns' crews here on board are to work in two watches, one closed up, one on standby. I want two officers and two petty officers on watch throughout the night. One pair in the conning-tower with the sentries, the other in the control-room. Hydrophones, search receiver and W/T to be continuously manned.'

'The search receiver and the hydrophones have limited reception, sir.' Kagumi was worried. 'The high land, the configuration of the creek, and . . .'

'Yes, yes. I am well aware of that, Kagumi. But limited performance is better than none.' With eyes once more on the portrait of the Emperor, Yashimoto ran a hand over his head while his mind searched for detail. 'There are to be no camouflage or fresh water parties tonight. I-357 is to remain at first degree readiness.'

'Tomorrow's flooding tests, sir?' Kagumi watched anxiously as the Captain weighed the question, one which soon brought an emphatic shake of the head. 'That will depend on how the situation develops'.

'The sick and wounded, sir? Must they be taken over to the huts tonight?'

Yashimoto regarded the First Lieutenant quizzically, as if wondering what lay behind the question. 'No. That too must be deferred for the time being.

A cautious smile relieved Kagumi's strained expression. He had not been happy about the Captain's intention to abandon the sick and wounded to the care of Maji's fishermen. Not only did the Africans live in primitive conditions

234

without medical facilities of any sort, but they had no reason to like the Japanese.

Yashimoto's manner relaxed. 'We must restrict our movement at night until this threat has passed. It seems likely that the British know our boat is in the creek. How they do, I can't imagine. But it is necessary to assume that they do. Our camouflage makes it unlikely that they know where the boat is moored. For that reason it is possible a Catalina may come over tonight and drop flares – check for signs of unusual activity. So far they've not done that. But we must be prepared for it. That is why I want no working parties ashore, or catamaran patrols tonight. Now get busy, Kagumi. At the double.'

'Aye, aye, sir.' The First Lieutenant turned to go, changed his mind. 'Do you really think the British destroyer will try to attack, sir? Breach Portuguese neutrality?' The question was asked with a diffident air, as if Kagumi feared he might have offended. He was soon to know that he had.

In the brief period since Petty Officer Hosokawa had made his disturbing report, tension had been building up in Yashimoto. 'How can you ask such a stupid question,' he exploded, half rising from the settee. 'After the orders I have just given. Get out and get on with them.'

With a last startled glance at the Captain the young man fled, astonished at the outbreak, for Commander Yashimoto, though strict, was rarely discourteous.

Twenty-seven

From the Captain's cabin the First Lieutenant went to the wardroom where officers off watch had gathered. Some were sitting about talking or reading, others were involved in games of darts and chess. Midshipman Galpin was stretched out in a corner, apparently asleep.

The Surgeon Lieutenant put down his book. 'Hullo, Number One. Long time no see.'

'Had my head down most of the afternoon. Been with the Old Man since.' The First Lieutenant looked round the wardroom, raised his voice. 'Anybody seen Andrew Weeks?'

'Playing Judo with AB Carmichael on the iron deck, sir.' Galpin, it appeared, had not been asleep.

'Tell him I want him up here, chop-chop.'

'Aye, aye, sir.' The midshipman got up, shook himself, ran a hand through tousled hair and made for the door.

'Care for a drink, Number One?' The Surgeon Lieutenant yawned.

'No thanks, Docker. Too early. And there's a busy night ahead.'

'Oh, what's on?'

The First Lieutenant lowered his voice. 'Quite a lot. We're going into battle, Docker.'

'Good heavens, Number One. *Quel drame.*' The doctor pulled himself up in the armchair. 'Who with?'

'You'll hear in due course. The Old Man's doing a fireside chat at 1830 – there'll be a briefing in here at 1900 – for the chosen.'

'Well, well. Going back to War, are we? Giving up the desert island jolly? How very exciting. Will I be among the chosen?'

The First Lieutenant took off his uniform cap, sat down. 'I doubt it. The Old Man hasn't given me the list yet. He's working on it.'

The doctor shrugged. 'Well, it all sounds very mysterious. Remember you can count on me for anything safe. Cut me out if it's not.'

After a moment's preoccupation, the First Lieutenant said, 'How would you define a psychopath?'

'Odd question, Number One. What's on your mind?'

'The Old Man used the word a moment ago. Talking about the *Fort Nebraska* massacre. He said the Jap captain must be a psychopath. I know roughly what the word means but wondered about its medical definition.'

'My dear chap, it runs to pages. Difficult to be brief but I'll try. In general a psychopath is someone emotionally unstable to an almost pathological degree, though he has no specific or marked disorder.'

'Can you enlarge on that? Sounds a bit obscure.'

The doctor looked surprised. 'I thought I'd put it in sufficiently simple terms for even a naval officer to comprehend. However, let's have another shot.' He scratched his chin. 'A psychopath is a mentally deranged, abnormal personality. Difficult to classify psychopaths. There are two main groups: the aggressive and the inadequate. The sadists, the killers, the hard men, belong to the former. The latter include the impulsive, the irrational and the unbalanced. Social misfits, minor delinquents, trouble-makers, Don Quixotes. They can be highly intelligent, gifted, but their behaviour is repeatedly abnormal, their attitude turbulent and emotional, particularly under stress. One often sees the beginnings of it in adolescents; the so-called difficult children. If the Japanese captain is a psychopath I imagine he'd come under the aggressive label. But he's probably not one. Simply conforming to the norms of Japanese militaristic behaviour. They're a pretty primitive lot in that respect.'

The First Lieutenant half smiled. 'I didn't mean you to write a book on the subject, Docker. But thanks all the same. Most interesting.'

Further conversation was interrupted by the arrival of an athletic-looking young man wearing loose, baggy, canvas jacket and shorts. 'Excuse my rig, Number One, but Galpin said you wanted me chop-chop. Carmichael's been giving me a work-out.'

'So I see.' The First Lieutenant eyed the red weal across Weeks's cheek. 'I'm due for the Last Dog tonight. I wondered if you'd do it for me. The Old Man's given me a job.'

'Yes, of course I will. I'm free until the morning watch tomorrow. Then I'm on with you.'

'That's why I asked you. Anyway, thanks for the help.' The First Lieutenant picked up a magazine. 'Better get back to your bruising.'

Lieutenant Andrew Weeks, RNVR, left the wardroom at the double.

'Incredible,' said the doctor. 'In this weather.'

'Mad dogs and Englishmen.' The First Lieutenant shook his head, put down the magazine unopened.

Sitting at the desk in his cabin, head in hands, Sandy Hamilton stared bleakly at the snapshot in the silver frame: a young woman in a bathing costume sitting on a beach towel against a background of coconut palms; tresses of fair hair trailing forward over brown shoulders, white rimmed sun-glasses giving a commonplace anonymity to a face he knew to be beautiful. The scrawled inscription, *Love, Camilla*, was the only clue to the subject's identity. But he wasn't thinking of anything as pleasant as the week-end at the Tuna Inn, nor the promise of a repeat performance on *Restless*'s return to Kilindini.

Something more serious, less pleasant, was occupying his mind; the conversation in the Captain's cabin shortly after the message drop. Barratt had given no hint of what was in the message, no indication of its origin. It was almost certainly from Navy HQ in Kilindini since it was an official drop, but why that and not W/T? Other than remarking that it was information, not orders, and that it had influenced his decision, Barratt hadn't referred to it. Nor had he mentioned it when outlining his plan of attack, a plan which struck Hamilton as harebrained, suicidal; the words he'd so nearly used to Barratt. The Captain had not gone into the details of *Operation Maji Mark Two* – 'You'll get all that at the briefing, Number One. Nothing to be gained by going over it now' – but its outlines were enough to fill Hamilton with foreboding. Not so much for the tactical disaster and the casualties he foresaw, as for the scale of the diplomatic consequences of so flagrant a breach of Portugal's neutrality, however much her sympathies might lie with Britain.

The Captain had made no attempt in recent weeks to conceal his attitude towards the Japanese. It was not the intense dislike of an enemy that was normal and rational; fiercer, more primitive than that, it was motivated, Hamilton suspected, by emotional stress. The whole affair, the way in which the hunt for the submarine had been conducted, the failure to answer signals from Captain (D), the refusal to obey orders, or to cooperate with the RAF, was so irrational, so abnormal, as to suggest a mind that was unbalanced.

It was not the captain of the submarine Hamilton had had in mind when asking for the definition of a psychopath: *. . . someone emotionally unstable to an almost pathological degree though he has no specific or marked disorder . . . impulsive, can be highly intelligent . . . attitude turbulent and emotional . . .* The doctor's words persisted in the First Lieutenant's mind. Did not Barratt's actions place him somewhere in that catalogue of symptoms?

The weather began to change soon after sunset, tumbling masses of cloud drifting in from the north-east, the barograph stylus tracing a steep downward slope as the glass fell.

In the chartroom Charlie Dodds watched the trace with frowning disapproval. Though not on watch he was in a constant state of anxiety with the destroyer close inshore in such hazardous waters, and a dark night with rainstorms still to come. A few minutes earlier the Captain had come to the bridge, looked at the weather and decided that the patrol line should be shifted a mile to the north-east to give *Restless* better radar coverage of the creek.

Dodds had pointed out that the alteration would make sighting of the destroyer easier for the Japanese each time she reached the north-eastern end of the patrol line, particularly if there was moonlight.

'I've no doubt we've been sighted, Pilot. By now they must have put a lookout on the headland.'

'Isn't that a bit of a snag, sir?'

'No. Good thing if they see us at times. What's more, unless this sky clears there won't be any moonlight. In that case we'll have to take steps to ensure that they do see us.'

That had sounded very odd to the Navigating Officer, but he decided against asking for the Captain's reasons. No doubt all would be made clear at the briefing. So he concentrated once more on the chart and the problems of the night ahead. The only shore light which would be of any use was on Tambuzi Island. With its ten mile range it would be visible briefly when *Restless* turned at the north-eastern extremity of her beat. Not that shore lights mattered much now that radar was once again in continuous operation. That, plus asdic and the echo-sounder, would make the night less hazardous. Nevertheless he hoped the sky would clear by the time the moon rose.

He switched off the chart-table light and went to the bridge for a chat with John Taylor who was keeping the first dog-watch with Peter Morrow. Having briefed Taylor on the navigational aspects of the new patrol line, he went down to his cabin for a shower and change. While doing so he thought about the coming night; the ship was buzzing with rumours about what was to happen, some more lurid than others. There seemed to be no doubt that there would be action of a sort before daylight; but how, when, and where would have to wait for the Captain's fireside chat. Notice of it had already been given by the Coxswain over the ship's broadcast system. Rubbing himself down in the shower, Dodds wondered if he'd be doing the same thing on the following night, or was this to be his last shower? The Biblical ring of that made him smile sheepishly. He supposed he was over-dramatizing the situation. But he couldn't deny the queasy feeling somewhere in his stomach. He knew it had nothing to do with hunger.

Yashimoto was entering the day's events in the War Diary, notably the sighting of the British destroyer, the circling Catalina, and the steps which he had taken to prepare I-357 for the possibility of a surprise attack that night. He had almost completed the task when, at his request, the Engineer Officer came to the cabin.

'Sit down, Chief.' The Captain's face was grave as he made room on the settee. 'There is much we must discuss. First, the repairs.'

'They're well in hand, Captain. We've got the better of that confounded hinge, but we've problems with fractured air pressure lines on the starboard side where the piping by-passes the lower hatch. Damage caused by the torn plating when the shell burst. We're replacing the damaged sections of piping. This will not delay the programme for tomorrow night's tests.'

Yashimoto shook his head. 'As long as that destroyer patrols off the entrance we may have to defer, or even abandon, those tests, Chief. They could interfere with our state of preparedness. We have to be ready to repel an attack at any time during the night. If it has not come by first light –' he paused. 'We must wait to see what tomorrow brings.'

The Engineer Officer drew a hand across tired, sunken eyes. 'So you think the British might attack, although this is neutral territory?'

After a brief examination of his fingernails, Yashimoto said, 'To be honest, Chief, I do not think they will. The British still take an old-fashioned view of the sanctity of neutrality. But I cannot count on that. The island is small, remote and unimportant. The coast hereabouts is also remote. Probably no more than a handful of Portuguese colonial officials spread over tens of thousands of square miles. The British might take a chance. Fortunately they can't know exactly where the boat is lying, and they must

241

appreciate the dangers of attempting to force the narrows.'

'Plunging gunfire?' suggested Satugawa.

'How? If they do not know where the target is? No – I regard an attack as possible but unlikely.' Yashimoto held up an admonitory finger. 'You must treat that as strictly confidential. The crew must believe an attack is imminent.'

'You may count on me, Captain. But what, then, do you think the British will do?'

'Watch and wait, I think. Ask their Fleet HQ in Kilindini for orders, though Keda tells me there have not yet been wireless signals of sufficient strength to suggest transmission from any vessel near us. But lamp signals were probably exchanged with the Catalina when it was over the ship. The clue to further action may lie in those signals.' He nodded, as if confirming his conclusion. 'In the meantime, as I've said, they'll watch and wait. The destroyer is patrolling off the headland now. Shinzo Nikaido tells me our search receiver is picking up intermittent radar signals. They occur at fairly regular intervals, their bearing always restricted to the sector opposite the mouth of the creek. The destroyer must be on a patrol line which brings her into that sector for short periods. Most of the time she appears to remain west of the creek where the headland masks the transmissions.' Yashimoto opened the desk drawer, took from it the box of Penang cheroots, held it out to the Engineer Officer. 'A cheroot, Chief?'

'Thank you, Captain.' Satugawa took one, produced a lighter, put the flame to Yashimoto's cheroot, then to his own. 'Little chance, I suppose, of attacking the British carrier?'

Yashimoto drew on his cheroot, inhaled, expelled a thin column of smoke from between pursed lips. 'It is evening of the 23rd November. The carrier's amended ETA off Mombasa is now 27th/28th. If we leave here even as late as the 25th we should be in time. Later than that might still give us an opportunity to attack. The carrier is bound for Durban. She must leave Mombasa in due course. If we can't get there in time to attack her on arrival, we must do so when she leaves.'

Satugawa found the Captain's confident tone, his calm demeanour, impressive. Once again he was grateful that a man of such quality commanded I-357. Nonetheless, he felt bound to ask the obvious question: 'But if this British destroyer remains on patrol outside, what d'you intend doing, sir?'

Through the thin curtain of smoke which hung between them Yashimoto contemplated his questioner through narrowed eyes. 'We shall put to sea sometime during the next forty-eight hours - even if we have to abandon the tests. We will choose the time, the moment for action. It will have to be dark. We will move into the basin and trim right down. At either midnight or four o'clock in the morning – times when the destroyer's watches will be changing and vigilance will be relaxed – we will make our move. Around those times the headland lookout will report by signal torch on each occasion that the destroyer reaches the farthest end of its patrol line. On receiving that signal at an appropriate moment, I will take I-357 through the narrows at full speed, diving to periscope depth within a mile of clearing the headlands. Sato's chart indicates that the depth of water shelves steeply after the first mile.'

Satugawa took the cheroot from his mouth. 'The destroyer's asdic and radar, Captain?'

Yashimoto shook his head. 'Their asdic is effective only up to fifteen hundred yards. Towards the end of that range signals are weak, particularly against the background of land and shoal water which we shall have. Within a few minutes of clearing the headlands the radar target will be no more than our periscope – too small to register. The destroyer's chances of detecting us will be slight.' Juggling with his lips, Yashimoto swivelled the cheroot into a corner of his mouth, leant forward, the pouchy eyes bright. 'Whereas,' he went on, 'our chances of sighting the destroyer will be excellent. We shall have chosen the moment – we will have the advantage of surprise.' He drew on the cheroot, puffed whorls of

243

blue smoke at the deckhead. 'I intend to sink that destroyer as we leave Creek Island, Chief. The Imperial Japanese Navy will give the British a lesson in tactics.'

Satugawa regarded the thickset, aggressive figure of his Captain with admiring eyes. 'That is splendid news, sir. But one point you have not mentioned. Our sentries? Presumably we embark them shortly before leaving?'

Yashimoto's expression was impassive. 'That would involve an unacceptable loss of time. We will not be able to recall them until after the warning signal from the headland lookout. To do so earlier would rob us of our eyes and ears at the most critical time. They will not be re-embarked, Chief. We shall have to manage without them.'

The Engineer Officer shrugged, his expression strained. 'I suppose so,' he said heavily.

Yashimoto's mouth tightened. 'It is war, Chief. No time for sentiment.' He drew on the cheroot, exhaled whorls of blue smoke. 'Tell me. Do you believe that those flooding and pressure tests are absolutely essential? His dark eyes narrowed, bore into the Engineer Officer's like twin gimlets.

Satugawa knew what the Captain wanted to hear. Loyally, he said it. 'Not absolutely essential, Captain – but highly desirable. If we do not make deep dives –' he hesitated. 'There should not be problems?'

Yashimoto smiled. 'Thank you, Chief. That is what I hoped you'd say.'

Twenty-eight

At 1830 *Restless*'s broadcast system crackled into life. The shrill whistle of the Boatswain's call was followed by the Coxswain's, 'D'ye hear there – d'ye hear there?' Next came Barratt's voice: 'This is your Captain speaking. I want to tell you about tonight's operation. As you know the Japanese submarine which massacred the *Fort Nebraska* survivors is inside the creek where they've been repairing shell damage. We're keeping the entrance covered by radar. The water outside is too shallow for a dive for about the first mile so the Jap will have to come out on the surface. Well trimmed down, no doubt, but still a radar target.' Barratt coughed, cleared his throat. 'I think we've got our nasty friends pretty well bottled up. We know they have sentries at the mouth of the creek – and probably on the headland since the Catalina's visit this afternoon. But that doesn't matter now. We want them to see us hanging around their front door. They'll be on the alert tonight, probably expecting something to happen. And they'll not be disappointed.' Barratt paused. 'But it won't come from where they expect it. No straight left to the chin. No Marquis of Queensberry rules. What they're going to get is a bloody great kick up the arse. And we're going to give it to them. So we'll be landing a shore party in much the same way as we did last night. Only this one will be a lot bigger, and its job a lot tougher.' Barratt's voice was hoarse. He stopped, again cleared his throat. 'I won't go into the where and how of the operation now, because I'll soon be giving a detailed briefing to the shore party and others concerned. They'll pass on the story in their messes *after* the briefing. So you'll get it all very shortly. There's one thing I want to stress – the shore party is, for obvious reasons, small in numbers. Each man has been chosen for his special skills, and each is a volunteer. But I want to emphasize that the attack is being carried out by *Restless* – it's her battle – and every one of you has an important role to play. And that's why I know the attack is going to succeed. Because this is a first-rate ship with a first-rate ship's company. We are going to destroy that –' he hesitated, searching for words, '– that submarine and as many of its bloody awful crew as we possibly can. Zero hour is 0200, two hours after midnight. That is all. Good luck and God bless you.'

The rumble of cheers from the messdecks reached many parts of the ship.

It was a hot night, made more sultry by low cloud which shut out the sky, and though the wind had freshened it was blowing down from the Equator bringing with it a front of warm air.

After the Captain's broadcast, Brad Corrigan left the stuffiness of the seamen's mess for the comparative comfort of the upper deck where he leant against the ladder to the searchlight platform. There, with folded arms, he looked out into the wall of darkness surrounding the ship, seeing nothing but hearing the rhythmic hum of the turbines, louder than usual because he was near the engineroom skylights, and the splash of the sea along the side as *Restless* moved through the water. At regular intervals the ship would heel over as she reversed course at the extremities of her patrol line.

Corrigan's thoughts were mixed: excited at the prospect of action, worried at the thought of danger, reassured by his own strength and skill, and proud in a diffident way about what the Captain had said that afternoon.

He'd begun by saying that the Japanese submarine was to be attacked that night, and hinted at how it would be done. 'I'm not pretending it won't be dangerous, Corrigan. It will be. But I want you with me because you're a long way the best man for the job. We'll have plenty of back-up, but you and I – just the two of us – will be on the sharp end. There are two reasons why I reckon we're the best pair for the job. One is that we both have a lot more reason than anybody else in this ship to loathe those bastards. The other is that you're a strong swimmer, you know how to look after yourself in the water. I'm pretty good there, too. Not in your class, but above average. Now I'm not taking anybody ashore who isn't a volunteer. If you volunteer for the job I'll be delighted. But if you don't – and I know you'd have good reasons for that – I won't think any the less of you, nor ask for your reasons.'

There hadn't been any hesitation on Corrigan's part. 'No way will I miss that chance, Captain. I'll be right there with you. And glad of it.' And he'd said it thinking of what the goddam Japs had done to Smitty Fredericks and all his other mates.

He looked at his watch – 1850. Another ten minutes and I'll have to go along to the wardroom, he thought. See who the other guys are and get the low-down on what's gonna happen. The Captain put me wise on what he called the Sharp End. But there's a helluva lot he hasn't told me. He said I'd get it all at the briefing. Then he shakes hands like we were buddies and I see from his eyes that he's all het up. Looking for a fight, I guess. He's not a big guy but he's tough all right. And he knows what he's doing. I'm glad it's him and not some kinda ordinary officer I'm going with.

A distant sheet of lightning lit the horizon and he could see the coastline of Africa, a low-lying, undulating strip of land. Don't need no goddam lightning, he told himself. Better it stays plenty dark. Looking up into the black, starless sky, he muttered, 'Hey, Mister God, keep it real dark will you.' His thoughts moved on to Sandport, Massachusetts. How's it there? he wondered, pictures of his parents sliding through his mind. After the briefing I better write a note to the folks, just in case. Tell them we got a fight coming in a few hours. Say I feel great. Think about them a lot. That's what they like to hear. Guess I'll ask them to pass my love to Mary Lou. Yeah. I'll do that. Just a few lines'll be enough.

*

247

But for guest nights, *Restless*'s wardroom was rarely called upon to accommodate so many people. Close on thirty officers and men, some sitting, some standing, had crowded in, the ventilation system struggling valiantly with tropical night and the heat of many human bodies in a confined space. Barratt sat at the far end of the wardroom table facing his audience, briefing notes in front of him. He was flanked by the First Lieutenant and the Engineer Officer.

'The object of *Operation Maji Mark Two*', he said by way of opening the proceedings, 'is to destroy the Japanese submarine I-357.' With a sombre look he added, 'The more Japanese we kill in accomplishing that object the better.' He went on to say that those present included the members of the shore party and the key personnel responsible for fighting the ship. 'The operation involves a two-handed attack on the enemy. *Restless* will do a lot more than landing and recovering the shore party. She will deal with any attempt by the submarine to leave the creek, and she will create a vital diversion. Without it the operation is unlikely to succeed.

'Before getting down to detail I would like to make a few observations. There were many more volunteers than we needed for the shore party. That didn't surprise me. But its members are limited and with a ship's company of two hundred and twenty men there were bound to be disappointments. I'm sorry about that. However, every man in *Restless* is involved in the operation in one way or another. In every way it's a team effort. In choosing men for the shore party I was influenced by our needs and their special skills. We've a poacher . . .' He looked at Angus McLean and there was a murmur of laughter. '. . . four men with marksmen's badges, some good swimmers, a county rugger player, a couple of Judo experts, and so on. Next point. No notes, please.' Barratt's eyes were on Andrew Weeks. 'I don't think anybody will be taken prisoner but we must guard against the possibility, however remote. So, no notes. When I get to what each of you has to do, commit your part to memory.'

With an embarrassed grin Andrew Weeks put away his notebook.

'Now for the shore party,' Barratt went on, looking round with eyes which seemed unusually bright. 'First let me say that all those who landed in last night's recce party have volunteered for tonight's do, so we've an important advantage. Not only have we got men who've already been on the island at night but, in place of the splendid Mr Katu –' Barratt hesitated, frowned, then smiled at the fresh ripple of subdued laughter, '– we have Aba Said, a Maji islander. He not only knows every inch of the island and exactly where the submarine is lying, but he's familiar with its routine, where the sentry posts are, *their* inspection routine, etcetera.' Barratt looked across to where Peter Morrow was doing a low-key simultaneous translation for the African's benefit. 'He's already given us marvellous information, including details like the submarine's pennant numbers. He saw them on one of their inflatables. He'll be invaluable tonight.'

Barratt consulted his notes. 'Right – let's move on. The shore party will be seventeen strong, split into four groups: the Pathfinders, three men; the Rig Crew, seven; the Beach Party, five men – and the Sharp End, two. Got that?' He glanced at the faces in front of him. 'Now this is where you chaps have got to listen very carefully because I'm going to give you the names of those in each group, and explain their duties. I'll also give the times for the different stages of the operation. They are, of course, approximate.' His manner took on a sudden gravity. 'Remember – there can be hitches, things can go wrong. It's the unpredictable in war which makes planning difficult. An awkward sentry for instance, or too much moon, too little cloud, too much noise. That sort of thing. So be ready to improvise if necessary.'

When he'd finished naming the men for each group and outlining their various tasks, he detailed the arms and other equipment to be carried, the signal arrangements and much else. That done, he explained the different stages of the operation, beginning with the beach landing, and ending with the destroyer's recovery of the shore party.

He dealt next with the part *Restless* was to play, stressing the importance of timing, of synchronizing her movements

249

as far as possible with those of the shore party. He spoke of the emergency signals, the circumstances under which they might be used, and the action the destroyer would take on observing them. At this point he said, 'I think I've covered just about everything. If you have any questions, now is the time to put them. I'll do my best to answer them.'

There were a number of questions, some of them important enough to require changes in the operational plan.

When Barratt had dealt with these he looked at the ward-room clock, compared the time with his wristwatch. 'It's almost 2000,' he said. 'Members of the shore party must have their gear, arms, etcetera mustered by 2130. It's important to get as much rest as possible between then and 0200 when you leave the ship. 'Wear dark clothing. Not too much, it'll be very hot. Blacken your faces and all other exposed flesh – your hair, too, unless it's black. See the Coxswain if you've not got enough blacking, he'll fix you up. If you run into a Jap sentry in the dark we want him to think you're an African.' Barratt's eyes glittered in a humourless smile. '*If* he has time to think before you kill him.' He ran a hand across his forehead, once more cleared his throat. 'Landing on the beach is, as I said earlier, scheduled for 0230. The attack itself round about 0320.' His eyes travelled over the curious, expectant faces. 'The First Lieutenant will command *Restless* in my absence, so the ship will be in good hands.' He stood up. 'Well, that's it. I haven't thrown in any pep talk. You probably dislike that sort of thing as much as I do. I just want to say that we've got a first-rate team, ashore and afloat.' He paused. 'When we sink that bloody submarine – I say *bloody* advisedly – I hope we'll give the Japanese some of the treatment they like to dish out to others.' For a moment his stare seemed to reach out over the heads of his audience, to something beyond the confines of the ward-room. 'That's all,' he said. 'So good luck and good hunting.'

The First Lieutenant, an attentive but privately critical member of the audience, could not have disapproved more of *Operation Maji Mark Two*. Nevertheless he conceded to himself that the Captain's planning was impressive. It's a pity, he thought, that he's put so much into a mad-hat scheme which is bound to end in disaster.

There was no doubt in Hamilton's mind that *Restless* under his temporary command would do all that was required of her, and for his part he would certainly do his utmost. But he was more than ever convinced that Barratt's judgement had gone. The strange, almost wild light in the Captain's eyes during the briefing strengthened Hamilton's belief that the man was on the edge of madness, if not already there.

The punkah flapped interminably, sweeping invisible waves of warm air over those in the Operations Room.

'The principle is absurd,' said Captain (D), eyeing it savagely. 'Hot air rises. That wretched contraption pushes it down again. Can't we open another window?'

'There aren't any other windows, sir.' Jakes's smile suggested happiness with his answer.

'Well, there ought to be.' Captain (D) patted round the wetter parts of his forehead, face and neck with a large white handkerchief. 'So, what is the news from the fighting front?' he asked the room in general.

Looking gloomier than usual, the SOO tugged at the lobe of an ear. 'Hutchison was about to report a message from the Duty Officer at 290 Squadron when you came in.'

'Oh, sorry if I interrupted. Let's hear it, Hutchison.'

The Flight Lieutenant, having twisted round to hold a whispered conversation with the Wren at the signals' desk, turned swiftly. 'Sorry, sir. I'm afraid I missed that?'

'Not surprised.' Captain (D) shook his head. 'Your antennae were trained in the wrong direction. However, I gather you have news from 290 Squadron. What is it? Japanese Fleet sighted, or something serious?'

'G-for-George landed at Port Reitz a few minutes ago, sir. Its captain, Don Tuke, reports that he sighted *Restless* at 1725 midway between Tambuzi Island and Cape Ulu, more or less where she's been for the last couple of days. There was thick cloud and heavy rain in the area during the after-

251

noon, but Tuke says he had a good low-fly look at the coast and islands in the vicinity. Apart from a couple of Portuguese coasters, some dhows and the usual rash of catamarans, he saw nothing worth reporting.'

'Did *Restless* attempt to communicate with him?' The SOO held his head back, his eyes focused along his nose as if it were a rifle barrel.

'I imagine Don Tuke would have told me had she done so, sir.' Hutchison spoke in a low voice. He looked across to the far end of the room to check whether Camilla had heard him. She was keying a cypher machine.

'I simply cannot make out what Barratt's up to.' Captain Pelly, the Chief Staff Officer, looked at the punkah as if the answer might come from somewhere within its languid flaps. 'Looks as if you'll be joining S-for-Sugar for tomorrow's ride, George.'

Captain (D)'s blue eyes twinkled with pleasure. 'Yes, indeed. Take-off at 0400. Spoil my beauty sleep, but it should be worth it. Bound to be cooler in the Catalina.' He chuckled. 'Cooler in the Catalina. Rather good. Title for a hit tune.'

'Let's hope the weather holds,' said the CSO. 'Don't like the sound of those rainstorms.'

A squeak of surprise from the cypher desk and the scrape of a chair was followed by Camilla sweeping across the room clipboard in hand. 'Signal from *Restless*,' was her triumphant announcement as she passed it to the SOO.

He took it, frowning as he read. 'H'm,' he said. 'That's better, but still a bit odd.'

'Come on SOO.' Captain (D) waved an imperious arm. 'Let's have it. Can't keep all the juicy bits to yourself.'

The SOO surveyed the faces round the operations table with an I-know-it-but-you-don't look. 'Usual address and other prefixes,' he said. 'Message begins. Intend to attack Japanese submarine I-357 before dawn tomorrow. Message ends. Time of origin 2231.' He handed the clipboard back to the cypher officer.

Captain (D) glanced at the wall-clock. 'That was fifteen

252

minutes ago. Does sound a bit odd, CSO. What d'you make of it? And how on earth does he know the Jap's pennant numbers?'

'It rather confirms what I thought,' said the Chief Staff Officer. 'Barratt knows where that submarine is. Can't get at it – neutral territory, that sort of thing – so he's been playing cat and mouse outside, waiting for it to put to sea. His tactics have evidently paid off. He must know she's coming out sometime before daylight tomorrow. Could be information picked up from African fishermen. They probably gave him the pennant numbers. You'll recall that *Restless*'s motorboat was seen towing a catamaran. Only thing that puzzles me is why Barratt has now decided to break wireless silence.'

Captain (D) blew out his cheeks before rapidly deflating them. 'I dare say he made a high speed dash – twenty or thirty miles out to sea before transmitting. That wouldn't alert the Jap if he's holed up close inshore. Plenty of traffic in the Mozambique Channel.'

'Pity Barratt didn't think of doing something like that days ago,' suggested the SOO.

The Chief Staff Officer's expression, the slightly raised eyebrows, conveyed mild disapproval. 'I've no doubt he'll explain it all when he gets back.' His eyes settled for a moment on the SOO. 'Our views may have been a little uncharitable. We could be sending him a signal of congratulation tomorrow.'

'So – do I or don't I go down there in the morning, CSO?' Captain (D)'s usually cheerful face was shadowed by disappointment.

'I think we might wait and see what happens before deciding on that, George.'

Camilla, standing beside the SOO, patted the clipboard. 'The Fleet W/T office acknowledged *Restless*'s signal,' she said. 'Are we to make any reply, sir?'

'No,' said the SOO, adding, 'unless either of you gentlemen care to?'

'I don't *think* so,' said Captain (D). 'Barratt's found the

253

submarine. He hasn't asked for help. Why not leave things as they are. He seems to be doing a good job.'

Greatly daring, Camilla fixed her attentions on Captain Pelly. 'Wouldn't it be rather nice, sir, to send *Restless* a "Good luck and good hunting" signal?'

The Captain melted under the appealing eyes of the cypher officer. 'Yes,' he said. 'It would be rather nice.'

Twenty-nine

Barratt went to the bridge after the watches had changed at midnight to find it wet and glistening from earlier rain. A clouded sky and distant lightning promised more. The weather continued to come from the north-east, the wind at times gusting to Force 6, building up a moderate sea, *Restless*'s bows throwing up sheets of spray each time her patrol line took her into the wind.

'Any sign of action ashore?' Barratt asked the officer-of-the-watch.

'None, sir. We've exposed a light several times. On each occasion for about ten seconds when the ship was opposite the entrance to the creek.' He lowered the night-glasses he was using. 'Once we blew off steam. With this wind I'm sure they heard us. But there's been no reaction.'

Barratt said, 'Good. That's what we want.' He went across to the starboard side of the bridge, stood with his hands on the coaming staring into the darkness, thinking of the coming hours. The attempt he'd made at rest had been hopeless. Far too tense for that, his mind too occupied, he'd soon given up. He imagined that others in the shore party were having the same difficulty. Rest and the immediate prospect of action were not easy bedfellows. It was good to be back on the bridge where things were happening. He checked a mental list of things to be done. He'd have a final session with the Torpedo Officer, get that side of things sorted out. Then another chat with Morrow and Aba Said. There were several more questions he had to ask the African. That would take him through to around 0100 when he'd go to his cabin, blacken his face and body, and put on the few garments he'd be wearing: the bathing trunks under dungaree trousers,

255

dark socks, ink-dyed canvas shoes and the webbing belt to hold the .38 revolver and the fighting knife. All that would have taken about forty minutes. Then he'd come back to the bridge, have a quick re-check of the drill for the night with the First Lieutenant – after that, standby for the landing.

For a moment his thoughts wandered in a confusion of emotions: foreboding, awareness of danger, of bloody action. But none were so powerful as the overriding determination for revenge.

When *Restless* had gone to the assistance of the southbound convoy he had attacked what was thought to be a German U-boat. But his emotions then and his emotions now were worlds apart; intense dislike for the Germans, coupled with respect for the skill and bravery of their U-boat commanders, bore no relation to what he felt about the Japanese. Nor did the methods of attack: the convoy battle had involved the usual asdic hunt, the dropping of depth-charges on a remote, unseen enemy represented by no more than a *ping* on the bridge speaker and a purple trace on the plotting-table.

The attack on I-357 would be the antithesis of that. He would see the Japanese submarine at close range, it would be a hand-to-hand affair, a visible killing and maiming, the ultimate in revenge.

Aware that his thoughts had wandered, that time was short, he went to the chartroom. There he found Dodds working on the tide-tables. After they'd discussed tides for the night, Barratt said, 'I'd like you to relieve Taylor for about twenty minutes. Tell him I want him here.'

Shortly afterwards the Torpedo Officer appeared. 'You sent for me, sir?'

'Yes, Torps. I'd like to run through the rig drill once more. I know Corrigan and I had a dummy run with you this afternoon, but I want to make sure I fully understand the nuts and bolts of the flooding arrangements. Don't want anything to go wrong, particularly at the assembly and launching stages.'

'You'll have the TGM with you for those, sir. McGlashan is the specialist. He designed the rig. Supervised its construction from the ground up.'

'The *ground up* presumably being my rough sketch,' Barratt remarked drily.

The Torpedo Officer's smile was apologetic. 'Yes, of course, sir. That sketch *was* the ground work.' He went on. 'The rig's really very simple and straightforward now. The engineroom staff have welded a longitudinal bulkhead into the DC drum. One half contains the Amatol charge, the other is free-flooding on launching. One of the two buoyancy drums has been cut in half and welded to the other, so their flooding now is done by a single bung with a topside vent to release displaced air. You can check the flooding at any time by shutting the vent.'

For some time after that they discussed the changes in the structure of the rig and the effect they would have on assembling, flooding and slipping. When they'd finished Barratt patted Taylor's shoulder. 'I must congratulate you and the TGM. You've done a splendid job. All that's necessary now is to put it to good use.'

The Torpedo Officer looked pleased. 'I've no doubt you'll do that, sir. I only wish I was coming with you.'

'You're needed on board, Taylor. The ship can't do without you *and* the TGM.'

In the early hours of morning Barratt turned *Restless* away from the southern end of the patrol line and brought her round in a broad sweep to sheltered water in the lee of Maji Island. About a mile south of the beach on which the landing was to be made he ordered *slow astern together* and, when the destroyer had all but lost way, *stop engines*. Having given orders for the motorboat and skimmer to be lowered into the water, he handed over command to the First Lieutenant. There was a minimum of formality. 'She's all yours, Number One,' he said. 'See you at the pick-up point at 0415 or thereabouts. God bless you and the best of luck.'

257

In the dim light of the compass binnacle Hamilton could see the whites of the Captain's teeth and eyes in the otherwise blackened face. 'Good luck, sir,' he said, an unfamiliar tremor in his voice. They shook hands, Barratt adjusted his webbing belt, checked the revolver and fighting knife it held. With a final, 'So long,' he went down to the waist where the shore party was mustering.

The embarkation took place without lights in total darkness. Although *Restless* was downwind of the island Barratt had stressed the importance of silence, so orders were given and difficulties discussed in subdued voices. To his concern these factors slowed the pace of embarkation and tried a temper already strained by tension. When the Coxswain reported that a rifle being handed down to the skimmer had been lost over the side, Barratt exploded. 'For God's sake, which bloody idiot was responsible?'

'Couldn't rightly tell in the dark, sir.'

'It was me, sir,' came in an undertone from a dark shape near Barratt who recognized the voice as that of a leading seaman, a man well liked on the seaman's messdeck. Barratt, who thought much of him and was already regretting his outburst, said, 'Never mind. We won't charge it to you, Johnson. Have another rifle put in the skimmer double quick, Coxswain.'

'Already done, sir,' said the Coxswain. 'I had spare equipment mustered in case of accidents.'

That incident out of the way, the embarkation continued. The five men of the beach party under the command of Lieutenant Weeks were in the skimmer with the rig, while the attack party of twelve men, including Peter Morrow and Aba Said, were with Barratt in the motorboat which was to take the skimmer in tow since the latter's outboard engine was too noisy for the landing operation. It would be used only on re-embarkation of the shore party or, if necessary, in an emergency.

Though to Barratt the time seemed a great deal longer, the motorboat bore off from the destroyer's side less than twelve minutes after embarkation had begun. Moving away with its tow at low speed it was soon lost to sight in the darkness.

The landing place chosen on the advice of Aba Said was a small beach on the southern side of the island. It had been selected for its tactical advantages; from Aba Said's information, confirmed by what Barratt and McLean had seen on the previous night, it seemed that the Japanese defences were based upon the possibility of an attack by a vessel entering the creek from seaward on the northern side of the island. The beach chosen had an added advantage; in a direct line, it was no more than five hundred yards from where the submarine lay. Because the creek was surrounded by a horseshoe of hills the distance to be covered by the attack party was considerably longer, involving as it did a climb and descent over rough, bush-covered terrain.

On this point, particularly, Said's advice had been invaluable. 'I have been to the beach many times,' he told Peter Morrow. 'The journey over the hill will take about twenty minutes. There is a rough track, but it is not easy to follow, especially in the dark. You say your men will be carrying heavy things, Bwana. In that case the journey must take longer.'

It was on this assessment that Barratt in his planning had allowed forty minutes for the journey from the beach, over the hill and down through the forest to the creek.

Piloted by Aba Said, who had fished the waters round Maji Island for at least fifteen of his twenty-one years, the motorboat and its tow reached the beach twenty minutes after leaving *Restless*. How the African found it on a black dark night was an unsolved mystery to Barratt who assumed it was a combination of night vision and instinct which the ordinary mortal didn't possess. Whatever it was, the white patch of beach showed up ahead soon after the African's warning to Morrow, 'We must go slow now, Bwana.' The motorboat's engine was throttled back, de-clutched and put astern. The bowman, sounding with a boathook, called out,

'Shelving fast, sir.' Seconds later the bows touched and disembarkation began. Once the motorboat had discharged its load, the bows of the skimmer were hauled up on the sand and unloading of the rig and other equipment took place. When this had been done the skimmer was again taken in tow by the motorboat which backed away in the darkness. Both craft were to lie off the beach until the return of the attack party. At the briefing Barratt had given the time of that return as 0400, stressing that it was no more than an approximation.

For the members of the shore party the journey to the beach had been an eerie one especially for the majority who had not landed the night before. Grouped together in the darkness, in silence, unable to see, each man's mind filled with thoughts of what the next hour might bring, was an experience which tested the nerves of the toughest.

Once on the beach and able to move again, much of the tension went as they got busy with their various tasks. Most important of these was the placing of the rig units in the carrier. This was done by the TGM, Petty Officer McGlashan, and the rig's crew. Working without lights of any sort meant that everything had to be done by touch; and in silence but for occasional whispers.

First the wooden carrier was laid in the sand. Much like a rigid, six-by-three foot stretcher, the projecting ends of its longitudinal and cross members provided handgrips for the six men who would carry the 200 lb load. Lengths of rope looped between the timber shafts formed the bed on which the parts of the rig were laid; the unprimed depth-charge, behind it the buoyancy drum, and last the canvas gripes to be used when the rig was launched. While McGlashan and his men were busy, others in the attack party were checking weapons and equipment. Some had service rifles or revolvers, a few had Sten guns, most had hand-grenades attached to their belts, and others bulging rucksacks over their shoulders. Every man had a fighting knife in his belt.

At thirty-seven minutes past two o'clock – seven minutes

behind Barratt's operational schedule – the attack party began to leave the beach. The pathfinders, Peter Morrow and Aba Said, led, followed by McLean and Carmichael. Barratt and Corrigan came next, the rig and its bearers immediately behind them. The rear was brought up by the TGM and Bob Stanley, a sickbay attendant who carried first-aid equipment.

The rain had stopped some time before they landed on the beach but there was still no break in the clouds, and the attack party climbed up the hillside in darkness, remaining in close order so that contact was not lost. Aba Said moved with the stealthy assurance of a bloodhound following a well-scented trail, pausing at times to peer into the night, touching the undergrowth as if its feel might carry clues. Occasionally he would stop, thrust his head forward and cup his hands behind his ears.

The stony track up which he took them wound its way through thick undergrowth where insects buzzed in protest as the rig carriers pushed it aside to make room for their load. At times there was the sound of a man stumbling, at others the crack of tinder breaking underfoot; occasionally the flap and screech of a startled bird would create alarm, but for the most part the only sounds were the scuff of feet, the wheeze of heavy breathing, and in the background the constant murmur of the sea. The low cloud ceiling intensified the night's heat, and the sour sweet smell of sweat hovered over the climbing men. At times when the going got steep McGlashan and Stanley would lend a hand with the rig, lightening the load for its carriers.

At the top of the hill they halted for a five minute rest, something Barratt had promised at the briefing. 'Don't forget,' he'd said, 'you may be short of puff when you reach the top, but a five minute rest will put that right. The descent should be a piece of cake.'

While they rested he moved among the men encouraging, advising, checking on their problems and patting backs for work well done. 'But the worst is over. The load will seem a lot lighter going down. And don't forget,' he laughed,

261

'it's strictly one way freight.' To all he again stressed the importance of silence. 'The nearer the target the greater the need,' was his whispered reminder. As he'd expected, the attack party's morale was high, their humour good and in spite of the unwelcome attention of swarms of mosquitoes, and undergrowth scratches on bare limbs, there were no complaints.

In a whispered conversation Morrow asked Aba Said how he had been able to follow the track so surely in the darkness.

'Bwana, for many years of my life I have used the path,' said the African. 'In the rocks by the beach where we landed there is good food in the sea shells. But since the Japanese arrived our people are not allowed to come to that beach.'

The luminous dial of Barratt's wrist watch showed 0302 when the rest period ended and the attack party began the descent led by Aba Said and Morrow, the others following in the order in which they'd climbed. They had not gone far when away to the north the horizon was illuminated by a sheet of lightning. Off the mainland guarding the entrance to the creek the dark silhouette of a destroyer had shown up momentarily against the brilliantly lit skyline. To Barratt and others who'd seen it, the sight of their ship, the reminder that they were not alone, was comforting.

Stars began to glitter through a break in the clouds and he cursed quietly. The last thing he wanted was a clear sky, particularly as the moon, risen at midnight, was still behind cloud. For the attack party's purposes the longer it remained there the better. The wind had backed north from north-east where the storm clouds had been gathering before darkness fell. He prayed that it would continue to mass them over the island.

The file of men threading their way down through the trees came to a halt. Aba Said went through his listening motions, head forward, peering into the darkness. 'Listen, Bwana,'

262

he warned. 'We are close to the water now. No more than fifty paces.'

Morrow listened, straining his faculties until he too could hear the faint murmur of water ahead. 'Where is the submarine, Aba Said?'

The African took his arm, aimed it left. 'That way, Bwana. About two hundred paces. The catamarans lie this side, behind the stern. Along the creek the mangroves are high. We must go towards the catamarans before it is possible to reach the water. There is a sentry at that place. He watches the catamarans.'

'Stay here, Aba Said,' Morrow replied. 'I will tell the Bwana M'Kubwa of these things.' He went back to where Barratt waited, gave him the news. The Captain hesitated before saying, 'Go ahead with Aba Said and McLean. Get McLean to deal with the sentry. Let me know when he has.' Barratt's tone was matter of fact, as if he were giving an order on *Restless*'s bridge.

Morrow disappeared into the night.

The three men went on in silence, keeping to the bank above the tangle of mangroves which lined the creek. At times they would stop to listen, only to hear the lapping of water, until they were closer to the catamarans when the subdued hum of machinery came from somewhere ahead. They moved warily, testing the ground underfoot with tentative steps before applying the weight of their bodies. They'd not gone far when the sound of a man coughing stopped them. Aba Said crept forward, leading the way down the bank through a break in the mangroves. For the first time they saw the water, its ruffled surface reflecting a slit of stars. Following the African's example they knelt behind the undergrowth which fringed the upper side of the bank. From their left came the sound of approaching footsteps. The scuff of feet came nearer, passed on, and they saw the dark shape of a man against the starlit water. He halted a short distance away. McLean whispered, 'You and Aba stay here.'

Crouching on all fours, McLean followed the line of the

undergrowth. A short distance on he stopped, took the fighting knife from its sheath and a .303 cartridge from his ammunition belt.

The footsteps sounded again, this time coming back along the bank. Soon the bulk of a man showed against the water. He was walking slowly, a rifle slung over his shoulder. McLean, rigid as a stalking cat, threw the cartridge far out into the water. At the sound of its splash the sentry stopped, stared into the creek, his rifle at the ready. McLean inched forward, came up behind the motionless figure. He was close enough to hear the man's breathing when he leapt and struck, twisting the serrated blade of the fighting knife, sinking it deep into the sentry's neck, the rasping noise of steel against gristle and bone deadened by the gasping sigh.

Thirty

'McLean killed him, sir. We pushed the body into the undergrowth.' The tremor in Morrow's voice was not as much excitement as shock. He'd stalked and killed wild animals on the Kenyan farm where he'd grown up, but never had he witnessed the stalking and killing of a human being. Black as the night was, the attack on the Japanese, a monochrome set against dark, star-splashed water, had been only too visible to Morrow's keen eyes.

A flat-toned 'Good' came from Barratt, followed by, 'Did you see the submarine?'

'No, sir. Still too dark in that quarter. Where the sentry was there's a stretch with no mangroves. The water comes right up to the bank. Aba was right. It'll be okay for launching the rig. He and McLean are in the undergrowth about eighty-five yards from the catamarans. Aba says they're moored fairly close astern of the submarine.'

'Right. Let's join the others.'

The cortège moved on, making its way gingerly down the slope towards the creek. Aba Said led, Morrow behind him, then Barratt and Carmichael followed by the men carrying the rig. McGlashan the TGM, with Stanley the sickbay attendant, brought up the rear.

In his planning Barratt had allowed five minutes for getting the rig into the water and trimming down. McGlashan, the acknowledged expert, had suggested three. 'Your tests were done in daylight, TGM,' Barratt had told him. 'We'll allow a couple more to make up for darkness.'

In the event it took less than four minutes. First the

buoyancy drum was lowered into the creek where Corrigan, up to his armpits in water, steadied it while the free-flooding lower compartment filled.

Next into the water was Barratt, minus the dungarees, black singlet and revolver he'd left in the undergrowth on the bank. His body, too, was blackened and nude but for bathing trunks. Both men wore belts with sheath-knives, and yellow armbands above their elbows for identification: 'So that you trigger-happy lot don't kill us when we come back,' Barratt had warned at the briefing.

McGlashan pushed home the depth-charge firing pistol, priming the charge to explode at a depth of fifteen feet. The canvas gripes were placed in position and the wooden carrier lowered into the water with the depth-charge where Barratt received it. The free-flooding chamber in the depth-charge filled, submerging its drum but leaving the carrier awash. Corrigan shoved the buoyancy drum into position above the depth-charge, the gripe ends were passed round it and secured on top with a Senhouse slip. Next to it was the lever controlling the air vent in the drum's upper compartment.

The two swimmers pushed the rig clear of the bank into deeper water. It was now submerged but for a few inches of buoyancy drum still above the surface.

The launching operation had taken place in silence but for minor sounds. With the Japanese sentry dead, and the submarine still the best part of a hundred yards away, all was well. Anything but loud sound reaching it would have been drowned by on-board noises and the slap of water against its hull.

On receiving the carry-on signal – three sharp tugs on a heaving line stretched between the rig and the men on shore – Morrow took charge of the attack party, moving his men back from the bank to re-group in the trees above the creek. There they prepared themselves, making ready weapons and adjusting loads. In a final whispered briefing he reminded them of the plan of attack. 'We should hear the explosion in about seven to ten minutes,' he said. 'The submarine is lying alongside the bank about a hundred yards ahead of where we launched the rig. Don't forget that its topsides are camouflaged with undergrowth, branches of trees, etcetera, so that's what you'll be looking for. Not a steel hull. Aba Said will lead us through the trees to a point opposite the boat. Keep close enough to each other to maintain contact in the dark. Once the fun begins, move quickly down towards the last lines of trees. According to Aba that'll bring us within about thirty feet of the Jap. Then spread out and take cover behind a tree from which your can do your stuff. One man, one tree. Okay? We do not, repeat not, open fire until we hear the explosion.' He paused. 'Unless, of course, the Japs open fire on the swimmers *before* that. In that case we'll give the bastards everything we've got. Finally, remember your prime targets: guns' crews, conning-tower and gangways. We'll move now, but for God's sake let's make it softly, softly.' He turned to Aba Said, spoke to him.

The African replied. 'I will go softly like a leopard, Bwana. Your men must follow like the children of the leopard.' Weaponless but for his fighting knife, Aba Said went ahead, The rustling of the wind in the trees filled the silence.

While the swimmers pushed the rig slowly forward to their legs providing the propulsion, direction was maintained by keeping the wind ahead and slowing at times for Corrigan to check the distance from the bank with swift underwater dashes. With their heads more often than not immersed in water as black as the night around them, they kept at their task, wind-fanned ripples splashing over the top of the buoyancy drum, the salt water stinging their eyes.

For most of the time there were only two things in Barratt's mind: an absolute determination to succeed, and a savage, almost sadistic satisfaction at the thought of what he was about to do to the Japanese.

They were well on the way to their target when the creek was illuminated by a sudden sheet of lightning. In that brief instant they saw the catamarans close ahead. Immediately beyond the three native craft lay the camouflaged bulk of the submarine, somehow bigger, higher and more massive than they had expected. It was no longer entirely covered with foliage. On the gun-platform abaft the tree-decked conning-tower the twin barrels of the anti-aircraft gun were trained forward to cover the creek; two men were standing by the gun, one leaning against its mounting, the other at the guardrail.

It was soon after the lightning flash that they felt the brig bump into the stern of a catamaran. Corrigan dived, came up between the catamarans, pushed two apart, making a gap through which they coaxed the rig. Progress was slow while the swimmers, fearing another lightning flash, edged the rig forward, the hull of one catamaran and the outrigger of another scraping against the submerged arms of the carrier.

When almost clear of the catamarans the rig stopped, snarled up on an obstruction on the port side. Barratt, nearest to it, dived under to come up immediately ahead of the rig. Groping under water in the darkness he found the trouble: the loose end of a fibre lashing on the outrigger's float had fouled a carrier-arm. With some difficulty he cut the fibre free. Diving again, he swam back to Corrigan. 'Okay,' he gasped. 'Push like hell. Another thirty feet, I reckon.'

As they forced the rig clear a rocket burst high above the creek and a parachute flare floated down, turning night into day. In the fraction of a second before they ducked beneath the surface they'd seen the lines of tracer bullets racing towards them. Though the two men did not know it, the 25mm shells struck the water well beyond them.

Still underwater, they continued to force the rig ahead. Coming up for air Barratt saw the parachute flare splutter into the creek as a second rocket burst and another flare began its descent. The tracers were passing overhead but he heard the unmistakable *spa-aa-aang* of rifle bullets splashing around him. In the moment between drawing a deep breath and submerging again, he had seen the submarine's stern less than twenty feet away. With fierce energy he and the

American pushed against the buoyancy drum, gasping, grunting, their scything legs forcing it onward. A few seconds later Corrigan poked his mouth up for air to be greeted by what looked like a Guy Fawkes night gone mad. For good measure it included the splash of bullets within inches of his head.

On the bursting of the rocket flare, and the sound of the submarine's twin AA guns opening fire, their tracer shells splashing into the creek astern of the submarine, Morrow and his men raced down the sloping bank and opened fire from the cover of the trees at almost point blank range. Concentrating on I-357's gun positions they had soon killed or wounded the Japanese crews. Thereafter, but for occasional rifle shots from the conning-tower, there was no response from the submarine.

On Morrow's shouted order, 'Bonfire,' the men in the attacking force who'd come ashore with bulging rucksacks over their shoulders, ducked out from behind the cover of the trees and hurled petrol bombs on to the undergrowth on the submarine's casing. Made from the wardroom's ample supply of empty gin bottles, they were closely followed by hand-grenades. Stacked with layers of sun-dried tinder, the submarine's upperworks were soon a roaring inferno. The Japanese crew began pouring out of the conning-tower, only to be shot down as they struggled through the fire. Unaware that the gangways had been destroyed by hand-grenades a few made for them, but most jumped into the sea on the far side, many with their scant clothing alight. A hand-grenade lobbed into the conning-tower closed that avenue of escape, forcing the Japanese to make for the fore and aft hatches where intense heat quickly drove them back.

As the sound of heavy gunfire drifted down from the mouth of the creek, Morrow muttered a hoarse, 'Thank Christ for that.' *Restless* was shelling the headlands, creating the planned diversion.

In the excitement of the action he'd lost count of time, but checking his wristwatch he found that only a few minutes had elapsed since the bursting of the first rocket. Blinded to any view of the creek by the fire on I-357's casing, he was wondering why the depth-charge had not yet exploded. Had the swimmers, exposed by the brilliance of the parachute flares, been killed in the water? He shook away the thought, concentrated again on the action which had become desultory; no more now than occasional rifle shots fired by his men at anything on the submarine which appeared to move.

He was about to give the order to cease fire when a huge explosion under the submarine's stern threw a column of water high into the air. A wall of compression hit the men on the bank with such force that those nearest to it were knocked off their feet, the cascading water dousing the fire on the after casing. The silence of surprise which followed the explosion gave way suddenly to a hoarse cheer from the men on the bank.

Satisfied that none of them had been injured, Morrow ordered the cease-fire. Leaving the Sten gunners and two men with rifles to keep the submarine covered, he set off with the rest of the party for the break in the mangroves where the rig had been launched, and to which the swimmers would return. The lagoon tests had shown that they could reach the bank and be out of the water within one and a half minutes of placing the depth-charge under the submarine's stern, whereas the flooding of the buoyancy tank would take two minutes once the air vent had been opened.

Thirty-one

Restless was in station off the mouth of the creek when a rocket burst over Maji Island and released a parachute flare. Since the shore party had none the First Lieutenant knew it must have been fired by the Japanese. Coming not long after sheet lightning had lit up the creek, he assumed they were either checking on *Restless*'s movements or, more likely, on something suspicious in the creek.

At the briefing it had been agreed that the destroyer should be ready to create a diversion from 0330 onwards by shelling the headlands.

'The whistle for the kick-off,' Barratt had said, 'will be the explosion of our depth-charge. If you hear general action ashore *before* then, get stuck in right away. Concentrate your fire on the mouth of the creek. It's got to look like covering fire for a landing party. The idea is to take the Japs' eye off the ball.'

Hamilton checked the time with Peter Dodds – it was 0342, but still no depth-charge explosion. *Restless*'s crew had been at action stations since 0320. With his binoculars trained on the flare-lit creek, he said, 'Tell Guns to keep his finger on the trigger. I think the balloon's about to go up.'

Dodds was passing the message to the Gunnery Officer in the control-tower when the sound of firing came from the creek. The first flare petered out and a second rocket burst high above. Its flare had begun to descend when heavy rifle and machine-gun fire, grenade explosions and other sounds of action erupted suddenly beyond the bluff which shut off the view from seaward.

The First Lieutenant at once gave the order to open fire. *Restless*'s formidable barrage started up, the crack and flash

271

of her guns, the acrid smell of cordite, the ship shaking from concussion, all combining in violent harmony. The response from the creek was quick, two Very lights arc-ing into the sky above the western headland. Seconds passed; *Restless*'s radar operator reported a small contact moving fast down the creek, its range opening. The cold white beam of the destroyer's searchlight settled on a catamaran making towards the bluff, a white squirt of foam at its stern. Had he not feared it might be crewed by islanders, Hamilton would have ordered its sinking. Instead he phoned Lawson in the control-tower. 'Hurry it along, Guns, but don't sink it,' he said.

Restless's pom-poms barked into action, fountains of silvered water leaping and sparkling astern of the scurrying catamaran which began a wild zig-zag. Down in the creek the night sky glowed in hues of orange and yellow, flame and smoke rising above the bluff from the hidden inferno.

Before long the tempo of action ashore slowed to no more than occasional bursts of machine-gun and rifle fire. The First Lieutenant was saying, 'I wonder what the devil has happened to that depth-charge?' when his question was answered by the muffled boom of an underwater explosion. The top of a great column of water leapt into the air above the bluff, its texture reflecting the light of the fire beneath it.

'Thank the Lord for that,' said the First Lieutenant. 'I was afraid something had gone badly wrong.'

'You've got to hand it to the Old Man.' The Navigating Officer's voice was nervous and edgy with emotion.

'Bloody marvellous.' The First Lieutenant lowered the binoculars. 'I thought his plan was crazy. But by God it seems to have worked.' He went to the compass platform, gave the order to cease-fire. The destroyer's guns fell silent, and he conned the ship round in a wide circle to regain position off the headlands.

When Barratt raised his head above water for the second time he saw in the light from the fire that they'd got the rig within ten feet of the submarine's stern. Mindful of rifle fire he took a quick gulp of air before ducking under. Totally obsessed with getting the rig into position, he was only dimly aware of Corrigan going up to breathe. Seconds later the American had ducked under and was alongside him again, the rig's forward progress responding to the powerful shove of the younger man. Looking through the few inches of water above them, Barratt saw the orange glow in the sky and his mind registered that the fire had come too soon. He supposed the shots from the submarine had triggered the action. The fire was meant to happen after the depth-charge had exploded, not before. The light it cast was a menace but nothing could be done about that, and they were close enough now. He tapped Corrigan's shoulder twice. The American returned the taps in acknowledgement. With the rig now almost under the submarine's stern they broke surface. Keeping low in the water Barratt reached up, felt for the air vent lever, attempted to depress it, but it wouldn't move. To exert greater pressure he pulled himself higher out of the water, pushed down on the lever with both hands. There was still no movement.

'It's jammed,' he shouted to Corrigan who pushed him aside, seized the lever and bore down on it. Strong as he was, the American failed to depress it. Vital seconds slipped by. Machine-gun and rifle fire began to splash around them. Barratt had realized it was coming from the shore opposite and not from the submarine when something delivered a violent blow on his back. He felt as if he'd been hit between the shoulder blades with a heavy instrument. He put his hand to the place, felt the broken flesh. No pain but his left arm had gone limp and unresponsive to any attempt to move it. He shouted to Corrigan, 'Get to hell out of it. I'll give you ninety seconds before I pull the Senhouse slip – that'll sink the bloody thing . . .' Before he could finish the sentence he had rolled over on his side, face downwards in the water. In the light of the flames Corrigan saw the crimson gash on the Captain's back. He reached out, pulled the limp body towards him, saw the closed eyes, blood oozing from the open mouth. He's dead, he decided, no way I can help him. He let the Captain's body go, ducking involuntarily as bullets whined and splashed around him.

The Senhouse slip, he thought. There's no other way. Christ Jesus give me strength. He took a deep breath, rolled on to his back underwater, raised an arm, ran a hand along the top of the buoyancy chamber until he felt the air vent lever. The Senhouse slip was just forward of it. His fingers found it, tried to slide the steel ring which held the tongue. It wouldn't budge. Have to get higher in the goddam water, he told himself. He pulled himself up, slipped the clip free. The gripes securing the depth-charge to the buoyancy chamber fell away and the chamber, freed of its load, rose in the water.

Corrigan made for the bank, his arms flailing the water in a desperate crawl. In the few seconds of life left to him he had managed to cover almost fifteen feet when he was blown out of the water by the violence of the explosion.

When Morrow and his men got back to the rig's launching site they took cover in the undergrowth. The fire on the submarine, burning less fiercely now, still cast enough light to show that I-357's stern was underwater while her bows had lifted.

Morrow touched McGlashan's shoulder. 'Look. She's down by the stern, TGM.'

McGlashan, kneeling beside him, said, 'Aye, the depth-charge must have blown the stern trimming tanks. Flooded the motor-room and stokers' mess, too, I'd dare say.' The TGM's tone suggested satisfaction with a job well done. 'The rudder and propellers must be in poor shape. They will have taken the full force of the blast.'

'Bloody good show,' said Morrow. 'Terrific.' His voice changed, betrayed anxiety. 'The Captain and Brad Corrigan should have shown up by now. Three minutes gone since the explosion.'

The sound of *Restless*'s guns had ceased and for the first time since the action began there was little to be heard other than odd rifle shots, and the occasional rattle of machine-gun fire coming from the direction of the Japanese sentry post on the beach by the huts. 'God knows what they're firing at,' said Morrow.

'Each other, I'd say.' McGlashan's response was unemotional.

A rocket sizzled into the sky from the far side of the creek, burst at the top of its climb to release yet another flare. McGlashan swore softly. 'Hope to Christ that doesn't show up our swimmers.'

McLean said, 'I'll go back along the bank, Mr Morrow. Check if they've come ashore further back.'

'Hold on for a moment, McLean. Let that flare die before you go.'

When it touched the water and spluttered out, the signalman left them.

McLean had not been long gone when yet another rocket soared into the sky; it burst and the parachute flare floated gently down. In the brilliance of its light Morrow and his men looked anxiously for some sign of the swimmers, but there was none. The flare settled in the water and the creek was again swallowed by a darkness relieved only by the subdued glow of ashes along I-357's casing.

Morrow looked at his watch: six minutes gone and still no sign of them. Though he tried hard to believe that all was well, he had a feeling deep down that something had gone desperately wrong. At the briefing Barratt had stressed that no more than four minutes at most should be allowed for the return of the swimmers. 'If we haven't got back by then the rest of the party must get to hell out of it,' he'd said. 'The Japanese mustn't be given time to mount a counter-attack. At the four minute mark get out double-quick and make for the pick-up point. That order is not to be disobeyed.' He had stopped then to glare at Morrow. 'The safe return of the attack force is a lot more important than attempts to rescue individual members who may have got into trouble. Is that understood?'

275

A general murmur of assent indicated that it was, and Barratt had gone on to the next item.

Four minutes – Morrow reminded himself – but six had already passed. Torn by anxiety, faced with an awful decision, he was wondering for how much longer he could ignore the Captain's orders when McLean appeared out of the darkness. 'They're dead, sir,' was the signalman's laconic report.

Morrow said, 'Oh, God. Are you sure?'

'Yes. Certain. I saw their bodies in the light of that last flare. Floating face downwards they were. Not far from each other. There were a lot of other bodies around. Jap bodies. The Captain had a bad wound. A big gash down the back. His body and Corrigan's looked all broken up. Kind of out of shape.'

Morrow said, 'Sure they weren't Japs, McLean? I mean – how could you be certain on a dark night? Our people's faces and bodies blackened – and all that?'

'Quite sure,' said McLean quietly. 'The yellow armbands showed up in the light of the flare. Apart from anything else their hair was too long for them to be Japs.'

'Christ!' Morrow's voice trembled. 'How bloody awful.'

In the darkness McGlashan put his hand on the Sub-Lieutenant's shoulder. 'It's war, Mr Morrow,' he said. 'One Japanese submarine and God knows how many Japs . . .' He hesitated. '. . . for the price of two of ours.'

In a businesslike voice McLean said, 'Shall I fire the recall?'

Morrow said, 'No point in hanging about, I suppose. Yes, do that.'

The signalman took a Very pistol from his belt, aimed it into the sky and fired twice. Two Very lights chased each other like green stars over the waters of the creek.

Thirty-two

For Yashimoto it had been a long day. Since Hosokawa's report of a British destroyer off the island, the Captain of I-357 had been busy ensuring that the defence measures he'd ordered had been properly implemented.

By midnight, physically and mentally tired but satisfied that every reasonable precaution had been taken, he went to his cabin to rest. The second degree of readiness had been instituted, skeleton crews for torpedoes and guns were at their stations, officers and lookouts were on watch in the conning-tower, and hydrophone and search-receiver operators were keeping a listening watch.

Secure in the knowledge that everything possible had been done, and much influenced by his belief that the British would not infringe Portuguese neutrality, he soon fell asleep. In his Night Order Book he had stressed that he was to be called immediately anything unusual occurred or was suspected, and particularly if the enemy destroyer made a close approach. The officer-of-the-watch was, in any event, to report to him at the end of each hour.

His last thought before falling asleep had, however, been concerned with something quite unrelated to these matters. On the contrary, it had to do with something both stimulating and agreeable, for he relived in fantasy the last bath he had taken with Masna in her fine house in Penang. The ornamental pool, its cool scented waters strewn with frangipani petals, had been an exquisite setting for that beautiful face and sensuous body; it was while contemplating these that the fantasy faded and sleep took over.

*

Lieutenant Nangi, on watch in the conning-tower, called the Captain by voice-pipe at 0200 to report that all was well. 'It is very dark, sir. Cloud still obscures the moon. There have been flashes of lightning in the north-east.'

Having thanked the Lieutenant for his report Yashimoto replaced the whistle in the mouthpiece of the voice-pipe beside the bunk. Inured by long experience to such interruptions, he slept until 0300 when Nangi again reported that all was well.

Forty minutes later the voice-pipe whistle shrilled once more. It was Lieutenant Sato, sharing the watch with Nangi. 'Captain, sir – on the bridge at once, please.' The note of urgency in Sato's voice was sufficient for Yashimoto to leap from his bunk and make for the conning-tower in nothing more than the singlet and shorts in which he'd been sleeping. Only his cap with its gilded peak identified him as he climbed on to the bridge.

'Please follow me, sir.' The voice in the darkness was Sato's. Yashimoto followed the Lieutenant past the periscope standards and down the ladder to the after gun-platform where men were standing by the twin .25 anti-aircraft guns. Sato stopped at the after guardrail, pointed into the black void astern. 'There was a flash of lightning a moment ago, sir. One of the gun's crews, Able Seaman Kamachi, says he saw something in the water, some movement between the catamarans.'

'What did you see, Kamachi?' rasped the Captain.

From the darkness round the AA guns came the reply, 'I saw movement, sir. Something there. Maybe a big fish disturbing the boats. I do not know.'

Yashimoto peered into the night for a moment. 'Fire a parachute flare,' he ordered.

The rocket soared away in a hissing, sparkling climb. Yashimoto and Sato moved clear of the barrels of the AA gun. 'Standby to fire on the catamarans,' commanded the Captain. The rocket burst high overhead and in the light of the descending flare Yashimoto saw that Kagumi had come

278

on to the gun-platform, revolver in hand. He was followed by a seaman carrying a rifle. The First Lieutenant is an excellent officer, thought the Captain; always does the right thing at the right time.

Astern of the submarine the three catamarans showed up as clearly as if daylight had come. It was Yashimoto who first detected the slight movement between them. 'Train on the outrigger float of the centre catamaran,' he ordered in a voice hoarsened by anxiety. 'Open fire.'

With an explosive rattle the twin barrels flashed into life, the tracer shells racing like brightly lit darts into the water beyond the catamarans.

'Bring down the range,' barked Yashimoto. 'Fire another flare.'

'The guns are at maximum depression, sir,' reported the gunlayer, 'We cannot . . .'

'Get rifles from the lookouts,' interrupted Yashimoto. 'Standby to fire another rocket.'

Kneeling, with the barrel of the rifle on the guardrail, Kagumi was firing single shots into the water beneath the float on the end of the outrigger. He stopped when the dying flare dropped into the creek. The second rocket hissed away, a fiery trail marking its passage. It reached the top of its climb, the parachute fluttered open and once again night became day.

From the conning-tower came the sound of a lookout shouting something unintelligible.

Yashimoto had turned to Sato, was saying, 'Find out what that man. . .', when the conning-tower and gun-platform came under heavy fire from the trees fringing the bank. Kagumi and most of the gun's crew were hit with the opening bursts. Yashimoto and Sato managed to drop down from the gun-platform and take cover on the layers of foliage on the offshore side of the conning-tower. Once there, they were pinned down by a hail of bullets. Noise precluded any attempt at voice communication. Confused, bewildered and power-less, Yashimoto crouched behind the conning-tower. His state of shocked anxiety was compounded by the intrusion of a new sound: heavy gunfire was coming from the mouth of the creek. At about the same time there were muffled explosions on the submarine's casing. The unmistakable smell of petrol reached him as fires broke out fore and aft along the length of I-357. Seconds later came the thump and flash of more solid explosives. Yashimoto took them to be shells from the destroyer's secondary armament until he realized they were hand-grenades thrown from the bank.

Flames were now reaching high above the casing where the stacked layers of brushwood and timber were ablaze, the roaring, hissing of the fire punctuated by the screams of men trying to escape. Many were jumping over the side into the creek, their scant clothing alight. There was a sudden explosion in the conning-tower close to where Yashimoto cowered. A hand-grenade? Sato, crouching near him, shouted something but the words were lost in the clamour of action. The fire was spreading rapidly towards them from both ends of the casing. The trees above them, 'planted' in the conning-tower and gun positions, were ablaze. The heat had become unbearable. Yashimoto was vaguely aware of Sato dropping on to the saddletanks and sliding down into the creek where men swam frantically in their efforts to get away from the fire.

With the flames scorching his near naked body, the heat beyond endurance, Yashimoto took off his cap, stood up and dived over the side, coming up clear of the saddletanks. Using an ungainly crawl, he swam away from I-357.

The water through which Yashimoto swam reflected the lurid hues of the fire – the breath of dangerous dragons, hell-fire, his mind told him. Unable to compass ordered thought, it fed him scraps of survival information: get away from the fire; swim towards the bluff; go ashore at the first break in the mangroves; walk on through the trees to the sentry post; you have armed men and a machine-gun there.

In the water through which he swam men were struggling to keep afloat, some silently, others noisily crying out for help. Passing them, passing corpses, some in grotesque attitudes, he swam on, never stopping, determined to survive. Survival was the dominant thought.

A small break in the mangroves showed on his left. He made for it, reached the bank. With difficulty he pulled himself clear of the water. Crawling on all fours, he found cover in a thicket. He waited there, exhausted. He would move into the trees when his strength returned. There would be less light from the fire then.

He was utterly confused. What on earth had happened? The main thrust of the attack had come from the enemy on the bank. There must have been – must still be, he corrected himself – many of them, judging from the scale and fury of the action. And the enemy swimmers in the water by the catamarans? What were they doing? How had the British got so many men into position without being detected?

How could their landing craft have come through the narrows without being seen by Hosokawa and his men? And by the other sentry posts? Could those inside I-357 have lessened the effect of the fire by flooding the ballast tanks? The tide was at half-ebb. There was less than two metres of water beneath the keel. Not enough to submerge the casing. No – flooding wouldn't have helped. If the casing hadn't been ablaze they might have fought off the enemy. The British had attacked with petrol bombs and hand-grenades. How had they known in advance that I-357 was covered with layers of brushwood and timber? Had an African told them? How would he have known, unless he was from the huts on the beach? How could he have got away from the island? What had happened was incomprehensible, unbelievable. Yashimoto gave up. It was too late now.

The enormity of what he'd done began to penetrate his consciousness. He had abandoned I-357, deserted his command while under enemy attack. His men, some of them certainly, must have witnessed the act of desertion, the dive over the side. That was not the act of a *samurai*. He should have stayed with his command. That he would quickly have burned to death was, he now realized, no excuse. That would be expected of a commanding officer in the Imperial Japanese

Navy. Death in action was sublime, the most noble end. Survival could be a disgrace. Yashimoto emptied his lungs with a tremulous sigh. There was only one way to purge dishonour: *bushido*, the code of the warrior, required that he should commit *seppuku*, the ritual act of disembowelment. He would have done that, of course, had he still been on board the submarine. There, before the Shinto shrine, he would have put on the white kimono, apologized to the Emperor, to his ancestors, to his natural gods, for his failure to defend his command and, thereby, his failure to attack the British carrier. After such expressions of regret and humility, he would have bared his stomach, plunged into it the ceremonial dagger and, with a violent sideways slash, completed the disembowelment. Now that that was no longer possible, he must reach the sentry post beyond the bluff, organize a counter-attack. The enemy on the bank would undoubtedly be in superior force. He would be killed in action. That would be good, but it would not purge dishonour in quite the same way that *seppuku* would have done.

These troublesome thoughts were interrupted by a vast explosion. A wall of pressure hit him, knocked him off the knees on which he crouched. Lying on his side he saw the column of water high in the air a hundred yards or so down the bank from where he lay. That the fire had detonated one of I-357's torpedo warheads was his first thought; or perhaps an ammunition magazine. Only something like that could have caused such an explosion.

The light from the fire had grown less brilliant, was diminishing, though he could still hear noises from it, crackles and explosive sizzles. He got to his feet, crouching low, and went towards the trees. The distant sound of pistol shots came to him. They were followed by two green Very lights which rose into the air over the creek. High above him another rocket burst and in the light of its flare he saw the line of trees. They were higher up the bank, farther away than he had thought. Feeling naked and exposed, he began to run. A burst of machine-gun fire came from the far side of the

282

creek. He knew it must be the sentry post by the huts. There was the high whine of approaching bullets and a dull thudding as they struck the ground around him. The idiots were firing at him. He redoubled his efforts, ran with furious energy. A dozen more paces and he would be in the undergrowth fringing the trees. He had almost made it when he felt an immense blow at the base of his spine. Its force lifted him from fast-moving feet and hurled him forward, arms outstretched to break his fall.

It was in this fashion that the dead body of Commander Togo Yashimoto reached the undergrowth in a last spectacular dive.

Thirty-three

A few minutes after they'd begun the climb up the hill the moon came clear of the clouds to help Aba Said lead the ragged file of men back along the track used on the outward journey. Without the burden of the rig, and the weight of petrol bombs, hand-grenades and ammunition expended, they found the going comparatively easy. But for yet another rocket flare and odd bursts of machine-gun fire from the sentries near the huts – fired in quite the wrong direction as it happened – there had been little Japanese reaction to the Very lights. Morrow and the Sten gunners, last to leave the bank, had stayed on to fight a rearguard action. But it had not been necessary and they'd soon caught up with the others.

The withdrawal was without further incident and within twenty minutes of leaving the creek they had arrived on the beach. The motorboat, lying a short distance offshore, came in with the skimmer in tow and by 0425 those on the beach had re-embarked and course was set for the pick-up point where *Restless* could be seen waiting in the moonlight. Before long the landing party, weary but excited, their dusky faces streaked with sweat, were back on board.

With the motorboat and skimmer hoisted inboard, *Restless* headed out to sea. The First Lieutenant handed over the watch to the Gunnery Officer and went to the chartroom where Morrow told him of the happenings ashore.

Listening in silence to the younger man's vivid, eager description of the action, Hamilton was visibly shocked when told how McLean had seen the dead bodies of Barratt and Corrigan.

'Bloody awful,' he said, the muscles in his face working, his voice strained. 'But I'm not surprised. They were taking incredible risks. When I heard that depth-charge explode well after the action had begun I was worried. Some sort of premonition, I suppose.'

In a voice that had lost its firmness, was on the edge of breaking, Morrow said, 'They were fantastically brave.' The whites of his eyes, the red of his lips, were exaggerated by the black, perspiring face.

The First Lieutenant saw the signs of reaction and quickly interrupted. 'You people put up a marvellous show. Well done. Now go and get some rest and remove that filthy blacking. You can fill me in on the details later.'

Morrow said, 'Are you going to tell Kilindini what's happened?'

'Yes. Of course. Right away.'

'Good.' Looking as if he were about to say something, the Sub-Lieutenant shook his head and left the chartroom.

The telephone on the cypher desk rang. Camilla picked it up. 'Who?' she said. Then, 'Oh, Fleet Wireless Officer. Sorry, sir. I didn't recognize your voice. The line's a bit woolly. Signal from who, did you say?' She frowned, listened intently. 'From *Restless*. Oh, splendid.' She looked across the operations room and smiled at Hutch Hutchison before beginning to write. 'Oh, how absolutely marvellous,' she said, adding, 'Sorry, sir, I won't interrupt again.' But she did, quite soon, with a quiet, 'Oh no, how awful.' When she'd finished writing she said, 'I'll read that back – to Deputy C-in-C, Eastern Fleet, repeat Captain (D), begins: Japanese submarine I-357 attacked and destroyed in Maji Island creek twelve miles south-south-east of Cape Ulu. Lieutenant Commander Barratt and Leading Seaman Corrigan USNR killed in action. Enemy casualties heavy. Surviving Japanese still on island. Lieutenant Hamilton, temporarily in command of *Restless*, requests instructions. Message ends. Time of origin 0458.' She paused, said a soft, 'Thank you, sir.' Putting the phone back on its rest, she looked at Hutchison with sad, clouded eyes. 'Isn't that dreadful. John Barratt and the American, Corrigan, have been killed.'

'Yes. Bad show. But they got the submarine. That's terrific. Can't make an omelette without breaking eggs, you know.'

Camilla turned away. 'That's a hateful simile,' she said. 'Cynical and unhelpful.'

The Flight Lieutenant looked solemn, shrugged. 'I dare say. But that's the price of war. Anyway, Sandy Hamilton's okay. That's something, isn't it?'

Her head was in her hands and he saw her shoulders shaking. He went over to the desk, touched her gently. 'Sorry. I'm not very strong on tact.'

A man came on to *Restless*'s bridge, went to the tall dark shape standing by the screen. 'Will you be using the Captain's day-cabin, sir?'

'Who is that?' asked the First Lieutenant.

'Captain's steward, sir.'

'Sorry, Betts. Your voice sounded different. No, I won't be using it.'

'Thought you wouldn't, sir. That's why I brought you this. Captain left it on his desk.'

With feelings of apprehension the First Lieutenant took the envelope, 'Thank you, Betts.' He tried to sound normal but knew he'd failed.

In the light over the chartroom table he saw that the envelope was addressed to *Lieutenant Alexander Hamilton RN*. It was marked *Personal* and headed, *To be opened should I not return*.

He must have expected it, thought a deeply troubled Hamilton, perhaps even wanted it. He opened the envelope, took out the single sheet of notepaper, held it under the light.

My dear Sandy,
I want you to know that I very much appreciate the

support you have given me for Maji Mark Two, notwith-
standing your belief that it was an unwise operation,
particularly because of the Portuguese neutrality aspect.
However, I've no doubt you will explain my views on
that.
We've gone to an awful lot of trouble to find this Japanese
submarine. Now that we're about to attack it, I trust we
will suffer few casualties.
But they are likely in war and if, as I believe, we achieve
our objective I hope they'll be seen to have been justified.
In great haste. We leave the ship shortly.
Yours as ever,
John Barratt.
PS: You can now safely break W/T silence and put dear
old (D) in the picture. Tell him I'm sorry to have been
such a bloody nuisance.